Trophy Wife

Trophy Wife

Nicola Thorne

HarperCollins*Publishers*

HarperCollins*Publishers*
77–85 Fulham Palace Road,
Hammersmith, London W6 8JB

Published by HarperCollins*Publishers* 1995
1 3 5 7 9 8 6 4 2

A catalogue record for this book is
available from the British Library

IS B N 0 00 224031 9

Typeset in Meridien
at the Spartan Press Ltd,
Lymington, Hants

Printed in Great Britain by
HarperCollinsManufacturing Glasgow

CONTENTS

PART I

A Contented Man

CHAPTER 1

Matt Ransom, eyes hidden behind large sunglasses, sat on the terrace watching the girl in white as with long, lithe strides she darted about on the tennis court below him. He was captivated by the grace of her movements, the reach of her arms skilfully returning the ball.

Now, standing at the baseline, she prepared to serve for the match. She raised herself like a ballet dancer on the tips of her tennis shoes, threw the ball high above her head, paused and then swung the racquet hard down to deliver an ace right into the court of the woman standing diagonally opposite her: Matt's daughter, Georgina.

Jenny Holstrom was partnered by her boyfriend George Hulme, Georgina by her husband Henry. Thanks to Jenny, she and George were two sets up and about to take the third, as Elspeth Ransom appeared through the french doors, carefully carrying a tray in her hands. Matt rose, reluctant to take his eyes off the almost mesmeric movements of the girl on the grass.

'She's lovely, isn't she?' Elspeth, nodding in the direction of the court, put the tray down on the table Matt had put in place for her.

'Who's that?' Matt, his tone deliberately nonchalant, began to take the glasses from the tray.

'Go on,' Elspeth smiled at her husband. 'I saw you looking at her. George's girl.'

'She's a very good player. She's wiped the floor, even with Henry. She's got a strong serve. Stylish.'

He stretched and then turned with slow deliberation as the players gathered up their cardigans or sweaters, towels, ball-bags and various other accoutrements and began to stroll in leisurely fashion towards the terrace where Elspeth was already pouring freshly squeezed lemon juice, heavily laced with thin slices of lemon and chunks of ice, into tall glasses.

'Well played, congratulations. Fine game.' Matt went towards the group and, as the first up the steps was his daughter, he kissed her cheek.

'But we lost, Daddy – ' she smiled ruefully at him and turned to Jenny, 'to a better player. Two better players,' she corrected herself to include George.

'You do play well, Jenny,' Matt smiled benignly at her. 'Most professional.'

'Oh, no!' Jenny laughed, throwing herself into a chair and vigorously towelling her hair, damp with sweat.

'Jenny's father played for Sweden.' George stood behind her and, in a proprietorial manner, gently took the towel from her and began to massage her hair with soft gestures that were like caresses. 'It must be in the genes.' He bent swiftly to kiss her cheek and Matt realised that he felt annoyed and turned away. He thought demonstrations of affection like this were bad form in public. At least that's what he pretended he thought. It would be quite absurd, on such a brief acquaintance, to call the emotion jealousy.

It was hot, a near perfect summer's day, in that typically English summer of largely indifferent weather, when beaches were deserted and those who had stayed at home wished they had gone abroad. But not for the past week. Each day the sun had shone from an intensely blue sky, and Matt had got home early from the office for the pleasure of enjoying a late afternoon on the terrace with his wife and a walk round the garden before drinks on the same terrace, then dinner, also taken outside.

'Well,' George threw down the towel and, taking the only vacant seat left on the terrace, looked at his watch, 'we must be getting back. Thanks for the game, Georgina and Henry. For your hospitality, Matt and Elspeth.'

'Delicious,' everyone murmured as George, a restless man, got to his feet and looked enquiringly over at Jenny. She, however, appeared in no hurry to leave. Matt glanced across at her. Her long, brown, slim legs were stretched out in front of her, her slender hands clasped the tall lemonade glass. Her blonde, almost white hair seemed to flow in an unbroken line across her brow, framing her oval face where it fell a couple of inches above the neckline. Her deeply recessed eyes were the colour of cornflowers, her nose aquiline, her mouth straight, sensually and slightly parted to show almost perfect white teeth. A tiny dimple softened her jawline. She wore a tennis dress with a V-neckline which enhanced her small breasts, a belt accentuating her narrow waist. It had been possible, Matt had noticed, just to see her white panties when she bent over on the court to collect the ball.

Matt was roused from his contemplation of her symmetrical beauty as she seemed about to rise from the chair.

'Why not stay for dinner?' he heard himself saying, while Elspeth looked at him in alarm. After all, there had been a lunch party.

'Just something cold,' Matt murmured, as if unaware of her agitation.

'Really thanks, Matt.' George, an inveterate watchgazer, looked at his wrist. 'We're dining in town.'

Jenny smiled, a lazy, rather rich smile; the smile of someone aware of her youth, her sexuality, above all her abundant power. A natural, graceful, God-given power that many beautiful women seem to have.

'Thank you so much, Sir Matthew.' She rose finally to her feet with the same easy, flowing movement with which she covered the court. Everything about her was effortless, graceful, as though she had some sort of inner propulsion.

What on earth did she see in a man like George?

'Please call me Matt. Everyone else does.' Matt only just managed to prevent himself putting an avuncular arm round her shoulders. Whereas he might have done it with an ordinary guest, a friend of his and Elspeth's or their children, with Jenny it seemed somehow to verge on trespassing. Instead he passed her her white cardigan and looked around with a deliberately casual air.

'Don't forget anything. Dinner another time, maybe.' It was important to make the invitation sound offhand. As he spoke he wandered across to Georgina, allowing his arm casually to encircle her waist as she and Henry went into the drawing room from the terrace and walked towards the far door.

'Everything all right, darling?'

'Fine, Daddy.'

'The children well?'

'Very well.'

Rupert and Alice were seven and five, both at school.

Matt stood in the hall chatting to his daughter while Elspeth followed with the guests. Henry had forgotten something on the court and disappeared to retrieve it.

It was five-thirty and George was obviously getting impatient. He put out a hand.

'Thank you for a lovely day, Elspeth. You must come to us soon.'

'That would be lovely.' Elspeth smiled graciously.

'We must collect the children.' Georgina looked round for her husband. 'They'll wonder where we are.'

'Here I am.' Henry appeared holding up the sweater he'd left on the court. 'And darling, we must hurry or – '

'I've just explained,' Georgina said. 'You're coming to us Tuesday, Mummy and Daddy.'

'Tuesday.' Matt nodded. 'I think it's Tuesday.'

'It *is* all right, Daddy?' Georgina looked across at him. 'We've asked the Harpers and the Moxons.'

'It is absolutely all right.' He leaned forward to reassure her. 'I'll come straight from the office.'

'Don't forget we've got a meeting with Birado on Tuesday, Matt. In the City.' George was solicitously helping Jenny on with her cardigan.

'That's in the morning.'

'It might go on all day.'

'I'll leave in time. Don't worry.' Matt smiled reassuringly at Georgina and leaned over to peck her cheek. 'Now you get back to those children and give them our love.'

'See you Tuesday.'

'Tuesday.'

'Thanks so much.'

'Lovely to have you.'

Kisses, smiles, handshakes, waves.

The older couple stood at the top of the porch as the younger people got into their respective cars, and stood watching as they drove slowly down the drive and, rounding a bend, vanished from sight.

'Nice couple,' Elspeth remarked as they turned back into the house.

'Oh, I don't think they're a "couple".'

Why did he feel it mattered?

Elspeth looked surprised. 'But I understood they lived together. Didn't you? "You must come and see *us*", George said.'

'Not necessarily.' They went back into the living room. Matt went over to the sideboard and removed the stopper from the whisky decanter. He felt strangely ill at ease, even angry with himself. 'I don't think he's known her very long.' He remembered then that his wife preferred sherry and turned to her. 'The usual, dear?'

'I think I'll have Campari with ice. Don't worry,' she held out a hand. 'I've got to go into the kitchen and I'll get it myself.'

'Bring me a few lumps too, please, dear.'

Matt went over to the television and switched it on, then, looking at the clock on the mantelpiece, switched it off again. 'Blast. Too late for the news.'

'I wish they'd have the news at the same time every day,' he murmured peevishly as Elspeth came back into the room. 'I always forget it's later on a Saturday.'

'I'm sure there's nothing on anyway.' Elspeth went to the sideboard where Matt's drink awaited its ice, put two lumps in it from the silver bowl in her hand, and took it over to him. 'You're a bit grumpy today, darling.'

'I didn't think I was.' He took the drink with a smile. 'In fact it's been rather a nice day.'

Elspeth returned to the sideboard and poured soda on to the red Campari that lined the bottom of her glass. Then she turned and gazed at the back of her husband's head as he leaned back, rather wearily she thought, against the chair, the glass in his outstretched hand visible, his legs in grey flannel slacks crossed; debonair, elegant, as always. Matt Ransom, her husband of nearly thirty years. There would be a big party at Claridge's in the following spring to celebrate the event.

Even after all this time, Matt still surprised her, always engendered in her a thrill, a feeling of pride. She knew he didn't know it, and that he imagined she felt about him rather as he felt about her – that she was a companion, a friend, but the heady days of being 'in love' had long gone. For him, maybe, yes; for her, never. Whatever the occasion she always considered him the best-looking man in the room: six foot three, trim figure encased in tailored, well-fitting clothes: business suit, flannels and blazer, black tie, whatever. His thick, slightly wavy hair was mostly iron grey, but flecked with dark patches, an interesting salt-and-pepper effect that enhanced his attractiveness, added to his distinction. He had strong, forceful features: a large straight nose, dark, almost black eyes under slightly bushy brows, a high, intelligent forehead, a square, smooth chin.

He thrilled her, always had; but he never made her feel inadequate or plain or dumpy, which she knew she was, had let herself become. She too was a strong, forceful personality, but she had never cared much for her appearance, took little interest in clothes or make-up. She had a good skin and she did little to embellish it; her hair, now quite white, curled naturally and her dress sense was minimal: tweeds for the country, a couple of good suits for town, a couple of evening dresses, and slacks for indoors — well-cut Daks' slacks, never jeans.

She looked exactly what she was: a caring, homely person; a good mother to their four children. Glamorous she was not, and never had been, but she knew she always had a special and abiding place in Matt's affections. She never questioned it.

She considered marriage more important than physical love: an enduring, transcending bond. She knew Matt so well, his moods, his likes and dislikes. He was a man of determination: steady, resolute, consistent, ambitious; a high achiever who by hard work had brought Ransom Engineering into the top one thousand companies in the kingdom, yet it was still — one of the very few — in private hands. It was run, as it had been for many years, by Matt. Their eldest son Maurice, a junior executive with the company, was being groomed to take over his father's place one day, probably far off.

George Hulme was Maurice's immediate boss. He was marketing director, a dynamic man who had been poached from a rival some years before. George was about thirty-eight.

'How old would you say Jenny was?'

'What?' Matt started, nearly spilling his whisky, but Elspeth observing his reaction as she wandered over to sit on the arm of his chair, merely thought that he had been nodding off to sleep.

'I was thinking that George must be in his late thirties. How old was his wife?'

'About the same age.'

'Did Jenny have anything to do with the divorce?'

'Not that I know of.' Matt raised his glass to his lips. 'In fact I know nothing about his private life, or hers if it comes to that, except that he's a bloody good salesman.'

'With an excellent choice in females. His wife was good looking too, wasn't she?'

'I thought so.' Matt lowered his glass, resting it on his lap. 'I can't see his attraction myself.'

'Oh, I can,' Elspeth said, to his surprise. 'Not *conventionally* good looking, maybe, but powerful. Women like a powerful man.' She put a hand gently on the top of his head. 'That is the secret of *your* success too, darling.'

'With women?' Matt looked at her in amusement.

'With me.' She lightly kissed the top of his head. 'Tell me,' she murmured teasingly. 'Have I been the only one?'

'Of course.' He reached for her hand.

'*All* these years?'

'The only one.' He held her hand tightly in his.

'Somehow I believe you.' She planted a kiss on the back of his hand – rather to his amazement because she was so seldom demonstrative – and, rising from the chair, went over towards the window. Beneath them the clear blue water of the pool was visible through the windows of the pool-house. 'I've been extraordinarily lucky, Matt.'

'So've I.' He smiled at her. 'A good wife is better than rubies, or whatever it is the Bible says.'

Later, in the cool of the evening, they sat on the terrace eating sandwiches, a bottle of wine on the table between them. The heady smell of summer roses came to them from the garden, and a few moths fluttered in and out of the lights.

They had few companionable evenings alone like this together. Theirs was a busy social and business life, entertaining, being entertained. They were both on the boards of a number of charities, good causes social and cultural.

They liked opera and went frequently to Covent Garden, usually entertaining business guests or friends in their box in the grand circle.

Then there were the children. Only Georgina was married. Maurice had a flat in Oxford. Philip, a computer expert, was in the States, and Elizabeth, the youngest, who was at drama school, had digs in London but often came home at weekends.

They ate about once a fortnight with Henry and Georgina. They and the grandchildren often came for Sunday lunch, but not tomorrow because there was a drinks party at the golf club of which Matt was president, which was why they had come today. George had been invited with his girl.

It was a busy, happy, fulfilling life, and Elspeth felt she was extremely lucky. She turned once more to look at Matt who was staring at her, a half-smiling, quizzical expression on his face.

'Penny for them?' he asked.

'I was thinking how happy we were. How *lucky*.'

'You can say that again.' Imbued with a sense of well-being, he raised his glass in a silent toast.

'Another sandwich?' She passed him the plate.

'Full up.' He patted his stomach. 'More wine, dear?'

'Just half.' She held out her glass. 'This is *very* fruity.'

'You can't beat Fleurie. I must order some more. It's excellent.' He leaned back in his chair and studied the colour, holding the glass towards the light. 'And tomorrow . . . '

'We have the golf club.'

'Couldn't wish for a better life,' he said. 'I'm a contented man.'

'Don't forget tomorrow evening,' we have the Buckhursts for dinner.' Elspeth reached for her spectacles and then for her diary, which lay on the table beside her. 'It's *such* a busy week.' She flicked over the pages. 'Sometimes I wish we had more evenings like this, when just the two of us are alone together.'

'Then *make* them, darling.' Matt leaned forward and took a sip from his glass. 'Turn down more invitations, don't entertain so much. *I* don't mind. I'm getting past it anyway.'

'Past it?' She threw back her head and gave a throaty laugh. 'You're just at the *peak*.'

'Don't say it. Don't tempt fate.' He smiled at her mockingly, placing his hand over his heart. 'I am at the age when men suddenly keel over with a coronary.'

'Oh darling, *don't*.' Elspeth looked alarmed. 'You're merely fifty-five. That's not the age . . . '

'Yes it is. Look at Michael Hamilton.'

'Everyone knew he had an unhealthy lifestyle. Also he was a womaniser,' she added with a sharp note of disapproval in her voice. 'And he was a *drinker*,' she went on, '*and* a workaholic – '

'All right, all right.' Matt waved a hand at her. 'I'm *none* of those things . . . '

She looked at him appraisingly. 'You work too hard, but on the whole you lead a very good, moderate lifestyle, to which I hope I may say, in all modesty, I contribute.'

'You do, darling, you do.' He reached out his hand and took hers. 'I am a happy, contented man,' he repeated, smiling, then his face grew solemn as he saw the look on her face. 'What *is* it, darling?'

'Don't tempt fate,' she whispered, pressing his hand, still clasped in hers. 'Just be glad for what we have. I am.'

They finished their sandwiches and wine almost in silence, then rose and, arms linked, wandered together round the garden, enjoying the cool of the night, the sound of the fountain cascading jets of water into the basin below.

Matt lay next to Elspeth, conscious of her warm, slightly abundant body next to his. The linen was cool, her skin fragrant after her bath. They drew back the curtains at night and the full moon shone into the room, making it almost seem like day, casting into deep, deep shadows the solid pieces of furniture, mostly antique. An owl hooted, its repetitious sound sometimes near, sometimes far, as it flitted between the trees, comforting however in its familiarity.

Chudleigh Court was a gracious Georgian house set in one hundred acres of Oxfordshire countryside. They had bought it when, due to the success of Ransom Engineering, Matt became a millionaire. His father had worked hard for it, and so had he, an engineering apprentice from the age of sixteen. In his day one didn't go to college, as Maurice had, but learned the job on the spot. He'd married relatively young, at the age of twenty-six. Elspeth was a year younger. Georgina was born almost nine months after their wedding, and their family was complete before they were thirty. They had not lived together, or even slept together before their marriage. Elspeth had been a virgin, but not Matt. In the fifties that was largely the way things were.

Matt became a father for the fourth time and a millionaire in the same year, and a year later they bought Chudleigh Court, twenty miles from Woodstock, and made it their main home. It had now been their home for twenty-four years. Matt thought about their celebration next spring of thirty years of marriage. For surely it was a celebration. Wondering why he was suddenly so thoughtful, so restless, Matt turned his head and gazed at Elspeth, her face lit by the moon, apparently sound asleep. Dear, familiar wife of his body, companion, friend. He reached out and touched her arm and, in her sleep, she seemed to smile.

Matt closed his own eyes and sighed, conscious for the first time for many years of a feeling of unease, almost of dissatisfaction. He could still visualise her in his mind's eye: vivid, alert, beautiful, young, her body pulsating with life, restless energy; those long, sweeping, effortless strides as she returned service or volleyed; the sight of her arm raised over her head as she served, the glimpse of a white, hairless armpit, before the racquet came thudding down on the ball.

Jenny.

From the tall tower, Matt looked towards the dome of St Paul's which had once dominated the City of London. Now it seemed like a tiny speck, almost insignificant among the high buildings and church spires, the old red Victorian buildings that remained in the Square Mile. In the background the voices continued talking, arguing, Spanish being translated into English, English into Spanish.

Birado SA was a medium-sized engineering company situated on the outskirts of Madrid, which he and George Hulme had visited several times since the previous spring.

Had he known Jenny then, Matt found himself wondering? Were they living together, or did she hover somewhere in the background? How had he met her? And why, above all, did it matter so much to *him*? His preoccupation with the girl irritated him, and he tried to brush away her image from his mind.

'So, if we could persuade you, Sir Matthew . . . '

Matt started.

Beyond was the broad winding ribbon of the Thames, the bridges of Blackfriars, London, Waterloo and Westminster, above which nobly rose the Gothic spires of the People's Parliament.

Guiltily Matt removed his gaze from the far horizon, and stared into the enquiring eyes of the female translator.

'I apologise,' he said with a shake of his head. 'I wasn't concentrating.'

'About the tender for the subsidiary company of Birado, Frontera SA,' George prompted him, his eyes on the notes he was making on the pad in front of him.

'Ah, yes.' Matt sat back and, with a knowledgeable expression, linked his fingers and gazed at the ceiling. 'We cannot complete the deal without the concurrence of *all* the participating companies . . . '

14

He launched forth into the ins and outs of the acquisition of the Spanish conglomerate, facts which he had at his fingertips. He was a master of his brief. It was a very intricate question which the advent of a single European market would make more, not less, complex.

'And it's nearly upon us,' he concluded, gazing at the board members of the Spanish company sitting opposite him, only one of whom spoke English.

Quickly the translator relayed the gist of Matt's remarks, upon which Señor Gonzalez, the managing director, launched into a long peroration in his native tongue.

Later, as the meeting broke up, George gazed at his watch and said, 'Have you time for a drink, Matt? I'm meeting Jenny at the Piccadilly.'

'Well, that would be nice,' Matt also glanced at his watch, 'if you don't think it's too late?'

'Oh no, I think it can be fitted in, and . . . we must get this business straightened out, and our offer finalised before the end of the week. We can talk in the car.'

'Quite so.'

The managing director of Birado stepped forward and held out his hand.

'So we will have your final offer at the weekend, Sir Matthew?'

'Oh, before I should think. Hulme and I are going to discuss it on the way home.'

'Perhaps you'd care to join us for a drink?' George said politely.

'Alas, thank you, no. Our plane is at seven. We too have a lot to do before the week is out, but it has been a most enjoyable and, I hope, profitable exercise doing business with you Sir Matthew, Mr Hulme . . . '

Señor Gonzalez and his co-directors bowed, smiled and shook hands before they dispersed to their cars waiting outside.

As Matthew and George got into the Jaguar, Matthew

sank back against the leather upholstery and ran a hand across his brow.

'Well.' He looked at George, who had been giving Peter the chauffeur instructions, and smiled. 'Tiring but successful.'

'We will have to up our bid.' George drew a notebook from his pocket and consulted it.

'But we expected that. We have made allowances for it in the budget.'

'Jeff seemed to think so.' Jeff Holland, the finance director of Ransom Engineering, had also been present at the meeting. George scribbled some figures on to the page.

The traffic in the City was building up as offices closed for the day and, as the car gently edged forward, Matt glanced out of the window. Now all the buildings could be seen from an entirely different perspective, as from the point of view of a fly.

'How long have you known Jenny?' Matt looked at George.

'About a year.'

'Is marriage on the cards then?'

'Oh, we're not thinking on those lines just yet. I'm not in a hurry to get my fingers burnt twice, and she's not in a hurry because of her age. You can't expect her to want to settle down. She's only twenty-one.'

'Really?' Matt experienced a sense of shock. 'As young as that? She's younger than Beth. She looks older,' he added after a pause.

'I was surprised too when I knew how old she was.' George slipped his notebook back into his breast pocket. 'She's so sophisticated.'

'She certainly is.' Matt rubbed a finger thoughtfully under his chin. 'Twenty-one. By God.'

By now they had reached Fleet Street and the car slowed to a crawl again as it negotiated the fork round St Bride's towards the Strand.

'Her father's a baron,' George said offhandedly.

16

'Really? I didn't think they existed any more.' Matt appeared amused.

'In Sweden they do. Don't forget they have a royal family. It's a very old title.'

'She doesn't have any trace of an accent.'

'She's lived here since she was a girl. Went to school here. The mother's English. Parents divorced.'

'I see.'

'You think Gonzalez will accept?'

Matt wasn't sure whether George deliberately wanted to change the subject away from Jenny, or whether his mind was, in fact, on the acquisition of Birado SA.

'Oh, I think so. We'd leave him on as MD, don't you think?'

'He seems very competent.' George nodded, and for the remaining few minutes of the journey the two men remained immersed in the facts and figures of the takeover.

'Shall I wait for you, Sir Matthew?' The chauffeur, having jumped out to open the door, leaned into the interior of the car.

'I'm not quite sure how long I'll be.' Matt looked at George.

'I'll wait in Swallow Street, Sir Matthew.'

'That's a very good idea.'

Matt got out of the car and stood on the pavement waiting for George. He looked around with an air of excited expectancy, feeling suddenly ridiculously happy.

Jenny was sitting in a corner of the bar reading the *Evening Standard*, her head bent concealing the contours of her perfect, oval-shaped face. She wore a white suit, no blouse, and a very small, even row of pearls at her throat.

As the men entered the bar she raised her head, her eyes immediately meeting Matt's, and to him they seemed to lighten up with pleasure. Then she saw George and her expression changed very subtly, becoming more matter-of-fact. She raised her head as he stooped to kiss her, saying, 'Pleasant surprise. Matt is to join us for a drink.'

Jenny gave her hand to Matt, who savoured the tenderness of her palm, the cool of her touch. His fingers seemed to tingle and he wondered if she felt the electricity too.

'How *very* nice to see you, Sir Matthew.'

'And very nice to see you.' He bowed slightly. 'And, please, Matt. Not "Sir Matthew".'

'Will it be champagne?' George rubbed his hands and looked round for the waiter.

'Oh, did something good happen?' Jenny looked at him with interest. 'You finalised the deal?'

'No, but we think it's in the bag.'

As the waiter came over, George ordered a bottle of Krug '81. The waiter bowed and withdrew and the men settled on either side of Jenny, who tucked the paper under her bag at her side, folded her hands in her lap and looked again at Matt.

'So the Spanish talks were a success?'

'We've got to discuss a final offer, but we think by the end of the week we shall have secured the foothold we've been looking for in Spain. Spain's on the verge of coming into Europe, so it will give us a strategic place in the European Community. Of course we've already got considerable French, German and Italian holdings: we can bring them all under one big umbrella. There will be an increasingly big role for George as group sales director.'

'And a lot of additional travel.' George reached in his pocket for his wallet as the waiter put down the tray containing champagne in an ice bucket and three tall glasses.

George paid the waiter, added a generous tip, and then started to fill the glasses, the first of which he passed to Jenny. 'To you, darling.'

'Thanks.' She smiled at him, slightly raising her glass.

'Matt.'

'Thanks.' As Matt reached across, his elbow gently brushed Jenny's breast. 'I do apologise,' he murmured, withdrawing his arm.

She looked at him but said nothing, while George, having filled his own glass, raised it and turned to Matt. 'To the success of Birado S A.'

'To the enlargement of the Ransom empire.' Jenny raised her own glass and they all drank.

'Well, not so much enlargement as consolidation.' Matt smiled his thanks and placed his own glass carefully on the table. 'It will certainly be big, but with all the component parts neatly dovetailing. We don't have anything we can't yet handle, anything too far from the core business.'

'Which is the manufacture of fine precision engines?' Jenny looked from one to the other.

'Fine precision machine *tooling*,' George corrected her. 'We manufacture parts for engines that do specialised jobs, in pharmaceuticals, chemicals, and so on. Anything that requires a special part, we can do.'

'You must come round the factory one day,' Matt said to Jenny, warming to the theme. 'I don't think you've visited us?'

'No. I'd love to.'

'And maybe one or two trips with me abroad,' George added, refilling his glass and Matt's, but not Jenny's, which was hardly touched.

Matt appeared to reflect on this. 'So long as it doesn't distract you from your work.' There was a note of mockery in his voice.

'Oh, don't worry, I'll keep his nose to the grindstone; that is if I can find the time to go.'

'Oh, you work?' Matt looked surprised.

'Doesn't everyone?'

'Well . . . not everyone.' He was thinking of Elspeth, who had never worked. But then she was a different generation. 'What do you do?'

'I work for a shipping line, Sverige/Norsk, nothing very important.'

'You don't mean you're a . . . ' Matt was going to say

19

stewardess, but thought it sounded patronising. He said instead, 'In full-time employment?'

'Baron Holstrom owns the line.' George looked at his watch.

'Oh, I see.' Matt sank back against the chair.

'Don't think I waste my time there,' Jenny said brusquely. 'It is not a sinecure. I work as personal assistant to the manager of the London office. Believe me, I take my job very seriously.'

'I'm sure you do. I apologise if you misunderstood me.'

'Matt, why not join us for dinner?' George said affably. 'We have a table booked at Langan's.'

'No, I wouldn't dream – '

'But we'd love to have you, wouldn't we, Jenny?'

'Of course.' Jenny reached for her bag and paper and smiled into Matt's eyes. 'It would be a great pleasure, Sir Matthew.'

'Then I accept, with pleasure.'

Matthew was aware of a ridiculous feeling of elation, as though he were a young man once again.

As Matt entered the bedroom, the light by Elspeth's side of the bed was still on. She sat up reading and, on seeing him, put her book down on her lap.

'Darling, it's *very* late,' he said, tiptoeing – though he didn't know why – to her side of the bed, his expression that of a guilty schoolboy.

Elspeth took off her reading glasses and laid them on the bedside table. 'Matt, where were you?'

'I had a business dinner, darling.'

'Couldn't you have *rung*?'

'I'm sorry. I should have.' Guilt turned to contrition.

'Georgina was very upset.'

'Oh my God!' Matt's hand flew to his mouth. 'I completely forgot.'

'It's unlike you, Matt.' Elspeth's tone was chilling. '*Most* unlike you.'

'I know, I know. I'll ring first thing in the morning to apologise.'

'She had some people there she specially wanted you to meet. It was all most awkward and – ' she stared at him for a few moments, as though trying to strip his soul bare, and repeated – 'and *so* unlike you. I can't understand it.'

'I'm afraid the Spaniards completely took over the meeting, dear.' He turned his back on her, not wishing her to see his face in case the lie showed. What a blissful evening it had been in Jenny's company. As well as guilt there was joy in his eyes too.

'Oh, it was the Spaniards.'

'Of course.' He turned to her again. 'You knew we were meeting them. A very important meeting, crucial to the future and well-being of the group.'

'Sara could have phoned.' Sara was his secretary.

'She didn't know.' He held out his hands placatingly. 'Please don't labour it, darling. I know it wasn't like me and I know it was rude. I am not proud of it and it won't happen again. But I just wanted you to know that there were justifiable circumstances.' With that he went into the bathroom and closed the door.

For a few moments, suddenly weary, he leaned against it, then went over to the basin and stared at his face close up in the mirror. He examined with great care the eyes, the slight pouches under them, the well-shaven chin but, above all, the lines of his face, the grey in his hair, the inevitable signs of the passage of age.

He was fifty-five and she was twenty-one. Thirty-four years' difference. He had completed his family before she was born.

He was an old fool, the sort of person who became the butt of jokes. There were so many of them and, in fact, he knew a few of them himself; men who discarded an older wife for a younger woman. Trophy wives, they were unkindly called. Old, successful men who paraded a young

21

wife on their arms not as a companion, lover and friend but as a trophy, a symbol of success and achievement.

And he, Matthew Ransom, had always been so upright, so loyal, so much a family man. Why, it was deeply ingrained in him. He loved Elspeth.

He had met many many beautiful women over the years, yet he had never been tempted to stray. Whatever happened he would always love Elspeth. He would never leave her.

He hastily undressed, cleaned his teeth, put on his pyjamas, opened the bathroom door, put out the light and walked over to the bed. Elspeth had already put out her light; he drew back the curtains as he always did and then climbed into bed beside her.

He could feel her stiff, as though the very lines of her body were somehow accusatory.

'Sorry,' he said, groping for her hand.

'It was so difficult for Georgina to *explain*. It isn't as though you did this sort of thing regularly. Some husbands do, people make allowances for it, but you don't. You are always *so* considerate, Matt. Always.'

'I know. I don't know what got into me.' He turned towards her and gently put his hand under her nightie.

'Matt?' Her tone was strained, alarmed, rather shrill.

'I do love you, you know.' His hand travelled along her thigh.

'Of course I know,' she said, but she put her hand firmly on his, preventing it straying any further. 'But really, dear, it is *very* late. What on earth has got into you tonight, Matt?'

'Sorry,' he mumbled and, removing his hand, kissed her on the cheek. Then he turned his back to her, pulling the bedclothes well over his shoulder.

But his mind, his feelings, were so confused, disturbed, so disordered that he knew he wouldn't sleep.

Until just before dawn his eyes closed, and even then he dreamt of her, of Jenny.

CHAPTER 2

Through one of the windows of the room, by stretching the neck a little, it was possible to catch a glimpse of Green Park, the trees now yellowing with autumn. It was a large drawing room, the windows bow-fronted, the whole place rather dark. Half Moon Street was so narrow, full of tall, terraced houses; but it was also so central, the heart of Mayfair. Besides, it was only for occasional use.

'A *pied-à-terre*, Sir Matthew?'

'Yes.' Matthew, his tall frame clad in a charcoal-grey overcoat, a grey pin-striped suit, stared down at the estate agent, hands in his pockets. 'Our main home is in Oxfordshire; but my wife and I come to town a great deal, and with the winter coming on . . . '

'Quite, Sir Matthew.'

'It is also possible we shall be opening an office in central London.'

Matt paused, irritated with himself. Why was he trying to explain himself, as if to justify his behaviour? Was it because he was nervous, slightly afraid? Trying to make excuses even to himself, trying to hide the *real* reason for wanting a flat in town, something that hadn't occurred to him for twenty-five years, hadn't been necessary and still wasn't? They usually stayed at the Hyde Park, Brown's, occasionally the Dorchester or the Savoy. He still didn't know what Elspeth would say, or even if he would tell her.

23

He knew it was rather a mad impulsive action – a bit in keeping with the night a few weeks ago when he had completely forgotten Georgina's dinner party.

The flat had three bedrooms, all en-suite, a well-fitted kitchen, dining room, large lounge, utility room. It was a high price for a short lease, but it was really just what he wanted. It had been the show flat of the newly refurbished building, and the carpets and curtains were included in the sale. It was thus nearly ready to move into, which was also just what he wanted.

'I'll have my solicitor contact you,' he said, thrusting his head once more out of the half-open window, conscious of the drone of traffic along Piccadilly.

He snapped the window shut, suddenly wondering how she would like it.

Jenny Holstrom obsessed him. There was little doubt about that. He hardly thought of anything else. He knew it was absurd, probably hormonal, and wondered if he should see a shrink. It had never happened to him before. It was like a bolt from the blue – untypical; even he admitted that. He felt different, he knew he was different. He had never lost control. Now the whole thing threatened to unhinge his life.

He made excuses to see her, always with George, but at least he had established to his satisfaction the fact that they didn't cohabit. Obviously sometimes he stayed with her and she stayed with him; but they didn't live together, they led separate lives. Thank heaven for that.

What was more, Jenny's flat was also in Mayfair, above the shipping office in South Audley Street, scarcely five minutes away from his new *pied-à-terre*. He had never been there, but when she told him where it was he had found himself on one of his nights alone in London going round to see, standing outside in the dark of the night, looking up at the windows, wondering if Jenny was there in bed, or maybe watching a late-night film on TV? He wondered what she would think if she should chance to look out of the window and recognise him across the street, for all the world like a peeping Tom, gazing helplessly upwards.

Silly old goat, she would probably have thought; silly old fool.

Back in the street, Matt said goodbye to the agent and told his chauffeur to take him to Claridge's where he was meeting a client for lunch, a businessman from the north for whom they did a lot of work manufacturing small parts for a vital piece of precision optical equipment.

It was a sunny, chilly autumn day, and he drove through the streets of Mayfair conscious of a strange new feeling in his heart: a compound of hope, anxiety, desire but, strangely, above all, fear.

What the hell was he doing? What impulse had dictated the agreement to buy the lease of the flat in Half Moon Street? What made him seek out the advice of estate agents, spend days surreptitiously looking at property? And why had he not told Elspeth, and what would she say if she knew? How could he possibly explain to her he'd bought a flat without consulting her? Would she not immediately divine some ulterior motive?

Maybe this was the reason for the prickly, uncomfortable sensation of fear? That for the first time for thirty harmonious, tranquil years of matrimony, he was upsetting the equanimity, the routine in which they had lived. Maybe destroying for ever their familiar lifestyle, and for what? For a woman he hardly ever saw but thought about constantly; but whom, in a way, he deliberately avoided seeing in order not to be tempted into a betrayal of his feelings. How could she not help but notice what he felt?

He was aware of Peter's face peering at him through the open door, expressing bewilderment, rather as though he had been standing there for some time.

'Claridge's, Sir Matthew,' he said patiently, maybe for the second time.

'Oh sorry, Peter, I was day-dreaming.'

Matt leapt out of the car with an agility that belied his years and hurried through the main door, acknowledging the nod of the doorman.

His client, Ted Openshaw, was already seated at Matt's usual table in a corner to the left of the door, studying the menu, a large gin and tonic in front of him. Matt hurried over to greet him.

'Ted, I'm so sorry to be late.'

'That's quite all right, Matt.' The burly ex-miner gave him a friendly handshake. 'I've had time to have a drink and look at the menu. Now this is on me.'

'No, on me,' Matt insisted as he slipped into his seat. 'I invited you.'

Ted chuckled comfortably. 'Well, we shan't fight about it. I think we can both afford the bill.'

'I think we can.' Matt smiled up at the waiter. 'I'll just have a glass of white wine, thank you.'

'Chablis, sir?'

'Chablis would be fine.'

'Shall we make that a bottle?' Ted suggested. 'I'm going to have fish for lunch.'

'Excellent idea. A bottle of a good Chablis.'

'Very good, Sir Matthew. I'll inform the wine waiter.' The waiter slipped the menu in front of Matt who glanced at it. 'I don't know that I'm really hungry,' he said, finally replacing it on the table. 'I think I'll join you in the fish, Ted. And something light to start.'

'Oeufs Benedict, I'm having.'

'Excellent. Are you staying here?' Matt joined his hands together and looked at Ted across the table. Ted Openshaw was a man he'd known for many years, a man his age with a similar family, a long-time wife and also four children, roughly the ages of Matt's. He too had a large house in a nice part of Cheshire, and a factory on the outskirts of Manchester. Their family backgrounds were, however, very different.

Ted was a former miner who had worked in the pit, until

26

his flair for invention had led him to night classes and engineering. At the age of forty he took over the company where he worked, becoming managing director and major shareholder.

The men were business colleagues, not friends, but they had visited one another's houses, Matt to play golf at Bramhall where Ted lived; Ted had brought his wife and stayed at Chudleigh for the weekend. Mavis Openshaw was a large, comfortable lady with whom Elspeth got on well. They shared a passion for gardening, were knowledgeable about roses and, of course, there was the ever-interesting topic of the children and grandchildren.

The meal ordered, the wine resting in an ice-bucket by their side, Ted put one broad hand over the other on the table and studied the man opposite him.'

'So. You look very well, Matt.'

'And you, Ted.'

'How's Elspeth?'

'Fine. Very well. And Mavis?'

'Couldn't be better. You know we have a fifth grandchild?'

'Really? No, I didn't know. That's excellent news.' Matt raised his glass. 'To you and Mavis. Boy or girl?'

'Boy, Simon. Mary's second.'

'Mary's,' Matt put his head on one side, 'Mary is Georgina's contemporary.'

'No, Mary is twenty-five. The same age as Beth.'

'Oh, yes.'

'And they all live near us, which is nice. It's Sarah who isn't married.'

'Mmm!' Matt joined his hands together under his chin and looked past Ted to the other lunchers in the large restaurant. As usual he saw one or two people he knew and, if they caught his eye, smiled. In the background, Ted was talking about his family: what they were doing, what their spouses were doing, how old the children were and, if old enough, where they went to school.

27

It was all very familiar. Very dull, very . . . well, ageing.

He saw himself then as he was: a middle-aged man with middle-aged friends and a life of increasingly geriatric concerns stretching before him . . . for how long? His father had lived until he was eighty-nine. Well, even if he equalled his record, he had another thirty-four years to go.

'You know we have acquired Birado, the Spanish engineering group?' Matt interrupted the stream of family statistics.

'Oh, it went through? I knew you wanted it.'

'Yes, everything was formalised about a month ago. I was in Madrid last week. It's an excellent operation. Streamlined, fully automated. They only employ a work-force of fifty, apart from the management and secretarial staff. I thought you might like to have a look over it, Ted? Maybe combine it with a trip to the coast and some golf? You know we have a house in Almeria.'

'Well, I think that would be lovely.' Ted looked delighted at the idea. 'Mavis would love it. When were you thinking of, Matt?'

'Maybe,' Matt drummed his fingers on the table, 'February? March?'

'Excellent.'

'Of course our wedding anniversary is in May. Thirty years.'

'A big party?'

'Of course. Here, you're both invited.'

'Thanks.'

'Birado, incidentally, is very compatible with the work you're doing . . . '

Then Matt saw, over Ted's shoulder, a swathe of thick blonde hair, the tall figure in a long black skirt, high-necked black sweater relieved by a thick gold necklace and gold earrings. Matt had missed her entry, but the waiter was holding back the chair for her as she sat down. And waiting to sit was a man with her; also fair, about thirty-five, with rather heavy Germanic features. Or maybe he was Swedish.

'Yes, compatible . . .' Ted encouraged him as Matt stopped suddenly in mid-sentence.'

'Sorry,' Matt looked apologetically at his guest, 'I just saw someone I knew.' He felt awkward, tongue-tied, slightly breathless, as though he'd had a shock. Ted was looking at him with what could have been concern.

'Compatible with the fibre-optics you're developing for Visionsmart.'

'But not a rival, I hope.'

'Oh, I don't think so.' Matt firmly grasped the stem of his glass. He was in control now. The sight of her – and it was her – had momentarily thrown him. He now raised his eyes and stared at her and, through the throng across the floor, Jenny saw him and stared back. Matt raised a hand and so did she. Then he looked across at Ted.

'George Hulme's very nice girlfriend.'

'Oh?' Now Ted turned round and Matt saw that Jenny was still looking in their direction, though appearing to listen to the man opposite her. Jenny, as if aware that she was the subject of the conversation of the two men on the far side of the room, smiled again. Then her companion looked round to see what was preoccupying her.

'*That's* not him,' Ted said turning to Matt.

'No. I don't know who it is. He looks foreign. She's half-Swedish, but I don't think he's old enough to be her father.'

'She's very young,' Ted said.

'How old do you think?' A mischievous smile played on Matt's lips.

'Twenty-five.'

'Twenty-one.'

'Go on, and he's what? George, I mean.'

'Thirty-eight.'

'She looks older than twenty-one.'

'That's what I think.'

'Why are we talking about her anyway?'

'Why indeed?' Matt was aware of an expression of curiosity in Ted's eyes. 'Well, she's a remarkably beautiful young woman and George is a very lucky man. I think so, anyway,' Matt said almost to himself, as though that justified his own interest.

Ted took up his glass, eyed the contents, smiled rather suggestively and looked across at Matt. 'Have you ever toyed with anything like that yourself?'

'Like what?'

'Well . . . ' Ted gave an uncharacteristically sheepish smile. 'A bit on the side?'

Matt was uncertain as to how to reply. It meant his relationship with Ted would enter a new dimension if he was honest. Instead he turned the question.

'Have you?'

Now it was Ted's turn to look nonplussed. There was a pause while they were served with the first course; each man dipped his spoon into the soft-boiled eggs and pronounced the dish good.

'I don't know that I ought to tell you, Matt.' Ted leaned his head over the table and lowered his voice confidentially. 'But I've had a relationship for many years with a very nice woman, no longer young, and we have a son of fourteen.'

Matt put down his spoon and stared across the table.

'I can see I've shocked you.' Ted took up his spoon, but the expression on his face was one of quiet self-satisfaction. 'She's very nice, very discreet. I bought her a house in Didsbury and she has everything she can want. It's quite near the works, so I see her and the boy regularly. He's a bright lad and goes to Manchester Grammar.'

'Does he know . . .?'

'That I'm married. He knows everything. It doesn't worry him. He loves his mother and he trusts me.'

'But doesn't love you?'

'Oh, I think he loves me.' Ted finished his dish and dabbed at his lips with his napkin. 'But we're not close. Not really. It's difficult to be with someone like that. Katie knows.'

'Oh, does she?' Katie was Ted's eldest daughter.

'She found out. It upset her at first. Maureen and I were having dinner at a place in Alderley Edge and Katie came in with her then boyfriend. Well, after that I told her the whole thing.'

'Has she met Maureen since?'

'No,' Ted shook his head. 'She feels it would be disloyal to her mother; but she has met Gerard, our boy, and he knows she is his half-sister. It makes him happy to know that he's got relations and that some time, maybe years hence, it will all be out in the open.'

'Mmm!' Matt too finished his dish, aware of a new development in his relationship with this blunt northerner whom he had only ever thought of before as a business colleague. He sat back and scratched his nose with the tip of his index finger. 'As a matter of fact, and I don't know whether I'm ashamed of this or proud, but I have never been unfaithful to Elspeth.'

'Never once? Not a little fling?' Ted looked mildly incredulous.

'No. Maybe I'm undersexed,' Matt murmured. Then he looked across at Jenny again and he knew for certain that it wasn't that.

As it happened, though she and her partner had started lunch after Matt and Ted, they all left the restaurant together. They stopped in the lobby and Jenny introduced her companion as the German agent of the shipping line. Matt introduced Ted. There was some small-talk and then Matt offered them all a lift. But Ted had his own transport and an afternoon appointment out of town, and the German had a car waiting to take him to Heathrow.

They all shook hands and Jenny and Matt stood on the pavement outside Claridge's waving to the two cars as they drove off. Matt felt quite light-headed at the thought that he had her to himself again; an unexpected, almost un-hoped-for treat. On the far side of the street, Peter waited in the Jaguar, keeping an eye on him.

'Can I give you a lift?' Matt said as he signalled for the car.

'Oh it's not far, Sir Matthew,' she smiled.

'I thought we'd dropped the "Sir Matthew".' He gently took her arm and propelled her across the road, skilfully dodging the post-lunchtime traffic.

'Sorry, Matt.' She smiled at Peter, who stood with the rear door open. Matt got in beside her.

'Look,' he said suddenly, 'I wonder if you can give me an opinion about something.'

'I'd be delighted.' She had opened her Filofax, as if to see what her next appointment was.

'Have you got half an hour?'

'What, now?' She glanced at the page open before her. 'Yes, I think so.'

'It's just that, well . . . ' He took up the mobile phone and dialled a number. 'Mr Giles? Sir Matthew Ransom here. I wonder if I can call in for the key? Yes, I have someone I'd like to see it. Thanks. No, not necessary for you to be there. We're on our way.'

He told Peter to return to the estate agency in Bond Street, then glanced at Jenny, who was looking mystified.

'I just want to know what you think. It won't take long.'

Having picked up the key and directed Peter to take them back to the flat, Matt sat back in the car, jingling the key between his fingers, curiously happy and excited.

'I take it this is a house or flat, or is it an office?' Jenny said.

'It's a flat.'

'You're going to take a flat?'

'I think so.'

She closed her Filofax and tucked it into the large, stylish handbag she carried. 'You want me to see it before showing it to your wife?'

'Something like that.'

'Or does she know?'

'No, she doesn't know, yet. It was just an impulse and, as I saw you, I thought I'd ask your opinion as a woman.'

'Oh!' Jenny leaned her head against the soft leather upholstery, her expression thoughtful. He glanced sideways at her and his heart filled with an inexpressible emotion, a mixture of hope and anguish, of yearning and desire. He wanted to take her hand and hold it, but he knew the time was not yet.

'How's George?' he asked instead.

'George is fine,' she said, looking at him gravely, 'but you know that yourself.'

Her solemnity was rather unnerving. He thought it must be the Scandinavian side of her. 'I mean personally.'

'I mean personally too.'

'He's a really nice fellow.' Matt looked out of the window.

'He is.'

Matt continued to gaze at the street, a plan about George coming almost unbidden to his mind.

Jenny leaned her head out of the window, as Matt had a few hours before, and sniffed the air.

'You can see Green Park.'

'I know.' He stood beside her, relishing the contact, careful not to make it too obvious. So tactile was the sensation that he could sense the quality of her skin, the fragrance of her body. A few inches away, the crown of her head gleamed in the pale, wintry sun. He resisted the temptation to kiss it.

The time was not yet.

Abruptly Jenny withdrew her head, firmly closed the window, and Matt stepped back too.

'It's nice,' she said, looking at him in the direct, rather

33

disconcerting way that seemed to suggest that she could read his thoughts. He had seen her only half a dozen times since the summer, if that, and always in the company of George and other people. This was the first time they'd been alone.

'Why do you need a *pied-à-terre*?' she asked, leaning back against the sill, hands folded in front of her, one foot, in its low-heeled black pump, twisted over the other.

'We spend a lot of time in town. You can't always get into a hotel. Even the Savoy was full last week.'

'What does Elspeth think?'

'I don't know.'

'But isn't it, forgive me for saying it, an *odd* thing to do without asking her?'

'It was done on an impulse. I was passing the estate agents on my way to Sothebys and saw it in the window. I love this area.'

'You don't *strike* me as being a man of impulse.' Her expression was grave again.

'Usually I'm not.'

He looked at her, at her mouth, her eyes, the smooth sheen of hair brushed back from her brow.

He came towards her, put a hand on her shoulder, drew her nearer to him.

She raised her chin, her mouth parted. Their lips touched and clung together, their tongues met. Matt enveloped her with his coat, pressing her against him, his hands touching her small, neat breasts. Then he broke away and said, 'Oh, damn.' Jenny merely looked at him, saying nothing.

CHAPTER 3

Matt stood in front of the large global map which decorated almost an entire wall of his office, and stuck a little flag in the far south-west corner of Europe.

'There,' he said, turning to George Hulme, who stood a few paces away gazing at the spot on the map, '*that's* where I want you for the next few months: Madrid.'

'Madrid!'

'I want you there running the show, George, keeping an eye on Gonzalez.'

'You mean you want me over Gonzalez, or equal with him?' There was a note of suspicion in George's tone.

'Well,' Matt fluttered his fingers, 'it will have to look equal, but really I want you there, in charge.'

George stuck his hands in his pockets and went over to the window, eyes brooding out across the bleak Oxfordshire countryside. Five years before, Ransom Engineering had moved to its new premises, built and landscaped with environmental considerations in mind. It was a low, two-storey building, and conformed to the best industrial architectural practice of the day.

Whatever one thought of its appearance — and there were some who criticised as well as some who praised it — the view from the windows on the first floor was superb. The site had once housed a stately home, and there was still an ancient lake full of carp and pike. Today it mirrored an icy blue sky, and its grassy verges bore traces of the thick hoar-frost of the previous night.

The news had come like a thunderbolt to George, and he was not sure how to take it; whether he welcomed it or not.

'How will it affect my overall position in the group?' he asked at last, wandering back to Matt's side and gazing at the map with its ever-expanding line of flags.

'How do you mean?' Matt returned to his desk. It was a semi-circular slab of highly polished mahogany, which had been designed to match the rest of the furniture in the room.

'As group sales director?'

'It won't affect it at all. You can continue to control the sales of the group from Madrid as well as London. It's no diminution in status at all, George. In fact it's a promotion. It also enhances the importance of Spain, which is no bad thing.'

'I see.' George slumped in one of the chairs in front of the desk and stroked his brow. 'Well, I shall have to think about it, Matt.'

'Of course.' Matt joined his hands carefully in front of him, his expression inscrutable.

'*And* consult with Jenny.'

'Ah!' Matt had not, for some reason, anticipated this.

'If Jenny doesn't want to come, I don't go.'

'I see.' Matt swallowed. This was something which had certainly not been in his calculations. 'Did you expect Jenny to wish to accompany you?'

'Of course.'

'But hasn't she got a job?'

'Well, she'll have to choose. It's not a very important job anyway. It just gives her something to do. She's not really interested in shipping.'

'I see, I hadn't thought of that. Well, of course, if it depends on Jenny . . . ' Matt set his lips in a stubborn line and gazed at George with a mulish air which George knew all too well.

*   *   *

'It's either Spain or no job,' George said to Jenny, lowering his voice so that no one else in the restaurant could hear.

'But he didn't say as much. Did he?' The news also came as a shock to Jenny.

'More or less. I don't know whether he's trying to get rid of me, or just what is going on.'

'He'd hardly send you to Spain . . . '

'Kicking me upstairs, you know. Like they do to politicians when they send them to the House of Lords.'

'I thought Sir Matthew had a very high regard for you.'

'So did I.' George picked disgruntledly at the roll on the side of his plate.

A silence fell between them, during which Jenny tried once more to rationalise her thoughts about George, about Matt, about the position into which she was sliding in relation to the head of the important group, her lover's boss, the great Sir Matthew Ransom himself.

Jenny Holstrom was a woman to whom life had always been kind. The adored only child of a wealthy, titled man, she had wanted for nothing except the vague desire – which most offspring of divorced parents have – that one day her parents would get back together. When they each remarried, that hope clearly became impossible, but the whole thing had been so civilised, had happened such a long time ago . . . Her parents had continued to love her more – were that possible – than ever. They wanted to compensate for what they'd done by making her feel more precious than before. She felt doubly precious, doubly loved.

She had been only four when her mother brought her to live permanently in England, at first with her grandparents, and then in a comfortable flat in Knightsbridge when her mother remarried, with weekend visits to the grandparents' country home in Sussex.

There had been a London day school, a girls' boarding school, lots of privileged, wealthy girls like herself. She was clever and there was a chance to go to university, which she didn't want to. She knew it was the one thing that her father reproached her for, that instead of being different she wanted to remain part of the herd.

But there had been something about university life that Jenny found uncongenial; the aura of the hippy, the great unwashed. Even the Zuleika Dobson image of Oxford didn't appeal.

At the age of eighteen, when she left school, she felt she was a woman. She wanted to do womanly things, not regress her life another three years while she got a degree.

And there were men. At first a stream of vaguely well-connected, wealthy young men: Swedes, English, assorted nationalities. Finally there was George.

Neither her father nor mother liked George. He was nobody and had come from nowhere. Yet to Jenny, meeting him at a conference of the CBI in London, he had glamour, was sexy, the image of the older man in the middle of divorcing his wife.

Jenny liked older men, and George was seventeen years older than she was. He was street-wise, worldly-wise, much travelled, and he gave her a good time. He was good in bed. He liked the fast life and so did she. He knew his way around. She liked going abroad with him and staying in expensive hotels, enjoying the night-life after George had done a hard day's work and she had been through the shops.

But *Spain*?

'It's only for six months,' George said at last rather despairingly, 'or thereabouts. They say Madrid really swings.'

'I'll be here when you get back,' she said with a kind of gritty edge to her voice. 'There are weekends.'

'I want you to come and live with me there, Jenny,' George said solemnly. 'We can give it a trial run.'

'What sort of a trial run?'

'Well . . . marriage if you like. Isn't it what you want, eventually?'

*   *   *

No, no, no. Back in her flat later that night she felt angry. There'd been a row, a scene, and afterwards an undignified tussle in the car. He'd wanted to come up. She'd said no. He'd obviously felt annoyed, rejected, and had driven off without seeing her to the door. He really, she decided, tugging at her earrings, was a peasant.

She put in her sleepers, ran them round the holes in her ears, aware of intense irritation, but also of something else: excitement, a feeling of adventure, fear.

The telephone rang and she stiffened, looked at the clock. It was ten thirty: the evening had ended abruptly after they'd left the restaurant.

She debated whether or not to answer the phone. Doubtless it would be George phoning from a call-box, contrite, wanting a reconciliation. She felt slightly contemptuous of him, and imagined the great Sir Matt stooping to such a gesture. Never. She seized the receiver and said abruptly, 'Hello?'

'Hello?' There was a chuckle in his voice. 'You sound *very* formidable. Did I wake you up?'

'Oh, *Matt*!' Her tone of voice changed completely.

'And who, may I ask, did you think it would be?'

'Well, certainly not you.' She felt rather kittenish and took the phone to the bed, stretching herself on it with a pleasurable sensation of anticipation.

'Come on. Who? George?'

She had the impression from his bantering tone that he was as relaxed as she was, probably lying on the bed with his tie undone.

'Where are you?' she asked.

'In my hotel. I had a dinner in the City. Elspeth stayed at home.'

'Oh!'

'The Savoy.'

'Oh!'

'The view is lovely, the lights from the Festival Hall shining on the river.'

'That's nice.'

'I could come over.'

No reply.

'Are you alone?' A trifle anxiously.

'Yes.'

'Did you see George?'

'Yes.'

'You don't sound very happy.'

'Happy with whom, or about what?'

'The prospect of going to Spain. I mean, I could come over to discuss it with you. Nothing else.'

'It's too late. Much, much too late.'

'Maybe you're right. Lunch tomorrow? I could stay over.'

'That would be nice.'

'Claridge's? One o'clock?'

'Lovely.'

'I shall look forward to it. Enormously,' he added.

'Goodnight, Matt.'

'Goodnight, my dear.'

Jenny lay on the bed for some time, the telephone pressed to her ear. Then she let it fall and lay staring at the ceiling.

What was she doing? Playing a double game with two powerful men?

Well, no, it was not a game. She knew precisely what she wanted. There was absolutely no comparison between George and Matt – none at all. One was finite. The other had a wife, family, and was over thirty years her senior. Attractive though she had to admit to herself she found him, the whole thing was quite, quite out of the question.

After lunch, followed discreetly by Peter in the Jag, they strolled through Mayfair towards Half Moon Street, stopping to gaze in the windows of a few antique shops. They were in playful mood; the lunch had been great. There had been a lot of banter, very little serious talk really, considering the potential seriousness of the situation. They simply seemed enormously to enjoy each other's company. George's name had scarcely been mentioned, Elspeth's not at all. The whole thing was rather unreal.

'I want you to see what furniture I've got,' he said.

'Already?' Jenny looked surprised. 'It's yours?'

'All signed, sealed and mine for forty-five years. It was a short lease, but it will see me out unless I can buy the freehold. It's really ideal for what I want, a place to unwind in. I might also be interested in some offices in St James's Street, a newly refurbished block just round the corner from St James's Square.' He was making this up, but it was nice to lend a little verisimilitude to the proceedings.

They reached Berkeley Square and paused to cross to the other side. Traffic came at them from all sides, but Jenny felt cocooned, aloof, protected from any danger by him. Matt maintained a steady grip on her arm and she felt cherished, as Daddy had cherished her. She pressed herself against him.

They strolled through the square into Curzon Street and then Half Moon Street. She could see how excited he was and stood back, smiling slightly, as he put the key in the lock. He looked like an impish schoolboy indulging in a prank. Which, in a way, he was.

They squeezed into the tiny lift and stood facing each other, he with his hands in the pockets of his coat, staring down at her. She, chin tucked into her fur collar, looked up at him. He put his hand out and touched her hair.

'I do adore you,' he said.

She let her head rest briefly against his chest, and the door of the lift slid open. He put an arm around her and ushered her out, pausing to unlock the door of the flat while behind them the lift gates slid quietly together.

The first thing she noticed was that the decor was different: a silk paper in a pale, opalescent green lined the walls.

'You've had it done over,' she exclaimed.

'Like it?'

'I forget what it was before.'

'It was paint, cream and a sort of white.'

He opened the door of the hall and she went into the lounge, which was partly furnished with new curtains. The central crystal chandelier had been removed to be replaced by discreet wall lighting and low lamps. It was very intimate.

It was also rich, opulent, comfortable. There was a long glass occasional table and, new in the corner, a Bang and Olufsen television and video recorder. A long sofa and two armchairs had an exotic bird motif of cages, cockatoos and tall pampas grass.

'Did your wife do all this?' Jenny meaningfully trailed a finger along the arm of the sofa.

'A very good firm in Mount Street recommended by the agents. Come and see the kitchen. Every gadget you can think of.'

He led her into the kitchen, which was instantly flooded with lights from the ceiling.

'The same firm?' Jenny enquired, noting the new fridge-freezer, washing-machine, dishwasher, double oven, gas-fired hob and microwave.

'I think they got it all from Harrods,' he said vaguely.

In the corner was a breakfast bar with a fruit squeezer, toaster and coffee percolator on the side.

'It's nice.' She looked at him nodding her approval. 'Has Elspeth seen it?'

'Not yet.' Matt, his face impassive, took her arm and, putting off the lights, guided her back into the hall. 'Shall I show you the bedrooms?'

'Please.'

The master bedroom had a four-poster, a couple of easy chairs and a dressing table of walnut veneer, clearly antique with delicate cabriole legs. The stool in front of it was covered in oyster satin. There was a chest of drawers which looked as though it had been crafted by the same *ébéniste* who had done the dressing table, and a double wardrobe with an elegant marquetry pattern on each door, French, eighteenth century.

The curtains here were of the same oyster satin as the stool, with ties of the same material.

'I like it all. It has style,' she said.

She then inspected the other two bedrooms; one double with bath en-suite, and one single with en-suite shower. At the end of the hall was a cloakroom with lavatory, bidet and basin.

'Plenty of loos,' she murmured as they wandered back into the sitting room. At the far end was a very small dining room which was, as yet, bare, and from this a door led into the kitchen.

'I don't know whether to make that a dining room or a study,' Matt said. 'I mean there are so many restaurants round here. More fun to eat out.'

'Or, occasionally, when one ate in, a salad or a hamburger in the kitchen,' she agreed.

'Or in front of the telly.' He stood and studied her expression. 'Like it?'

'Hm!' she nodded emphatically. 'I can't get over the speed at which it's all been done.'

'That's what these people are there for.'

Matt stood with his back to the window and looked at her as, hands deep in her pockets, she perched on an arm of the sofa. 'What did you tell George?'

'I said I couldn't go to Spain. I didn't want to. I've resisted living with him as a . . . mistress. I wouldn't dream of it. It's not my style.'

'Good.' Matt smiled with satisfaction.

'George says he won't go.'

'I think he will.' There was a slight edge to Matt's voice. 'He has the best job in the world, and he knows it. He wouldn't get the salary or the status anywhere else.'

'He's angry. I think he might leave.'

'Then I don't mind.'

'You don't *mind* losing George?'

43

'Not if I can get him away from you.'

'Matt!' She shook her head.

'Yes?'

'You're very devious.'

'I'm not devious. I am a man who wants something, someone. I have a way of getting what I want. That's all.'

'You're doing *all* this merely to get George away from me?'

'George will be very good for the new company. He is innovative, full of ideas. I seriously want George there; but I also seriously want him away from you.'

'Which is the reason for showing me round this flat?'

'I hoped you'd like it. I wanted a woman's opinion.'

'But not Elspeth's?'

'Elspeth . . . ' Matt paused, 'that *is* a very delicate matter.'

'I should think it is delicate.' Jenny's lip curled slightly. 'You've bought and furnished a flat in London your wife knows nothing about. Yet you've brought me to see it twice.' She stood up, shoulders thrust back, her hands on either side of her neat, narrow waist with its broad black belt. She must have been aware of her allure, her attraction, as she stood there, swaying slightly on her high-heeled boots, face partly concealed by the high fashion collar of her coat.

'Matt, I should tell you I have no intention of being your mistress, if that's what you have in mind.'

'I could give you everything . . . ' he began. He had dreaded the moment and now it was upon him.

'But I've got everything. I'm not short of money. Daddy gives me all I need. I have a very good life, my independence, freedom. I know you won't leave Elspeth, Matt, and I don't want you to, not for me.'

'But George . . . '

'George is attractive, sexy, but I don't love him. Frankly I'm not sorry he's being exiled to Spain. It will enable the affair to fizzle out. He was becoming too possessive, so you

44

did me a favour. I may go back to Sweden and work in the offices in Stockholm.'

'I thought you might care for me,' he said softly. 'The kiss . . . '

She bowed her head. 'I think you *are* very attractive. Most attractive. I have always liked older men, but age has nothing to do with it.'

'Then maybe I might be allowed to take you out for dinner occasionally? Lunch sometimes?'

'I have no objection to that. I'd like you as a friend, Matt, sincerely; but as anything else . . . ' She shook her head. 'I hope you're not too disappointed.'

Matt reached for the lights, led her from the flat, closed the door. Far from feeling rebuffed he felt they had barely started. She was negotiating terms and they had just begun.

He felt excited, full of anticipation.

Besides, wasn't love a game, and who wanted a woman who was easy to get?

'I really don't know what's the matter with your father.' Elspeth kept a steadying hand on Beth's leg as she attached some coloured balls to the top of the Christmas tree.

Term had finished and Beth had been home for a week. Philip would not be back from America, but apart from him they would be one big happy family as usual at Christmas time.

'Oh?' Beth paused in the act of fixing a translucent ball and gazed down at her mother, an expression of concern on her face. 'Isn't Daddy well? I thought he was fine when I saw him last week.'

'He's so restless. Not like him. I hope it isn't a warning of something wrong. High blood pressure; you know, the usual things men get as they get older.'

'Oh Mummy!' Beth finished decorating the top of the tree and carefully climbed down the stepladder, one hand still in her mother's. 'It's not like you to worry.'

'I know, and it's not like Daddy to be so . . . well, I don't know how to describe it. Sometimes I think his mind's on something else, far away.'

'But it is. It always is, more so with the business expanding. He was telling me all about the acquisition in Spain. Also, Mummy, he's got so many things to do.' Beth hopped off the bottom step and moved the ladder to the next part of the huge, sixteen-foot tree that had been delivered and erected the day before. 'President of this, chairman of that. I think he takes on too many things. Now there's a hint there is to be a London office.'

'Oh?' Elspeth paused in the middle of untangling Christmas tinsel taken from the box that was brought down from the attic each year. 'He never mentioned a London office.'

'Didn't he?' Beth looked surprised. She thought her parents shared everything. 'Maybe it was only a thought.'

'Totally unnecessary.' Elspeth did in fact feel rather aggrieved that Matt, who always *said* he consulted her about everything, hadn't mentioned it.

'Maybe it's the male menopause, Mummy.'

'I don't believe in that nonsense.'

'A lot of people do.' Beth, tinsel in her hands, carefully mounted the stepladder again and began to drape it tastefully around the higher branches of the tree.

Beth was the most artistic of all the Ransom children. In fact, the only artistic one. Maurice was a businessman, Philip thought of nothing but computers, and Georgina seemed happy in her role of mother and farmer's wife, enjoying her involvement in village affairs and the farming community in general.

Beth had always been different. Dark, vivacious, very like Matt in looks and, Elspeth sometimes suspected, his favourite, though he protested that he loved all his children equally.

Beth, a late entry, was in her third year at drama school, and had her eye on the gold medal. After that, who knew?

A career in television maybe? But of course, at first, the obligatory few years in rep.

Christmas had always been an exciting time in the Ransom household. Elspeth had been making preparations since October, when she started the Christmas cake, then a huge Christmas pudding, sausage rolls and mince pies, various casseroles, sauces and desserts ready for the deep freeze. The massive turkey had been delivered by the same farmer who supplied the Christmas tree, and there was a sirloin of beef, a loin of pork, and a leg of lamb in the cold larder.

Yet Matt this year had seemed to be less excited by Christmas than he usually was, more preoccupied, restless. It hardly seemed as though he had Christmas on his mind at all, but something else.

Maybe it was the idea of a London office and the impending departure of George Hulme for Spain, because in Elspeth's opinion Matt would miss him. George had always been his right hand, a loyal lieutenant, and Elspeth wondered whether Matt had done the right thing in insisting that George took up the post in Spain he clearly didn't want, especially as that pretty young girl-friend of his had apparently declined to accompany him.

The tree finished, the two women went round the house adding finishing touches to the decorations, some of which had been in place for days. Sprigs of fresh holly and mistletoe were stuck over the pictures, and a large bunch of mistletoe hung strategically in the hall. The lights were tested on the Christmas tree and found to be in working order. Wasn't it just the worst thing when they blew on Christmas Day and no one could find a spare bulb?

Matt would be home that night for the holiday, not returning to the office until the new year. Maurice would arrive the next day, and Henry, Georgina and the children on Christmas Eve. They would stay one night only: it was always difficult to get away for longer because of the animals. After all, the farm-workers wanted their holidays too.

Elspeth experienced the familiar surge of excitement she always had at Christmas and, as preparations progressed, that nagging sense of anxiety about Matt gradually evaporated.

That night he came home around six, with arms full of presents, Peter behind him similarly encumbered. Elspeth had taken the pudding and some of the mince tarts out of the freezer, and they lay on trays in the larder defrosting. That night there was goose for dinner, and its succulent smell permeated the kitchen. Matt had a piece of tinsel around his neck, and seemed in unusually good humour, maybe a little drunk from the office party.

Peter was offered a sausage roll and a drink. As he never touched alcohol, he had a coke, while Elspeth and Beth had sherry and Matt a glass of beer.

They all went into the drawing room to admire the tree and, as night had fallen, the lights were ceremoniously switched on, according to custom, by Matt.

The room had been dark, illuminated only by the log fire leaping in the huge grate, and now the myriad twinkling, multi-coloured lights shone on their awestruck faces; the magic of light, of Christmas, as usual casting its spell.

'Happy Christmas,' Matt cried, raising his glass, and they all replied, toasting one another, the family embracing.

Elspeth took Peter to the kitchen where he was presented, again according to custom, with a turkey, a Christmas pudding and a bottle of sherry for the family.

The others said their goodbyes to Peter in the hall, but Matt went to the car with him and, after he had got into the driving seat and turned on the lights, Matt leaned through the window, his hand outstretched.

'Again a happy Christmas, Peter, to you and the family. And thanks for everything.'

'Thank *you*, Sir Matthew.' Peter shook his hand, but

instead of switching on the engine, sat staring ahead as if he had something else to say. 'A happy Christmas to you and *all* your family and . . . Sir Matthew . . . ' He paused, looking embarrassed.

'Yes, Peter?' Matt, who had been about to turn back to the house, looked at him enquiringly. 'Is there something else?'

'It's not for me to say really, Sir Matthew,' Peter's prominent Adam's apple rose and fell, 'but I would like to say that you have a *very* nice family, sir, something precious. Lady Ransom is one of the nicest ladies I know . . . '

'One of the nicest I know too, Peter,' Matt said coldly. 'Have no doubt about that.'

'No, sir. Happy Christmas, sir.' And without looking at his employer again, Peter started the car and quickly drove away. Matt stood watching him until the lights were out of sight. He felt irritated by the presumption of his underling. The cheek of the man! No doubt about what, or rather whom, he was referring to. The impudence. He decided to wander round the garden, despite the cold, and the fact that he'd left his overcoat indoors. The waters from the fountain were still, the statue of the mermaid glowing whitely in the bright lights from the house. Beyond, the trees looked sepulchral, and the freshly turned earth of the herbaceous borders glittered with the tiny crystals of an early frost. Matt turned morosely towards the house and gazed at it.

It was a place, a scene he loved. He loved Christmas too, and his time with the family, the arrival of the children and grandchildren, the beagling on Boxing Day, all the fun and tradition of Christmas time.

But this year was different. This year he felt uneasy; happy, but also tense. Peter might have spoken out of turn, but he had a point. He knew Matt well, and seemed to be able to see to the very centre of his heart.

This year Matt wondered if it was the last time he would spend Christmas like this, in the bosom of his family.

*   *   *

George said, 'I don't think you love me any more.'

He propped himself up on both hands, gazing down at the face on the bed, his eyes devouring her body, the sight of which made him almost sick with desire.

'Sorry.' Jenny also raised herself on an elbow. 'Not in the mood.'

While George collapsed sulkily beside her, covering himself with the duvet, she swung herself off the bed and sat on the side staring at the floor.

'I can't just turn it on and off,' she said.

'You can try.'

'Do you want me to pretend?' She turned and looked at him, one hand clutching the nape of her neck. Her body formed an arc from the top of her sleek head to the neat, rounded curve of her buttocks. She stared at him with a rather chilly indifference and then turned her head to gaze at the floor.

'It's our last night,' he said.

'Only for a time. Why are you being so dramatic, George? Look, you'd better go. I've got to pack and various things.'

'I'll take you to the airport.'

'I'd rather you didn't, thanks.'

'Why not?'

'I just don't. It's so sentimental.'

'I can't understand you.' He sat up and lit a cigarette. 'I thought we had it made. Damn Matt.'

Imagining that somehow he had read her mind, Jenny started involuntarily.

'What's Matt got to do with it? It's got nothing to do with him.'

'Sending me to fucking Spain.'

'You didn't have to go.'

'I did. He laid it on the line. I think the bugger wants me out of the way.'

Jenny put her other hand behind her neck so that her fingers linked. She had never thought George especially perceptive, but now she wondered. 'Why should he want that?'

'If only I knew. He's a devious bastard.'

'You've never said that about him before.'

'I never thought it before; but now I begin to wonder. I think he wants Maurice in my place and he's moving me on. Know what I mean? He's *demoting* me, not promoting me. I can't speak a word of Spanish. I'll be hopeless and I'll have no direct control over the sales force. He's leaving it wide open for Maurice, believe me.'

'Isn't he a little *young*?'

'Yes, he is. But he's a Ransom. Well, if I don't like it in Madrid I'm going to chuck the whole thing in. Of course, if *you* were coming with me it would be a different ball-game.'

'I'll come out, I promise.' She knew she sounded apathetic.

'And I'll be over here once a month.' His tone was more cheerful. 'You'll see, time will soon fly.'

She felt his hand round her stomach and her mood altered. Why not . . .? Maybe it would be the last time.

Poor George.

The plane for Stockholm left at three, and Jenny had got to Heathrow in good time. She travelled light, just a small suitcase and presents for the family. She kept a full set of clothes in her father's apartment, and the next day, Christmas Eve, they were going to their chalet in the mountains for a skiing holiday. Her mother was in Italy with her second husband, who was an antique dealer.

Jenny took her place in the check-in line, looking without much interest at her fellow travellers, passport and flight tickets in her hand. She felt tired, a little jaded, a little unhappy. Sex with George had not, after all, been very satisfactory, and when he left at three in the morning, he was in a foul mood. There was no remorse in her heart when she said goodbye.

51

But maybe for the time being she would do as her father suggested and stay on in Stockholm. There was no point in rushing things; besides, it would put her quarry off the scent. She knew he was a man who couldn't resist a challenge, who would relish the chase.

She had plenty of time.

At that moment, as if with a sense of *déjà vu*, she raised her eyes to find herself staring at the object of her thoughts. Were she the blushing type, she might have blushed guiltily. Instead she gave him an ice-cold stare.

'Matt!' she said matter-of-factly. 'How *nice*!'

He fleetingly touched her cheek. 'I just had to see you to say goodbye.'

'But how did you know the time . . .?'

He put a finger to his lips. 'I have ways of finding out. I wanted to see you. I thought George might be here so I kept out of sight.'

'I came alone.'

'I know. I saw you arrive by cab.'

'Matt, is it *wise*?'

'No. It's very silly.' He took his place beside her as they moved up the line. 'But let's talk about it when we have a drink.'

The formalities soon over, he took her to the V I P lounge and placed her in a corner while he collected two glasses of champagne.

'Isn't this fun?' He raised his glass to her.

'Very unexpected, very *surprising*.' She too raised her glass, the icicles in her eyes melting.

'But aren't surprises nice?'

'I don't know.' Her lips brushed the rim of the glass and she looked at him without drinking.

'Did you see George last night?'

'Yes.'

'To say goodbye?'

'Of course. He leaves in a few days.'

'I suppose you'll miss him.'

'I suppose so.'

She looked at him for a long moment almost relishing the jealousy in his eyes. 'Matt, I think George is beginning to suspect why you are sending him away.'

'Oh?' Matt seemed interested rather than concerned.

'Your chauffeur wouldn't have said anything, would he?'

Matt shook his head. He finished the champagne in his glass and went and got two more. As he came back, Jenny looked at her watch.

'They'll be calling me soon.'

'Look, Jenny.' Matt carefully replaced the glasses and then clasped her hands between his. 'I want you to think about us over Christmas.'

'What shall I think?' She looked at him coolly, appraisingly.

'You know.'

'I will never be your mistress.'

'You were George's.'

'That's different.'

'How am I different?'

She rose, leaving her drink untouched, looked behind her to pick up her handbag and soft, black kid gloves.

'I'll miss my plane, Matt.' She swept past him and he followed her.

In the lobby, in front of the passport control, they stopped.

'Happy Christmas,' she said, putting out her hand.

'May I telephone you?' He produced his chequebook and a pen, preparing to make a note on the back. But she shook her head.

'It will be better when we meet,' she said.

'When will that be?'

'I'll phone when I get back.'

She looked towards passport control, as if suddenly really anxious that she might miss her plane.

'I'll phone. I promise.'

She kissed the tips of her fingers and held out her hand, but before he could touch it she had fled, waving her passport, blonde hair flying.

Gone.

CHAPTER 4

Rupert Timperley was a sturdy, independent child, tall for his age and mature. He was clever, ahead of his class in school, and his parents were going to send him to Charterhouse or Haileybury. His father had been to Charterhouse, the Ransom boys to Sherborne, but Matt had been at Haileybury.

It was more likely at this stage that Rupert would be a businessman or perhaps an academic than a farmer, but who could tell? Neither Henry nor Georgina minded, as long as he was happy, healthy, and led the best kind of life that, as parents, they could give him.

Alice, his five-year-old sister, was a very different sort of person – beautiful, clinging, loving. She had the spoiled air of one who expected – and would undoubtedly get – a lifetime of adulation. Already she received it from her grandfather, who openly adored her. She was able at this young age to manipulate him, and sat curled up on his lap, an arm round his shoulder.

The traditional family Christmas. What could be better? What could be more guaranteed to take a man's mind off the vision of a beautiful young woman kissing her fingertips at him, tantalisingly waving as she disappeared through passport control?

He found himself brooding about her, staring into the fire. His arm tightened about Alice. Back to reality.

Lunch was over, the turkey carved by him as he sported a paper hat. The pudding had appeared like a ball of fire. Everybody had eaten too much.

There had been a phone call from Philip, and now Maurice and Henry were playing snooker. Rupert alternated between crawling round on the floor playing with his new toys, and rushing off to see his father and uncle in the billiard room. Georgina and her mother sat side by side on the sofa sipping coffee, too full for mince pies. Alice dozed while Grandpa daydreamed. Only Beth seemed restless, a bit bored and, coffee cup in hand, wandered restlessly around the room, pacing from the fireplace to gaze up at the huge Christmas tree, or gazing broodingly out of the window at the darkening scene.

They were not at all alike in temperament, Matt thought, returning to his obsession. Only a couple of years separated Jenny and Beth. They did not resemble each other either. Beth was dark and Jenny blonde. Beth was passionate, temperamental, mercurial, whereas Jenny . . . Well, she was ice-cold, aloof, composed. She was the elusive enchantress of the fairy-tale, the woman who all men wanted, but who wanted none of them.

Not that his daughter Beth didn't have her mysterious side. Her family knew very few of her friends, and if she had an intimate side to her life, they knew little about it. She seemed to spread her favours quite liberally, but her family didn't know how deeply. She lived in a small flat in Swiss Cottage, and Matt had only been there once.

He suddenly wondered what would happen if he were to leave them all? What would the family be like in a year's time if he was no longer here?

It was a fanciful idea which made him jerk suddenly. Little Alice, finger in her mouth, looked sleepily up at him.

'Sorry, darling.' He leaned his head against her. 'You go back to sleep.'

Georgina looked up and around at them and, putting her

coffee cup down, rose and came over to them, arms extended.

'Maybe she should have a proper sleep, Daddy. She had the most enormous meal.'

'Would you like that, darling?' Matt tenderly stroked her hair away from her brow. 'Have a little lie-down?'

'Or maybe we should be going?' Georgina looked at the clock. 'It's nearly milking time.'

'Oh Georgie, on *Christmas Day*.' Her mother also put her cup down and rose to warm her behind in front of the fire.

'Cows have to be milked on Christmas Day as well, Mum, as on every other day.'

'I know, but couldn't Michael . . .?' Michael was the farm manager who had been left in charge.

'Mummy, Michael has a family too; he milked the cows yesterday and this morning. We want to keep him, not drive him away. He's too valuable. It's been a lovely day, anyway, Mummy. It's been a great break for us.'

And non-stop work for Elspeth too, Matt thought as Alice, awake now, clambered off his knee and ran to the door in search of her brother. There had been a family dinner the night before, and now a huge Christmas lunch. It was really a lot to expect, but all the young people joined in, men as well as women, everyone except the paterfamilias; the titular head of the family: Matt.

His mind flew to a household in Sweden, or maybe it was a chalet or lodge in the mountains. What sort of household did the Holstrom family keep? Jenny was an only child; her father had remarried but had no children. Were there just the three of them in the skiing lodge, or maybe a crowd of young people to keep Jenny entertained? Blond, young Swedish men? Matt shook his head in irritation with himself, and the gesture was seen by Beth, who went up to him, encircling his shoulders with her arm.

'Something wrong, Daddy?'

'Nothing wrong, darling.' Affectionately he put his arm around her. 'Just thinking.' He kissed her cheek and she snuggled up to him, and suddenly he wondered what the youngest, the beloved, would think if she knew the turmoil that was going on in the mind of her revered father? Because he knew she did revere and respect – as well as love – him. 'Love you, darling,' he mumbled and kissed her again, holding her very tight.

How he loved women! Needed them. His daughters, his granddaughter, his wife . . . Jenny. There it was again, that name. Never very far away.

A blast of cold air greeted them as the doors opened and the Timperley family prepared to make its departure. Rupert staggered under the weight of a huge box which contained just some of his new toys, and some of Alice's. She was also hugging a great big bear that was a gift from her grandfather. It had a blue-spotted bow and was almost as tall as she was. He'd bought it himself at Hamleys. Henry in a duffle coat fussed over the two youngsters, while Georgina went methodically round the house to ensure that nothing was left behind.

There were affectionate kisses and hugs on the steps, and then Maurice went down to see them into the Land Rover while Matt, Elspeth and Beth stood huddled in the porch waving goodbye.

It was five, pitch-dark and cold.

'I should imagine Michael has already started milking,' Elspeth said as she pushed the door to after Maurice had come in blowing into his hands. 'He's very good.'

'And they're very good to Michael,' Maurice said. 'He has a comfortable house, a good job, and lots of extra perks which Henry is not bound to give. Safe employment, eh, Dad?'

'I should think so.' Matt produced his pipe from his top pocket and puffed at it preparatory to the leisurely business of filling it.

'By the way, Dad, I took a call from George Hulme.'

'Oh?' Involuntarily Matt started, nearly dropping his pipe.

'He's in the locality and would like to pop in and say goodbye. He's off tomorrow, I believe.'

'I think he wants to settle in before the New Year,' Matt murmured. 'The Spanish take a shorter holiday than we.'

'Oh it'll be nice to see George,' Elspeth murmured. 'Maybe he'll stay for supper? When did he say he'd be here, Maurice?'

'He didn't give a time.'

'I wonder if that lovely girlfriend will be with him? What was her name, Matt?'

'Jenny,' Matt answered woodenly. 'Jenny Holstrom.'

'Is she going with him to Spain?'

Matt began to walk back into the drawing room, wondering if there was any purpose behind Elspeth's questioning.

'I don't think so,' he called over his shoulder. In front of him, Beth was putting more logs on the fire.

'They seemed so fond, I thought, in the summer.' Elspeth *did* seem to want to go on!

'Really, dear,' Matt said irritably. 'I don't see why George's relationship with his girlfriend is of any interest to you . . . Or us,' he added so sharply that Beth paused in the act of feeding the fire and looked up, first at him, then at her brother, who put his hands in his pockets and shrugged.

Maurice was twenty-seven. After Sherborne there'd been Trinity College, Cambridge. He'd entered his father's firm at the age of twenty-one, beginning at the bottom as Matt had before him.

He was like his father to look at, slightly shorter in stature and not unlike him in temperament, a man who thought before he leapt; determined, ambitious, yet careful. He was a confident man, good at games, popular with his peers and with a steady girlfriend, Shirley, who was a nurse at the Radcliffe and on duty over Christmas.

'George will no doubt tell us himself.' Maurice smiled good-naturedly at his father. 'Care for a game, Dad?'

'Why not?' Matt was determined to disguise his agitation at the totally unexpected arrival of George, and went into the billiard room with his son, with whom he stood chatting for a few minutes while he chalked his cue.

Beth and Elspeth went into the kitchen to begin the supper, the dishwasher having effectively disposed of the lunch dishes.

'I see what you mean about Dad,' Beth observed to the back of Elspeth, who had the door to the larder open and was taking stock of what was left.

'Oh?' Elspeth didn't turn round.

'He *is* kind of restless. Maybe he needs a holiday, Mum. Why don't you suggest it? A cruise or something.'

'A cruise!' Elspeth brought the cold turkey over to the kitchen table and studied it. 'You think your father would go for a cruise when this Spanish deal is not yet completed? Dad would be insulted to think you even considered him the age for cruising.'

'Yes, I suppose so.' Beth laughed uneasily. 'Yet, there couldn't be anything *worrying* Daddy, could there, Mummy? Not money or anything like that?'

'Money?' Elspeth straightened up and gazed in astonishment at her daughter. Elspeth had on a red frock, a colour which, though Christmassy, did not become her, accentuating her full figure. Her cheeks were red, no trace of make-up remained on her face, and her grey, wispy hair hadn't had the attention of a comb since the morning.

'Daddy worried about money?' She tucked a wisp of hair behind her ears. 'Oh no, not that I know of. He tells me everything.'

Does he though? Beth wondered to herself . . . She thought of the strange disappearances, the secretiveness, restlessness; in short, untypical behaviour. What did it all mean? Some kind of mid-life crisis?

60

'What do you think George will say about cold turkey?' Elspeth prattled on. 'Do you think he'll mind? I'll add some slices of beef,' she looked round, 'and salads, of course. Maybe smoked salmon to start if there's any left.' She walked back to the larder, again trying vainly to anchor a stray wisp of hair.

Beth smiled ruefully at her mother's back. How typical of her to dismiss intangibles from her mind while worrying about more practical, material things. She was comfortable with her husband, with the unquestioning familiarity of half a lifetime together.

Suddenly an awful coldness seemed to seize Beth's heart. Supposing her father was ill? Hiding something from his loved ones – something terrible?

Her mother still in the larder, Beth escaped to the billiard room where the two men were deeply engaged in their game. Matt, his face bent over the table, was earnestly appraising the position of the balls in relation to the six pockets, looking cheerfully happy and relaxed. He wore a sweater over his check shirt and grey flannels. Christmas lunch was never a time for formal dressing, unlike dinner on Christmas Eve, when it was black tie for the men, and the women displayed their finery. A lock of iron-grey hair hung over his brow and, in the ferocity of his concentration he looked formidable, handsome. No, no shadow of illness there, Beth thought, dismissing her dark forebodings.

'Penny for them, darling?' Matt appeared not to see her, but now she knew he had.

'I thought how *good looking* you were, Daddy.'

'Thank you, darling.'

He aimed his cue, took a shot at the red ball and missed. 'Blast,' he said, straightening up and smiling. 'I think you were sent by the enemy to deflect my aim.'

'Mummy's already fussing about supper. Cold turkey, cold beef and salad.'

'God help us!' Maurice rubbed a hand on his stomach. 'She seems to think we'll all starve. We – '

61

The doorbell pealed and Maurice, about to take a shot, paused in the act.

'Will that be George?' he asked.

'Who else?' Matt chalked his cue, suddenly uneasy again.

'Shall I answer?' Beth said.

'Would you, darling? Give him a whisky and bring him in while we finish the game.'

Elspeth had already got to the door, however, and was helping to divest George of his coat and scarf.

'Still cold outside, George?'

'I think it may be freezing,' he replied. 'I do hope I haven't disturbed you.'

'Not at *all*,' Elspeth insisted, a hand on his arm. 'Georgina, Henry and the children went a couple of hours ago. Matt and Maurice are playing snooker.'

'Daddy says you're to have a whisky and join them.'

'Thank you.' George rather sheepishly produced a packet wrapped in Christmas paper from behind his back. 'This is for all of you. Nothing much. Everything has been so hectic.'

'George, how sweet!' Elspeth took the present from him and began to unwrap it, managing to disguise her dismay at the revelation of about the fourth box of chocolates she had received that Christmas. Though her family thought she was unaware of it, she knew she was too fat. She was much more conscious of her deficiencies — and worried about them far more — than her family knew. 'Chocolates! How lovely!' she exclaimed. 'My favourite.'

She led the way into the drawing room. George immediately went over to the fire, holding out his hands in front of it.

'That nice girlfriend not with you?' Elspeth added the chocolates to the heap of open presents still lying at the bottom of the Christmas tree.

'No, she went back to Sweden to be with her father.'

'Oh dear, poor George. You'll feel lonely without her. Will she join you in Spain?'

'I'm not sure.' George produced a handkerchief and blew his nose. 'She works, you know.'

'Oh, does she?'

'Yes, in her father's shipping business. I dare say she'll come over for the odd weekend.'

'She was so beautiful,' Elspeth said, straightening up. 'So very, very beautiful. I can understand you being smitten.' Hearing movement she turned to the door. 'Here *is* Matt. Darling, look what George brought.' She indicated the large, ornate box of Swiss chocolates lying by the tree.

'How very nice of you, George,' Matt said politely. 'Happy Christmas.' He went over to his subordinate and shook hands.

'And you, Matt.'

'All packed up?'

'Yes. I've just been to say goodbye to my parents.'

'Of course, they live in Somerset.'

Matt stooped to throw more logs on the fire. Maurice was at the drinks table, the whisky decanter in his hand.

'Whisky, George?'

'Just a very small one. I'm driving.'

'What a pity you can't stay the night,' Elspeth said. 'If we'd known . . . I thought your friend might be with you.'

'I've got to go back to the house and do all those last-minute things.'

'Someone taking you to the airport?'

'Peter is coming with the car, I believe,' George looked over at Matt, who nodded.

'Peter will be at your place about lunchtime. Your plane's at four, I think.'

'How *exciting*.' Beth curled up on the sofa and hugged her knees. 'I wish someone would send *me* to Spain.'

'Well, it's a mixed blessing.' George looked ill-at-ease. 'Of course I'll miss Jenny, and who knows what it will do to our relationship? But then she *is* very young.'

'Is she?' Beth looked interested. 'Everyone is talking about this mysterious Jenny, and yet I've never set eyes on her.'

'Not *everyone*.' George looked around.

'Oh well, we mentioned her at lunch today as a matter of fact.' Elspeth looked embarrassed and fiddled with those irritating wisps of hair. 'I wondered if she were going with you, but Matt said he thought not. That was all, but I so vividly recall her that summer's afternoon, playing tennis . . . '

Matt suddenly looked towards the fire, aware of an ache in his heart, a longing. That was the moment he believed he'd fallen in love with Jenny. Love at first sight, something he'd never believed in. No doubt about it.

'How old *is* she out of interest?' Beth asked. 'Everyone seems so fascinated by her.'

'Twenty-one.'

'Twenty-*one*!' Beth sat up. 'But *I'm* twenty-five.'

'Yes, but she seems much older than you,' Matt said sharply. 'I mean, she's more like . . . ' He looked helplessly at George, afraid that he might have given himself away, 'twenty-five or so.'

'Yes, but I mean twenty-*one*!' Beth's youthful laugh was derisive. 'George, you're a baby-snatcher.'

'Well, this one got away, I think,' George said ruefully. 'I think Spain will administer the *coup-de-grâce*.'

'Oh, poor George.' Elspeth put a comforting hand on his arm and frowned at Beth, looking at the clock on the mantelpiece. 'Now, if you're in such a hurry to get home, we've some cuts all ready . . . '

'Really I couldn't, Elspeth,' George protested, patting his stomach.

'But you must. I insist. We couldn't let you go without something to eat, could we, Matt?'

'No indeed,' Matt said. He put an arm round George's shoulder as they walked across the hall to the dining room, where somehow, miraculously, Elspeth had managed to lay the table again with clean linen and sparkling silver. 'Look here, I thought I'd send Maurice out in a couple of months' time, just to see how things are going.'

'Oh, not to relieve me? Not to stay?' For a moment George's eyes gleamed hopefully.

'Afraid not.' Matt shook his head. 'You'll have to be there the full six months, George, at least. We want to get Birado S A well under way, part of the group.'

'That's great news, Father,' Maurice said with enthusiasm, shaking his napkin into his lap. 'You never told me.'

'I haven't quite made up my mind. It all depends how the reorganisation over here goes.' As Matt began to fill the wine glasses round the table, Beth giggled.

'I suggested to Mummy that you needed a cruise. She said you never would, and I think she was right.'

'Need a cruise?' Matt paused, looking at her in astonishment. 'Me? Why on earth do I need a cruise?'

'Because you are restless, dear; not quite yourself.' Choosing her words carefully, because she knew how touchy he could be, Elspeth began to put slices of beef and turkey on the top plate of the pile in front of her, which Maurice, next to her, passed round.

'Oh, you go on about this. It does *irritate* me.' Matt replaced the wine bottle on the coaster and sat down. 'Look, we've had a busy year, a lot on our plates. We have fearful competition from Europe *and* Japan.'

'*I* think Matt's fine.' George looked at them with surprise. 'He's right on top. I'm afraid it will be a very long time before Maurice succeeds him.'

'Don't tempt fate,' Matt said with a smile. But he knew it was a mask; a mask that was intended to deceive them all, because in his heart he had for the first time a feeling of terror, as well as disloyalty towards a close colleague and friend.

Pehr Holstrom sat on a bench at the top of the ski lift, his arm around the shoulders of his daughter, his beloved only child, Jenny. His wife Ingrid was in one of the cars coming slowly up on the cable together with her son Sven, two friends, Eric and Lars, and Lars's German girlfriend, Eva.

65

It had been a jolly house party, the weather excellent for skiing, and now it was almost time to think of returning home to Stockholm.

His fingers tightened around Jenny's arm.

'I wish you wouldn't go back, my darling. It's not necessary.'

She shifted away from him along the bench.

'To London.'

'I know where you mean. Sometimes I wish that too.'

'Then *stay*, my darling,' he urged her.

'In Stockholm?'

'Why not? Are you *so* attached to London?'

She didn't reply.

'Or is it George?' Her father's tone changed, became frosty. He had never liked George, considered him far too old for his daughter, and perhaps socially inferior. In short, simply not good enough.

'George is no longer there.' She straightened up. The cable cars began to disgorge their passengers.

'What?'

'He went to Spain the day after Christmas Day.'

'For good?'

'For at least six months.'

'Why, that's terrific!' Pehr looked genuinely pleased.

'I knew you'd say that,' she said sulkily and, rising, began to fasten her boots on to the waiting skis. 'You and I never agreed about George, Daddy.' She gingerly tested her boot in the ski socket.

'My dear, George was *not* the man for you.'

'I knew that. Of course I knew it. Anyway, it's finished. All done. Gone. His boss sent him to Spain and I decided it was time to end it anyway.' She dusted snow from her fingers, as though she was symbolically getting rid of George too.

'Good, then I hope you will find someone of your own class, more your own age and . . . ' He paused.

'Settle down, Daddy?' she suggested.

66

'If you like. But twenty-one is no great age. I accept that. You have lots of time for that. Have fun. Relax. Enjoy yourself.' He rose suddenly and, opening his arms wide, flung them round her. 'Jenny dearest, you have no idea how pleased I am to hear about George. It would have made my Christmas if you'd have told me that before.'

'You didn't ask,' she said rather childishly. 'Did it really matter?'

'It mattered that you might have thought of marrying him.'

She looked at him slyly. 'Perhaps that's why I didn't say.'

He held her away from him, carefully studying her face. In many ways his daughter was an enigma. She always had been; a wise, knowing child almost from birth, secretive and aloof. She was very like her mother, although this shared characteristic of coldness was considered very Swedish.

It was so difficult to read Jenny's mind. There was something rather regal in the way she expected tributes from people; maybe it was the reason for George's success. He had been so clearly, almost foolishly, devoted.

Pehr Holstrom too had led a fortunate life, except for the collapse of his marriage when his only daughter was three. But even that had not been such a disaster, because his wife, Miranda, was a very balanced, civilised woman, and they had agreed on an amicable parting.

The wrench for him had been to be separated from Jenny, but he saw her several times a year and they remained close, some said too close. They could almost read each other's thoughts. Almost more like brother and sister, confiding in each other, sharing the same wry amusement at the antics of the world. This rapport was supposed by some people to have made Ingrid extremely jealous.

However, as Ingrid now alighted from the cable car and came towards them, there was no suspicion of resentment that Pehr and Jenny had left her behind and gone together in the first car; only laughter, a sense of anticipation, as she pointed to the pristine slopes around them and exclaimed:

'It is really wonderful up here. My goodness.' She shaded her eyes. 'The snow looks untouched.'

'That's because there was a good fall last night.' Pehr too rose and began to fasten his skis. 'And it is still early enough in the morning for us to benefit from it.'

Sven was Ingrid's son by her first marriage. He was nineteen, at university in Uppsala, a keen and accomplished skier since his youth. He and Jenny had a friendly rather than fraternal relationship. In the same way, Ingrid never attempted to take the place of Jenny's mother. Careful not to show it, she had nevertheless been more than relieved when Jenny had gone to London to work.

Behind Ingrid came Eric. Eric Jorgensen was an athlete and sportsman who worked at a riding stables. His father had been one of Pehr's oldest friends and had died in a car crash together with his wife a few years before. Pehr had been of enormous help and comfort to Eric, who had come to regard him as a second father. Lars and Eva completed the party.

They were all good skiers and spent the day on a long cross-country run, returning to the Holstrom chalet in the late afternoon. This was a spacious dwelling that had been in the family for many years, and was frequently visited throughout the season by Pehr and Ingrid, or by Sven and his many friends, though on this occasion Lars and his girlfriend were staying in a hotel in the village, one much patronised by skiers for the *après-ski* entertainment.

Lars and Eva went back to the hotel while the occupants of the chalet showered, changed and gathered in the main room for drinks before dinner, which was to be eaten at a local restaurant. Pehr insisted that Ingrid and his daughter shouldn't have to cook during their holidays.

He was busy at the bar as Ingrid came into the room wearing a black top with a heavy gold border, velvet slacks and high-heeled sandals.

'Good news. Jenny may be persuaded to stay on in Stockholm after the holiday.'

'For good?' The expression on Ingrid's perfectly groomed face was inscrutable.

'Well, I'd like her to stay for good.'

'That's excellent news.' Eric, who had been lounging, got enthusiastically to his feet.

'I didn't say "yes".' Jenny accepted a glass from her father. 'It's just an idea.'

'She's tired of London,' Pehr explained.

'But don't you have a *boyfriend* there?' Sven said slyly.

'The boyfriend has gone to Spain.' Pehr didn't attempt to hide his satisfaction. 'Which is good.'

'Really, Daddy,' Jenny said sharply, 'I'd rather you didn't air my personal business in public.' Jenny looked annoyed.

'Sorry, darling.' He was immediately contrite. 'It's just that I'm so pleased if it comes off.'

'Nothing's decided,' she said firmly. 'You merely suggested it and I said I'd think about it.'

'Would you actually like to remain in Stockholm?' Ingrid settled by the side of her stepdaughter, stirring her champagne cocktail with a swizzle-stick. 'You've never lived there for any length of time, have you?'

'Not since I was small.' Jenny looked at her quizzically, knowing quite well that she wouldn't be very keen on the idea. 'Of course I wouldn't live with you or Daddy, Ingrid. I'd get my own apartment.'

'Then it really is a possibility?' Eric continued to look excited.

'No, it's merely an idea,' Jenny said coolly, 'and if you don't mind, tonight I really don't want to talk about it.'

Jenny didn't want to talk about it, but the idea remained in her thoughts for the rest of their holiday. After she returned to Stockholm, she cancelled her plane reservation for London and began to look for an apartment to rent. She checked with her cleaner that she would continue to look after the London flat, and with the staff in the London office that they would cover for her in her absence.

She went into the Stockholm office with her father, who was delighted at the idea of his daughter appearing to take an active interest in the business. Much as he loved her, Jenny's motivation remained obscure to him; he didn't really know what it was she was looking for.

Since she was eighteen she had seemed restless and unfulfilled, clearly not wholly cut out for a life of pleasure, but not ambitious enough to find any meaning for her life in a career.

Shipping was not a glamorous business, and Jenny's role as assistant to the MD in the London office had been a sinecure consisting mainly of lunching and dining clients, the sort of PR exercise that was duplicated by the agency employed by Sverige/Norsk to do just that. Being the chairman's daughter, however, added a cachet to the exercise. It was easy for her and potential clients felt flattered to be entertained by someone so close to the top; the men enjoyed being seen in public with such a beauty.

In Stockholm her father found for her very much the same sort of role. It was a well-run office where all the jobs dovetailed. Computers had largely taken over work previously done by people, and although Pehr would dearly have loved to find a real job for Jenny, there was not very much for her to do.

Ingrid Holstrom also worked. A former newspaper editor, she was now a freelance journalist working from home.

Ingrid would very much like to have got to know her stepdaughter better, but it was difficult. She was so idolised by Pehr that he wanted her to himself whenever she was in Stockholm.

Ingrid was a woman of forty-five who, in her ten years of marriage to Pehr, had determined not to be jealous of his devotion to Jenny. But Jenny, though always perfectly friendly and civilised, was hard to get to know. She shared with her father that quality of detachment, of excluding others. When they were together, they were so clearly

70

absorbed in each other that some people considered it unnatural.

Ingrid was at work in her study when the telephone rang and the masculine voice at the other end of the line asked in English for Jenny.

'I'll see if she's in her room,' Ingrid replied in English. 'Who shall I say?'

'Matt. I'm calling from London.'

Ingrid repeated the name to herself and went along the corridor to knock at Jenny's door. No reply. She returned to her study and lifted the receiver.

'I'm afraid Jenny's not in. Have you tried the office?'

'I rang the office and they gave me your number,' the man replied politely.

'Is it business or personal?'

'It's quite urgent,' Matt replied testily. 'When do you think she'll be in?'

'I expect her for dinner tonight,' Ingrid answered coldly. 'I'm her stepmother.'

'How do you do? Matt Ransom.' His tone became conciliatory.

'How do you do, Mr Ransom? If you give me your number, I'll make sure Jenny calls you.'

'No . . . Tell her, if you would, that I'll call her tomorrow. Tomorrow morning at about ten.'

'I'll tell her you'll call at ten. Goodbye.' Ingrid's voice remained chilly.

A short while later there was the sound of a key in the lock and Jenny entered, closely followed by Eric. Ingrid went to the door to welcome them.

'Eric, how nice to see you.'

'And you, Ingrid.'

'Did you have a good lunch?'

'Splendid.'

'I've come back for a few things,' Jenny said offhandedly. 'We're going to friends of Eric's in Bjorko for the weekend.'

'The Hajams, you know them?' Eric asked politely.

71

'Of course. That's nice. When will you be back?'

'I'm not sure.' Jenny swept her hair back from her forehead. Ingrid thought she looked tired and rather unhappy. Maybe she was trying to make something with Eric. Heaven knew he was keen enough on her. Always pounded after her when she was in Sweden.

'Oh, by the way,' Ingrid consulted the pad on her desk, 'there was a call for you from England.'

'Oh?' Jenny looked up sharply.

'Someone called Matt.'

'Oh! Did he say he'd ring again?'

'Tomorrow at about ten.'

'Well, I shan't be here.'

'Shall I tell him to call you at the Hajams?'

'No.'

'What shall I say then?'

'Just say that I've gone away and you don't know when I'll be back.'

Jenny, suddenly transformed, her expression triumphant, abruptly left the room while Eric and Ingrid looked thoughtfully after her.

There was more skiing that weekend, with the large Hajam family and an assortment of friends, both contemporary and older.

Jenny loved skiing, and threw herself wholeheartedly, tirelessly, into vigorous activities, then partied afterwards. Eric was never very far away from her, and once, when they had outdistanced the others by several miles on the cross-country run, and paused to collect their breaths, he leaned against a tree, pushed up his goggles, and looked at her.

'Who's Matt?'

'Just someone.'

'Something personal?'

'Not really.' She too pushed up her goggles and, shading her eyes, looked over the beautiful landscape surrounding them, seeming preoccupied by it.

72

CHAPTER 5

Pehr Holstrom's secretary said, 'May I have your name please?'

'Sir Matthew Ransom.'

'Have you an appointment, Sir Matthew?'

'No. I really came to see Miss Holstrom.'

'She's not here, I'm afraid.'

'Oh!' Pause for consideration. 'When will she be back?'

'I've no idea. She's skiing.'

'I see. Is her father here by any chance? I'd like to make his acquaintance.'

'I shan't keep you a moment, Sir Matthew.' The secretary jotted his name on a pad and disappeared through the door. After a few seconds, Pehr came to the door, a hand outstretched in welcome.

'Sir Matthew Ransom? How do you do?'

'How do you do, Mr Holstrom. I'm afraid this call is a bit out of order.'

'Not at all.' Pehr politely insisted that his unexpected guest should precede him into a large, pleasant office overlooking the harbour. 'I understand you know Jenny?'

'Slightly.' Matt looked round, feeling foolishly like a young boy, his heart on his sleeve. Supposing he told her father that the thought of his daughter obsessed him; that her lack of contact or of any explanation as to why she prolonged her stay tormented him? 'I knew her through my sales manager, George Hulme.'

'Oh!' This news didn't appear to go down well with the father.

Matt undid the top button of his jacket and took the seat opposite Pehr. 'I am here basically to do business in Sweden. I'm sure you are the man to point me in the right direction.'

'Business?' Pehr stroked his chin. 'What sort of business, may I ask?'

Matthew opened his briefcase and, producing a glossy folder, pushed it across the desk towards Pehr who, with a polite expression on his face, opened it.

'Ah, Ransom Engineering. I have surely heard of it.'

'We are one of the most successful private companies in the United Kingdom. Just now we have embarked on an extensive programme of expansion. We have taken over Birado SA, the Spanish manufacturer of precision tools. It is possible we may seek a Stock Exchange quotation in the not too distant future, though, frankly, I'm strongly in favour of remaining independent.'

'And in what way can I help you, Sir Matthew?'

'Well, shipping and engineering are not so far apart. I would value any contacts you have in Stockholm, or other parts of Sweden. As well as selling our machines, we are also prepared to invest in the right company.'

Pehr looked interested. 'On what terms?'

'Well,' Matt shrugged, 'naturally a percentage, maybe a majority of the shares. It depends.'

'Well.' Pehr sat back and regarded his visitor. He was a tall, imposing sort of man, the epitome of the successful English gentleman. 'I may be able to put some business your way, Sir Matthew.' He reached for his diary and turned over the pages. 'How long are you here for?'

'It depends. I really shouldn't have barged in like this . . . '

'Please.' Pehr put out a deprecating hand. 'It is my pleasure. Of course I have many contacts in the engineering industry; some of our shipbuilding friends are also greatly in need of fresh capital. Are you free for lunch?'

'Not today.' Matt looked regretful. 'But tomorrow . . . '

'Ah!' Pehr's face fell. 'I can't make tomorrow, or the next day.'

'Then maybe I can make today free.' Matt produced a diary from his breast pocket and flicked over a few pages.

'Perhaps we can make it dinner.' Pehr made a brief note on his pad. 'I'll get my wife to call you. You are staying at . . .?' Matt gave him the name of his hotel. 'I should think Thursday or Friday of this week.' Pehr looked up with a smile.

'That sounds fine.' Matt returned the smile. 'And maybe Jenny will be there?'

'Who knows?' Pehr shrugged ruefully. 'She's a law unto herself.'

Jenny opened the door.

'Hello, Matt. How nice to see you again!' She held out her hand, her smile brisk, impersonal, friendly.

'Very nice to see you.' Matt caught his breath as he gripped her hand.

'I'm so sorry I was away when you arrived.' She led the way into a long room which had a spectacular view of the bay. An elegant woman of about forty-five rose and came towards him.

'My stepmother, Ingrid.' Jenny ushered her forward. 'And this,' she gestured to a man who had had his back towards them but who turned as soon as they entered, 'is Eric Jorgensen, a friend of the family.'

Eric was young, tall, blond and very handsome. Matt felt an instinctive dislike of him.

'It's just us and my father.' Jenny glanced at her watch. 'He should be home any minute.'

'What will you have to drink?' Eric asked, his manner, his tone of voice, seeming an indication of how relaxed and at home he felt at the Holstrom residence.

75

'Doesn't one drink aquavit?'

'Not everyone.' Eric had the same laconic casualness of manner as Jenny. 'But of course we have it.'

Matt noted the 'we'.

'Eric and I have just returned from a ski trip.' Jenny seemed to enjoy twisting the knife. 'Do you ski, Matt?'

'Not as well, I'm sure, as you and Eric.' Matt accepted the glass from the irritatingly smooth young man with a smile. 'My elder son Maurice is very good.'

'Oh, you have children?' Ingrid was also smooth, urbane, charming.

She wore a beige dress of soft Angora wool, belted at the waist. She was tall, very slim, and her pepper-and-salt hair was straight in the front and wound in a soft bun at the nape of her neck. Her face was thin and lined, her eyes very blue, mouth wide, and when she smiled the light caught a gold inlay in one of her teeth. She looked alert, intelligent, perceptive.

Matt gave a run-down on his children, what they did, how old they were. He sat next to Ingrid, intent on hiding his sense of unease. It wasn't like him, after all, to lack confidence. It wouldn't do at all to show it. He was aware of Jenny sitting opposite him. Her dress, also wool but not Angora, was dark brown with a high polo collar, adorned with a gold chunky necklace. From her ears dangled the inevitable large earrings. He could have sworn she was watching him, her eyes glinting wickedly. She looked dangerous, alluring, very lovely. His desire for her was a desperation that was almost painful. At one time she held up her hand to Eric as he passed in a casual, intimate gesture, and he clasped it briefly before releasing it. Matt was sure she was doing it deliberately for him.

Shortly afterwards Pehr came in and, as it was already quite late, they sat down to dinner. The food was simple but excellent, Smörgåsbord, fillet of beef and fresh vegetables, apparently all cooked by Ingrid with the same effortless ease with which she appeared to do everything.

76

The talk was mainly about the Common Market, the advantages and disadvantages of the European Community, and gradually Matt felt himself relax, unwind; his confidence returned, and his sense of power. He knew Jenny was riveted by him, watching him. He knew he had to perform well for her, like a peacock spreading its feathers.

Yes, he had, of course, met Mrs Thatcher. He had been her host at dinners given by industrialists, and sat next to her frequently. They were on Christian-name terms. She certainly enjoyed conversation, but had no small-talk. Almost everything had to have a purpose, a meaning. It was quite hard to entertain her. Yes, and her predecessor Edward Heath; he had no small-talk at all. Oh, and the foreign secretary? He knew him fairly well, but the chancellor better. Well, the Queen? He had met her, of course, shaken hands several times. Oh yes, and of course the Princess of Wales . . . Well, she was *very* beautiful close to, but so painfully shy, not a good conversationalist; no, it was difficult to tell whether or not she and Charles were happy . . . But then Royals weren't like other people, were they? Except perhaps in Sweden.

After dinner Jenny seemed to make a point of placing herself next to Matt as they sat on the low, comfortable sofa facing the window, the beautiful view of the bay with its twinkling lights before them. In the background came the strains of a late Beethoven quartet from the hi-fi.

'I'm so glad you could make it,' Jenny said with obvious sincerity. 'When do you go home?'

'Tomorrow.' He stirred his coffee before putting the cup to his lips. 'Will you be returning to London?'

'Oh, I suppose so. Eventually.'

'Have you seen George since he went to Spain?' Tone of voice deliberately non-committal.

'No.' No attempt to elaborate. He didn't press her. This terseness of hers, absence of small-talk, was part of her attraction.

'Well, we shall all miss you if you don't come back to London.'

'All?' She looked at him oddly, a teasing light in her eyes.

'And we shall miss her if she does.' Pehr joined them on the low sofa, evidently oblivious of the undercurrent between them. 'My daughter is a restless young woman, Sir Matthew. I don't think she really knows what she wants to do.'

'Maybe a ski instructress.' Eric, pacing restlessly a few feet away from the sofa, paused and stared at them, as if what Pehr had missed he knew. 'Jenny really is *very* good.'

'I just want to enjoy myself.' Jenny clasped her knees, her head tilted to one side. 'Why not? Life is so short.'

'I thought you told me you enjoyed work?' Matt glanced at her quizzically.

She pretended to groan. 'Mmm, sometimes yes and sometimes no.' She tossed back her head, teasing again, and smiled at him. 'Oh, I shall return. Eventually.'

It was that 'eventually' which was so provocative – and didn't she know it?

A short time later, Matt took leave of the family, at the same time reluctant to leave Jenny, yet anxious to as well. He was uncomfortable with her, dreaded being away from her.

He was a man in torment.

Maurice's secretary stuck her head round the door.

'Someone wants to speak to your father, Maurice. He wouldn't give his name.'

'Oh? Strange.' Maurice raised his head from the set of figures on the computer print-out. 'Did you tell him Father was away?'

'Yes. He said it was quite urgent, but of a personal nature, and asked if I knew how he could get hold of him.'

'Put him through.'

'It's on line one, Maurice.'

The secretary disappeared, and Maurice picked up the receiver. 'Maurice Ransom speaking.'

'Oh!' Pause. 'Is Sir Matthew available?'

'I'm afraid he's abroad on business. Can I help? '

'Well. It's of a personal nature. I'm not sure – '

'I am his son,' Maurice said peremptorily. 'I think there's very little in my father's life I don't know about.'

'Oh well, in that case . . . It's about the building insurance on the flat your father's bought. There's been some query . . . '

'Flat?' Maurice frowned. 'I'm afraid I don't understand.'

'In Mayfair.' A note of doubt crept into the voice. 'It's Robert Giles of the Giles, Wilyard estate agency. The insurers have asked me if your father was aware that the insurance has to cover the outside as well as the inside of his apartment. It's unusual, but the landlord hopes eventually to sell the freehold to the leaseholders.'

Maurice thought quickly. 'I'd better come and see for myself,' he said. 'Give me your address, will you?'

'Thirty-two, Old Bond Street, Mr Ransom. I would be so glad if you could deal with this matter as quickly as possible. It's a matter of the legality . . . '

'Of course. I shall be in London tomorrow. Could we say eleven in the morning?'

'Shall I meet you at the flat, Mr Ransom?'

'I'll pick you up at your office,' Maurice replied. 'Peter probably knows where it is, doesn't he?'

'Oh, Sir Matthew's chauffeur knows us.' Mr Giles sounded confident. 'Looking forward to meeting you, Mr Ransom. I hope it is not inconvenient.'

'Not at all,' Maurice replied.

Maurice looked out of the window towards Green Park. It was a good view. Already there were signs of spring about, crocuses and snowdrops dotted among the trees. Above them rose the tower of Westminster Cathedral.

'Well,' he stuck his head back in, 'very nice.'

'You hadn't seen it before, sir?' Mr Giles looked surprised.

'No. I very rarely come to town. Now, let me see, when was the purchase completed?'

'Just before Christmas. Sir Matthew was anxious to get it done as quickly as possible. I have seldom known a purchase go through with such speed. No reason not to, of course. But usually they don't.'

'Exactly.' Maurice, his tone non-committal, scratched his chin.

'I hope Lady Ransom is pleased with it. I think it was to be a surprise for her.' Giles was anxious to be helpful.

Suddenly the penny clicked and Maurice felt a sense of relief. 'It's a surprise for their thirtieth wedding anniversary,' he said. 'I think she'll be thrilled to bits.'

'Oh well, I'm very glad about that.' Mr Giles too experienced a sense of relief. 'If we could just get the matter of the insurance sorted out . . . '

'No problem at all.' Maurice sounded reassuring. 'My father will be back tomorrow. I'll get on to it straight away.'

Matthew spent his first morning back at work going through the list of contacts he'd made in Stockholm, only one name missing from the list.

'There's a chance of some really good business,' he said at last, leaning back in his seat. 'The Swedes are very keen on the EC. Now these people,' he bent over a sheaf of documents he had produced from his briefcase, 'are in a similar situation to Birado. May be worth considering investing, or even buying them altogether.'

Maurice took the papers from his father and sat studying them for some minutes. His expression was impassive. The telephone rang, and for several minutes Matthew was engaged in conversation.

'Oh, by the way, Father.' Maurice deliberately sounded non-committal as Matt replaced the receiver. 'About the flat in Mayfair . . . '

The effect on his father was remarkable. Maurice had a sense of satisfaction at scoring a bull's-eye.

'How did you know about that?'

'Oh it *is* a secret?' Maurice smiled. 'I thought so. Well, I promise, not a word. I presume it's a present for your wedding anniversary?'

Matthew leaned back in his chair and fiddled with his pen. 'All the same, I'd like to know how you found out about it, Maurice?'

'The agent, Mr Giles, wa͟͟͟ to talk to you about the insurance. The leaseholder has the responsibility for the whole building, not just the flat.'

'Nevertheless, Giles had no right to speak to you. This is a confidential matter.'

'Father, don't say it's a present for *me*.' Maurice feigned surprise.

Matthew rose from his desk and began angrily to pace up and down. 'It is *not* a present for anybody. I've bought a flat in London to have a little privacy.'

'For yourself?' Maurice stared unbelievingly at him.

'Precisely.' Matt sat down and glared at him. 'A *pied-à-terre*.'

'But I simply don't understand . . . '

'What is there for you to understand? I am fifty-five. I am wealthy. I can well afford to spend my money, and spend it how I like.'

'But surely Mother should have been brought into a matter like this?'

'Why?'

'Well, is it a secret from her?'

'No.'

'She does know about it then?'

'No, she doesn't.'

'I simply don't understand,' Maurice repeated.

'It's actually none of your business. I spend a lot of time in London. I may spend more. If we continue to expand there will be a London office, probably in the City, Mayfair

81

or the West End. I saw that flat and I happened to like it. It was an impulse.'

'I must say I'm surprised,' Maurice said stiffly. 'I thought that, as a family, we shared things. Does Beth know?'

'No one knows. Now you know, and I'd be glad if you'd keep the information to yourself.'

'But Beth could well do with a decent place to live in London.'

'Beth is very well sited in Swiss Cottage. Mayfair is far too expensive for students. I don't suppose she'd want to live there anyway.'

'You're probably right . . . You're a dark horse, Father,' Maurice said thoughtfully as he got up and pointed to the documents scattered on the desk. 'I thought I knew you, but it appears I don't.'

'You're making a mountain out of a molehill.' Matt waved a hand expansively towards the scattered documents. 'Now be a good fellow and follow these up if you would. And, Maurice,' he folded his hands, leaning forward confidentially across his desk. 'I'm sorry if you think I should have told you about the apartment; but honestly, sometimes I think families share too much; we tend to live in one another's pockets. It's not terribly healthy. Is it?'

'It's always seemed all right to me. I thought we were an open, honest and loving family. Now I'm not sure. I think Mother would be very hurt if she knew.'

'Well, there is no need for her to be hurt. Maybe I'll hurry up the process of getting a London office, then I'll tell her.'

'I don't think there's any *need* for a London office, if you don't mind my saying so, Father. The expense will be considerable.'

'Huge tax advantages.'

'Dubious advantage.' Maurice had accountancy qualifications. 'Extra staff, high wages. I think we, the management, should be consulted. Even though I'm a junior member of the management team, I think that.'

'Everyone will be consulted in good time,' Matt said blandly, looking at the map on the wall and, momentarily, blinking his eyes. 'Maurice, I may ask you to go to Glasgow for a few months, or perhaps Belfast. How do you think you would like that?'

The children looked so sweet, the girls in their flimsy dresses, the rows of boys forming the two back rows in blue shirts, blue striped ties and grey shorts. Their childish voices raised to the rafters of the school hall, and Miss Proudie, the music mistress, conducted from the piano at the right of the stage.

Sometimes her small charges lost their way, or a wrong note was heard above the rest, whereupon she would look up in exasperation, wagging an admonishing finger at the offender, while continuing to play with her other hand. She never seemed to miss a key.

Little angels. The parents, friends and relations who filled the room were clearly enraptured by the well-rehearsed performance of the five-to-seven-year-olds of the Wolverton school — fees five hundred pounds a term — one of the best of the many private primary and junior schools in the area. Parents, both men and women, looked on with pride, while the older generation of grannies and grandpas, if present, blew hard into their hankies.

There was something so beautiful, so touching, about innocence soon lost and never to be regained.

Matt, chairman of the governors of the school, was as captivated as anyone. Arms folded, he sat gazing proudly first at Alice, then Rupert, then back again, as they burst out their little hearts in song. He sat between Georgina and Elspeth, with Henry and his mother on Georgina's left.

It had been a happy day, a family day, culminating in the half-term concert for which the pupils had been rehearsing for weeks. By the end of it there was loud, enthusiastic applause, and the head stepped forward to usher a smiling, nervous Miss Proudie forward. She, in turn, applauded her

83

pupils, who were showing signs of restlessness now that the big moment was over, and were beginning to fidget.

The head, Mrs Muir, then made a short speech, laudatory to all concerned before concluding, 'And finally I would like to *ask* Sir Matthew Ransom, the chairman of the governors, to say a few words . . . '

Willingly Matt went up the stairs to the platform, where he added his praises to all concerned, particularly Miss Proudie, and to the parents who had had the wisdom and good sense to send their children to Wolverton, 'which I think I can say without any fear of contradiction is the very best school in this area. We are very fortunate to have as head . . . ' and so on and so forth. The speech, as did the occasion, varied little from year to year.

Yet listening to him, Elspeth felt that familiar sense of pride she always had when she saw and heard him on a platform. He was so commanding, so self-assured, a born leader, an accomplished speaker, at ease in public.

For Matt was a public figure and did a lot of public speaking. He was chairman of the governors of two schools, of the local branch of the Red Cross. He was president of the golf club and on the committees of any number of local societies and voluntary bodies devoted to good works. This was apart from his business interests and the many top level organisations and societies connected with industry and engineering.

His voice was resonant, he projected himself well. He could win an audience, sway them if necessary (and today of course it wasn't, as most of the parents and grandparents were as well off, as self-assured as he).

Yet he was just as adept at appealing for money for a good cause. People seemed willing to empty their pockets and handbags after an emotional, if rational, appeal from Matt. Animals and human beings all benefited from having a charity devoted to them favoured by Matt.

After he finished, the choir eagerly broke its ranks and rushed over to be reclaimed by proud parents. Alice and

Rupert remained on stage to receive a hug from their grandfather. 'Splendid,' he said, 'splendid. I never heard "The Little Drummer Boy" better sung.'

Watching them below, a fond smile on her face, Georgina said to her mother, 'Dad's awfully good with kids.'

'Always was,' Elspeth answered. 'You all adored him.'

'He was an ideal kind of father, really, and grandfather.'

'And husband,' Elspeth murmured. 'I'm so lucky. When you think of some people . . . '

'And *he's* lucky to have you, Mum.' Georgina squeezed her arm. 'You're an ideal wife, an ideal mother.'

'Oh no, not ideal,' Elspeth protested, flattered. 'Your father could have had anyone, you know. He was so good looking. I never really *know* why he chose me.'

'Mum,' Georgina looked at her in concern, 'that's not like you. Dad loves you.'

'I was never beautiful,' Elspeth wandered on, 'not particularly clever . . . '

'But look what a smashing couple you've made. A lot of people envy you, Mum. They really do.'

'I was a tiny bit worried about your father before and around Christmas time,' Elspeth murmured with a frown. 'But he seems better now.'

'Worried? In what way?'

'He was so restless, not himself. Beth and Maurice noticed it. You wouldn't because you weren't at home. I didn't want to worry you, but I wondered if he was sickening for something, but he seems more settled since he returned from Sweden.'

'Unless it's the male menopause.' Georgina giggled. 'They say men have them as well, don't they? Daddy's at the right age.'

'I think he takes on too much,' Elspeth said. 'He doesn't realise he's ageing. He is chairman of about half a dozen organisations, vice-chairman of a dozen more, and on the board, or committee, of a dozen more than that.'

'Still, he's *loaded* with honours, so he has some compensation. I hear Oxford might even give him an honorary degree.'

'Really?' Elspeth's eyes lit up with pleasure. 'He'd love that.'

'He must have given *millions* to the university over the years.'

'Well, the firm has, not Daddy; but it has benefited the area, the town and, yes, the university itself.'

'And the Ransom bursary in engineering.'

'Yes, that was important.' Elspeth still had her eyes on the stage as Matt, clasping Alice and Rupert by their hands, carefully ushered them down the stairs. Once on the floor they let go of his hands and raced towards their mother.

'Mummy, Mummy, how did you *like* it?'

'Did you hear *me*?'

'I heard you. You were wonderful.' Georgina kissed first one and then the other, and then it was Elspeth's turn. When she rose from kissing them, her face was glowing.

Matt stood in the background, looking on with approval.

'Well, wasn't that lovely?' He turned as the head came up, hand extended.

'Thank *you*, Sir Matthew, so much for generously giving your time to come here this afternoon once again and,' she lowered her voice, 'your most welcome gift.'

'Gift?' Rupert pricked up his ears at the word. 'What did Grandpa give?'

'Your grandfather very kindly gave a large sum of money to our scholarship fund, so that the children whose parents cannot afford to send them here and receive the benefit of a private education may be enabled to do so.'

'Oh, is that all?' Rupert's tone was offhand.

'It's *very* important.' Mrs Muir's tone was reproving. 'You are extremely lucky to have a mummy and daddy who – '

'Oh, well, never mind that,' Matt said uneasily, anxious to change the conversation. He held a hand out to Rupert. 'Now have we all said our "thank-yous" and "good-byes"?' He looked over at the head. 'And do have a nice holiday, Mrs Muir. Oh, and the next meeting of governors is . . . '

They both got out their diaries and looked up dates, while friends gathered round the younger children, and more parents wandered up to greet the Ransoms. Apart from Matt's eminent position, Georgina was on the parents' committee, and Henry assisted his father-in-law in the fund-raising appeals.

There was more chatting on the steps, by the cars, and then further kisses and hugs as the Timperley family got into their large Range Rover, where they were ecstatically greeted by their two golden retrievers from behind the dog grille at the back. Matt and Elspeth waited to see them off and then got into Elspeth's Metro. Matt settled back at the wheel, still wreathed in smiles, while Elspeth strapped herself in beside him.

'Well, that *was* lovely,' she said contentedly as Matt positioned the car in the queue to get out of the school grounds. 'Those little concerts are so *sweet*. Do you remember Maurice and Georgina in the nativity play?'

'Well,' Matt screwed up his eyes and took a left turn out of the drive, 'I think *that's* stretching the memory a bit, dear.'

'Oh Matt, they were so *dear*. How could you forget? Georgina was one of the angels and Maurice was a shepherd. The Virgin Mary couldn't stop giggling – nerves of course – and the infant Jesus shook in her arms. Surely you remember?'

Yes, looking back, far back, Matt did remember. It was a medley of childhood memories, a long way back. Thirty years.

As if reading his thoughts – and who else was better able to read them? – Elspeth said:

'Matt, about the party. Claridge's want to know if we want a band. I don't *think* we want a band, do we, darling?'

'No dancing?' Matt looked surprised. 'I thought one always had dancing at these shindigs?'

'Oh yes, I suppose . . . Well, O K, a band, but a small one. I'll ring them tomorrow. Oh, and Matt, they want to know . . . '

Thirty years married. His memories wandered back even further than the nativity play. To meeting Elspeth. That had been at a party too. The office party, when Ransom Engineering, as it had been then, had been headed by Matthew's father, Edmund.

Elspeth, a trainee teacher at a college in London, had actually been brought to the party by another employee, a trainee engineer like Matt. He remembered her as she was then: fresh-faced, practical, and exuding a friendliness and warmth that had been immediately appealing to a man who had been very close to his own mother, who had died when Matt was ten. His father had been preoccupied with building up his business, and Matt, an only child, keenly felt the lack of a close female presence. He'd begun to date his colleague's girlfriend; the colleague had subsequently nursed a grudge, rather as George Hulme might well do now, over thirty years later. Matt had been married at twenty-six, a father at twenty-seven. Elspeth was just a year younger than he, and for nearly thirty years they had shared everything.

How could he have ever imagined, *thought* about a younger woman?

He felt especially fond and protective of her as the memories came flooding back and, because of it, they spent a particularly close evening, both seeming aware of the ties that had bound them for so long; they had a drink by the fire, a meal in the kitchen, a short period in front of the telly, and bed. The mood of the evening, based on tenderness and harmony continued, and they made love very gently before falling asleep, still clasping each other.

*   *   *

His secretary said:

'There's a call for you, Sir Matthew. It's personal.'

'Oh!' Matt smiled at her.

'Line three.'

'Thanks.' He took up the receiver and, in his most professional manner, said, 'Matthew Ransom speaking.'

'Oh, Matt . . . ' The voice, so clear, could have come from the room next door. 'It's Jenny.'

'Jenny!' His heart skipped a beat. 'Where are you?'

'In London.' Short on information, as usual. Terse and to the point.

'That's great. Great news.' His heart quickened. 'For how long?'

'I don't quite know. Matt, this is a business call really. My father wanted me to say "hello", send greetings and all that sort of thing, but he also wondered if you would be interested in acquiring the rest of the lease of our premises?'

'Your what?'

'The premises in South Audley Street.'

'You're moving out?' Utter, total panic took over.

'To somewhere bigger. Father's got his eye on a floor in a new block in the City.'

'Oh!' Relief.

'It was just a thought. There are seven years to run on this lease. It's not much, I suppose.'

'It's worth looking at,' Matt said quickly, anxious to keep her talking. 'Why don't we meet and I can see over the place?'

'You really think you might be interested?'

'Yes, definitely. Would – ' he reached over and flicked through his diary – 'tomorrow suit you, and then maybe lunch?'

'Why, that would be nice, Matt.' Her voice sounded, as usual, terribly detached and impersonal. 'Shall we say eleven, eleven thirty?'

'Say eleven thirty and I'll get my secretary to book us a table at Claridge's.'

'How lovely.' For a moment her tone grew warmer. 'I'll see you then, Matt.'

'Lovely, looking forward to it.'

He was about to write her name in his diary and then, with a sudden feeling of guilt, thought better of it. Instead he just wrote: 'Lunch. Claridge's, 1 p.m.' and sat gazing for a few seconds at the entry over which he seemed to see imposed the magical name 'Jenny'.

His reverie was interrupted as Maurice came through the door, a sheaf of papers in his hand.

'Dad, about the visit . . . ' It was then that Matt saw the word Bristol underneath the new diary entry which, in his excitement, had escaped him. 'Bristol tomorrow,' Maurice went on, as if reminding him. 'I'm wondering if we can have a conference . . . '

'Sorry.' Matt shut his diary firmly. 'I can't make it. Something else has just come up.'

'But Dad,' Maurice looked incredulous, 'it's tremendously important. How could you fix something else?'

'Sorry. I just did. It means I'll be in London.' He reached out for the papers in Maurice's hand. 'Anything we can sort out now? It will be a test for you.' He gave him a confident smile.

'But Dad,' Maurice perched on the side of his desk, 'I simply can't understand you. This has been fixed for ages. Mark Dawson will be livid.'

'I'll talk to him. I'll say I want you to handle it. After all, Maurice, you want more control, don't you?'

'Yes, but I'm not in a position to finalise a deal worth millions of pounds that we've been talking about for months. I haven't the stature or authority and neither Jack, Jeff or the rest of the team will be very pleased. Can you . . . say what it is that is more important than putting your signature on a multi-million contract for the firm?'

'I have to go to London, that's all I can say. But I can tell you, it's important too.'

'I suppose it's nothing to do with the flat in Mayfair, Dad?'

'Don't be impertinent,' Matt said sharply.

'I don't think I'm being impertinent.' Maurice, his face very pale, got off the desk. 'I think this *is* very much my business. This meeting tomorrow has been in your diary for at *least* six weeks. It comes at the end of a crucial period of negotiation involving endless hours of our time and expertise on costs. You are a personal friend of Mark Dawson and you could help sway it.'

'I'll have a word with him on the phone. It will be all right, you'll see.'

'It's not the same, Dad. He will feel that something more important than him has turned up. If so, I think *I* have a right to know what it is.'

'Very well then.' Matt stood up and walked to the window. 'I'm going to look at some offices. I told you I was thinking of a London office . . . '

'And *that's* more important than the Dawson deal?' Maurice looked at him incredulously. 'I can't believe this, Dad.'

'They belong to the Swedish shipping line which I visited on my Scandinavian trip. They're offering them to me on an advantageous lease, but I have to make up my mind very quickly.'

'I don't believe this.'

'Well, it's true.' Matt began to be aware that he was losing his temper. 'And, Maurice, I must ask you *not* to flout my authority at every turn, question everything I do. I warned you some time ago. I suggested then that a few months away from here might do you good, put things in perspective. I think highly of you, Maurice, you know that, but I don't think you are quite ready to step into my shoes just yet. You're only twenty-seven, after all.'

'But if I suddenly decided, Dad, to absent myself from a meeting of critical importance to the company, made weeks before, what would you say?'

91

'I wouldn't be pleased,' Matt said imperturbably. 'But then you're twenty-seven and I'm fifty-five, and the absolute head of this company. I would expect *you* to consult me and tell me what you were going to do. Well, I have told you what I'm going to do. I consider it important to meet Pehr Holstrom and see the offices. I've got business dealings with him, too, that might even supersede the Dawson deal.'

'Oh!' Maurice's expression changed. 'He's over here, is he?'

'Yes. I thought we could combine looking at the offices with business.'

'Why didn't you say so then?' Maurice's manner of stiff formality relaxed. 'It alters the situation. So long as you explain to the others.'

'I will tell them that I'm meeting an important overseas contact who is only here for a short time. There's no need to say anything about offices.'

'Which, anyway, I don't think we need.'

'I'm not so sure.'

'I think it's a complete waste of money, Father. I think . . . ' he paused and stared at him hard for a moment. 'I don't know what's happening to you. I really don't.'

'Well, I assure you you will be fully consulted when the time comes, and so will other members of the management team.' Matt sat down at his desk and ran his hand across his forehead. 'I would be awfully grateful if you could drop your criticism of your father for the time being, Maurice, and maybe ask the others to come in so that we can consult about the Dawson deal which, as you say, is *very* important.'

The offices were hopelessly small, but then he had known they would be. They consisted of the ground and first floors of what had once been a townhouse in this prestigious part of Mayfair. But this was not the point. Even if he had been genuinely interested in a London office, he

92

would have gone to the City, as Pehr Holstrom was doing. Mayfair was altogether the wrong ambience. There was rather a nice receptionist sitting at a desk at the entrance, and inside about half a dozen people scattered about, working at VDUs.

'Very nice,' he said turning to Jenny. 'Lovely.'

She looked at him quizzically. She had on a fashionable fake-fur coat which she clasped to her as though she felt the cold, and high leather boots. Her hair seemed more golden than ever, her skin more translucent, her eyes more blue. If he thought his obsession had gone, or been diminished, he was wrong. Seeing her again reinforced it, only made it stronger. He was no longer the tender husband, devoted grandfather, reflecting on thirty years of happy, contented marriage as he had done only a few days before. What was he? His bewilderment must have shown on his face because her expression changed too.

'What is it, Matt?'

'Well!' To cover his confusion. 'They are very nice offices; but I don't think they'd quite suit us. They're not big enough for us, either.'

'There's the flat,' she said.

'Oh, the flat.' He paused. 'You wouldn't be keeping that on?'

'No, it's the lease of the whole building. Come and see.'

'I'd like that.'

She opened a door that led back on to the staircase and they continued up to the next floor, which was partitioned from the rest of the house by a door. This Jenny opened, and stood back to allow him to enter. The feeling of her presence there was overpowering, the knowledge that this was the place where she lived, breathed, ate, slept.

The entrance led straight into a large room furnished in the modern Swedish style: bleached parquet blocks covered with thick rugs, leather armchairs, a huge leather sofa facing a large, expensive television. In the corner was a round dining table with four chairs, and beyond this a

93

gleaming kitchen furnished with all the latest gadgets. Back in the living room, she pointed to two doors.

'Bedrooms. Like to see?'

'If I may.'

She opened the door of one and he peeped through.

There was a double bed which, like the rest of the furniture, was of natural Swedish teak or afrormosia. There were blinds at the windows rather than curtains. It had an impersonal atmosphere, like that of a hotel room, and he asked, 'Yours?'

She shook her head. 'The guest room. Mine is far more untidy. I'd rather you didn't look in, if you don't mind. I didn't make the bed.'

'Don't worry, that's O K.' He looked round then, re-turning to the corridor, followed her back to the drawing room. At her invitation he sat in one of the deep chairs and clasped his hands.

'Still won't do?' She leaned against the sill, her back to the window.

'I'd have to think about it, but I think it will be "no". Sorry.'

'Pity.' She gave a rueful yet detached smile. 'Am I still owed lunch?'

'You're always owed lunch,' he said. 'Oh, and thanks for thinking of me.'

'How about an aquavit for old times' sake?' She glanced at him sideways and selected a bottle from the drinks table.

'Delighted.' He joined his hands behind his neck, gazing at her. He felt a curious sense of peace just being here, at home in her flat, her company. He was blissfully content to watch her slow, graceful movements, as if everything was done in slow motion. She disappeared for a moment into the kitchen, returning with two glasses.

'I didn't really think you'd want it,' she said, turning to him as she poured the drink. 'I just thought it would be nice to see you again. It seemed a good excuse.'

His heart beat more quickly. He felt suddenly hot. He struggled out of his overcoat, then, straightening his tie, sat back and made a determined effort to compose himself.

'You don't need an excuse, Jenny,' he said very softly.

'Well, I hadn't heard from you.' She seemed strangely shy.

'I'd the idea you didn't *want* to hear. You'd call the shots.'

She grimaced and didn't reply.

'How's — what's his name?' Matt clicked his fingers. 'The young man who was with us at dinner.'

'Eric?'

'Eric. That's it. How's Eric?'

'He's fine.'

'And George. Have you seen George?'

'George's absolutely finished.' She gave him his glass and sat opposite him, hers clasped between her hands.

'He must be very disappointed.'

'He didn't reply.'

'Oh, you wrote and told him?'

'More or less.' She sounded nonchalant. 'He asked when I was coming over and I said I had no plans.'

'Poor George,' Matt mused, looking into his glass, feeling extraordinarily happy. 'So that leaves just Eric.'

'Matt, don't be so jealous!'

'I'm not jealous, I assure you. I mean I envy the luck of these younger men.'

'Has anything changed?' She made a sudden movement towards him, her eyes disconcertingly direct.

'Changed?' He swallowed.

'I had the impression you were . . . well, keen.'

'That hasn't changed.' He nervously sipped from his glass. 'What I want to know is, how do you feel?'

'How do you think? I came back, didn't I?' As if responding to an implied invitation, he got to his feet and, leaving his glass on the table in front of him, went to

95

perch on the arm of her chair. He leaned over and, letting his fingers run through her hair, gently brushed it with his lips.

'You don't know how often I've wanted to do this.'

She caught his hand, pressing her cheek against it. 'Sometimes these things have to happen,' Matt continued in a caressing tone.

'Yes, but you can always prevent them happening, try and stop them. That's why I stayed on in Sweden.'

'But you had to come back?'

'I didn't *have* to, but Daddy is actually quite serious about disposing of the office. I also . . . ' she hesitated, and he resumed stroking her hair with long, slow strokes as if she were a cat. 'I suppose what I'm trying to say is that I can't keep away from you.'

'I feel the same about you.' His elation now knew no bounds.

'Matt,' she jerked her head abruptly away from him and looked up at him, 'we both know we *can't* go on with this. It will seriously jeopardise your marriage.'

'Not necessarily.' He paused. 'Anyway, the marriage was over long ago.'

'What do you mean?'

'What I said. You can't "be in love" for thirty years.'

'But I thought,' hesitantly, 'when I saw you and Elspeth together you seemed very happy.'

'One has to keep up appearances. As a matter of fact, they become second nature.'

'You mean . . . it's all a sham?' Her tone changed to one of incredulity. He noticed her manner was changing too; almost visibly she was relaxing.

'Naturally I'm fond of Elspeth; but it's hardly a life, is it?'

'No sex?' She barely whispered the word.

'No, nothing . . . just an amiable companionship. It's like being half dead. When I saw you I felt that I'd come to life again, like Lazarus.'

'I see.' Her relief was palpable; her acceptance of his falsehood was palpable. She turned towards him as if she were offering herself, a gesture he found decidedly provocative, and casually he slipped an arm round her neck.

He was aware of her legs, her knees, her thighs, the burning centre at the heart of her. She turned her head and, as he bent lower, he was conscious of the curve of her neck, the contour of her chin, the opaque lips suggestively parted. He reached out and roughly pulled her towards him, and the kiss this time seemed like drinking from a tall glass with the taste of aquavit deliciously still on her breath.

Claridge's was forgotten. He had tasted her. Dived deep into her. Unbelievable. An unbelievable experience.

They lay together on the bed in the spare room, naked, fingers entwined, both staring upwards. His emotions had drained him, leaving him incapable even of the exultation of conquest.

'I love you so much,' he murmured, not quite believing the sound of his own voice.

She didn't reply, and this lack of an answer worried him. He turned his head and, although she looked as though she was still staring at the ceiling, her eyes were half closed, her long pale lashes lying on her pale cheeks. The nipples of her neat round breasts were erect and taut, her stomach dipped at her navel. Her pubic hair was like a small thicket, quite black. He yearned to bury his face in it and feast.

He had never seen anything, anyone, so beautiful in his life.

'What are we going to do?' he asked, putting a hand, brown and hard-looking against her whiteness, on her taut, flat stomach.

'What do you want to do, Matt?' She opened those astonishing eyes that were the colour of blue quartz, and stared at him.

'I want you,' he said. 'That's all I can think of. You could have the flat, you know that. It's for you. It was always meant for you. No strings.'

'It would certainly *be* very convenient if we disposed of the lease of this building, which Daddy wants to do. But there *are* strings, Matt, aren't there?'

'What do you mean?'

'We're lovers. I'd be your mistress.'

He was silent, thinking what a lovely, dangerous word 'mistress' was.

'You know I don't *want* to be a mistress, Matt.'

Still he didn't reply.

'Matt?' After a while.

'Yes?'

'Did I upset you?'

'Yes, of course you upset me. You throw out a lifeline to a drowning man and then . . . '

'I didn't mean it to happen. You must believe that, and now I feel deeply guilty that it did.'

'Oh, my darling, don't feel *guilty*.' He turned towards her and buried his face once again in her hair. 'This was the most marvellous thing that ever happened to me.'

'Even if it never happened again?'

'Yes.' He paused. 'I suppose what you are trying to tell me is that you'll go back?'

'There really is nothing for me to do here. Besides, if I go away, it will give you a chance to get over me.'

'I will never get over you, especially not now.' He flung an arm over her, as if to try and keep her by his side, imprison her for ever. 'What would you do if you went back?'

'Pehr suggested I might go to university.'

'What a terrible waste,' he murmured, thinking of Beth and her student friends: not exactly unwashed, but casually, sometimes shabbily, dressed, and living in an environment far removed from what he imagined for Jenny. The thought of Jenny as a student was appalling, somehow shocking.

'There's absolutely nothing to keep me in England, apart from you. I have lost touch with all my school friends.'

'All?'

'They were mostly Americans, Arab princesses, the daughters of foreign diplomats or businessmen who now live abroad. Besides, Daddy would have a fit if he knew about you and me. One of the things he objected to about George was that he was so much older than I.'

Matt felt offended, rebuffed, and withdrew his arm. He saw she was capable, perhaps because she was still so young, of wounding him deeply.

'Does it matter to you so much what your father says?'

'Yes, it does. He's always given me good advice, and he loves me for what I am, not for what he can get out of me.'

Matt sat up, feeling suddenly vulnerable, capable indeed of being deeply hurt by this goddess beside him.

'I love you for what you are. Far, far more than you can ever guess. Only I feel I'm going to lose you and I don't know that I can bear it, Jenny. Please, please be kind to me.'

He reached out for her and she folded her arms around him, holding him tight, feeling deeply bewildered, rather frightened, wondering what would become of them.

Wanting, and not wanting.

Beth, hurrying along the street, was late for her audition. If she got this part it could mean TV. TV at such an early stage in her career . . . Best not to think of it.

She ran across Grosvenor Square, still muttering lines to herself. Important to get them *exactly* right.

She reached the safety of South Audley Street and paused to look at the paper in her hand, checking her directions to the house of the producer which was in one of the mews between here and Park Street.

Head bent, concentrating on her lines, she looked up just in time to see a couple emerge from a doorway a few paces in front of her. They immediately turned to their right,

99

going away from her in the direction of Curzon Street. The man – tall, distinguished looking – wore a grey overcoat and was carrying a briefcase in one hand. The other arm was round the woman, also tall with a striking profile and blonde hair swinging over the collar of her fur coat. They were pressed so close together you could hardly have inserted a hair between them, and then the man turned and either whispered something in her ear or nuzzled it. It was hard to tell.

But the one thing Beth knew, without any doubt at all, was that the man in question was her father. The woman looked about twenty years his junior, maybe more. It was hard to tell without seeing her close up and, walking quickly, they were receding.

Beth experienced a sensation she had never felt in her life before or needed to summon up as an actress: fear, repugnance, a sense of unreality.

She didn't know whether to run after her father or continue on her way to the TV producer's house. What, after all, would she say to him? 'Daddy, what do you think you're doing with another woman?' And then it occurred to her that her father was fifty-five, a hugely rich, successful man. Didn't a lot of men have affairs? Didn't one read about them all the time, and why should he be any different?

But he was. He was Daddy; loving, affectionate Daddy; a family man, if ever there was a family man, a doting father, a loving grandfather and, hitherto, as far as they were concerned, a devoted husband.

Maybe he still was. Couldn't people have affairs and still love their families? Wasn't it what the play that she was about to rehearse herself in a few minutes was about? An Alan Ayckbourn comedy of relationships in which couples were tossed around, ending up in one another's bedrooms, one another's beds? Silly to pretend it didn't happen all the time.

The couple stopped by the traffic lights, where Mount

Street bisected South Audley Street. A couple of hundred yards behind them, Beth suddenly stopped too, wondering what she would say if her father looked around.

But he only had eyes for his companion. And then, as she turned towards him, Beth could see she was very young indeed, maybe as young as she was. Very beautiful; very, very beautiful. Her father bent towards her and she raised her mouth. Their lips met.

Beth rushed into the shelter of a doorway, not wanting to be seen for fear she would shatter a moment that was profound, private, almost sacred but, to her, infinitely disturbing, like a gentle, insinuating wind that presages the beginning of a violent and destructive storm.

PART II

Happy Anniversary

CHAPTER 6

After the Prime Minister with her entourage had left the atmosphere in the party relaxed. Not that she was ever formal; her studied graciousness was well known to Matt, who served on a number of government committees. He and Elspeth were fairly frequent guests at Downing Street; but even then he felt flattered when there had been a flurry at the door and a flushed functionary rushed in to tell him the PM had arrived, on her way to another engagement, of course. She had told him she would look in if she could, and indeed she had.

Now she had departed, and the high moment of the party arrived in the crowded ballroom at Claridge's. The band struck up the 'Anniversary Waltz', and Matt took his wife by the hand, leading her onto the middle of the floor. Then, while everyone gathered round and clapped, he put his arm tenderly around her, gazed deeply into her eyes and, together, they completed several turns of the floor before being joined by Henry and Georgina, Beth partnered by Maurice. Gradually, other couples joined in.

Elspeth wore a long powder-blue gown, specially made for the occasion. She had also paid a rare visit to her hairdresser, and her snow-white locks curled deftly around her head. She looked sweet, pretty, dumpy, grandmotherly. She looked ten years older than Matt, but if some rather catty people commented on it (and there were quite a few of those there) the bulk of their friends and acquaintances knew what a singularly happy, devoted couple they were, and envied them for it. Some were on their second, third or even fourth marriages. Very few had lasted the course for as long as the Ransoms'.

'You look very well tonight.' Matt smiled reassuringly down at her, his hand tightening round her waist.

'So do you,' she said, gazing up at him. 'You're the best-looking man in the room, and I'm very lucky. What a nice party it is, Matt, to have all our friends with us. Wasn't the PM charming?'

'Always is.' Matt looked around, trying to make out faces in the concourse. 'That is the secret of her success. She . . . '

The rest of what he was saying was drowned by the noise of the band as it reached a crescendo. Gradually, as if acting on a hidden signal, the couples began to leave the floor, until only the anniversary pair remained still waltzing, as if oblivious to everyone else.

When the last couple had left and Matt and Elspeth were alone, the band stopped abruptly; there was a roll on the drums and the lights dramatically went out to an appreciative gasp from the crowd. Almost immediately, however, a glow came from the wings, and a huge wedding cake was rolled in by two chefs in white aprons and tall white hats. Thirty candles burned on the three tiers of the cake, atop of which was a couple dressed for their wedding day, the woman slim and beautiful, the man tall and handsome.

Mesmerised by the surprise, which had been organised by their children, Matt and Elspeth could only stand and stare, totally nonplussed, a little embarrassed, until the orchestra very gently resumed the bars of the 'Anniversary Waltz'. Georgina, Beth and Maurice appeared in the beam of light which suddenly shone over them as they embraced their parents and led them to the cake-cutting ceremony on the edge of the dance floor.

Matt stood beside his wife, his hand covering hers as they prepared to cut the cake. He could sense that Elspeth's hand was trembling, and had turned to give her another reassuring smile when his eye was caught by someone standing, also smiling, on the edge of the crowd. He looked at her and she looked at him. The man beside her didn't appear to notice the silent encounter, his own eyes fixed upon the group centre stage. Matt's hand suddenly trembled too, and Elspeth looked at him in surprise.

'Are you nervous too, dear? Then let's both do it,' and she plunged her hand holding the knife into the thick, creamy sponge mixture, while everyone burst out singing, 'For *they* are jolly good fellows', and a renewed burst of applause followed.

Matt hardly saw the cake. He felt confused. Gone was the laughter, and the trembling that had started when he looked into Jenny's eyes didn't cease.

'I never thought *you'd* be so nervous.' It was Elspeth's turn to be reassuring, and she stepped back as the chef expertly took over the cutting of the cake into portions for the guests. Champagne also appeared, though there had been no lack of it before, and glasses were refilled.

Streamers were thrown, and balloons started to tumble down from the ceiling where they had been caught up in a net. The anniversary pair were assailed on all sides by guests wanting to kiss them, shake their hands, wish them well.

Right at the end of the queue, and reaching them only as people had dispersed and the dancing had started again, were George and Jenny, the latter dressed in a black dinner dress slit up to the thigh on one side. With no sleeves and a high neckline, it looked extremely sexy. Her thick curtain of hair shadowed one side of her face, which made her seem infinitely mysterious and alluring. She stood just behind George as he embraced Elspeth and shook hands with Matt.

107

'Congratulations,' he said, then, turning rather diffidently to the woman by his side, 'it was too late to ask if I could bring Jenny. She only just reappeared from Sweden.'

'Of course you could,' Elspeth turned graciously to her, 'and we're delighted to see you.' She gave her a quick peck on the cheek. 'How are you, Jenny? You *look* very well. Have you been sunning yourself somewhere?'

'Only on the ski slopes,' Jenny began as Elspeth turned to Matt and took his arm.

'Darling, you remember Jenny, don't you?'

'Of course I do.' Matt, a polite, almost impersonal smile on his face, reached for Jenny's hand. 'I thought maybe you'd been in Spain?'

'No, definitely skiing.' He thought her voice contained a hint of mockery.

'Jenny was once nearly junior champion of Sweden.' George had a proprietorial note in his voice which Matt found irksome.

'Skiing, as late as May?' he enquired caustically.

'Well, not *quite* as late. I had to get myself together.'

'And you only just arrived?' Matt hoped the disbelief in his voice didn't show.

'Just!' She smiled mockingly again. Could he believe her?

'And how *are* things, George?' Elspeth seemed genuinely pleased to see him, and stopped a passing waiter to give him and Jenny a glass each of champagne.

'Oh, fine. I like Madrid.'

'And he's done very well there.' Matt was making a desperate effort to sound normal. 'I'm hoping he'll want to return.'

'Oh, not "ordering" me, Matt?' George's tone was ironic.

'We'll see,' Matt said mysteriously.

'May I take Elspeth away for the pleasure of a dance, Matt?'

'Of course.' Matt bowed to his wife, giving her hand to George. 'And may I?' He turned to Jenny, who was watching the two go on to the dance floor.

'Of course, Sir Matthew,' she murmured, reaching up her arms to put one hand on his shoulder. Her movements seemed intimate, sexually charged. He held her very tight.

'And did you *really* get back today?' he murmured as they began to dance in perfect synchronisation.

'Well, this week. I did try and ring you. You've been constantly busy.'

'I didn't get a message.' He cautiously pressed her body closer to his, imagining the act of sex.

'I didn't leave one.'

'Ah, that would explain it. I thought you'd deserted me.'

'Why should you think that?'

'March, April.' He pressed his fingers individually into the small of her back, as if counting.

'It's only May now.'

'Have you come to London for good?'

'I'm not sure. It depends.'

'On what does it depend?'

'A lot of things.'

'Where are you staying?'

'At the Connaught.'

'May I ring you there?'

'If you like.'

He looked into her eyes and was sure she was teasing him. To be so close yet not be able to make love. He pulled her imperceptibly nearer again and brushed his cheek against hers.

'I adore you,' he whispered. They continued to revolve as the music played, jostling against other couples, but Matt took no notice. For him there was only one other person in the room, and he held her in his arms.

Beth had a number of young men she dated, one or two she went to bed with, but she had no steady boyfriend. She

109

wanted to avoid the fate of her sister, or even her parents, and become locked in an early marriage, even if happy. Her sister's undoubtedly was; but her parents'?

In time she began to wonder if her eyes had deceived her that day in Mayfair. Had it really been Dad? After all, she had never seen the man's face. But one knew one's father, how he dressed, those little nuances of walk and gesture, even from behind.

She wished she wasn't sure, but she was. It haunted her, but there was no one in whom she could confide. Georgina, no; nor Maurice. Certainly not Mum.

Beth had brought a fellow drama student called Tim Edgcumbe to her parents' party as her escort, but a number of other young people had also been invited, the children of friends whose ages roughly corresponded to the ages of the Ransom offspring. They had a table to themselves in a corner of the room, well away from the dance floor.

The food had been good, the drink plentiful, and the young people were in good spirits. Beth liked Tim. He was one of the men she sometimes went to bed with, but not too often in case he got serious. Now they sat holding hands loosely, watching the crowded dance floor, wondering whether they should join the throng.

'Should we?' Tim looked at Beth, who screwed up her nose.

'I wish they'd play something more lively,' she said.

'I think this is mainly for the older ones.'

'Maybe we'll sit it out until it hots up. I . . . '

The couple on the fringe of the dance floor were dancing very slowly, almost as though the beat of the music mesmerised them. The man had his hand on the woman's back. Her left hand covered his. There was very little space between them. There was something charged, very sexual, about the couple which caught the attention. The woman was lovely, almost as tall as the man, her golden hair tucked behind an ear. Her eyes seemed to be fastened

110

on his throat, but he was gazing at her face. No doubt about that.

It would be impossible to suggest that there was anything between the couple, but equally impossible to suggest that there was not. The man tucked the woman's hand against his chest in a close, intimate gesture.

The man turned and Beth knew who he was, always had. But the woman fascinated her. Without a shadow of a doubt she had last seen her that cold February day in South Audley Street.

She sat looking at them for a few moments, but now they only had eyes for each other. Her eyes searched for her mother but she couldn't see her. Of Georgina or Maurice there was no sign either.

'There are *so* many people in here,' she said, turning abruptly to Tim.

'Anyway, let's dance.' He tugged her reluctantly to her feet and led her on to the dance floor while, at the other side of the room, she could still see her father.

'What are you staring at?' Tim murmured, trying to put his cheek comfortably against hers.

'I've just seen my father with someone. I want to know who she is.'

They revolved so that Tim could look at the far side of the room, but he shook his head. 'I haven't a clue. She's gorgeous.'

'That's what I think.'

'Oh, don't be silly, Beth. You know your father is devoted to your mum. Besides, she's young enough to be his daughter.'

'I'm not suggesting anything,' she said. 'I just wondered who she was.'

'Well, let's go and find out,' Tim began, but the music came to a sudden stop with a flourish of drums, and the band leader announced a short break.

Her father and the woman broke immediately, looked around innocently for their respective partners. Then Beth saw her mother appear as if from nowhere with George. They were both talking animatedly despite the din. In the middle of the floor they collided with her father and the woman and, with much laughter, they changed partners again.

By this time Beth and Tim had joined them, and Matt, a fatherly arm around her, drew her off the floor.

'Enjoying yourself, darling?'

'Yes, Daddy. Are you?'

'Very much. By the way,' he turned abruptly to the couple just behind him, 'did you know George was back?'

'Hi Beth, how are you?' George said with his cheerful, familiar smile. 'How's the acting going?'

'Fine thanks, George,' Beth said, not looking at him but at the woman at his side.

'Jenny, did you ever meet Beth, Matt's younger daughter?'

'Hi!' Jenny said, giving her a friendly grin.

'Hi!' Beth held out her hand. 'No, I don't think we ever met.'

'I don't think so,' Jenny agreed.

'Beth's an actress.'

'Oh!' Jenny didn't seem very interested, really. Her expression was inscrutable, polite, rather bored. She didn't so much as glance at Matt.

Yet Matt, clearly still excited by her proximity, as though he'd won first prize in a raffle, steered her in the direction of the family table, where Georgina and Henry had just rejoined Maurice and his girlfriend Shirley.

The men rose as the new arrivals approached, and Jenny was introduced to the people she didn't know. While George hovered, Matt pointedly held out a chair for Jenny, then beckoned to the waiter to serve her with champagne. He then sat down next to her, taking the chair which had previously been occupied by Elspeth.

His behaviour had by now become rather obvious.

Georgina and Henry exchanged glances, while Maurice leapt to his feet to give his mother his chair.

112

'We need another,' he said, beckoning to a waiter, who instantly hurried forward with a chair. Maurice scowled at his father and said something to Shirley, who shook her head as if she didn't understand. But Matt seemed oblivious of the dark looks from the members of his family; he was still concentrating his whole attention on Jenny.

George now appeared rather agitated, as though wondering what was going on. The only one who didn't seem to notice anything was Elspeth, who was engaged in a long discussion with Tim.

When the music started again, George rose immediately and held out a hand to Jenny. Matt then asked Beth to dance, but she declined, and instead he whispered in Georgina's ear and she got up, smiling at Henry, who at once asked Elspeth if he could have the honour. The couples made their way to the dance floor, while Beth and Tim remained at the table, staring after them.

'What got into you?' Tim asked. 'You were in a good mood when you came. Something's upset you.'

'It's just so big, so crowded.' Beth shook her shoulders. 'Something I saw.'

'What?' Tim was intrigued.

'I can't say. Not yet.'

And, spontaneously, she tucked her hand in his for comfort.

The following morning, breakfast in the Ransom household was late. As usual Elspeth was first down. She never drank much at parties, or at any other time, so she never suffered from the headaches or hangovers that afflicted other people.

It was a lovely morning and she felt very happy. She thought the party had been a great success. It had broken up about two o'clock but, after all the farewells had been said, it had been nearly four when Peter had deposited them at the door of their house. As it was the weekend, they preferred to come home than stay the night in town.

A few hours' sleep and here she was in the kitchen, in her housecoat, brewing coffee in the percolator, putting frozen rolls in the oven for breakfast. Or it would be brunch, really, as there was still no sound from either Matt or Beth asleep upstairs. The couple who looked after them always had weekends free.

It was a bright, sunny morning. The garden looked lovely. Elspeth had already been on a tour of inspection, with her morning tea mug clasped in her hand, a feeling of contentment and happiness possessing her as she inspected the proliferation of flowers in her herbaceous border, a hobby which she indulged with the help of a full-time gardener. Then there was her bird table to restock and, at last, she'd wandered back, glanced at the clock, and begun preparations for the late breakfast.

The door of the kitchen was quietly pushed open and Beth, looking tired and dishevelled, came in, yawning. She slumped down at the breakfast table, rubbing her eyes. Then she glanced at the clock on the wall.

'Golly! I didn't know it was that late.'

'It's nearly midday,' her mother said breezily. 'I thought we'd make it a sort of brunch with coffee and rolls, scrambled eggs if anyone wants them.'

'I couldn't eat a *thing*; but coffee I'd love.' Beth yawned again and stretched her arms. 'Daddy up yet, Mummy?'

'No. I can't ever remember him sleeping so late.'

'Well, it was after four when we got to bed. What time did you get up?'

'Oh, about nine.' Her mother grinned. 'Late for me. I might have a little nap this afternoon.'

'I don't know how you do it. Always bright and cheerful.' On an impulse Beth got up and threw her arms around her mother, surprising her so much that she nearly dropped the mug into which she was pouring coffee. 'I *do* love you, Mummy.'

'And I love you,' her mother gasped, taking a step back.

'I love you, and I appreciate you and, and . . . thank you!'

'But, darling . . . ' Carefully Elspeth put the mug down, happy but surprised by this unexpected and uncharacteristic outburst. 'I love you too. And thank me for what?'

'For being my mother, for being so wonderful, so good, so kind and caring. We're all . . . all terribly lucky to have you.' And she embraced her mother again, just as Matt appeared, also rubbing the sleep from his eyes and saying:

'Hey, what's going on here?'

'Just telling Mummy how much I love her and appreciate her.' Beth unfastened her arms from around her mother's neck. 'And how lucky we *all* are to have her. Aren't we, Daddy?'

'We certainly are,' Matt agreed, looking longingly at the percolator on the table. 'I'd love some coffee. Any to spare?'

'Freshly made,' Elspeth said cheerfully. 'Are you hungry, darling?'

'Not yet.' Matt picked up the *Sunday Times* and glanced at it. 'In about half an hour.'

'It's such a lovely day,' Elspeth chattered on. 'Why don't you both go and sit outside and I'll have my bath? I thought we'd have brunch at about half-twelve or so?'

'Good idea.' Matt looked up and, taking the mug from her, smiled. 'Thanks, Elspeth. A very successful evening, I thought.'

'Wonderful.' Elspeth sat down at the kitchen table and gazed at him. 'It was a terrific party. I think everyone enjoyed it. Didn't you, Beth?'

'Lovely,' Beth said, but her tone was stilted and non-committal.

'Did you *really* enjoy it, darling?' Her father peered at her. 'I thought you looked a bit peaky. A bit off-colour?'

'No, I was perfectly all right,' Beth snapped back rather sharply.

'Something with Tim?'

'Oh, Daddy, for God's sake, no.' She swept up her mug and left the kitchen by the garden door, while her father and mother stared at each other.

'Well, what brought that on?' Matt wondered.

'I thought she was very quiet and moody last night. Perhaps she'll tell me later on. Now, why don't you take your coffee outside and maybe she'll tell you?'

'I will in a minute.' Matt scratched his head. 'Beth is getting too old for these tantrums.'

'Darling,' Elspeth protested, 'darling, don't forget she's an actress. I think her temperament and moods are something we shall always have to live with.'

'She was never easy.'

'She never was,' Elspeth agreed.

'Do you think there's anything with that Tim?'

'I don't expect so.'

'Do they sleep together?'

Elspeth looked surprised. 'I don't know, and I would never *dream* of asking.'

'She didn't bring him back.'

'That doesn't mean they don't sleep together.'

'No, I suppose not.' Matt moodily drank his coffee.

'Wasn't it a nice surprise to see Jenny again?' Elspeth said brightly, and Matt looked at her suspiciously.

'Why do you say that?'

'Because it was. Don't you think?' Elspeth reached over to pour more coffee.

'Not particularly.'

'I thought you liked her?'

'Why should I like her?'

'Well, you've always paid her a lot of attention when we've seen her with George, and I thought you did last night.'

Matt leaned back in his chair, his hand round his mug. 'Are you suggesting anything, Elspeth?'

'Oh, darling.' Elspeth's expression was one of contrition. She hurried to the chair beside him. 'Of course I'm not. I'm just saying that I thought it was nice to see Jenny again because I like her, and I thought you did too. I can't blame you. She's a very pretty girl. In fact, last night *I* thought you were very gallant and now you say you weren't particularly pleased to see her.'

'I didn't.' Matt, looking confused and also angry, ruffled his hair. 'I didn't say anything. You said wasn't it a nice surprise to see her again, and I merely said "not particularly".'

'Well, it seems a funny remark to make when you so obviously *were* pleased to see her.'

'Well, I didn't. I wasn't . . . Oh, Elspeth,' Matt pushed back his chair, 'I just think you're reading all sorts of things into this that aren't there.' He refilled his mug and, the paper under his arm, went over to the kitchen door while Elspeth looked on in surprise.

'Matt, I'm doing nothing of the sort. I'm sorry I mentioned her.'

'So am I.'

And with a grimace he eased himself through the door and shut it after him.

Elspeth sat there for a few seconds, aware of sensations and, above all, emotions she had never known before. One moment she had been so happy, now . . . now there was a doubt in her mind, a large question mark looming in front of her.

Matt *had* been particularly attentive to Jenny. There was no doubt about it. His face had seemed to light up when he saw her. She couldn't help noticing how closely they danced, and was sure others had noticed it too. And then when they returned to the table, why, he'd actually given her – a much younger woman – her, Elspeth's chair. It was Maurice who'd leapt up and made sure his mother was seated.

Maybe Matt thought that, as Jenny's escort, it was up to him to see . . . Oh, what the hell. Put it out of your mind. Don't let it spoil your happiness, Elspeth told herself, running her hands through her hair, looking at the clock; then, taking the rolls out of the oven and leaving them to cool, she went up to run her bath.

No use, no point at all, for the first time in thirty years, and especially on her anniversary, even *beginning* to torment herself with a smidgeon of jealousy.

Matt carefully put the news section of the *Sunday Times* and his coffee cup down on the patio table. Then he gazed thoughtfully at his daughter before bending to ruffle her already tousled hair.

'What's the matter, chick?' he asked, sitting down next to her, but she angrily brushed his hand away and moved as far down the bench as she could, putting as much space between him and herself as possible.

'Beth?' he asked anxiously of his favourite daughter, his favourite child.

She didn't reply but sat, arms folded, scowling into space.

'Well, this isn't very nice for our anniversary,' her father said, feeling annoyed. 'Trying to spoil things, are we?'

'*I'm* not the one spoiling things,' she muttered under her breath.

'Well, who is spoiling things? What on earth has happened to you? Is it a tiff with Tim? I think he's – '

'It's *nothing* to do with Tim,' she exploded, turning to look fiercely at him. 'It's you.'

'Me? What did *I* do?'

'You and that woman!'

Matt waited a moment and then said quietly, 'What are you talking about, Beth?'

'Jenny.'

'Oh, Jenny.' He sat back as though to pass the remark off.

'Yes. "Oh, Jenny".' Beth gazed at him witheringly. 'Don't think *I* don't know.'

'Just what do you mean?' He attempted to sound scornful.

'I know that you're having an affair with her.'

118

Matt took a deep breath. 'And how,' he said, 'do you know that?'

'Because I saw you. The way you danced with her . . . '

'My dear, is that all?' He laughed with relief. 'Can't I dance with a pretty woman without people thinking I'm sleeping with her? I hardly know the creature.'

'*Everyone* noticed. I don't know what Mum thought.'

'Did you ask her?'

'Of course I didn't.'

Matt, beginning to feel angry, pointed towards the kitchen door. 'Then go and ask her. Go on.'

'I wouldn't dream of upsetting her on her wedding anniversary.'

'Then why are you upsetting me?'

'Because it's true.'

'It is not true.

'It is.'

Matt made as though to get up, then changed his mind and, seizing his coffee cup, swallowed the by-now-cold contents.

'You're being absurd.' He shook out the paper and stared intently at the front page, but the words formed a curious blur before his eyes.

'I saw you in South Audley Street. With her.'

The blur got worse and Matt shook his head and tried to refocus.

'You were kissing. You'd come out of a house or shop or some place and I followed you – '

'You were spying . . . ' He spun furiously round at her.

'I was *not* spying,' she said shrilly. 'By one of those curious coincidences that happen in life, I was on my way to audition at the house of Marty Frank who lives nearby. I was so upset I didn't get the job.'

Matt swallowed. 'Coming out of a house doesn't mean a thing.'

'You stopped at the corner of Mount Street and you kissed. A long, lingering kiss.' By now her voice was so

119

loud, her tone so hysterical, that Matt looked nervously upwards towards the house. 'But you can't deny it, Daddy, because I saw you. I was there. And then you have the effrontery, the sheer *nerve*, to ask her to your wedding anniversary party.'

'I did not ask her,' he said thickly. 'I was as amazed as anyone to see her with George. I didn't know she was coming. Of course I didn't ask him to bring her. I didn't even know she was in this country. I – '

'Why do you make all these excuses?'

'I am not making excuses.' He tried to keep his tone level and unemotional. 'And will you please stop shouting? I don't see why your mother should be brought into all this . . . all this hysteria.'

'Why did you *do* it, Daddy?' Beth suddenly leapt up and flung her arms dramatically in the air. 'Why did you do it? You're so lucky to have someone like Mummy; a family who love you, a place like this,' her arms embraced the house. 'Why do you have to chase after a woman the age of your daughter? Why? *Why?*'

'Shut up!' Matt hissed. 'Shut up. You don't know what you're saying. I am not "having an affair" with Je . . . the woman in question.' He looked nervously towards the house again.

'Then what were you doing in South Audley Street?'

'The offices of the shipping company where she works are there. I'd been to see them as I was thinking of London offices for us. I know her father . . . '

'It doesn't mean you have to kiss her, does it? You stopped by the traffic lights, your arms entwined, and had a passionate embrace. Anyone could have seen you . . . '

'Anyone did,' Matt murmured sotto voce. 'Unfortunately, the worst person in the world . . . '

'And last night, as you danced, you were pressing yourself into her in a most unpleasant and suggestive way. I was quite disgusted. God knows what everyone else thought. Mummy must have been terribly hurt . . . '

'I don't think your mother noticed anything. She was dancing with George. That ballroom was so crowded. Anyway, I'm not having an affair with her.'

'You'd only like to?' Beth's lip curled with derision.

'I'm not answering any more of these stupid, idiotic questions, submitting to this interrogation, this third degree. I love your mother. I have been married to her for thirty years. I'm staying married to her, so that is that. No more nonsense, please!'

Up in her bedroom, Elspeth emerged from the bathroom towelling her hair, humming an air under her breath, feeling suddenly happy. The tune was the 'Anniversary Waltz'.

She sat in front of the dressing table and wound her towel into a turban, then sat forward and inspected her face carefully in the mirror, tracing the deep lines with her forefinger.

Her mood changed.

Yes, she did look old, much older than Matt. She undid her bathrobe and submitted herself to a good, frank inspection. It was not only the face, the snow-white hair, but it was also the way she had filled out, let herself go because of her skill in the kitchen, all those official dinners, all that entertaining. Her breasts were full but they hung, and the skin puckered at the sides, as did the skin of her arms.

She put a hand on the rolls of her stomach. Sitting as she was she had to peer over to see her pubic hair. She was much, much too fat. She resolved to go on a diet. Maybe visit a beauty parlour, have a few sessions, see what they could do for her. She fastened her robe and seized a pot of face cream, unscrewed the lid and began to apply the contents vigorously all over her face, as if to atone for those many years of neglect. For a moment she stopped, cocked her ear and listened. Maybe she was going deaf too.

But no there *were* voices raised in anger on the terrace. Beth was shouting something to Matt; she sounded angry. Beth angry with her adored father? It seemed impossible. And yet Beth had been very withdrawn the evening before, and Elspeth had noticed her frowning across the table in Matt's direction. What had happened between them? Maybe she too thought he'd been over-familiar with that woman – Jenny. Maybe it was something completely different.

Had he, for instance, threatened her allowance? Surely not. He was the most generous of men. Maybe he'd said something about Tim? Well, Tim was very nice, but a bit wet. Mind you, any man had to try very hard to upstage Matt, or be thought in any way superior to him, at least in the eyes of his youngest daughter.

It was strange, most unusual.

She crossed the room stealthily, then surreptitiously opened the window, feeling a bit sneaky, whereupon the voices immediately became louder. She peeped over the sill and was amazed to see Matt and Beth confronting each other on the terrace below. Matt's face was an unhealthy red, whereas Beth's was very white and she had her arm flung out in the direction of her father.

'*And* you make yourself a fool *and* an idiot, everyone laughing at you . . . '

'I say shut up.' Matt wagged his finger violently at her. '*Shut up!*'

But nothing, no one now, was going to stop Beth.

'Chasing around after a woman young enough to be your daughter. You'll be the laughing stock of the whole world, Dad. Everybody, but everybody – ' she paused and spat out the words – 'will say how perfectly ridiculous you are.'

By this time her voice had risen to a crescendo and Matt advanced, fist raised. 'Shut up!' he hissed again. 'I tell you – '

And then he looked up towards the window and

saw Elspeth, her mouth agape, staring down at him.

And in that minute their eyes locked.

Elspeth sat on the side of the bed, head still bound in a towelling turban, clutching her robe around her, eyes thoughtfully cast on the ground. No tears.

'It never entered my head until last night,' she said eventually, looking up at him. Matt had the bulk of his body propped against the sill, probably so that she would not see his face.

'I tell you there was, *is* nothing.'

'But Beth said she saw you kissing in the street.' Elspeth's normally calm, controlled voice betrayed extreme indignation.

'It was a peck. Look, she's a lovely woman . . . '

'But what were you *doing* with her?'

'Looking at her offices.'

'And did you take them?'

'No. They weren't suitable.'

'Did *anyone* take them?'

'I suppose so, eventually. I don't know.' Matt uncrossed and recrossed his arms. 'Look, Elspeth, you're making a mountain out of a molehill, needlessly causing yourself distress . . . '

'But on our wedding anniversary. Of course I noticed. Tried not to think of it.'

He went over to her and perched on the bed beside her, one arm gently encircling her shoulders. 'At this time, of all times, you're hypersensitive. There *is* nothing to think about,' he straightened and looked grimly towards the window, 'and it will be a long time, a very long time, before I can forgive that young woman for causing all this mischief.'

A very long time indeed before he would forgive the beloved daughter.

CHAPTER 7

Matt stood in the stern of the punt, heaving hard down on the long pole in his hands. In the prow, one hand trailing in the water, the other holding a parasol to shade her eyes from the hot sun, lay Jenny. Except for their very modern dress, they could have been a couple from an Edwardian or Victorian scene, immortalised by an Alma-Tadema or a Sisley, as the punt was propelled slowly down-river, passing the houses of the wealthy with their lush gardens fronting the water's edge. Sometimes there was a boat or a dinghy moored by the jetty, the long trailing branches of weeping willows kissing the shiny surface of the water like Narcissus.

It was breathlessly beautiful and, for the lovers, more beautiful still, as their eyes sent secret messages back and forth. Matt wore grey slacks and a white shirt open at the neck. He looked trim and elegant, with white sneakers on his feet, no socks. Jenny wore jeans and a sloppy top, a large sun hat crowning her head. Both wore sunglasses; both were contentedly, blissfully at ease.

'Did you punt at university?' Jenny asked, breaking a long pause.

'I never went to university.'

'Oh!'

'You didn't either.'

'No. Daddy wanted me to. I was too lazy.'

'What did you want to do?' He drew the long pole out of the water, moved it across to the other side of the boat.

'Difficult to say.' She lifted her hand from the river and held it languidly before her, watching the minute drops of water drip into the boat.

'Get married?' He looked at her sideways.

'Well, that was an option, one day.'

'Most women seem career-minded or want to marry. Yet you don't seem mad-keen on either.'

'There's still time.'

'Of course.' He smiled down at her. 'Will you make shipping your career?'

'Shipping is extremely boring.' She dangled the damp hand in the water again. 'Skiing, maybe.'

'A professional skier?'

'Or a ski instructor. I'm considered quite good. Or horse-riding, maybe.'

'You like riding?' Matt seemed interested.

'Passionately. I like eventing. I've taken part in competitions. With Eric; he's *very* good.'

'Anything special, ever, between you and Eric?' Matt asked, turning his head sideways.

'Uh, no.' Jenny shook her head firmly. 'He's a familiar friend; like a brother. My father is his guardian.'

'I see.' Matt looked at her again and nodded, but he sounded unconvinced. 'The trouble with you is you don't need to work. Do you?'

'It's no "trouble".' She stared up at him. 'It's rather nice. It makes me free. I have my own money from my grand-father who founded the firm. It left me well off and inde-pendent.'

'So there,' she seemed to be saying, and silence fell again as she settled back on her cushion. Matt dug the pole deep into the river bed, invigorated by her presence so close to him. Inscrutable, intangible – impregnable?

He hoped she had taken care of that. Yet the erotic images he had of her made him look sharply away, as if in

125

fear that she could read his mind, turning his gaze towards the other craft plying up and down the river.

'Why did *you* never go to university?' Jenny resumed her inspection of the water. 'I thought all men like you did.'

'I wanted to be an engineer. In those days, just after the war, it wasn't considered necessary if you wanted to do something practical. I was an apprentice in my father's factory and did my exams stage by stage. I never felt deprived of a university education.'

'And yet both your sons went to university?'

'These days they do. I don't think they're any better educated than I was.'

'Maurice is nice,' Jenny said absently. 'What's Philip like?'

'Rather like Maurice.' Matt steered the craft towards the bank, stowed his pole alongside and quickly dropped anchor before it drifted out again into midstream. 'They're *fairly* similar to look at, and both have a scientific bent, though Maurice did engineering and Philip computer studies. I think Philip is considered the better looking one.'

'And the girls? Your girls, I mean.'

'Well, Georgina took a secretarial course, but she married young, at nineteen. Henry never wanted her to work but, of course, as a farmer's wife she works very hard.'

'And Beth?'

'Beth went for drama.'

Matt sat down beside her and put his arm round her shoulders.

'Don't let's talk about the kids. Let's talk about us.'

She removed her glasses and gazed at him, her clear blue eyes appraising. He could see the faint down on her cheeks and upper lip. He leaned forward and kissed her.

Someone from a nearby boat called out something, and Matt drew away and looked up as a couple of young men in a punt a few yards away made some ribald signs and cheered.

'I do *hate* that sort of thing,' Matt said irritably, wiping his mouth on the back of his hand.

'Oh, let them,' Jenny said offhandedly. 'Let's go back and do it in the hotel. More comfortable anyway.'

She smiled at him wickedly. His heart turned over.

The chosen one.

It was one of those famous Thameside hotels with two Michelin stars and a celebrated chef. They had stayed there for two nights as Mr and Mrs Douglas Frith. Matt was supposed, by all and sundry, to be *en route* from the Far East, but had returned days early for his rendezvous with Jenny. The following day they would be leaving; they would have then to face up to the future.

What future? They had still not come to a decision, mainly because, in the enjoyment of each other's exclusive company for the first time, they had not wanted to break the spell by decisions. Decisions which would be hard; the consequences both pleasant and unpleasant.

Matt felt like a man reborn. He realised that from about his mid-thirties or so, he had been half dead. He had regained his youth, making love to and satisfying a woman who was the epitome, the wellspring, of youth.

Spurred on by visions of her nudity, he steered the punt vigorously the last few yards towards the jetty, and then put out the pole towards the hotel boatman, who grasped it and pulled.

'Nice trip, Mr Frith?'

'Terrific.'

'Not too much traffic on the water?'

'Well, enough.' Matt jumped agilely on to the jetty and reached down for Jenny's hand. She rose gingerly and gave it to him, carefully watching her step.

'Enjoy the trip, Mrs Frith?'

'Yes, thanks,' Jenny replied curtly. She hated the silly name, this ridiculous deception.

Matt gave the boatman a tip and he and Jenny walked

arm in arm towards the hotel across the lawn, where already guests were assembled for tea.

'Do you want tea, darling?'

'Not particularly.' She shook her head.

He steered her past the guests, then through the hotel doors into the main lobby, where he collected their key from the desk.

He was on the point of asking if there were any messages, and then realised, of course, that there wouldn't be. He was here incognito, officially still in Hong Kong.

They went silently up in the lift, along the corridor of the third floor to their suite with its wide view of the river. They had a bedroom, bathroom and a sitting room, one of the more expensive suites in the hotel. Matt had had to take out a large amount of cash to pay for it.

He unlocked the door, threw it open, and ushered Jenny in. She took off her hat, threw it on a chair, and removed her sunglasses. Then she opened the french doors on to the balcony. She leaned over the rail for a moment, gazing at the river. Matt joined her, an arm placed carelessly round her waist.

'Penny for them?'

'You know what I'm thinking.' She turned to him and he leaned against her, grasping her waist, hungry for her lips.

'Oh Matt, don't,' she said irritably, pushing him away.

'Darling?' He looked at her interrogatively, and then, as she went back into the sitting room, pushed the open windows carefully shut behind them, not wishing to re-enact the awful day when Elspeth had heard the row between him and Beth out of the bedroom window.

'You know what it's about.' Jenny flung herself petulantly onto the sofa.

'I know.' He sat down beside her and folded his hands in his lap.

'I told you I would never tolerate being your mistress.'

'You did.'

'I feel I've fallen into a trap.'

'No trap, I assure you. I fell into it too.' Matt rose and began roaming the room. 'I felt we were destined to be together.'

'And are we?'

'Yes.' He stopped, turned and looked at her.

'You do mean to divorce Elspeth, then?'

'I . . .' he paused. He had always hesitated at that final, terrifying act of committal. 'I realise I will have to consider – '

'You will *have* to do it if you want this to go on, Matt.' Jenny stood up and peremptorily, minutely, examined her face in the mirror, as if searching for signs of those tell-tale lines of age. 'I'm perfectly serious, Matt,' she said, not looking at him.

'I know; but you *have* to give me time.'

'Only so much, and no more.'

She went into the bathroom, and he could hear the bath running. His heart sank. The mood of the boat, the moment for romance, had irreparably gone. Running the bath always came after, not before. She was drawing in. Telling him that this had to stop. He felt she meant it; it was not just a gesture. Not just an empty threat.

The dining room overlooked the river, and they had their special table in the corner with a view.

After all, the bath had been a ploy, and she had emerged nude, gone over to the bed, turned over the linen sheets and waited for him.

Divine. The best time yet, the most magical. He had lost himself in her and thought that, for the first time, she had been lost too; swept up, overwhelmed by the passion that she tried so hard to resist, as if to stop herself feeling as much for him as he felt for her.

Now all was tenderness and romantic glances over the superb food, the vintage champagne, amorous eye contact across glittering candles. Bathed, refreshed, fulfilled, their hands frequently touched on the white, damask cloth; feet and legs became entwined beneath the table.

Talk about nothing, light, frothy. Lovers' talk. Plans suspended. That would come tomorrow, she thought. Would have to come some day. But not now, not tonight.

A voice suddenly cut into their intimate, self-centred world. 'Fancy seeing *you* here tonight.'

Matt rose, automaton-like, and extended a hand.

'Simon, how very good to see you. Is Doris with you?'

'Yes.' The unwelcome visitor pointed to a table in the middle where his wife, who was not only a contemporary, but also a close friend of Elspeth's, waved rather self-consciously at him.

'I don't think you've met Jenny Holstrom.' Matt, with an air of impenetrable calm, indicated his companion. 'A friend of the family. Jenny, Sir Simon Harvey, head of the Harvey Pharmaceutical Group.'

'We were at school together,' the jovial Sir Simon explained earnestly. 'How do you do, Miss Holstrom?'

'Jenny is the daughter of a business friend, Pehr Holstrom of the shipping line.'

'Of course I've heard of them,' Simon mumbled.

'We're here to discuss a spot of business.' Matt's voice sounded strained.

'Of course,' Sir Simon smiled effusively at Jenny. 'Well, maybe you'll have a drink with us after dinner?'

'That would be nice.'

'You staying here?'

'No,' Matt said quickly. 'We've just driven over for dinner. Jenny's father . . . had a tummy upset and couldn't accompany us.'

'What a pity. Well, he missed a treat. The food here is as good as ever.'

'It is.'

'He'll come another time,' Jenny said sweetly. 'So nice to meet you, Sir Simon.'

'And you, Miss Holstrom . . . Well, anyway, after dinner, Matt.'

'I think maybe we'd better be getting back.' Matt looked importantly at his watch. 'It's already quite late. Another time, Simon, and best regards to Doris.' He gave her a wave and, as her husband wove his way across the room between the tables, Matt sat down, eyes on his lap.

For a moment there was silence.

'Sorry,' he said at last, glancing up. Jenny had her back to the Harveys, so they couldn't see the unconcealed anger on her face.

'I really *am* sorry,' Matt mumbled. 'What else could I do?'

'You said we weren't *staying* here,' she hissed.

'I know. Well, we can't now.'

'What do you mean?'

'We'll just have to leave.'

'You mean *they're* staying here?'

'Of course. They live in Newcastle.'

'Well, I think this is absolutely disgusting, Matt.' She flung her napkin down on the table. 'Disgusting *and* humiliating.'

'So do I. Please, *Jenny*. Not a scene. Not here. Just for our sake, for *your* sake, for our future, try and be normal.'

'Future? You think we have a future?'

'Yes, I do.'

'It's already ten o'clock.'

'I know. We'll simply have to go.'

'Where do you think we can go at ten o'clock at night?'

'We'll have to go to the flat. It will be one o'clock when we get to London. My darling,' he groped under the table for her hand, 'I'm most terribly sorry.'

'It's the last humiliation . . . '

'I know. It will be. I promise.'

The rest of the gourmet meal tasted, to him, like sawdust.

*   *   *

131

For the moment there was peace. The children had been got safely off to school, and Henry and most of the men were in the field, or in the cowsheds where some of the herd were about to give birth.

This was the time of the day that Georgina most enjoyed. Well, not most. Life was mainly pleasurable and she enjoyed ninety per cent of it. The other ten consisted of those small trials which came to every married couple, most particularly those with children. The people, if they existed, to whom life was one long pleasure trip were lucky.

Georgina had been married for eleven years. Nineteen had been far too young, she knew that now, but on the other hand, if you were going to opt for marriage and children rather than a career, why not begin early, as her parents had done? Not that she had reasoned like that; not at the time when she had been so madly in love with Henry. She drew her coffee cup towards her and opened the pages of the morning paper, an inveterate reader of the tabloids, eager to digest the gossip of the outside world.

She turned the pages of the paper, coffee mug to her lips. Not a lot to titillate, really. So much trouble in the world, so many things going wrong. They were lucky. Two nice kids, happy, healthy . . . Well, everything was not quite hunky-dory. They were, for instance, a bit worried about Dad. There had been that awful row between him and Beth, overheard by Mother, who had been splendid, of course, about the whole thing, handling it superbly, as one would expect her to. She said it would be most extra-ordinary if someone like Matt, high powered, attractive, successful, didn't have the odd fling with a woman. So many of the women they knew openly flirted with him.

But *had* he? No one was quite sure, and Dad vehemently denied it. Yet they had all been aware of Dad's rather obvious behaviour with Jenny on the night of the anniversary. What an occasion to choose to flirt with another woman! So unlike Dad, too, especially in public.

Well, anyway, it had blown over, though George had left somewhat peremptorily for Spain without his customary farewell drinks at the house; the girl was apparently back in Sweden, and Dad now on a trip in the Far East.

Georgina rose reluctantly from the table. The cat was stretched alongside the Aga, and Rufus, one of their golden retrievers, left the spot he'd been occupying in the sun by the open door and came over for a pat. She looked out on to the yard where a few hens pecked disconsolately away, and was suddenly glad about life; glad and grateful for herself, for the kids, for Henry, for her parents.

Sometimes, she thought, it was a good thing just to pause, take stock and give thanks.

She went over to the sink to rinse out her mug, aware of a commotion going on in one of the outbuildings. One of the cows, probably, having a difficult labour. Poor thing. Her own two labours had been none too good, and she had balked at having more children. Henry wanted a large family, but for Georgina two was enough. Good-natured Henry gave in, agreed. After all, they were not *wealthy*, and you could do so much more for two than you could for three or four.

Henry's family had no money, and her father paid the children's school fees, had promised to look after all their educational needs. Generous, lovable Dad.

As if to confirm the presence of protracted labour pains, she heard a loud, prolonged bellow, then the sound of running footsteps in the yard. She turned as Michael Nesbitt, the farm manager, hurried in, his face tense with anxiety.

'Trouble, Michael?' she asked as he rushed into the kitchen.

'I'm afraid so.' He paused, looked at her awkwardly.

'You'll want to telephone the vet.' Calm, practical Georgina pointed to the apparatus on the wall.

'I'm afraid it's Henry,' Michael blurted out. 'He's had a nasty kick on the head. One of the cows went slightly berserk . . . '

133

'Oh, my God!' Her hands flew to her face. 'Is he . . . ?'

'He's unconscious, but we daren't move him until we see the doctor. Sam has made a pillow from some straw for his head.'

She was aware of the furious beating of her heart. But she must keep calm. She was calm. She was a calm person, like her mother, and at times like this, calm was what was needed.

'You phone Dr Hastings,' she said in a practical tone of voice. 'I'll go over and see Henry.'

As she went through the door Rufus ran at her heels; even the cat followed, apparently curious. She walked very slowly, trying to still the rapid heartbeat, the awful sense of impending doom.

She stood for a moment by the open door of the cowshed, aware of the unnatural, chilling stillness inside after all that noise. The rampant cow was still, a small creature wriggled at its rear end. She walked into the barn, her pace quickening towards the recumbent human figure lying on the floor, no visible sign of hurt on his ashen face. No blood.

Sam was kneeling by his side, and the other men were attending to the aftermath of the birth of the new calf which was now struggling to stand up.

Life and death. Oh not death. Henry . . .

She knelt by his side, gazed at his face. His eyelids didn't flicker and she put a finger to the pulse at his neck. It beat quite strongly. Relief surged through her.

'Concussion,' she said as Sam pointed to the back of his own head.

'Was a nasty blow, Mrs Timperley. He went down and out like a light.'

Very gently, Georgina turned his head and then she saw the nasty gash, the matted hair congealed with blood on the side. She felt slightly swoony, sick.

'Happened so sudden like. We could do nothing . . . '

'I'm sure he'll be OK,' she said, tenderly smoothing

Henry's brow, as if trying to relay to him the news that she was here. 'I'm sure he'll be OK.'

Then she stooped and gently kissed him, letting her cheek linger against his.

Maurice put down the telephone and frowned.

'Hong Kong says that Dad left the office days ago. He should be back here by now.'

His secretary, Mary, looked concerned. 'I hope *he* hasn't met with an accident.'

'We'd have heard if he had.'

'Maybe he stopped off somewhere.' She accepted the reprimand. 'Only trying to be helpful,' she said.

'Call the travel office and see if you can trace his movements.'

'Yes, Maurice.' Mary was grateful to have something to do. The sudden news about Henry had been dreadful. Rushed to hospital. The surgeons had had to operate for subcutaneous haemorrhage. He was still deeply unconscious and the prognosis hard to make. All the family except Philip, who was in the States, and Sir Matthew, who couldn't be found, were at the hospital to support Georgina.

A morning on the phone and there was still no news of Matt. According to the agency that the firm always used he should have arrived at Heathrow three days ago. Yet no one had been told to expect him, no Peter at the airport to meet him.

'We can't tell Mum that Dad has gone missing,' Maurice said, grimly pursing his lips. 'She couldn't take it at this moment.'

'But he isn't missing, surely, is he, Maurice?' Mary looked deeply shaken. 'I mean . . . '

Mary of course knew nothing about the row over Jenny, the suspicion that Dad had a mistress young enough to be his daughter.

Maurice consulted his watch. 'Call the hospital and see

135

what the latest news on Henry is, would you? I'm going to go up to town.'

'And if Sir Matthew telephones?'

'Just tell him what's happened and ask him to go straight to the Radcliffe.'

'Henry *will* be all right, won't he?' Mary's eyes suddenly filled with tears. Good, sensible, reliable Mary, so like the women in his family who were expected to show practical good sense in times of crisis; were expected to and, invariably, did. Even Beth had abandoned her theatrical histrionics and calmed down.

'Oh, I expect so,' Maurice said. 'No reason why he shouldn't. He's young. Time is on his side.'

And he looked at Mary as though he were talking about a mere mishap, and not something that was to do with brain surgery where life hung by a thread.

Matt turned gently in bed, trying not to disturb the sleeping woman by his side.

More like the Sleeping Beauty, he thought, looking adoringly at her. She lay, head turned to one side on the pillow, the thick swathe of hair spread out like cloth of gold, lips slightly parted, long lashes resting on her cheeks. Stunning.

He stole a glance at the clock by the side of the bed and saw it was nearly midday.

Good grief. He propped himself up on an elbow and shook his head, as if trying to expel the last vestiges of sleep. They hadn't got to bed before three, and then they hadn't gone to sleep at once, the humiliating events of the evening, not unnaturally, keeping them wide awake. The furtive departure from the hotel, Jenny furious, Matt at a loss at such unexpected bad luck.

Even now it was sure to get around. Simon Harvey was a great gossip. His waspish wife even more so.

And it *had* been hard to explain their exit at after ten o'clock at night. There had been no phone calls. Matt supposed, with an awful sense of futility, that the hotel management knew the reason why. Perhaps they always had, there being an inbuilt facility for sniffing out adulterous couples, like police dogs searching for drugs.

If he was not careful he was going to lose Jenny. He knew she still felt guilty, worried about Elspeth, what his family and her father would say. He felt that if he didn't tie her down she would take off, run away again, especially after what had happened last night. Here was a woman who had to be convinced of his love, then subdued and captured, like some primitive replay of a far distant past.

Somehow it made her even more desirable in that quirky, ridiculous way of the unattainable goal, the treasure just out of sight or out of reach.

He was gazing, besotted, at her sleeping face when the doorbell rang. The noise was violent, intrusive. Jenny's eyes flickered, opened wide.

'Who's that?' she murmured drowsily.

'I don't know.'

'Who knows we're here?' Eyes focused accusingly on him.

'No one, as far as I know.'

'You didn't tell your office, did you?'

'Of course not. Anyway, the office doesn't know it exists.'

Then he remembered Maurice, and an uneasy thought came to his mind, but he stayed silent.

'Better answer it, I suppose.' He threw his legs over the side of the bed. 'It can't be anything important.'

'Just tell them to go away.' Jenny closed her eyes again and he bent to kiss her brow.

'I will.'

He went through the hall and paused by the intercom at the side of the door. It had a video but he hadn't yet had it connected. Now he wished he had done so, he could have seen who the caller was. Instead he said: 'Yes?'

'Father, is that you?'

Maurice. He clutched his dressing gown across his chest.

'Father,' the voice continued at the other end, 'I've something important to tell you.'

'Come right up.' Matt tried to keep his voice as normal as he could, and then he pressed the door release.

From the bedroom Jenny called, 'Who is it?'

Matt padded along the hall and paused on the threshold.

'It's Maurice.'

'Maurice?' She sat up in bed. 'What does *he* want?'

'He says it's important. I'll shut the door. You just lie here quietly.'

'Matt,' Jenny said furiously, thrusting aside the duvet as she got out of bed. 'You can't just *shut* me away.'

'Please, darling. Please,' he begged, his tone fretful, urgent, and he shut the door firmly behind him just as the doorbell rang.

'Maurice!' he cried, opening the door and forcing a smile. 'What on earth brings you here?'

As Maurice stepped into the hall his expression was hard to define. He looked around suspiciously as if, metaphorically, sniffing the air.

'You here alone, Father?'

'Come in.' Matt beckoned him in. 'Come on in.' He opened the door of the drawing room. 'Nothing *wrong*, I hope?' His tone was anxious.

'Very wrong, I'm afraid, Father,' Maurice said gravely, facing his parent, noting the dressing gown, the night's growth of beard. 'Henry's had a very serious accident.'

'Oh, my God!' Matt clapped his hands to his head.

'The whole family are at the hospital.'

'It's as bad as that?' Matt sank into a nearby chair. 'What? Where?'

'He got kicked in the head by a cow in labour. He's had brain surgery.'

'My God, that's *awful*. When did it happen?'

'Yesterday morning. We've been trying to get hold of you.' Maurice, his eyes accusing, sat in the chair facing his father. 'It was really awful not knowing where you were.'

'I got back last night,' Matt said.

'The agency said you got back *several* days ago. Have you been hiding up here with that woman, Father?' Maurice turned deliberately towards the door. 'If you have, I think it's *deeply* irresponsible of you.'

Matt didn't know what to say. His son had never talked like this to him before, never used this particular icy tone of voice, and he didn't know how to deal with it. To feel that you were being ridiculed by your child was worse, he was sure, than facing dislike or even hatred. Maybe they would follow.

'I needed a break after a long, hard tour,' Matt said at last. 'A few days on my own.'

Maurice shook his head. 'I suspect you're not on your own.'

'It's no business of yours if I'm not.'

Maurice rose and stared down at him, his mouth curled contemptuously. 'Yes, it is. It *is* my business when the head not only of the family but a large organisation goes absent without telling a soul. Anything can happen, and something has . . . '

'But I don't see what I could have done. Of course I'm concerned and will go at once; but what could I actually do?'

'It's the principle, Father,' Maurice said scornfully. 'Surely you realise that?'

'Yes.' Matt rose, head bowed. 'Yes, I do see. I'll go and get changed and be with you in ten minutes or so.'

'Has Peter got the car?'

'I'll call him,' Matt said. 'He'll be here in no time. Here, Maurice, you do it for me like a good fellow.' And, handing him the phone, he went quickly back to his room.

Jenny had put on jeans and a T-shirt and was standing by the window.

139

'Henry's had a terrible accident.'

'I know,' she nodded, 'I was listening. I'm sorry. You'll have to go at once.'

'Do you want to say "hello" to Maurice?'

'No.' Jenny shook her head.

'I didn't tell him you were here, but he knew.'

'Of course he knows.' Jenny's tone was sharp, contemptuous, like Maurice's. 'You can always *sense* the presence of a person in a place, and presumably your son doesn't think you go with prostitutes. They know, Matt.' She turned to him, her expression disdainful. 'You can be sure they all know. Your whole family knows and, after this, heaven knows how you'll face up to them.' She turned to the window again, gazing broodily across Green Park to the high tower of Westminster Cathedral. 'God *knows* what you'll tell them.'

Matt got clean underpants and socks from his drawer, went into the bathroom, ran the electric razor along his cheeks and chin and went back into the bedroom. Jenny was still standing motionless by the window.

He took a clean shirt from its polythene cover, selected a tie, put on the suit he had worn the day before, then sat on the bed while he put on his shoes. Then he went up to her and put both hands on her shoulders, nuzzling her cheek.

'I'm *so* sorry. I'll ring you as soon as I know.'

He kissed her cheek twice, but she still said nothing.

She was cold, immobile, unresponsive.

He knew for certain that if things went on like this, he would lose her.

CHAPTER 8

An extraordinary silence seemed to hang over the house, a silence that was tangible, that one could hear, feel, almost *see*.

From outside came the whirr of a lawnmower as Jack, one of the gardeners, worked on the lawn on the far side of the house.

It was a brilliant day. The sun streamed through the windows, the open doors, the air seemed so fresh, sparkling, vibrant. The highly polished parquet floors and furniture shone, huge bowls of flowers decorated the rooms, the fragrance mingling with the smell of old wood and polish.

Elspeth sat alone on the sofa in the middle of the drawing room, the paper on her knee. Georgina had said she shouldn't look at it. Beth had begged her not to, but the papers were delivered every day to the house, two tabloids plus *The Times* and the *Financial Times*.

The picture of Matt and Jenny in colour dominated the front page of one of the tabloids:

TYCOON SWAPS OLD MODEL FOR NEW

Sir Matthew Ransom, fifty-seven, head of the giant engineering concern, Ransom Engineering, pictured here at Marylebone Registry Office with his wife Jenny who, at twenty-three is four years younger than his youngest daughter. She was only twenty-one when the tycoon met her and fell head over heels in love with her. Blonde, stunningly beautiful, the new Lady Ransom is the daughter of Swedish millionaire shipping magnate, Baron Pehr Holstrom, but neither he nor any of the bridegroom's family were present at the wedding, which was a very quiet affair. After lunch for a few close friends at Claridge's, the couple left for an unknown destination.

Sir Matthew's marriage shocked and surprised many of his friends, who had always supposed Sir Matthew and his quiet, grey-haired wife Elspeth the perfect couple. They have four children, none of whom would comment about the wedding. Maurice, 29, a business executive, is tipped to one day head the family firm.

Pehr Holstrom's family were also tight-lipped. The new Lady Ransom's mother is married to Count Angelo di Francobello, an antique dealer. 'I wish her the best of luck,' was all she would say from her home in Rome's swanky Borghese Gardens district. 'She'll need it.' Both the Countess di Francobello and her husband are younger than Jenny Ransom's husband, as is her father Pehr, who is reported to be distressed at the marriage. His daughter's money, however, is believed to be safely in trust and cannot be touched. In her own right, the new Lady Ransom is considered a very wealthy woman. The marriage was obviously for love.

The couple have a flat in Mayfair, but are reported to be looking at a substantial mansion in Knightsbridge.

The door behind her opened quietly, but Elspeth didn't turn round as footsteps stole softly across the floor. The paper was whisked away from her and she turned to see Beth looking sternly down at her.

'I *told* you not to read it, Mummy.'

'I can't help reading it, darling. It's on the front page.' Elspeth's voice remained unnaturally calm. 'Anyway, what does it matter now? It's all over, it's done. Finished with. Forgotten.'

She stood up and went over to the table where an also-forgotten pot of coffee stood. 'Here, have some coffee. It will be a bit cold.' She looked at her daughter, who in turn was scrutinising the front page of the tabloid. 'It's a good picture, isn't it? Well, she's a very beautiful woman, and your father has never looked his age.' Her hand instinctively went to her hair, as if she were recalling the cruel phrase. 'Quiet, grey-haired wife.' Definitely an implication of dowdiness here. The dowdy older woman who couldn't keep her man, swapped for a younger model.

It was a handsome picture of a handsome pair. The age difference discernible if not embarrassingly obvious. As Elspeth said, Matt looked younger than his years. They stood on the steps of the registry office, half turned towards the cameras. Casual, elegant, Jenny in a white suit, no hat, the usual heavy costume jewellery, which she so liked, at her throat and ears. Her head was flung back as if in delight, and the sheen of that glorious hair was captured even in the poor quality colour of the picture. She was smiling at Matt and he at her, and no one could have doubted they were in love. He had on a well-cut grey suit, white shirt and club tie. They looked like a couple who could have stepped out from the pages of a Hollywood glossy. Maybe the next step would be to invite *Hello!* magazine to inspect their new home in Knightsbridge, which was bound to be fabulous with all that money and glamour around.

Beth finished studying the piece and flung the paper angrily aside. It seemed revolting to think that this was *her* father. She sat down and took the cup offered by her

143

mother. Having slept badly, she was still in her dressing gown and had not breakfasted.

Elspeth stood, her eyes on the scene outside. The gardener operating the mower could be seen in the far distance, by the edge of the lake. Another was hoeing the herbaceous border. She wondered for how long all this could be kept up, though Matt had said he would do nothing to interrupt her lifestyle or the quality of her life. Eventually, though, he had hinted that if he and Jenny had a family, Chudleigh Court would be very nice, provided a suitable alternative could be found for Elspeth.

One couldn't have asked for a more civilised divorce. Under pressure from his family, and also due to his own instinctive good manners, he wanted to make it as easy for his ex-wife as he could, given that the situation was painful, deeply resented, and unwelcome both to her and his children.

She put the cup to her lips but the coffee was cold. Mrs Hewitt, her daily, had brought it in half an hour before and was now upstairs making the beds.

'I'll make some fresh,' she said, turning to Beth and holding out her hand. 'Give me your cup.'

'Mum don't be so *brave*,' Beth burst out. 'It makes it all so much worse.'

Elspeth took her cup in silence and put it with her own on the table. 'Darling, I've known about this for over a year. It was in May last year, don't you remember? After the anniversary party? Do you remember you and Daddy had a row and I heard it from the open window upstairs . . . that's when it began.'

'Of course I "remember". I often feel I started the whole thing. If I'd shut up – '

'Beth,' her mother sat down beside her and reached for her hand, 'your father was determined to have this woman. He was obsessed by her from the day he saw her there – ' she pointed to the tennis court beyond the open window – 'when George first brought her. He tried to tell

144

himself it was an old man's obsession, that she was your age and so on, but he couldn't. He even went to a psychiatrist.'

'Did he?' Beth looked surprised.

'Yes for a short time. He said so anyway. The psychiatrist said there was nothing wrong with him that he could do anything about. In fact if you ask me Daddy just didn't want to do anything about it, darling. He wanted Jenny and now he's got her and we must make the best of it.' She looked around, removed her hand from Beth's and sighed again. 'He's left me well off. I'm not in poverty. He's behaved with generosity, if you like, which is what I'd have expected from him. He doesn't *want* to hurt me, though he knows he has. I can't just reject him out of hand. I still think of him as my best friend . . . '

'I don't know how you *can*.'

'Daddy and I grew up together. It has nothing to do with sex, you know. That passes as one gets older. Your love grows gentler and expands to embrace your children. You feel about each other in a different sort of way. That is why so many men do go off with younger women. Trophy Wives, as you see the papers call them. They make them feel virile, young again. They change their lives in a way they never expected. It's one of the ironies of nature that Daddy is capable of fathering a child and he and Jenny will probably go on to have a family.'

'I still think it's obscene, and I will never *ever* speak to Daddy again.'

Elspeth looked at her fondly, thinking how ironic it was that his best-beloved daughter had been the first to abandon her father. All the children had been disapproving, but Beth the most. One would have expected it might be Georgina, because Matt had dropped the bombshell so soon after Henry's dreadful accident. It had seemed terribly selfish to everyone that, with Henry scarcely convalescent, Matt should announce that he, who had always been the bulwark of the family, was about to desert it.

145

Even many of his friends had never forgiven him *that*.

Leaving Beth curled up again with the paper, Elspeth carried the tray into the kitchen, threw out the remains of the cold coffee and ground some fresh beans. She then refilled the percolator and plugged it in. Upstairs she could hear the sounds of hoovering. Molly Hewitt had been a tower of strength, so had the children, her friends, many of Matt's friends. She had had letters as though for a bereavement, some of them almost embarrassing. She had been conscious of the love and concern surrounding her from the time of the announcement of the separation and subsequent divorce, which was a 'quickie' effected with her consent. Useless to hang on to a man who no longer wanted you.

But it had been hard. It had taken its toll. She felt older and knew she looked it. She'd grown even plumper because food was a kind of consolation, and many of her clothes no longer fitted her. More than ever she looked like the granny she was.

Nevertheless, in the quiet of the night, that fateful hour around four, when she automatically seemed to wake up, the feeling of rejection was awful. It weighed her down. Matt had told her he loved her, but what use was that kind of love? A sort of general love that one gave to one's children, some of one's friends, sometimes animals. It was a non-specific love, not the deep, personal, intimate love shared by husband and wife. The trust, the understanding . . . All that had gone, broken, and she knew for certain that, however much they pretended, neither of them would ever experience it again. She would almost certainly not remarry, and Elspeth doubted that Matt's marriage with a woman like Jenny could possibly last.

Elspeth made the coffee, took a cup into Beth, who was still deep in the morning papers – having moved on from her father's marriage – and then went upstairs with one for Molly who was cleaning the guest bedrooms.

'A fresh cup for you, Molly,' Elspeth said, putting it on a table as Molly switched off the Hoover.

'Thanks ever so much, Lady R,' the cheerful Molly said. She had been with the family for over ten years, but would never have dreamt of referring to her by anything other than Lady Ransom, or occasionally Lady R. If Molly had been disapproving of Matt – and most people were – she never criticised him either. In a way, she was the perfect domestic, the old-fashioned sort, who knew her place. There was, however, a deep feeling of sympathy on Molly's part which Elspeth couldn't help but detect, a gentleness, an added kindness.

Elspeth stood in the middle of the floor and gazed around. 'This place is going to be too big for me, you know, Molly. Philip settled in America, Maurice thinking of marrying. It will only be Beth, and she will soon be travelling around if she gets a job.'

'Oh, but Lady R, you could never . . . I mean, you've lived here for so long. It's your home.'

'Yes it is, and I love it; but it's a large home. I'll have to ask my hus – ' she corrected herself quickly – 'Sir Matthew what he thinks when he gets back from honeymoon.'

Even that was a strange word. Honeymoon. It sounded almost obscene, and she noticed that Molly seemed shocked by it too. Matt on honeymoon with a woman thirty-four years younger than he was. How would she feel if Beth married someone Matt's age? Well, she'd hate it . . . and the irony was, so would Matt. Apparently Jenny's father hadn't been too happy about it either, and had made an excuse not to come to the wedding.

'I hear Mr Timperley's coming along ever so well,' Molly said brightly, energetically applying the duster to the already gleaming dressing table.

Elspeth grimaced. 'Well his memory isn't good, and of course he has a bad limp. But thank God no other function, nothing else, was seriously harmed. In the circumstances we were lucky. Very.'

They both knew what the 'circumstances' were. The year had been dominated by Matt's decision to divorce his wife, and even with her reluctant cooperation there were so many things to do, think about. Molly thought that Lady R should have given her husband a harder time; but everyone who knew her also knew it was not in her nature to be mean or vindictive. She came from a good family, she had gone to a good school, she had been brought up in an age when manners mattered, when the concept of the stiff-upper-lip in adversity ruled. Never in her wildest dreams would it have occurred to her to have tried to resist, or even show Matt how deeply she cared.

There were some who said she lacked feeling: a woman of the upper-middle class who never really seem to care.

They didn't know about the dark and lonely nights, the clock hands pointing to around four, the sweat that came, the fear . . . and the tears.

Later that morning, she and Molly went into a spare bedroom discussing further matters of detail to do with the house, and then Elspeth went into her own room. There, once again, she stood looking around. Nothing had changed. It was still the same bedroom, the same bed she had shared all those years with Matt. He'd removed all his things one day when she had been out, cleared the lot. Considerate of him. His wardrobe was emptied completely, drawers and shelves emptied. Hairbrushes, combs and so on removed from the dressing table, bath things, shaving kit and lotions from the bathroom. One moment everything had been there, and the next it had all gone.

And even then she hadn't cried.

She sat down and stared hard at herself in the mirror. But maybe now that the day she had been dreading had finally arrived, the day she had hoped against hope would be avoided, had come . . . Maybe now it would all sink in that she had lost him. Matt had gone for ever.

It had been a busy time viewing properties after they got back from honeymoon. So much to do. The Mayfair flat, once considered suitable as a love nest, was quite hopeless as the main residence for Sir Matthew and the new Lady Ransom.

They'd looked at Mayfair, Belgravia, Knightsbridge, the better parts of Kensington and as far west as Chiswick. Then they'd gone to Hampstead, Highgate and north to Barnet.

Barnet. Even though it was near the constituency of the prime minister, it was considered much too far out. Mill Hill? Well, it was really rather middle class, too near Hendon and Edgware anyway to be smart, and then one's friends would have to go all that way up the busy Finchley Road, along the crowded Hendon Way to see them. Out of the question.

After a great deal of inspection, toing and froing, St John's Wood seemed an ideal spot; five minutes from the West End, fifteen from the City, easy access to Oxford via the motorway, and near one of the prettiest and most gracious parks in London.

The choice was now between a duplex on Prince Albert Road, overlooking the park and with a magnificent view as far as Greenwich and beyond. It was a highly prestigious, recently built block, with a circular terrace on both floors and a roof garden. It was priced at well over two million pounds.

Also in that bracket, but further towards Swiss Cottage, in one of the pretty roads that ran between Avenue Road and Primrose Hill, was a neo-Georgian house set in its own quarter-acre of ground, with five bedrooms, three with en-suite bathroom, drawing room, dining room, study, cellar, quarters for servants, and every mod con in the kitchen it was possible to think of. It also had a walled garden, a high spiked, electrified iron fence in front, garage for three cars, and the latest in security and surveillance systems.

And here was their first disagreement since the marriage three months before. Because Jenny obviously preferred the luxurious apartment, whereas Matthew, essentially a

149

homebody, loved the traditional design of the newly refurbished house. Perhaps it was here that age showed.

Jenny couldn't get over the spectacular view from the top floor of the duplex.

'It surely must be the best view in London.' She turned enthusiastically to her husband, who was busy prowling around the large, light room. He joined her eagerly, putting an arm tenderly round her waist.

'It's absolutely beautiful,' he said, leaning his cheek against hers.

'Well, then, darling, let's have this.'

Staggeringly lovely in a lilac outfit, a dress with a round neck and two rows of buttons and a matching coat, she gazed at him, head flung back, teeth parted. For all the world like a model in one of those spectacular advertisements for a special brand of dentifrice.

He still couldn't believe it. Didn't think he ever would. They were married. She was his.

'How can I resist you anything?' He bent to brush her lips with his.

'Then it's "yes"?'

'Darling.' He stepped back, still gazing at her. 'I don't know *how* to say this, but do you think the duplex is really suitable for . . . children?'

'Children?' She screwed up her nose in bewilderment. 'You mean your grandchildren?'

Matt lowered his voice. 'Our children, Jenny.'

'Oh, Matt!' She turned towards the window again with an irritable shake of her head. 'Don't be so foolish.'

'Jenny.' He felt rebuffed, hurt.

'Well, darling,' she turned to him, 'be reasonable. We've only just got married.'

'But eventually . . . '

It was something they'd never talked about, God knew why. But when the divorce had come through – and they'd never been quite sure if Elspeth would delay it or not, despite her promises – the wedding had taken place immediately. Then it had been off to the Bahamas, Mexico, Venezuela. Far too exciting and frantic a time to talk about children.

But Matt, aware that an unwelcome tension had come between them, went up to her and rested his chin in the nape of her neck. 'Sorry.'

She reached up and stroked his chin, and when she turned she was smiling. She put her arms round his neck and kissed him.

'I can't think why you're in such a hurry to have a family,' she murmured as they broke apart.

'Aren't you?'

'No.'

'Not ever?'

'Not necessarily.' Cautiously. 'I just never thought *you* would. It never occurred to me.'

'But *I* thought *you* would.' He looked perplexed.

'Why?'

'Most women do.'

'I suppose you want to turn me into another Elspeth, so that you can then go off with a younger woman.'

He felt stung, took several steps back. 'Jenny!'

'Well, I'm sorry, Matt. I really am.'

'That's a *dreadful*, hurtful thing to say.'

'Darling . . . ' She held out a hand placatingly. 'She *is* rather plain and dumpy. Don't say it hadn't *anything* to do with you falling for me?'

'I'm extremely fond of Elspeth.' Huffily. 'We were married for over thirty years – '

'You still left her.'

Yes, he'd left her. What excuse could he give for that? What excuse had he ever made, or tried to make, to himself? He'd deluded himself, cut himself off from reality, alienated his family.

But to reach heaven on earth, to hold it in one's arms, had been worth it. Jenny represented that heaven for him. He was continually, perpetually in love with her, obsessed by her, every minute of the day. Only at night when he slept did he get any respite, and when he woke it was to find himself staring at her beautiful face, usually in profile. Then he ached for her, would reach out and take her.

'Darling.' He went over to her again. 'We agreed we wouldn't talk about the past.'

'It is there, Matt. You've just said so. Thirty years of Elspeth and only three months of me.'

'I know which I prefer.'

'Was it any good with her?' Curious, Jenny turned and stared at him, almost as though she were looking at a stranger. 'I mean, the being in love bit. Sex.'

'I suppose at one time when we were young.' Matt seemed to be searching the deep recesses of his memory. 'But I was never as obsessed by her as I am with you. That I swear.'

'But I mean, was she good looking? Had a nice figure?'

'It was about the right time for me to get married,' he said. 'That's all I can remember.'

'Sounds very dull and prosaic.' She smiled.

'It was. Living in Oxford was rather dull. I needed a mate, someone to look after me. Most men do, you know. That is the real, the original reason for marriage. Now with you . . . I don't need you to look after me. In fact, I want to look after you. I want to devote the rest of my life to doing that, and pleasing you . . . '

'Then you will buy me this apartment,' she said firmly.

And, of course, he did.

So much to do: a new wife, a new house, new life . . . and a business to be run. He had been kept in touch, of course, during his honeymoon; during the frantic toing and froing looking for houses, during which time they lived at the flat in Half Moon Street. Now that was up for sale.

On his first full day back at the office Matt felt a little apprehensive as Peter stopped in front of the main door, rather like a boy starting a new school.

152

'Welcome back, Sir Matthew.' The receptionist half rose from her chair as he went into the hall, briefcase under his arm.

'Thank you, Jean.' He gave her a brief, business-like smile.

'Did you . . . ?' she paused awkwardly, conscious of old family loyalties.

'Very nice, thanks.' He knew what she meant. A lot of people would find it very awkward to ask him if he'd had a good time.

He walked up the stairs to his office on the first floor. Sara, his secretary, leapt up as he entered the outer office.

'Welcome back, Sir Matthew.'

'Thank you, Sara.' He kissed her lightly on the cheek. She had remained a staunch ally. Of others he was not so sure.

'How is Lady Ransom?' Sara asked politely.

'Looking for furniture.' Matthew smiled as he stopped on the threshold of his office. 'But we decided on the duplex in St John's Wood. It has the most fantastic views, right over London.'

'How lovely.' Sara gathered her sheaf of files and followed him into his room, where he stood looking round.

'Mmm. Seems strange to be back.' He glanced at a few things put neatly on his desk. 'Anything urgent?' he enquired.

'I think your son wants to see you urgently, Sir Matt. He asked me to let him know as soon as you arrived.'

'Ah. Well.' Awkward pause.

'And these,' Sara pointed to an envelope on his desk, 'came from your solicitors, about the City offices.' She paused again, looking at him askance. 'I don't *think* Maurice is too happy about that.'

'Isn't he?' Matt squared his shoulders and took his seat behind his desk.

'Shall I tell him you're here now, Sir Matthew?'

153

'Let him wait for a bit.' Matt reached for the first letter on top of his in-tray. 'And maybe bring me a cup of coffee, would you, dear?'

'Certainly, Sir Matt.' She smiled at him, rather envying the woman who had been so fortunate as to capture his heart.

Yes, it was good to be back. Quite a few things needed his attention, but nothing really urgent. A place like this with capable management ran itself. Later in the day he would call a meeting of his management team: Jack Clark, the managing director, Harry Adams, deputy managing director, Jeff Holland, financial controller, Maurice, deputy marketing director. He sighed. Some decisions would have to be made in that sphere soon. He couldn't keep George abroad for ever. Besides, now there was no need.

He drew a recent report from George towards him. George had made a good job of Spain. Indeed he covered the whole of Europe pretty well from his base in Madrid. He had been out there a year and a half and seemed to enjoy it.

Suddenly the door burst open and Maurice walked in, followed by Sara with the coffee.

'Really, Father, I said it was urgent . . . '

With an air of quiet authority Matt pointed to a chair.

'Maurice, do sit down. I've only been here about half an hour. Coffee?'

'Please.'

'Another cup for Maurice, if you'd be so kind, Sara, and perhaps you'd hold telephone calls?'

'Yes, Sir Matthew.' She smiled knowingly at Maurice and withdrew.

'Now, what is it that is so terribly urgent?' Matt sat back in his chair and regarded his son.

'Well, Father, seeing that you have been away three months . . . ' Maurice began, clearly in a temper.

'Not *quite* three months,' Matt corrected him. 'July, August,' he began to count on his fingers. 'I have also kept

154

in touch by phone and fax. Can't a man have a decent holiday?'

'You were the man who would never take a holiday, never leave the office . . . '

'Yes, well,' Matt inspected his fingernails, 'that was in the past. I've seen the error of my ways. I was overdoing it. Your mother always used to say I was overdoing it. She urged me to take a cruise . . . well, I did.'

'Yes, but I think she meant you to take it with her.' Maurice seemed pleased with his wit.

Matt held up a hand. 'Please, Maurice, don't get on to that subject again. We have had several discussions, all rather unpleasant, if I recall . . '

'Well, what can you expect?'

'And I consider the matter closed.' Matt banged his fist down on the desk. 'Is that understood, Maurice? I am divorced from your mother, a woman I still greatly respect and admire. In the meantime I have remarried, to a woman whom I love, and with whom I am very happy. We are starting a new life together, a new home. The past is the past . . . '

'You can never undo the past, Father, or forget it.'

'Rubbish!' Matt said firmly. 'Anyway,' he looked up at his son, 'you said you wanted to see me on a matter of urgency. Could you come to the point: I've a lot to do.'

'It's about the City offices on London Wall.'

'Yes, what about them?'

'I see you've made up your mind. That – ' Maurice pointed to the thick buff envelope before his father on the desk – 'seems to be a draft lease.'

'Oh, good!' Matt eagerly reached for the envelope and began to slide the contents out of it. 'Yes, it is.'

'Father, neither I nor anyone else in management has seen them. I know I'm only junior management, but – '

'There is no need.' Matt donned a pair of reading spectacles, glanced through the pages of the lease and looked up at his son. 'This is a private company, Maurice, as I

155

shouldn't have to remind you. I am the owner and chairman. I can do what I like with it and, what I like, now that I am to be domiciled in London, is an office base there. I also think it is pretty vital to our global image. You're very welcome to go and see the offices any time you like. They have a most attractive view of the City of London and beyond.

'And also, Maurice, while I'm on the subject – ' Matt straightened his jacket sleeves and fiddled with some objects on his desk – 'I think you overstep the limits sometimes. I really do. I know you are my son and, naturally, you hope to succeed me one day. Doubtless you will. It is what I hope for you, as Philip shows no interest in this business at all, and neither, of course, do your sisters. I think I've given you rapid promotion, which you deserve. You work hard, you're imaginative, business-like, yet . . . ' He paused and looked at him keenly. 'You are a little overbearing, Maurice, if I may say so. You are, as you observed a moment ago, only a junior member of the managing team. I expect to rectify that in a matter of months, if all goes well. But – ' his gaze became severe – 'and a very strict "but", that time is not yet, and may well be postponed if this criticism and constant carping from you goes on: about my divorce, my wife, my lifestyle, the City offices and so on. Really, Maurice, it is a non-stop stream of abuse I get from you, and I'm tired of it.'

'That's not true, Father.' Maurice reddened, bit his lip.

'It *is* true. Many of your faxes appeared to me critical in tone, not warm and friendly as one would expect between father and son.'

'I didn't know you were going to be away so long. There are many things needing your decision.'

'Then where was Jack? Isn't he managing director?'

'Well . . . Jack seemed to think you were away rather a long time too.'

'Oh, did he?' Matt looked at his watch. 'Anyway, we have a meeting this afternoon and, as George won't be here, I think you should attend it. I can then deal with all your criticisms at the same time.'

'Thank you, Father.' Maurice stood up but was clearly not ready to leave, and hovered around his father's desk.

'Is there anything else on your mind, Maurice?' Matt's voice contained a note of impatience.

'Well, maybe it's not the right time to make the announcement, Father, but I thought you should know that Shirley and I have decided to get married.'

'My dear boy,' Matt rose from his desk, expression transformed, his face gleaming with pleasure, 'but that is absolutely splendid news. I'm so glad you've decided to tie the knot. When is it to be?'

'It's not quite decided but, well . . . We both want children, eventually. Shirley's nearly thirty. Time to get settled.'

'Excellent. I couldn't agree more. I would be very happy to think of you and Shirley settled and happy. You are ideally suited, she's a dear girl.'

'Thank you, Father.'

Gratified, Maurice bowed his head. 'She likes you too.'

'I can't tell you how happy I am for you both. Is she to leave the hospital?'

'Not at the moment.'

'They'll miss her when she does.'

'I think they will, and we've a lot to do yet. Of course I want to give up the flat and get a house. That's why I'm worried about London, Father.' Maurice, his expression and manner appearing more relaxed, sat down again. 'You see, if the offices are moving to London, I don't want to be looking for a house in Oxfordshire.'

'Ah yes, I do see.' Matt also sat down again and joined his fingers at the tips. 'It all becomes very clear to me now, that and your manner generally. I can see that approaching matrimony yourself you were naturally upset at what happened to us, your mother and me.'

'We all were. It's not just me or because I'm getting married.'

'Quite. It's an upsetting business, no one denies it. It upset me. I sometimes think, you know,' he settled back in his chair, his expression ruminative, 'that the old idea of polygamy was not such a bad thing.' Noting the shocked look on his son's face he continued hurriedly, 'All men, Maurice, not just older ones like me, are inclined to polygamy. Why do so many have mistresses? Have you ever asked yourself?'

As Maurice didn't reply he continued. 'A man wants variety, a woman wants fidelity. Both the sexes are after different things. With several wives, a man could continue to look after them all.'

'But why did it take you so long?'

'I don't know and, believe me, I never had a mistress or even a fling in all the years I was married to Elspeth.'

'Then why now, Dad?'

Matt shrugged. 'I don't know. I loved Jenny the moment I saw her. I was obsessed by her. I knew it was foolish, irrational, but I was and still am. I don't think I ever really and truly loved before, and that's the truth, Maurice.'

He gazed solemnly at his son for a moment and then smiled. 'Anyway, about you and Shirley. It's great news. Does your mother know?'

'Yes.'

'She's pleased?'

'Very. She suggested . . . ' Maurice paused and looked at his fingernails. 'She suggested we might like to move into Chudleigh with her.'

'Oh!' Matt's expression became thoughtful. 'Is that so?'

'Don't you think it's a good idea?'

'Not particularly. Do you?'

'Well, not to *share* it with her. Mother thought we might divide the house. In that case I would think it an excellent idea. Shirley does too.'

'You mean physically divide it?' Matt leapt out of his chair with the agility of a man half his age.

'Yes.'

'Two entrances and that sort of thing?'

'Yes. We even had an architect look over it.'

'I think you've got a bloody nerve.'

'I *beg* your pardon?'

'Chudleigh is not your mother's house to divide, or yours. It is mine. All mine. Bought and paid for with my own money.'

'But you agreed Mother could live there. It was part of your divorce settlement.'

'But I didn't *give* it to her. It remains my house and, as a matter of fact, it is not unlikely that Jenny and I may want it as our country home.'

'But Mother – '

'Oh come, Maurice, it is much too large for your mother.'

'Which is *why* she thought of dividing it.' Maurice's tone became heated.

'Not *hers* to divide.'

'I'm sure she would talk to you about it.'

'I've heard nothing from her solicitor. And if she is determined now to stick to our arrangement, then I suppose she can. If she wants to rattle round in a house with ten bedrooms, that's her affair. Join her by all means,' he pointed a finger at his son, 'but no division, Maurice. I will not allow my house to be touched in any way at all, and if Elspeth wants to see me to discuss it we can talk about a suitable alternative for you to live in – with her too, if you wish.'

'Father, why so unreasonable?'

'Because Jenny happens to love Chudleigh as much as I do, and what she wants I want. Do you understand that, Maurice?'

'I understand it, Father,' Maurice said quietly. 'Indeed, I am beginning to understand all too well.'

CHAPTER 9

'That's great news about the wedding.' Jenny, squatting on one of the boxes that littered the drawing room, glanced up at Matt from the book of colour swatches she was carefully considering, thoughtfully turning over one page after the other, right hand thrust into her hair. She wore tight black pants and a baggy shirt, no make-up except, perhaps, a trace of blusher, her long blonde hair draped casually about her shoulder. As usual she looked adorable.

She'd worked hard on the apartment, having flown over a designer friend from Sweden, and already the thick Wilton carpet was down, a rich, luxurious grey through-out, except for the kitchen which was tiled and the bath-rooms which had cork floors.

The whole place was bare and it would be some months before they could move in, but all day long consultants, tradesmen, women, workmen and experts of various kinds kept up a continuous procession through the duplex with its huge windows, its spectacular views over London.

Now they were alone. Matt had driven over after work to pick her up. His rather unpleasant morning with Maurice, the stormy meeting in the afternoon with the management team about the London office, were behind him.

It had been unpleasant. It was that kind of day. Un-pleasant.

Jenny had seemed cool too as she greeted him, pre-occupied, more than usually distant. But this remote-ness was part of her, such a contrast to the passion she was capable of displaying in bed, a hot cauldron of seemingly insatiable and unappeasable desire. Fire and ice.

He sat down beside her, glancing at the patterns she held in her hands.

'They're not quite sure about the date.'

'Mmm,' she nodded, eyes on the pages of the book.

'Darling, they want to live at Chudleigh. What would you think about that?'

Jenny stared at him and snapped the book shut. 'Who does?'

'Maurice and Shirley do.'

'With your wi . . . with Elspeth?' she corrected herself.

'Yes.' Matt looked uncomfortable. 'But not sharing.'

'What do you mean "not sharing", Matt?' She joined both hands behind her neck.

'They want to divide the house.'

'Divide the house!' She threw the pattern book on the floor and jumped up. 'And what exactly did you say to that?'

'Well, of course I said I was against it.'

'I should think so. It would ruin it.'

'Exactly.' Matt wilted beneath Jenny's accusatory gaze. 'That's what I told him.'

'And what did he say to that?'

'Elspeth wants to talk to me about it.'

'Mmm,' Jenny grunted, walking to the window where she stood brooding, arms akimbo. 'I expect she wants to wheedle you into agreeing.'

'Oh, darling.' He walked over to her, gently placing his arms around her shoulders. 'Try not to be unkind about poor Elspeth.'

'I am *not* being unkind to "poor Elspeth".' Spinning round she faced him as his arms fell helplessly to his sides. 'Matt, I do hope we're not going to start this "let's be kind to Elspeth" business, just as you've got what you want.'

161

'What do you mean?'

'Well, you've got me.'

'I know, darling, and very grateful too.'

'And one of the things we agreed was that, whatever happened in the past, your marriage to Elspeth was over.'

'Which was just what I told Maurice today.'

'Oh, did you? So he brought it up?'

'Well,' Matt, still wriggling, groped for words, 'it came up with the house, the wedding. There was a lot to talk about.'

'Elspeth's bound to want to cling.'

'Jenny, try and be more understanding.' Matt returned to the box in the centre of the floor and sat down heavily upon it, hands to his throbbing temple. 'It has been one hell of a day. I was away from the office for nearly three months, as you know. It was a long time.'

'Well, it didn't seem like it. I don't think a day passed without a dozen faxes, all needing your urgent attention. It was hardly a holiday. They never left you alone for a moment.'

'Oh Jenny, darling . . . I am, after all, chairman of a large company, and one of the complex problems they say we haven't faced is whether to go public or not. It came up at the meeting this afternoon.'

'Go public?' She screwed up her eyes.

'Float Ransom Engineering on the Stock Exchange, raise millions to finance our acquisitions and, incidentally, make me even richer than I am at present.'

At that she was silent, thoughtful. 'Then why don't you?'

'Because it means I lose control. It has always been a family company, and I want Maurice and his children to succeed me. The family can maybe keep the majority share, but it means we are always answerable to shareholders. Then,' he swallowed nervously, 'Maurice doesn't like the idea of London Wall, and nor do the other directors.'

'I'm surprised you take any notice of them, if you're the head of the company.'

'Well, quite. In a way I agree with you. They're thinking parochially and not globally. They are too small-minded. But it's a sticking point.'

'Can't you go ahead without them?'

'Of course I can.'

'Then do. Show your strength, Matt.' Jenny quickly crossed the room and knelt beside him, grasping his arm. 'Darling, *I* believe in you. You're a great man. That's part of your attraction, your power. You're strong, you're virile and, Matt –' she hesitated just for a second – 'I *do* love you.'

She held up her mouth and he bent down to kiss her. His hands travelled along her neck, across her shoulderblades on to her small breasts. She scarcely ever wore a brassière; Matt found that sexy and exciting.

She lay back on the floor and he lay beside her. Dusk was falling, the last rays of the sun spreading across the treetops into the room. He undid her top, then drew down her pants. She kicked them off, high into the air, to the other side of the room.

It was over very soon, climactic in every sense.

The pace of the heart slackened, the fire inside him abated. She lay very still, eyes closed. Matt gently licked her on the face like a cat, little loving gestures behind the ears, below the eyes, around the mouth.

'You're absolutely perfect,' he murmured. 'Perfect in every way.'

Lazily she put her hand inside his shirt, her great blue eyes open, staring at him.

'I wish I knew that you *really* loved me,' he murmured, staring straight into them. 'I wish I could be sure.'

'I do love you,' she insisted, and curled her legs tightly around his.

The restaurant in St John's Wood High Street was one they frequently slipped into after Jenny had spent a day working at the apartment. Matt had changed into casual clothes kept in reserve in what was to be their bedroom. They left the car in the underground car park and, hand in hand, wandered up Allitsen Road towards the High Street. Inside the restaurant, they were greeted with customary deference by the restaurateur.

'Good evening, Sir Matthew.'

'Good evening, Sandro. Have you a table for us?'

'Of course, Sir Matthew. Good evening, Lady Ransom.' Deep bow.

'Good evening.' Calm and poised as usual.

Jenny looked round. It was still early and there were only a few diners. 'Good evening, Lady Ransom.' She liked it. She was slightly ashamed of herself, but she loved the deference. She didn't know why she liked it so much, but she did. It was maybe one of the reasons – though not the only, nor the most important one – she had married Matt. 'Lady Ransom' had a wonderful ring to it. There was defer-ence too in people's attitudes on the telephone. Their voices changed when you acquired a handle. Miss Holstrom . . . Lady Ransom. A great deal of difference. Yes, indeed.

Sandro showed them to a corner table, bowing and scraping. The other waiters, cloths folded over their arms, stood obsequiously by. One or two diners looked curiously at them. Sandro swept back the chair and Jenny sat down, folded her arms on the table, looked up as Matt seated himself opposite her.

He had taken a shower after their lovemaking and wore crisply pressed flannels, an open-necked blue shirt and a blazer. His thick, iron-grey hair was brushed back, a deep natural wave on the crest of his head. He looked hand-some, appealing, very masculine. The firmness and suppleness of his body for a man of his age had surprised her. There was nothing repulsive, nothing that she, a twenty-three-year-old woman, found distasteful. On the contrary. Physically Matt turned her on. His experience,

164

consideration and expertise was so much greater than that of many a younger man who had failed to satisfy her.

As Sandro presented the menus with a flourish, Matt reached in his top pocket for his reading spectacles. Before putting them on he smiled at her, as if he could read her thoughts. It was a deep, contented smile. Matt made love with the firmness and mastery with which he conducted his business. He was a leader, in control.

Jenny liked that.

She liked slightly less the way people fawned on him. You couldn't keep from slightly despising them. Everyone ran around at his beck and call. Chauffeurs jumped to attention, commissionaires rushed to open doors; everyone knew what an important person Matt Ransom was. His platinum card presented at a store was an 'open sesame' to lavish attention, as well as evidence of unbridled wealth. 'Lady Ransom' inscribed on it was evidence of her power, too, and his glory reflected on her.

She smiled into his eyes and saw, as usual, the adoration that lurked there. Adoration, love, lust. There was no question of it, or of which came first.

Lust, love, adoration: what did it matter? He had what he wanted, and so, she had to admit, did she: a title, power, limitless wealth, the means and incentive to gratify every wish. It made up a great deal for defying Pehr to know that here was a stronger, even more powerful man to protect her.

Suddenly she frowned.

'What is it, darling?' Immediately Matt looked concerned. 'Nothing you fancy on the menu?'

'Oh, nothing as simple as that.' She replaced the menu on the table and smiled. As usual there was plenty of choice. 'I was just thinking what you said about the house. Surely you're not going to break it up and divide it into two apartments?'

'Well,' Matt took up his fork and began to scratch on the

pink tablecloth, 'I don't want to, of course. I've been thinking it over, and really – ' he held out his arms, gazing at her – 'we have everything we could possibly want; above all each other. Poor Elspeth . . . Well, really all she has left is the house.'

'Plus her children,' Jenny said indignantly. 'Besides, she could easily buy another. My goodness, the settlement you made on her . . . ' Jenny blew out her cheeks, as if her mind boggled at the thought. 'Or *you* could buy her another if she feels that badly about it.'

'Or *we* could buy another?' He lowered his voice, leaning towards her as if to emphasise their intimacy, the intensity of their affection for each other.

'We!' Jenny exclaimed. 'Why should *we*! Heavens, as if we've time. Elspeth has all the time in the world, for goodness' sake.'

'I know. But Chudleigh has special meaning for Elspeth. We bought it after our last child was born, when I'd made my first million. We lived there all our married lives.'

'All the more reason for her to move then,' Jenny said firmly, 'so that she can make a new beginning.'

Matt reached for her hand, loosely played with the wedding ring on her finger, revolving it round and round.

'Darling, let *us* make the new beginning. The agents have sent me details of an exquisite Queen Anne house in Wiltshire. It's near Salisbury, only a couple of hours from London.'

'Matt, you're not giving in?'

'No, I'm not. Of course I'm not. But why is Chudleigh so special for *you*?'

'Because I like it. Also, it's where we first met.'

'Oh, I see.' His eyes beamed with pleasure.

'Besides, I don't see why Elspeth should start dictating to *you*.'

'She was my wife. It isn't only her. Maurice grew up there. He'd like to live there too.'

'Are you ready to order, Sir Matthew . . . Lady Ransom?'

Pad in hand, pencil poised, Sandro looked from one to the other with just the right mixture of respect and servility. Not too little, not too much.

'Yes.' Matt picked up the menu, one hand indicating Jenny. 'My wife will have baked scallops to start, and was it veal to follow, darling?'

'Osso bucco,' she said.

'Well, osso bucco. And I'll have the same, I think.' He returned the menu to Sandro.

'And to drink, Sir Matthew?'

'Verdicchio, darling? Is that OK?'

'Anything's OK by me,' Jenny said.

'Half a bottle of Verdicchio.' Matt looked at the menu again. 'And a bottle of Barolo, maybe, with the osso bucco. Does that sound all right, darling?'

'That's fine.' Jenny, who drank little, joined her hands under her chin and nodded.

'And may I ask how the apartment is coming on, Sir Matthew?'

'Very well.'

'Will you be moving in soon?'

Jenny shook her head. 'I don't think until the spring.'

'As long as that?' Sandro gave a silent whistle.

'It's got to be just right, you know.' Matt pointed again to Jenny. 'Lady Ransom is particularly keen that everything will be just so.'

'I can imagine that,' Sandro said, retrieving the menus. 'And then I hope you will not desert us.'

'Of course not.' Matt looked at him in surprise. 'Why should we?'

'For the pleasures of dining at home,' Sandro looked meaningfully at Jenny, 'in the company of the beautiful Lady Ransom.'

'We won't desert you,' Matt said, feeling flattered. 'At least once a week.'

167

Sandro beckoned authoritatively to the wine waiter. *'Mezza bottiglia di Verdicchio per Sir Matthew. Pronto,'* and snapped his fingers twice.

'Creep,' Jenny muttered as the restaurateur went briskly back to the counter.

'Don't you like him? I thought you did.'

'I think he's a creep.'

'Well, anyway, the food's very good.' He put his hand on hers again. 'You've got to get used to creeps, darling, in our situation. There are a lot of them about.'

'So I've noticed.'

'But in a way one must also be grateful for them. They oil the wheels. Make life easier. It isn't always so, you know, at the top.'

'You're thinking of business again, I suppose.'

'Well, there are disagreements.' Matt broke open one of the crisp rolls that had been placed in a basket in front of him.

'About London Wall? Assert your authority, Matt.'

'I have. I am. But it is nice to take the management along with me.'

'They're so bloody idle, that's the point. Liking a nice soft option in the country . . .'

'No, I don't think it's that, quite.' Matt, besotted by love as he was, never hesitated to correct Jenny if he thought she was wrong, especially in matters of business. 'Strictly speaking there is no need for an office in London. We do very well as we are. People come to us and we can get to them. No problem there as far as that's concerned.'

'Then why?' She looked puzzled.

'It's the prestige . . . you know what I mean. It simply looks good.' He lowered his head. 'Frankly, also, at the time I thought of it, I was looking for ways to spend more time with you, justify the Half Moon Street flat.'

'Where you'd hoped to install me as a mistress. Tell me, Matt – ' Jenny paused as the waiter appeared with the first course – 'would you have been quite content to have

168

me there as a mistress, for ever maybe, while you remained with Elspeth?'

Matt didn't reply, his eyes on the dish set before him.

'Go on, answer.'

'That may have been my intention at first.' Finally he looked at her. 'I didn't dare believe my luck that you would ever want to marry me.'

'Usually a mistress, tucked away in some flat out of harm's way, needs the money. I didn't.'

'No.'

'Is that why you knew you had to marry me?'

'No. I wanted to marry you. But of course I had to think of Elspeth . . . '

'I say, if it isn't Matt Ransom.'

Matt, interrupted, turned angrily around and stared. Advancing towards them was a large man, hair *en brosse*, obviously an American, dressed in grey flannels and a loud check jacket, face wreathed in smiles.

'Matt!' He stretched out his hand. 'It *is* Matt Ransom? I thought, I'd know that back anywhere.' There was a sonic boom of a laugh and Matt half rose in his chair.

'Bud . . . Bud Osterhauser, how very good to see you.' Matt took the man's hand. 'What brings you here?'

'Business, Matt, business,' the American informed the dining room.

'I hadn't heard you were coming.'

'I thought I'd wait until I got here before telephoning.'

'Well, it's very good to see you, Bud.' The insincerity of his tone seemed lost on Bud, who was busy gazing at Jenny, an even wider smile on his face.

'And this, if my eyes don't deceive me, is your pretty little daughter Beth.' He turned to Matt. 'My how she's grown since – '

'Bud,' Matt spoke urgently, leaning towards him, 'could you lower your voice? We don't want the whole restaurant to know our business.'

'Oh gee, Matt, I'm so sorry. Did I say something wrong?'

169

'This is my wife, Jenny.'

'Oh, your *wife*.' The expression on Bud's face turned from comedy to tragedy. 'Oh Matt, I didn't *know*. I'm terribly sorry. I guess I hadn't heard . . . ' He extended his hand to Jenny.

'Lady Ransom, please *do* forgive – '

'There's nothing to forgive,' Jenny said sweetly. 'Matt, why don't you ask Sandro to pull up a chair for your friend?'

'Well, that's very kind of you, er, Lady . . . '

'Jenny,' Matt said.

'Jenny, but . . . my wife Mary Louise is with me.' He pointed to a corner where a comfortable, elderly woman sat looking at them with interest. 'She's called Lulu.'

'Maybe a drink afterwards?' Matt said smoothly, wondering how often history could repeat itself, preparing to resume his seat after waving to Lulu.

'Matt, why don't I give you a ring in the office? I don't want to spoil your meal.'

'Not spoiling it at all.'

'I'll telephone,' Bud began to back away, 'and Lady Ransom . . . Jenny, very *nice* to meet you.'

'I hope to see you again,' Jenny said still smiling.

'Sure. So do I.'

Bud waved and half walked, half stumbled back to the table in the corner where he leaned over urgently imparting all this interesting information to his obviously curious wife.

Matt gazed solemnly at Jenny. 'Sorry, darling.'

'It's the first time it's happened,' Jenny's voice was deadly calm. 'It will probably happen again.'

'I thought everyone knew. My secretary blew it somewhere.'

'What you mean she wrote to everyone you knew and told them . . . '

'I had a card printed for business acquaintances, people I didn't know very well. So many people *know* Elspeth. I wanted to avoid this sort of thing.'

'Well I'll be blowed.' Jenny threw her napkin onto the table and leaned back, arms akimbo. 'You felt you had to *explain* to people, Matt, for divorcing your wife of thirty years and marrying me?'

'It wasn't an explanation. It wasn't like that at all. It just happens that Bud's wife Lulu was very friendly with Elspeth. The same age . . . '

'And the same type.' Jenny looked in the direction of Mrs Osterhauser, who was still in deep conversation with her husband, obviously on the subject of her.

'Personally I think that a most tactless blunder. Beth doesn't look at all like me. She's dark for a start.'

'It's *ages* since he saw her; she was only little.' Matt's voice was placating.

'It was just plain rude.'

'I'm sure it wasn't meant, darling.' His hand groped for hers again. 'This is our first row, and it's over such a trivial matter. Please put it right out of your mind.'

'It's *bound* to happen again. It *will* happen again.' She paused and gazed at him. 'Do you think people consider us objects of fun? Of pity?'

'Envy more like,' he protested. 'Jenny, what's got into you? It's not that bad, that awful. After all, I am over thirty years older than you. That's the truth. If you're taken for my daughter, maybe it's natural, but frankly I'm very proud that you're my wife.'

'Let's change the subject,' Jenny said, as Sandro re-appeared with a bevy of waiters to remove the empty plates and serve the main course.

'Everything satisfactory, Sir Matthew?'

'Very.'

'*And* Lady Ransom?'

'Yes, thanks.'

Surreptitiously she looked round the room and saw with relief that the Osterhausers had gone.

Gone, but not forgotten. All at once she felt in-secure, uncertain, vulnerable to the snubs of Matt's friends, from which not even he would be able to protect her.

The tension among the board of management was apparent as they waited for the chairman to enter the room. Rumours had abounded for some time that change was in the air. The London office was now a fact. The new Lady Ransom had transferred her energies from the apartment in St John's Wood, now nearing completion, to the ninth floor of the offices on London Wall, overlooking the church of St Giles, Cripplegate, where incongruously Oliver Cromwell was married and the poet Milton buried. Nothing could be more different than the huge modern glass and concrete rising above it, which looked as though it wouldn't last the century.

Present were Jack Clark, managing director, Harry Adams, deputy managing director, Jeff Holland, financial controller, Arthur Griven, chief executive, George Hulme now director of European affairs, Michael Hall who had succeeded him as marketing director, and Maurice.

Most of them had been with Ransom Engineering for at least ten years. Jack Clark was the oldest and nearing retirement. He had been an apprentice with Matt when his father ran the firm.

Except for Maurice and George, it was a grey-haired bunch of men, a board, some might have thought, ready for new blood.

They were men who, although experienced, were set in their ways and in their way of life. With the exception of George and Maurice, they were family men, grandfathers like Matt, none of whom wished to leave the comforts of the Oxfordshire countryside for London.

Then there was the question of going public. The advantages of a private company were obvious, but it limited expansion; however, on this issue Matt was outnumbered. Most of them knew that going public would make them millionaires, as they all had shares in the company, and it would be a nice little nest-egg for their eventual retirement.

Harry and Maurice stood by the window talking. Jeff was at the table doing some last minute calculations with the help of his calculator. George stared moodily into space and Jack Clark and Arthur Griven, sitting next to each other at the table, exchanged pleasantries.

Suddenly the door shot open and Matt came in accompanied by two men, only one of whom, Gerard Singer, was known to the assembled company. Gerard was a senior partner of the merchant bank, Singer, Dulwich and Hood, which advised the Ransom Group on mergers and acquisitions. Gerard was about forty-five, the man following him younger. He was clearly quite at ease in the strange company, and stood looking around him with complete confidence. Matt ushered him up to the table and then beckoned to his secretary to take her place beside him.

The men round the table all rose at Matt's entry, they didn't look at him though, but at the two men with him, who were given chairs next to Matt.

'Please sit down,' Matt said, remaining standing. 'Gentlemen, I would like to introduce a new member to this meeting, Andrew Rose.' He pointed to the self-confident stranger on his left, who smiled agreeably round the table. 'Gerard Singer you know. I have asked Gerard to attend because this is a rather important meeting, at which I wish to announce a new direction of company policy. This will mean a few changes.'

He then sat down and joined his hands before him, looking relaxed and confident, in control.

'As the changes affect most of you, I have decided to announce them at a meeting rather than to individuals. As you know,' he cleared his throat, 'when the prime minister makes Cabinet changes, she asks every minister to see her individually. I don't propose to do that because we are a much more closely knit group. I've asked Gerard

173

to come because, as our outside financial adviser, he has to approve of our new strategy, and I think he does.'

Gerard nodded, though he carefully kept his eyes on the table.

Matt cleared his throat again while, slightly behind him, Sara sat scribbling notes.

'The point, gentlemen, which has been exercising us for many months, if not years, is whether to take the company on to the Stock Exchange or remain private.

'Now Ransom Engineering has an excellent record for profit-making and low borrowings. The trouble is that, at the moment, we are an awkward size – ' he wafted his hands in the air as though indicating the extent of the dilemma – 'neither big nor small. Yet our expertise is second to none and our business is worldwide.

'I have thus decided, after consultation with Singer's, to reorganise Ransom Engineering; the first major re-organisation in recent history. I propose to offer half the shares on the Stock Market, which should result in exten-sive recapitalisation and reduce our borrowings. Half the shares will be retained by me, my family and employees in a way that I shall announce in due course.'

Those present glanced at one another and shuffled in their chairs. Matt, unperturbed, continued.

'Now as you know, we have completed the purchase of a lease of offices on London Wall, which in future will be the registered offices. In order to enhance the importance of these moves, I have decided to appoint a new supremo who will report solely to me.' He paused and indicated the man next to him. 'May I introduce Andrew Rose, who was deputy chief executive at Win-nowing's, the electronics people. Some of you may know him by name. He has a very high profile in the industrial world.'

Betraying his first sign of nerves, Andrew Rose smiled round, but was met only by hostile stares.

'This of course affects you all, particularly Jack who must

wonder what his role will be, and Harry.' He smiled charmingly at both of them.

'I propose to leave Jack as managing director, with responsibility for the operations here in Oxford. Harry also remains as his deputy. Jeff,' he glanced at a sheet of paper in front of him, 'remains as financial controller and George as marketing director, Europe.' He paused and his smile turned into an expression of regret, 'I'm afraid that leaves me with no vacancy for Arthur, whom I shall have to ask to resign. Maurice will move with me to London as my personal assistant with a seat on the board and that,' he glanced again at his list and looked around, 'concludes my announcements, gentlemen. I realise you might like to pause for reflection. Sara has organised coffee . . . '

He was interrupted by Jack Clark who, eyes blazing, rose to his feet.

'I need no pause for what I have to say, Matt, and I daresay this applies to every member of this board, except perhaps your son. I don't know if he was privy to this – this plan, or not . . . ' He looked at Maurice, who violently shook his head. 'Maurice says not. Well, all *I* can say is that I think the whole thing is perfectly disgusting, disgraceful, a travesty of the trust we have all displayed in you and a betrayal of our loyalty to the company.'

'Please, before you go any further, Jack – ' Matt held out a hand but, ignoring him, Jack's fist came down firmly on the table.

'I will *not* be interrupted, Sir Matthew. I must have my say, speak my mind. To have reached such momentous decisions without consulting *any* member of the board, not one, not your managing director, financial controller, not even your son, who we all assume will one day head Ransom Engineering is, to my mind, disgraceful. Disgraceful and immoral. I wish I could say it was also illegal, but I'm sure it is not. It smacks to me of cowardice, frankly, Matt. Not to take one of us,' he leaned across the table, glaring at Matt, 'into your confidence. Well, who *did* you

175

tell?' He cocked his head on one side. 'Who *did* you consult? Your young wife, I suppose . . . '

'Please leave my wife out of this . . . '

'I would like to, Matt, but I can't because it seems to me that, since you met the present Lady Ransom you have gone clean out of your mind. You have behaved in a dictatorial, high-handed way, in a way that has appalled members of your staff, not least those who were fond of the first Lady Ransom – very fond, I may say. Until last year when you married again, Matt, you were a man we all looked up to. Now I'm sorry to tell you that that no longer applies. I'm glad Ransom Engineering continues to make a profit, but I must say I'm astonished because your hold on the company has slackened atrociously. You went off on honeymoon for three months, leaving the ship virtually rudderless. Thank heaven that, because of your devoted management team, we kept the ship on a straight course. But since then we've hardly seen you; don't know where you are. You take on enormously expensive London offices, strictly against the advice of your financial controller. The opinion of your board goes for nothing.

'Well, Sir Matthew, I for one shall not be staying. I intend to resign as from now, and my solicitors will be in touch with you about adequate compensation.'

Then, with trembling hands, he put his papers in his briefcase and made for the door, standing aside to let in one of the secretaries who was bringing in the coffee.

'Well!' Obviously rather shaken, Matt rose and went over to the sideboard and opened the cupboard. 'I rather think that I need a drink after all that. Perhaps something a little stronger is indicated? Andrew? Sorry about all that unpleasantness.'

'Coffee is fine, Sir Matthew.' Rose spoke in a strong, clear voice, but nevertheless betrayed signs of unease.

'Harry? Jeff?' Matt looked up as Sara and the other secretary moved round the table putting a cup of coffee in front of each man. Sugar, milk, and a plate of biscuits were placed in the centre of the table. There were no smiles, each remaining locked in thought. The girls, too, sensing the atmosphere, seemed eager to be gone.

'Do you still need me, Sir Matthew?' Sara murmured.

'Yes please, Sara. I hope you're getting everything that's being said?'

'I think so, sir.'

'Good. Then let's continue.' Matt, who had also decided against an alcoholic stiffener, put his coffee to his lips, and then replaced the cup in its saucer.

'Well, I am very sorry about that outbreak. I think I can understand it . . . '

'Will you ask Jack to change his mind?' Harry's voice trembled slightly. 'The emotion of the moment . . . '

'I don't think so, Harry. A man, especially of Jack's experience, should have learned by now to control his feelings. After all, he still has a job.' He looked over at Arthur, who was staring at his cup. 'Your redundancy terms will be *very* generous, Arthur. I think you will like the package we have drawn up for you; Gerard will let you have details after this meeting.'

'Thank you, Matt.' Arthur's tone was expressionless.

Jeff, who had been vigorously stirring his coffee, now leaned towards the chairman.

'Matt, while trying not to express my point of view with quite the violence we heard from Jack, I must tell you that I am *deeply* dissatisfied with what has happened and the way this has been handled. I don't agree with you. I think it could have been handled with more delicacy; people affected should have been summoned individually. We have, in a sense, all been demoted by the appointment of a man none of us knew about. I pity Andrew Rose in his new position. As financial controller I think I should have been privy to all that you have told us. I was not taken into your confidence for a second. I think, therefore, that I have no alternative but to follow the example of our late managing director and tender my resignation . . . '

'Oh Jeff, come.' Matt leaned back, his face registering alarm. 'I can't have you *all* doing this.'

'Why not?' George Hulme raised his voice for the first time. 'It seems to me, Matt, that you have devised a very neat way of getting rid of almost everyone with the possible exception of your son. We all seem to me to be to some extent expendable. From being overall marketing manager, I am now only in charge of Europe. Am I not to be offered my job back?'

'I'm afraid not, George . . . but, believe me, we think you are doing a splendid job in Europe and don't want to lose you.'

'By "we", I suppose you mean the triumvirate of yourself and the two men – could we call them stooges, Matt? – on either side of you.'

'I do object to that description, George,' Matt said quietly.

'I don't apologise for it, Matt, because the fact is that you have acted as a one-man band for too long in this company, consulting nobody. I know I once had a personal interest in your present wife, but I would not wish to bring her into the matter at all. Your private life is your own affair, and I think Jack was in error mentioning it. Personally I wished you both well. No, in my opinion you have become too dictatorial and, like my two colleagues, I shall also be offering my resignation and consulting my solicitors. I think it will take you a very long time to sort out the mess you have got your company in, Matt. Mass resignations will not look good in the City, and nor will your attempt to float the company in the Stock Exchange.

'I think you're in for a very sticky ride indeed. I don't envy you your press when the papers get hold of this.'

PART III

Fire and Ice

CHAPTER 10

Jenny looked round the chairman's office with a smile of quiet satisfaction. The blinds were drawn against the evening sun, slatted blinds that enabled the sun to be kept out without obliterating the view.

The chairman's great solid desk, brought from the Oxford offices, commanded a position centre floor. In front of it were two well-upholstered executive chairs, a long, low sofa and an occasional table which was nearly the length of the sofa and handy for documents, notes, books, coffee, and so on. The carpet was a muted beige, the furniture polished mahogany.

She walked to the secretary's room next door and checked that everything was in order. Then she went through that door to the offices beyond. Andrew Rose's office was the last one along the corridor, giving him a view over the west of the City. There were offices for the new marketing director, the new financial controller and, next to Matt's, an office for Maurice, the only member of the board not to have resigned in the cataclysmic aftermath of Andrew Rose's appointment. Yet against the prophecy of George, Ransom's had not only survived, but seemed stronger. And how glad Jenny was to have *him* out of the company. No more would those baleful, knowing eyes follow her around at office parties. The fact that she had once been intimate with the man was now a source of embarrassment to her.

There had not been an outcry in the financial press which, indeed, had seemed to welcome the move, and there were headlines such as: SIR MATTHEW SHOWS STRONG LEADERSHIP. The indication seemed to be that many financial journalists thought this cleansing of the Augean stables was well overdue. Moreover, the appointment of Rose was a masterstroke. He was considered a strong executive, a man not of the family who would pull Ransom's together and refit it for its emergence as a global company. The old guard were considered just that: too old. Put them out to grass; forget about them

And now there was a party to show off the new offices, the new staff, the new marketing director, William Lumsden, a recommendation of Andrew Rose's; the new financial man, Mark Strong. Gone was all the dead wood. In came the new.

Jenny heard a click from the far end of the corridor and went towards the door. That would be the caterers, and not before time. She walked up the corridor to find Maurice letting himself in. He seemed surprised when he saw her.

'Oh . . . I'm sorry.'

'Whatever for?' Jenny smiled at him. 'I've just been checking that everything is all right before the caterers arrive.'

'I see.' Maurice nodded peremptorily and was about to walk past her, towards his office, but Jenny barred his way.

'Maurice.'

'Yes?' He paused and looked at her.

'Can't we be friends? I know you don't like me, but I wish you'd try and change your mind. I'm here to stay. In fact I have done all I can for you, Maurice. Your father really did want to send you off to Belfast, you know.'

'In the hope that I might attract a sniper's bullet?'

'Oh, that's *very* unfair, Maurice. Your father loves you.'

'Then why did he want to banish me to Belfast?'

'I think at the time he thought it was a good move for you to gain experience.'

182

'In *Belfast*?'

'Well, yes. Why not?'

'Tell me, does Dad consult you about everything?' He leaned casually against the wall, arms folded, looking at her with an expression that could have been contempt.

'The major things, yes.'

'So you OK'd this wholesale slaughter of loyal colleagues of my father?'

'Well,' Jenny shrugged, 'we didn't know they would go, did we?'

'You must have had a pretty good idea.'

'Your father had thought very long and hard about what he did. I know he thinks highly of Gerard Singer, and so do I. He's been to dinner many times.'

'But not me?'

'I beg your pardon, Maurice?'

'I wasn't invited to dinner?'

'Well, if not it was because you made your dislike of me so obvious. How could we invite you to dinner? We were nervous of being rebuffed. Personally I'd love to be friends. I would love to meet your fiancée. I'd like to get to know *all* your family. To bury the hatchet, to let bygones be bygones. Why can't we all be civilised about this?'

'Because we didn't think Dad's behaviour was very civilised towards Mother.'

'I'm sorry,' Jenny sighed, 'but these things do happen. They happen all the time. You only have to open a newspaper – '

'That doesn't mean we like it to happen to us,' Maurice said coldly. 'Nor do we like Dad's idea to eject our mother from the house she has lived in all her life . . . '

'Maurice, there is no idea of *ejection*, none at all. It was simply that your father didn't want it divided into two.'

'*You* didn't want it divided into two.' Maurice stuck out his finger at her.

'Well, who wants to divide a lovely Georgian house into two apartments?'

'Lots of people do, when houses become too big. That happens all the time too.'

'Well, it's a pity if it's not necessary, and in this instance we didn't think it was. We should like to live there. Your mother was being unreasonable. With ten bedrooms it's much too big for her. If I were her – '

'Which you're not, thank heaven,' Maurice said coldly, and then, 'please let me pass. I would like to go to my own office.'

The snub made the blood rush to Jenny's face, and she stepped aside quickly as he brushed past her and, entering the room next to his father's, shut the door.

Jenny lay in bed, thinking about the party, Matt still asleep beside her. All in all she thought it had gone well. Most of the financial press had come, and many of Ransom Engineering's suppliers and customers. The trade minister had been there. Champagne had flowed and they'd run out of canapés. Maurice had left before the party without seeing her again, yet the whole evening had been ruined for her because of the bitterness and acrimony of their conversation.

Matt stirred beside her and reached for her. He always wanted her in the morning. Never underestimate the power of the morning erection, and he was often too tired at night. So much had their social life increased that they scarcely went to bed before midnight, usually much later.

But today she didn't feel like it. Today she wouldn't even pretend, so, as his hand strayed towards her thighs, she drew herself up in the bed and threw her legs over the side.

'Darling?'

She turned and saw Matt's eyes wide open, staring at her.

'Not *every* morning, darling,' she said a little crossly, reaching for her wrap at the foot of the bed.

184

'But I thought you enjoyed it.'

She didn't reply, but went to the dressing table and began brushing her hair. The static clung to her head and she took a good long look at herself in the mirror: pale smudges under the eyes. Too many late nights.

'Is there something wrong, Jenny?' Matt's voice from the bed was plaintive, wheedling.

She turned towards him, hairbrush in her hand.

'It just becomes a habit, Matt, every morning.'

'It's a nice habit.'

'I don't always feel like it.'

'Oh!' He put his hands behind his head while she went on brushing her hair. She could see him looking pensive.

'Just because I say "no" once . . . ' She turned to him but he held out a hand placatingly.

'Don't worry, don't worry . . . *I* don't want to do anything you don't want to do.'

'Just because a man gets an erection in the morning . . . '

'I know, I know,' his tone was teasing, 'it's nature's way.'

'Nature's way of what?' She finished brushing her hair and went and sat on the bed.

'Nature's way maybe of ensuring the continuity of the species.'

'Oh Matt, not babies again. All those innuendoes . . . '

'But darling, don't you want a baby?' His expression concerned, he propped himself on one arm.

'There is so much to do and I'm still young.'

'Yes, but I'm not. In two years I'll be sixty.'

'So?'

'My son or daughter will be twenty when I'm eighty. It's not fair.'

'It's not fair now.'

He looked shocked. 'Do you really mean that?'

'Yes, if you like. If I became pregnant today you'd be fifty-nine when the baby was born. Seventy-nine, eighty, what's the difference?'

'Do you mean you never want a child?'

'Matt, I can't see why you do. Christ, you've got *four*, and none of them is particularly pleasant to you. They've given you an awfully bad time since you married me.'

'They're protective of their mother. I *can* understand it.'

'They won't accept me. Maurice was extremely rude to me yesterday.'

'Maurice? When?' Matt's eyebrows shot up.

'At the office . . .'

'But he wasn't at the party. I must say I was expecting him . . .'

'He was there just before. I don't know why, to get something from his room. He seemed surprised to see me. I asked again if we could be friends.'

'And what did he say?'

'He went on about Belfast and my influence over you.'

'But you don't influence me.'

'He said the staff change was my fault.'

'What balls.'

'It wasn't very nice.'

'My precious, I can imagine that.' Matt stretched out his arm for her and this time she lay down beside him and he cradled her head.

'I said we'd like him to come to dinner. I did all I could, but I do think he hates me.'

'It's not you as a person. It's because of Elspeth. Maybe we should let her keep the house and forget it, darling?' He looked enquiringly at her.

'But why should we?'

'Maybe the family would come round.'

'Just give in? Because of them?'

'Well, if you want things to be better, that might be one of the ways. I don't care all that much about Chudleigh. It's not as though it's been in the family for centuries. There are another dozen houses, just as nice, that I'd be quite happy living in, as long as it was with you.'

Jenny sat up and, pulling her robe right round her,

raised her knees, leaning her chin on them. 'I think it's principle, Matt. It *is* too big for her.'

'It's too big for us . . . without children.'

'Is this a sly idea of yours to make me breed?' She turned and smiled at him.

'Well, Jenny, it would make me very happy.'

She lay back on the bed, unfastened her gown, sighed. Tomorrow she would come off the pill.

He put his arms around her, murmuring into her ear. 'Very, *very* happy. I never knew what bliss really was until I met you.'

'Sounds like a song,' she murmured, closing her eyes and smiling.

As usual they sat in the front row of the Grand Tier, guests of an eminent industrialist, a patron of Covent Garden. At the interval there would be supper in the private dining room behind the Royal Box, and afterwards they could meet the cast if they wished.

Jenny, as usual, looked beautiful in an evening dress of ivory satin with a large orchid at the throat, a gift from her adoring husband. As usual she wore little make-up, except for startling blue eye-shadow and a very pale pink opalescent lipstick, almost the colour of the dress.

Jenny was bored by opera, especially Mozart. The undoubted beauty of the music did not compensate her for the ins and outs of the plots, the shenanigans of the players. Even the majesty of *The Magic Flute* she thought absurd. Yet Matt loved opera and, besides, Covent Garden was the place to be seen, especially in the company of such a beautiful young wife. He enjoyed their social life and they hardly spent a night at home.

They were at all the first nights, the best parties afterwards. As patrons of art they were invited to private views and the junketing that accompanied these. Now that they were installed in their apartment, they sometimes entertained there. They had a live-in Cypriot house-keeper, Maria, who was a wonderful cook.

Life was full, joyous, successful. The new management had settled down in the London office, and now plans were going ahead for the Stock Market listing in the summer.

All that was wanted now, in Matt's opinion, was a baby – and Chudleigh. One seemed to be dependent on the other.

Tonight they were attending a performance of *Don Giovanni*. The trouble with Mozart was that there was only one interval, an hour and a half of excruciating noise and boredom before you could eat. Not that she was par-ticularly hungry. She let her eyes rove round the faces in the semi-circular front row, some straining eagerly for-ward, absorbed in the drama on stage, others looking as bored as she was.

It was noticeable that on the whole the men seemed more interested in opera than the women, or was it that they only pretended? That, like Matt, they enjoyed being seen in their tuxedos with a beautiful or distinguished woman by their side?

Not, she had to admit in all modesty, that many of them were beautiful, and hardly any of them were young. They were mostly the middle-aged wives of middle-aged men, like Elspeth who, incidentally, had adored opera, according to Matt, and was very knowledgeable. There was a very stout party next but one to her, the wife of Matt's dreadful northern friend Ted Openshaw who had been on a tour of the new offices that day, and whom Matt had managed to squeeze on to Jon Herberson's guest list. There were always one or two spare seats for last-minute people of influence. Anyway, as sure as hell Ted's wife *didn't* enjoy opera. She was fast asleep, her head sagging on to her comfortable bosom while her husband, his mind distracted by his wife's behaviour – presumably in case she should snore – kept on glancing at her anxiously. Finally he nudged her and she shook herself awake. Jenny leaned forward and gave them a sympathetic smile.

At last the final quartet gave its all centre stage, the curtain dropped, the audience burst into ecstatic applause, and the members of the cast appeared in front of the curtain to take their bows.

Thank God. The interval.

The lights came on and the audience rose, stretched itself and, amid the gaggle of noise, began to make for the exits, champagne and smoked salmon sandwiches.

'Enjoy it, darling?' Matt looked at her.

'Very much. Beautiful,' she nodded enthusiastically, still clapping.

'Enjoy it, Jenny?' Jon Herberson leaned across, also clapping.

'Lovely, Jon. Beautiful opera.'

'*Don Giovanni* is one of my favourites, if not *the* favourite.' Jon's arm came out to steer Jenny into the aisle, towards the back of the Grand Tier, then round to the private dining room. 'Tom Allen is one of the great Dons.'

'Oh, definitely.'

People seemed to stand back for her as she passed. They always did; women gaped, and men looked at her slyly. Her dress was a new couture creation from Yves St Laurent, and she knew she looked wonderful. Occasionally she heard the words pronounced, very quietly, 'Lady Ransom.' Tomorrow there might be a paragraph in one of the dailies.

> 'Sir Matt Ransom and his beautiful half-Swedish wife were guests of the American industrialist, Jon Herberson, at the first night of *Don Giovanni* at the Royal Opera. Mr Herberson's other guests were . . . '

Jon was very good at that sort of thing, discreet publicity for himself and the large conglomerate of which he was the head, here in Europe on a visit. He was currently unmarried and always had an attractive woman companion, this evening the only real rival to Jenny, Celia Felton, also American, a rather bitchy journalist over on a European tour, and currently tipped to be Mrs Herberson number three.

They moved towards the dining room. The chairman of the opera with his guests was emerging from the Royal Box. They stopped to chat. Inside, the buffet was laid; waiters advanced with champagne.

Celia Felton waited for Jenny as she came through the door, whispering *sotto voce*:

'I say, I do admire your dress. St Laurent?'

'How clever of you to guess.'

'I recognise his style.'

Celia was about forty, elegant but wide mouthed, with spiteful, malicious eyes. She was very smart in red, striking. Jet black hair coiled like a snake, large red talons for nails.

'Matt looks *rejuvenated*,' Celia said suggestively. 'You'd never think he was – '

Jenny was about to pass on when she saw Mrs Openshaw ahead of her. Matt was talking to Jon, the chairman of the opera to the wife of the head of a grocery chain. Oh for some champagne, some air. Her throat felt suddenly dry.

Suddenly the voices became very loud, then dimmed. The room began to swing around, she saw people turn to her, their faces grotesque, registering concern.

She thought it was an earthquake or a bomb, the room began to disintegrate . . . Matt's arm was suddenly under her, supporting her as she fell back. There was a cry of dismay from the crowd . . .

The man standing over her wore evening dress. She was on some sort of couch in a room, an office, not very large or tidy. Behind the man was Matt, and behind him Celia Felton. All three were gazing at her with concern.

Her eyes focused and she looked at them. 'I'd like some water,' she said, and immediately the unfamiliar man in the tuxedo handed her a glass. Celia moved forward to prop up her head as she drank. Matt, perched uneasily by her side, attempted to take her hand.

'Darling, you gave us a terrible fright . . . '

She put her hand to her head. It was throbbing. 'What happened?'

'We don't quite know, but we think you fainted.' Matt looked at the man handing her the glass of water. 'This is Dr Stallworthy, who happened to be in the audience.'

'Were you feeling unwell before, Lady Ransom?' His eyes narrowed as she handed back the glass of water to Celia, and he put his fingers on her pulse.

'I felt fine; but I was thirsty. I remember feeling very thirsty.'

'Have you been passing water a lot recently? This thirst, has it been frequent?'

'No, not at all. I think it was very hot in the auditorium.'

'It *was* hot,' Celia said, fanning her face with her hand.

'Very hot,' Matt agreed.

'Well I think you're OK, Lady Ransom,' the doctor smiled and, putting her hand back on her stomach, patted it. 'Maybe you're not eating properly. I think Sir Matthew should get you home and into bed, and tomorrow maybe your doctor should give you a thorough check-up.'

'She's all right, then?' Matt looked relieved.

'Her pulse is very strong. I don't think it was anything to do with Lady Ransom's heart – ' he gazed at her critically – 'but she *is* very thin.'

'She's been overdoing it,' Matt said, but then he thought of something else and burst out: 'Could my wife be pregnant, doctor?'

The doctor smiled.

'That *is* a possibility I'd considered, Sir Matthew. Why don't you get your doctor to give her a thorough check-up?'

191

'Pregnant!' Celia gasped, looking at Matt. 'Golly!'

'It's what we both wish,' Matt said fervently. 'But it's not the sort of thing we'd want in the gossip columns, Celia. Not yet, anyway.'

'Oh, I wouldn't dream . . . ' Celia began as the doctor took her firmly by the arm and steered her to the door.

'Would you be so kind as to inform the company that Lady Ransom is all right and Sir Matthew is taking her home? Maybe someone would call his car?'

Obediently Celia went.

'Thank you very much, doctor.' Matthew made as if to escort the physician to the door.

'I'd like to see my patient safely into your car,' the doctor insisted.

'And of course you must let me have your account.' Matt lowered his voice. 'Send it to . . . ' he produced a card and tucked it in the doctor's hand.

'I wouldn't dream of it,' the doctor waved the card away. 'It was a pleasure.'

'Then if you would leave me your card, I hope you'd find a pair of tickets to an opera acceptable?'

'That *would* be very nice,' the doctor smiled. 'Now, Lady Ransom, do you feel well enough to try and get to your feet?'

Jenny sat upright and gingerly tried her feet on the floor. Then, Matt holding one hand, the doctor the other, she stood up and pronounced herself fine, except for a slight woozy feeling in the head, which the doctor thought was perfectly natural. She drank another glass of water and said she was still thirsty.

'A urine test will answer a lot of questions,' the doctor advised, gripping her tightly by the arm. 'And maybe it will show the results you're both hoping for.'

The private physician, summoned from Welbeck Street, sat between Matt and Jenny, who still had on her dressing gown.

'I'm happy to tell you that I can find nothing wrong with Lady Ransom. Her blood pressure is normal, if a little low; her urine shows nothing untoward, her blood count is excellent. I can only attribute the fainting episode to the heat of the opera and, maybe, the slightly lowered blood pressure. Had you eaten that day, Lady Ransom?'

Jenny screwed up her nose. 'Nothing much. Maybe a sandwich at lunchtime.'

The doctor nodded. 'That's what I thought. I imagine you have a very frantic lifestyle. Lots of shopping expeditions, parties, late nights . . .'

'Well, yes, I suppose so.' She smiled at Matt. 'If he can take it, I can.'

'He may be used to it, and you may not be; but I can run the rule over him too, if you like.'

'I'll make an appointment to see you at your office,' Matt said, but there was a look of disappointment on his face. 'Then Jenny is definitely not pregnant?'

The doctor shook his head. 'I've ruled that out. The urine shows no sign of pregnancy. Have you been . . . hoping?'

'Well, *we* are hoping.'

'For how long?' The doctor assumed an expression of tact.

'Three or four months,' Jenny said.

'Oh, then there is plenty of time. Give it another two or three months, and if you still have no success we'll do some tests. Have you been on the pill, Lady Ransom?'

'Yes.'

'Well occasionally that inhibits ovulation for a time.' The doctor rose and picked up his bag. 'I'm sure that within a year you'll have good news, but if in the meantime you want to come and see me . . .'

'We'll give it a few months.' Matt got up to escort the doctor to the door. 'And in the meantime I'll come for a check-up myself.'

*   *   *

the legend ran, and underneath it in black type:

It is understood that Sir Matthew Ransom, the prominent industrialist, may become a father for the fifth time. His young wife, Jenny, twenty-four, fainted at the opera the other night, and it was whispered afterwards that she might be anti-cipating a happy event. Sir Matthew divorced his wife of over thirty years and married the beautiful half-Swedish Jenny — who is four years younger than his youngest daughter, drama student Beth — in June of last year . . .

'Shit!' Matt said, throwing the paper on the floor. 'Wait until I get hold of that Celia Felton . . . '

'You should never have brought her into the chairman's room.' Jenny, still pale, looked at him across the table, her fingers clasping a cup of coffee.

'I couldn't keep her out. She was there when you fell.'

'Anyway, we want a baby, don't we?' Jenny studied her cup. 'And if the doctor's right, soon we'll have one.' She looked up at him again. 'It's too early to feel disappointed, you know, Matt.'

'Of course I'm not disappointed, darling.' He got up and kissed her reassuringly.

'I suppose Elspeth got pregnant immediately.'

'Well, she did as a matter of fact.'

'Lucky Elspeth.'

'Of course there was no pill in those days, and I do think what the doctor said about the pill . . . '

'Well, I'm not on it now.' Jenny sipped her coffee and looked restlessly out of the window, where the trees in the park were now in full foliage. 'Matt, when you see the doctor, why don't you have a sperm count? It might be you, you know.'

'But, Christ, I've had four children,' Matt said in-dignantly.

'Yes, but as you get older, darling . . . you know, just to see before *I* have to start undergoing any hideous tests.'

'Well, all right,' Matt grunted, reaching for the pile of letters Maria had brought in and placed on the breakfast table. He began sorting out those that were for him and those for Jenny.

'The usual round of invitations, I suppose,' he said with a sigh, slitting the first envelope open with a paper knife. He withdrew an embossed card and stared at the invitation.

'Well, I never did, Maurice is getting married.'

'But you knew that.'

'Yes, but not when.' Matt smiled. 'Well, I'm glad. Maurice has acquitted himself very well since the reshuffle.'

Jenny smiled at him and reached for the invitation. 'May I see?'

Matt passed it over and slit open the next envelope.

'A note from Celia Felton to hope you've recovered.' He tossed it to Jenny.

'How kind of her,' Jenny said acidly, letting the note lie on the table while she studied the card from Maurice.

'A June wedding like ours, I see . . . but I'm not invited.'

'What?' Matt paused in the act of opening another envelope and stared at her. 'What do you mean, you're not invited? Of course you're invited.'

'It *says* "the pleasure is requested of the company of Sir Matthew Ransom", not Sir Matthew and Lady Ransom . . . '

'Well, of course it means you.' Matt leaned over and took the card from her.

'Do you really think it does? Then it's not very politely put, is it?'

'But he couldn't leave you out. He'd know I wouldn't come. I made that quite clear to them all.'

'Matt, you can hardly miss your elder son's wedding. Besides, I wouldn't really *want* to be there. I'm sure Elspeth would hate it, to say nothing of your children.'

'It's time we healed the wounds,' Matt said testily. 'They

can't keep up a continual embargo on my wife, whom I expect to accompany me wherever I go.'

'But not family occasions.'

'Then they do without me.'

Jenny went over to Matt and put her arms round his neck, her cheek against his.

'Matt, it is kind of you; but it's not what I want. I don't want to alienate you from your family; I know how they feel. I would like nothing more than to have them as part of an extended family. After all, I always got on very well with my stepmother. I hope in time, and if we have our own children, they will come round and become part of our family too.'

'It's very sweet of you, Jenny,' Matt pressed her hand, 'very generous.'

'And besides, if you see Elspeth alone, if you *appear* to want to fit in, you might persuade her to leave Chudleigh. That way, if you're nice to her, we may get what we want.'

'What a brilliant idea.' Matt looked at his watch and jumped up. 'We'll have to see about that. I'm going to be late for a meeting. It will also give me the opportunity to have a word with Maurice. Thank you, darling – ' he bent and kissed her – 'for being so sweet and understanding and,' he pointed his finger sternly at her, 'don't you *dare* emerge from this place until the doctor gives you the all-clear. I want you to have a complete rest, do you understand?'

Jenny smiled, but gave no indication as to whether she understood or not.

After Matt had gone, Jenny sat for a long time at the table, thinking over the events of the past thirty-six hours. She had never fainted in her life, and her first thoughts had been that she was indeed pregnant. The feeling of relief that had swept through her when the doctor told her she wasn't had made her feel guilty, disloyal to Matt.

But the truth was that she had a feeling of revulsion towards motherhood, though it was hard to explain why, certainly to her husband. Matt's desire for children had

196

surprised, and then embarrassed and worried her. Unlike most younger couples contemplating matrimony, it was not something they had ever discussed.

Maybe it was he who had deceived her.

Jenny rose from the table and wandered to the window again where, drawn by the beauty of the day, she promptly decided on a walk in the park, whatever Matt thought.

She changed from her night things into jeans and a sweater, thick socks and trainers, and went down in the lift and out of the block, crossing Prince Albert Road at the traffic lights and going across the bridge into the park.

The outer circle was busy with traffic, some doubtless on its way to work. Other cars idled along, waiting for the time when they could take up the few free parking spaces available in central London.

Jenny walked briskly through the gates into the park and headed towards the lake. On either side of her, gardeners were busy planting flowers in the gardens; a grey squirrel boldly swung from the branch of a tree, ran along the rails and started unashamedly to beg.

Fleecy clouds scudded across the sky, and in the distance rose the high buildings of central London. The clock tower at the junction of Park Road and Baker Street; the Post Office Tower further in the distance, while, to the right, gleamed the fairly new dome of the Mosque on Park Road, and to the left rose the curious rock shapes of London Zoo.

Already a football team was playing, and one or two energetic joggers puffed past her. People strolled to and from home or their places of work singly or in pairs; small groups of mothers perambulated with their babies for an airing, and the odd solitary person drifted by, complete with their worldly possessions. The flotsam and jetsam of a large city.

Jenny had always been a man's woman, and had few intimate female friends, whose absence she now felt keenly. She had been too busy, too peripatetic all her life, to form close bonds with members of her own sex, except when she was at school; and they had all dispersed. How nice it would be now to be able to ring up a girl friend for a chat, suggest lunch or an afternoon visit to a cinema; but no, all she had to do was idle her day away and wait for Matt, as though she only became alive when he was there. But that was the way it had to be. Somehow she knew he would be horrified if she wanted to work. Besides, what could she do? She couldn't even type. Her work for her father had largely been social; taking clients for lunch or entertaining them in the evening.

Of course there was nothing to stop her now from going to a cinema alone, or a gallery, or on a shopping expedition; anything she liked. But basically she was alone, without close female friends, dependent solely on the company of one man. It was rather like being a concubine without the advantages of the company of other women.

Her mother used to live in London, and she wished she did now; but since her marriage to Angelo di Francobello, she'd lived in Rome, and had become an even more aloof figure than she had been before. Mummy was not the sort of chubby, cuddly mother – like Elspeth, for instance. She was a rather grand, very beautiful figure, remote, someone to admire and look up to; someone, perhaps, whom Jenny would emulate when she became a mother herself. Perhaps the reason for her mother's aloofness was that she had been as reluctant to bear children as Jenny was now.

Jenny went round the broad circumference of the lake, across the two bridges, toyed with the idea of going down Baker Street to look at the shops in Oxford Street, but decided it was too far. She was beginning to feel tired.

But she also felt lonely; lonely and alone. A woman waiting for she-did-not-quite-know-what to happen, still strangely nervous and uncertain about her role in life, her place in the scheme of things.

It was hot in the office, too, despite the air-conditioning. All the men were in shirt-sleeves. Gerard Singer was there from the bank, and the new management team headed by Andrew Rose, who was proving an excellent choice with his logical, incisive mind. He and Maurice got on well, too, which was good. The average age of the new team was forty-two, that of the old had been fifty-five. Youth showed, but so did experience, Matt thought as he sat at the head of the table, chin in hand. He was still the controller, the guide, the one who, ultimately, made the decisions.

But that would not last for much longer. They were going to go public in the autumn. Half the shares were to be sold, half to remain in private hands. Of that half, a quarter would go to Matt, a quarter to Jenny, a quarter to the workforce, the remainder to the rest of the family. It had taken a long time to work out, but now, it seemed an eminently sensible arrangement, and the vote to be taken at today's meeting was to accept it formally.

Matt started the meeting by putting the issue at once to the vote. Expecting all hands to rise, he was surprised when Maurice sat there with his hands seemingly firmly anchored to the table.

'Maurice?' Matt, recalling the wedding invitation, did not feel disposed to deal gently with his son. 'You're not voting?'

'I think Mother should have a larger share, Father. I've already spoken to you privately about this.'

'You have,' Matt kept his voice calm, 'and I have told you that I think your mother is, well, generously provided for. Even a quarter of a quarter is a lot when it comes to the Stock Market.'

'It's a fifth of a quarter, Father. It is *not* a lot.'

'I'd like to have a word with you privately about this, Maurice.' Matt looked round the table and at his colleagues, who tactfully avoided his eyes.

'Even if Maurice abstains,' Andrew spoke up in his clear business-like voice, 'the vote is carried.'

'Carried then, with one abstention.' Matt nodded in satisfaction and turned to Mark Strong, the new financial adviser. 'You and Gerard will have to put your heads together to produce a prospectus, Mark. You think that's the best time to go, Gerard. The autumn?'

'I think so.'

'Hopefully in time for your new baby, Matt?' Andrew said with a smile. 'We couldn't help reading . . . Congratulations.'

'Well,' Matt uneasily shuffled his papers, 'it's not confirmed. Nothing official. You know what these newspapers are. Now, gentlemen, there being no other business, I call this meeting to a close.' He glanced sharply at his son. 'I think you and I have things to talk about, Maurice.'

'Yes, Father.'

'Then please stay behind.'

The boardroom slowly cleared as the members shuffled towards the door. Matt, still in shirt-sleeves, sat watching them leave. Yes, a good team, a young team. He didn't miss Jack or Harry or Arthur or Jeff. He certainly didn't miss George. He had been carrying a lot of dead wood, and now the company was run by a finer, fitter team.

Maurice saw the last member to the door and then shut it behind him. He turned and walked slowly back to his place at the table.

'I'm sorry, Dad, but you know how I feel.'

'You do accept the board's decision, though?'

'I must; but I think I must also indicate how I feel about Mother. I must show an objection. Mum hasn't been well.'

'Oh!' Matt looked up, concern on his face.

'She's depressed.'

'Still?'

'Yes, of course "still". A year since your "quickie" divorce. She was very generous to you, good to you.'

'She accepted the inevitable,' Matt said. 'She was wise, and I was good to her. I couldn't help not loving her any more. She didn't want to keep me against my will.'

'Well, she has no intention of giving up the house, Dad. It's the matrimonial home, after all.'

'All right then,' Matt folded his arms. 'I shan't fight her.

Now, about your wedding . . . was it *really* your intention to ask me without Jenny?'

'Yes.'

'Then I think it was very rude.'

'We don't want her,' Maurice glared at his father. 'It must be obvious why.'

'She would not have come. She is a woman of great sensitivity. But it would have been nice, polite, to have included her.'

'Sorry, it was a matter of principle, Dad. We didn't know she wouldn't come.'

'Well, I'm not coming either.'

'I'm very sorry.' Maurice's face clouded.

'No doubt that was your intention?'

'No. I want you to come. Of course I do.'

'But first you insult me by not asking Jenny.'

'I told you the reason. I'm sorry if I offended you, and her. I see now that it could have been better handled. Shirley thought I should have talked to you about it.'

'Well, I'm glad Shirley is a sensible woman.'

'She is a *very* sensible woman, and she would still like to live at Chudleigh. Keep Mum company.'

'Maurice, I'm not fighting you on this, but I have no intention of *dividing* Chudleigh. However, as your wedding present, I intend to make you and Shirley what I hope you will consider a handsome gift. Your own choice of a country house,' he waved an arm expansively in the air, 'anywhere you like . . . and take your mother if you wish. You'll do me a favour.'

'Well!' Maurice looked nonplussed. 'I don't know what to say. You really mean that? It's most generous.'

'A place big enough, maybe with a cottage or a dower house attached. Why should she object? Just to spite me?'

'No, I think she might like it.' Maurice grew more enthusiastic. 'It will be a break with the past. I'll try and talk her into it.' His sullen expression vanished and he stretched out his hand. 'Thank you, Father. It *is* generous of you and . . . well, this is hard for me to say, but I do hope you'll change your mind and come to the wedding. Henry is nearly ninety per cent fit. We all miss you. It will be a chance for a family reconciliation, but I'm afraid, just yet . . . Jenny *is* a problem; if she comes, Mum won't.'

'I understand that,' Matt nodded sympathetically. 'Of course I do, and so does Jenny. But I must warn you that this is the last time I will come without her. I want to heal the family rift, and I know Jenny would like to. She wants you all to like her, especially if we do have a baby . . . '

'Oh, it is true then?' Maurice's face now registered mixed emotions.

'Well, we want one; but she's not yet pregnant.'

'Didn't she faint at the opera?'

'Heat, and low blood pressure. Nothing wrong. She's been overdoing it. We lead a pretty active social life. However, yes, we both would like a child. Like every woman, Jenny wants to be a mother.'

'Then I hope you're successful.'

'Thank you, Maurice – oh, and . . . it would make me very happy if you'd just write a note to Jenny. I'm sure she'll appreciate it. You know, explaining that – well – this once only . . . '

Maurice grimaced. 'I'll do it, Dad. I'll do it for you. But I can't force the family to like or accept Jenny if they don't want to. And I very much doubt if Mother would ever want to see her, whatever the circumstances. It wouldn't be natural.'

'Do what you can.' Matt rose and pressed his son's shoulder. Then, his arm around him, he saw him to the door and, after closing it, went over to the window, where he stood gazing out at the concrete towers of that unbeautiful structure, the Barbican.

But his eyes didn't see it. They saw blonde, beautiful Jenny with a small blonde, beautiful child by her side, running along the seashore, the wind in their hair.

He knew then that he wanted that bond with her more than anything else in the world.

202

CHAPTER 11

Peter got Matt to the church with seconds to spare. Just as the Jaguar drove off to park round the side of the church, the bride's Daimler appeared and Matt hurried into the church and up the aisle. Despite the absence of music, and thus the near certainty that this did not denote the arrival of the bride, heads turned, and Matt was scrutinised with as much curiosity as if he had been. Most of the stares were not friendly, though. Many were surprised he'd turned up at all.

Conducted by the usher, he slipped into the front pew on the groom's side beside Elspeth, and flashed her a nervous smile. She didn't look at him, but continued to stare resolutely towards the altar, her cheeks flushed pink. Maurice turned and gave him a friendly grin, but Matt's eyes were on the man standing next to Maurice. His son Philip had flown over from the States to be best man, and Matt had not seen him since his remarriage.

Philip appeared to wish to ignore his father but, as Maurice gently nudged him in the ribs, he too turned and smiled at him perfunctorily. Matt squared his shoulders. He'd known it was going to be a bumpy ride, the whole day fraught with pitfalls.

At that moment the organ crashed out the conventional, but somehow always thrilling and inspiring strains of Mendelssohn's *Wedding March*, and Shirley Livingstone, on the arm of her father Major Livingstone, MC, TD, began her stately, fateful journey down the aisle.

All heads turned to watch her; smiles were wide. Matt also turned to look at this woman who was to be his first daughter-in-law, a powerful and important member of the Ransom family.

Shirley was not conventionally pretty. She was a ward sister at the Radcliffe, and had a sensible, good natured face; merry, dancing eyes and a ready smile. Her ash-blonde hair, worn short, curled slightly. She was a person not concerned with fashion or much about her looks. Her skin was good, her figure slim, her legs, hidden by her long dress, shapely when seen. She was a nice, friendly, open-natured girl with all the potential of being a good wife and mother. Any man would be proud of her.

In many ways she resembled Elspeth, in nature if not in looks though, maybe, as the years advanced, she would grow more like her mother-in-law: plump, motherly and old-fashioned.

Maurice and Shirley had lived together in a flat in Oxford for about five years, known each other longer. They had decided to marry because Shirley thought it was time that she had a baby if she was to have one at all. Maurice agreed. He felt ready to start a family and settle down.

Thinking of babies made Matt think of Jenny. Still no sign of one for them. His sperm count was perfectly normal. Now Jenny had agreed to have tests. Oh, if only it could have been as easy for them as it was for some people. Well, only a year since their marriage. Plenty of time.

The bride reached the altar where the groom and his best man now awaited her. She wore the complete bridal outfit, including veil, and carried a large bouquet which she handed to one of her five child bridesmaids, who included Alice. The sole male attendant was Rupert, who looked solemn and in charge.

Maurice gripped Shirley's hand as she took her place beside him, and her father stepped back. It was a pleasing moment, a note of warmth and intimacy. Matt smiled his approval. As the last notes of the *Wedding March* sounded on the organ, the vicar intoned the equally solemn words of the marriage ceremony.

'Dearly beloved, we are gathered together in the sight of God . . . '

However, as the ceremony progressed and, despite his apparently relaxed air, Matt gradually began to regret his decision to come.

He felt not only the family but the whole congregation was against him. It showed in the glances, the averted faces, the way Georgina peered round her mother to stare at him, or Beth deliberately avoided eye-contact with him; the stiff stance of Henry, leaning on his stick.

And then there was Philip. Philip, who had written his father a letter from the States to say how badly he thought he had behaved towards his mother. This was the first time he and Philip had met since then, and the auguries were not good.

Well, he would go to the reception, as he had promised, and then he would leave as soon as he decently could, certainly before the departure of the bride and groom.

'Maurice James Ransom, will you take . . . ?'

The bride and groom signed the register, accompanied by both sets of parents and the best man. Then they processed down the aisle towards the open door and the glorious sunshine. It was the sort of golden summer's day on which Matt and Jenny had been married, but that had been a brief affair in a register office. Whereas Matt and Elspeth had married on an unseasonable spring day when it had rained all the time.

There were the photographs: the bride and groom alone, with the bridesmaids and the page, with the best man, bridesmaids and page, with both sets of parents and, finally, with all the relations.

Elspeth had managed to avoid Matt's eye until, after the photographs, and as the cars drew up to take the party back to the house, he turned to her and said:

'Can I give you a lift back to the house, Elspeth?'

'Well . . .' As she hesitated, Alice ran up and seized her grandfather's hand, giving him a huge hug.

'Grandpa take me, take me!'

'Darling,' Matt returned her hug and kissed her on both cheeks, 'lovely to see you.'

'And can Clarissa . . . ?' Alice tugged the hand of a fellow bridesmaid who stood shyly by with her finger in her mouth.

'Well, does Rupert . . . ?'

'Rupert's going back with Daddy and Mummy.'

'Right!' Matt glanced at the door, which was being held open by Peter, seeing a solution to his dilemma. 'You and Clarissa jump in the back with Grandma, and I'll ride in the front with Peter.'

Elspeth also looked relieved, and flashed Matt a grateful smile as he bundled the two small girls into the back of the car.

Matt sank into the seat beside the driver, thankful for the non-stop prattle of the small girls in the back.

'Wasn't it a lovely wedding?' Elspeth was the first to break the silence between the grown-ups.

'Lovely.' Matt half-turned towards her. 'So lucky with the weather. Do you remember we . . . ?' He paused and looked ahead again.

'It was such an awful day,' Elspeth said. 'Poured with rain.'

Yes, but there had been a warm glow about it. It was a happy day and they'd hardly noticed the weather. But that wasn't the thing to refer to now.

'Where's your . . . ?' Alice piped from the back, then stopped. ' . . . The other lady?'

'My wife,' Matt said firmly, 'Jenny.'

'Where's Jenny?'

'She's in London.'

'Why didn't she come?'

Silence. All psychologists agreed that it was unwise to lie to the young. In the old days you could have fobbed them off with anything, but not now.

'She's not really one of the family,' Matt said cautiously, 'at least not yet.'

'But aren't you *married*, Grandpa?' Alice sniggered, and so did her loyal friend.

'Oh yes, we're married. But it takes time. Well . . . '

He waited, hoping Elspeth would help him out, but she maintained a stony silence.

'All sorts of things,' he concluded, noting with relief that they were turning into the gates of Chudleigh. Shirley's parents lived in London, but it had been decided to have a country wedding, hence the choice of Chudleigh for the reception, and Chudleigh church nearby.

The bride and groom had already arrived, and so had most of the guests. Cars of all makes, colours and sizes were parked outside the imposing porch; the Rollses as well as the Minis, the Ferraris as well as the MGs. The bride and groom were once again posing for photographers on the steps, and Matt had an odd feeling as he looked at them, a curious sense of being once again in the place which for so long had been home and would, he hoped, soon be again.

As soon as they stopped, Peter was out of the car and opening the rear door, helping Elspeth to emerge. She wore a rather insipid beige dress, quite the wrong colour for her, and a hat that didn't become her. Either the dress had been bought before she had put on weight or, if a recent purchase, the *vendeuse* had got the measurements wrong. It looked rather as though she had been squeezed into it and then sewn in at the sides. She kept on clutching herself at the waist, tugging at the sides as though she felt something wasn't quite right. Then she tilted her hat to one side, knowing that didn't do the trick either. From the steps, Maurice was waving to them.

'They want us for another photograph,' Matt said to her, and then to the two bridesmaids, 'Come along, little ones.'

As they ran ahead, he waited for Elspeth to catch up.

'I feel a mess,' she said.

'You look fine,' he replied reassuringly.

'You know that's not true, Matt.'

'It's unlike you to get so concerned about your appearance, Elspeth.'

'Maybe I should have given more thought to it years ago.'

'Don't be silly. You're fine.'

Matt, of course, looked splendid. Tails, starched white collar, pearl-grey tie. Jenny had said how good he looked just before he left, handing him his top hat with a light he now seldom saw in her eyes.

Maurice and Shirley were kissing as they joined them on the steps. Shirley held out her hand for Matt, an expression of genuine friendliness on her face, for which he was grateful. He stood beside her while Elspeth ranged herself next to Maurice. The children gathered at the feet of Shirley, her train spread out before her. Maurice then called for Philip, who was talking to a good-looking man of about his own age whom Matt didn't know.

'Who's that?' he asked Shirley, pointing at the stranger.

'A friend of Philip's. I think they came over together.'

'Oh!'

Philip then joined the family group. After a few shots so once again did Georgina, Beth and Henry, and the whole process, concluding with all the invited guests, was repeated.

Finally into the house, and Matt was dying for a drink. Elspeth had taken off her hat and gone straight into the drawing room, where champagne and canapés were being served. These were to be followed by a buffet lunch in the marquee that had been erected on the lawn, connected to the house by a covered way.

'We didn't know what the weather was going to be like,' Maurice explained, shepherding his father towards the drawing room. 'Couldn't leave it to chance.'

'Of course not,' Matt nodded approvingly. 'Your mother looks well.'

'She's very nervous.'

'So are we all, and Philip has hardly spoken a word to me.' Matt paused. 'Shan't stay for the lunch, Maurice. I feel it's best if I go. I'll have a drink . . . '

'Just as you like, Dad.' Maurice's face fell. 'Only I did think it would be a good opportunity . . . you know, all the family here.'

'Well, if you want me to.'

'I think we'd all like you to, Dad.'

'Even your mother?'

'Well, I know Mother's worried about the house.'

'But it's all settled, Maurice.' Matt looked alarmed.

'Well, she's still not happy.'

'My dear boy,' Matt suddenly felt highly irritated, but succeeded in keeping his voice low, 'I hope I haven't bought you a country home, complete with separate cottage for your mother, if she's now going to say she isn't leaving Chudleigh.'

'Maybe you should have talked about it with her.'

'You don't *mean* that? I thought it was all agreed.'

'I don't say it isn't, Dad. It's just that Mother isn't happy.'

'Well, I'm very unhappy if that's the case,' Matt said angrily. 'I assumed it was all settled. Jenny wants to move in in the autumn, start doing the place over as soon as she can.'

'Then you'd better stay and talk to Mother.'

'All right. I will.' Matt continued to look grim. 'Who is the man with Philip, by the way?'

'A friend.' Maurice glanced at him.

'Came with him from America?'

'Yes.'

'Oh!' Matt looked thoughtful. 'Are they going to tour or something?'

'No idea. His name's Russ . . . Russ, something like that. Dad, you know Major Livingstone, don't you?'

'Of course.' Matt, who had the ease of a chameleon in changing his expression, assumed one of great charm and shook the hand of Maurice's new father-in-law. 'How do you do, Major?'

'Very well, thank you, Sir Matthew. And you?'

'Very well. I must say your daughter looked lovely.'

'She's a lovely girl,' the major agreed proudly.

'And her husband is a very lucky fellow.'

'You remember my wife, don't you, Sir Matthew . . . ?'

Oh yes, he did. And she didn't approve of him either. There were so many strained expressions on the faces of so many people gathered round him. Some, who went to great pains to avoid him, were largely the members of the county gentry, the pillars of the Conservative Association, the Hunt, the various do-good societies with which the area abounded.

In the eyes of these people, the mores of the twentieth century scarcely existed, and Matt had done the unforgivable, raised between them and himself a barrier that was to all intents and purposes impenetrable. He had forsaken his wife and married a woman younger than his daughter. Dirty old so-and-so. Disgusting carry-on.

Matt had one glass, then another, in rapid succession. He was taller than most of the people present, and they seemed to swirl about him; his eyes levelled with Philip and he beckoned. At first Philip seemed intent on ignoring the signal, then he turned to the man next to him, murmured something, and together they made their way through the crush towards Matt.

'Dad, may I introduce my friend Russ Kietel to you?'

'How do you do?' Matt stretched out his hand.

'How do you do, Sir Matthew? I've heard a lot about you.'

'Have you indeed?' Matt gazed at him curiously. He was an extremely good-looking man, with hair almost as blond as Jenny's and compelling blue eyes. His morning suit was exquisitely cut, pearl grey with a floral waistcoat and a pearl-grey cravat. 'Do you and Philip work together?'

Russ looked at Philip with amusement, as though sharing some kind of joke.

'Not exactly, Dad . . . '

'Hello, Daddy.' Beth stood fiddling with her hands, looking shy.

'Beth, my darling.' Matt reached out for her, clasping her shoulders. 'So good to see you. So *very* good.'

'Sorry I haven't been in touch, Daddy. But . . . I'm glad you came.'

'So am I, very glad.' His eyes brimmed with emotion. 'Jenny and I wish you'd visit us in London. We'd love to see you, any time.'

She ignored the invitation rather pointedly. 'Are you going to stay for lunch?'

'Of course.'

'Mum said she thought you weren't.'

'Well, I am.'

'Good.' She gazed at him, unsmiling.

'See you around, Father.' Philip, preparing to move away, vaguely waved a hand at him.

'Philip,' he called sharply, 'how long are you here for?'

'Here? You mean in England, or here at Chudleigh?'

'Both. I'd like you to meet Jenny.'

'I'd like to have a talk with you first, Father.' Matt's face fell. For a moment he had hoped everything was going to change, turn out well.

'Here, later, after lunch?'

'I think Russ and I will be leaving early. Maybe I'll give you a ring in a day or two?'

'Perhaps I can give you a lift back to London?'

'Uhuh,' Philip shook his head, 'Russ has friends in Oxford. We're dining with them.'

211

'Oh, I see. Call me then, Philip. I'd love to see you.'

Beth carefully watched Matt following Philip's progress across the room, still deep in conversation with the American.

'He's very good looking, isn't he, Daddy?' she asked slyly. Matt turned enquiringly to his daughter. 'Russ, Philip's friend,' she continued.

'Well, I suppose . . . '

Matt suddenly stopped and stared at his daughter. 'You don't mean . . . ?'

'Didn't you *know*, Daddy?'

'Know?' Matt stopped a passing waiter and took another glass of champagne. 'Let's go and talk,' he said urgently to Beth. 'Let's go to my old study.' Clasping his glass in one hand, Beth's in the other, they made their way across the crowded room, through a door at the far end and into the room which, for over twenty years, had been Matt's sanctum.

It was greatly changed. Gone were the desk, the bookshelves, the tray of pipes, though Matt had only occasionally smoked a pipe.

'I think Mummy uses it as a sitting room now,' Beth said sensing his reaction. 'Didn't you know?'

'Well, I'd like to know what she's done with the desk.' Matt felt angry. 'This, after all, is still my house and, moreover, one to which I hope I'll be returning . . . very soon.'

'Does *Mummy* know?' Beth sank into one of the chairs and joined her hands beneath her chin. She looked very pretty, very modern in a long, trailing ethnic garment, possibly a purchase from Camden Lock or Petticoat Lane. Her hair had had a crinkly perm and, unlike Jenny, she wore lots of make-up: heavy eyeshadow, mascara, purple lipstick. It was very theatrical; not to Matt's taste but, he supposed, suitable for an actress.

'Just who is this Russ, darling?'

'Philip's *boy*friend, Daddy.'

'*Boy*friend!' Matt repeated the words sitting down in a chair facing Beth. 'You mean "boyfriend"?'

'As in boyfriend, Daddy. Lover.'

'I see.'

Matt gripped the arms of the chair with both hands and stared in front of him. 'I never knew that Philip was . . . queer.'

'Gay, Daddy. Gay is the word.'

'Well, in my opinion it's a misnomer.' Matt finished the wine in his glass and carefully placed it on a small occasional table by his side, which also carried a portrait of Georgina and her family.

'It's more friendly than "queer". You mustn't think of it like that anyway, Daddy. It doesn't matter now; but I thought you would have known, must have suspected. Surely Mum – '

'Your mother never said anything to me.'

'Well, she knew.'

'She knew?'

'You remember Phil had that trouble at school?' At one point the head had summoned Matt and Elspeth to discuss the subject of Philip's intense friendships; possibly, also, the smoking of cannabis.

'We just thought that was all adolescent nonsense. It blew over.'

'Phil was always gay. He knew when he was about twelve.'

'Did the others know?'

'We all knew, but we didn't talk about it. I suppose that's why we thought you knew.' She leaned forward, hands spread out earnestly. 'You know, Daddy, that was the trouble. As a family we never really *talked*, did we? We thought we were close and we weren't.'

'I thought we *were* close,' Matt said defensively.

'If we had been we could have stopped you and Mum from splitting.'

'Nothing could have stopped me falling in love with Jenny. It was meant.'

'Daddy,' Beth gave a derisive laugh, 'you are a silly old so-and-so. These things are never "meant". You were just a silly old man falling for a dolly bird.'

'Beth!' Matt passed his hand across his brow, which was beginning to throb. 'I can't have you talking like that about Jenny. She is not, emphatically not, a dolly bird.'

Beth ignored him. 'Daddy, lots of men do it when they get old and powerful. They ditch their old trusted wives for a bit of crumpet . . . '

Matt heaved himself out of his chair. 'Darling, I do love you; but I can't put up with this.'

'It's how *you* see it, Daddy,' she pleaded. 'It's how *we* see it.'

'You have never even tried to get to know Jenny. We have invited you, and you haven't even replied. Jenny's very upset. None of my children have even visited our home. You have all refused to accept the fact of Jenny's existence. How, as your father, do you think I feel about that?'

Beth remained in her chair, staring at the floor. Her beloved father's reproachful expression embarrassed her. Because he was beloved still. She loved him so much, but there was also that loyalty to her mother, a sense of females sticking together, a bond which she felt was important too.

'I'm glad you came to the wedding,' she said, slowly getting up. 'It's a chance for us to try and understand. You see, Daddy, we didn't know how you could leave Mummy. She has been very, very unhappy.'

'I know, I know.' Matt's expression too was sombre. 'Don't think I don't know, or understand; but it's so hard to get near your mother, explain anything to her. She's hardly looked at me since I arrived.'

'You can't blame Mummy, especially as you want her to move out of here – ' Beth looked at him reproachfully – 'the family home.'

'But darling, be reasonable. It's much too big . . . and if

Jenny and I have children, as we want to, it's ideal. I've done everything I can to try and make it easy, but I have my life to live, too, and I feel ostracised and spurned by my own family.'

'Better get back.' Beth held out a hand. 'People will wonder where we've disappeared to.'

'I'm glad we've had this chat.' Matt felt happier, more hopeful, as she led him to the door. 'And please do keep in touch, darling. I'll telephone you and hope you'll come to dinner. Or we can all eat out, whichever you prefer. Jenny is such a sweet person, and she'd love to get to know you. She's very vulnerable,' he said suddenly, 'quite lonely, hardly any women friends.'

'The reason for which one can possibly understand.'

And, without explaining her caustic remark, Beth pointedly preceded her father from the room.

The drawing room was emptying as people made for the marquee on the lawn, mostly strolling through the open french windows on to the terrace and down the steps. Waiters were putting out tables and chairs in the bright sunshine and already guests were emerging with plates of food, precariously balanced wine glasses. Groups of people who already knew one another were forming, drawing up tables so that they could be together. Matt stood for some time with Beth by his side, surveying the scene. He felt the atmosphere towards him thawing, maybe under the mellowing influence of food and champagne. Faces became more friendly; there were even smiles. Observing that his family spoke to him, former friends and acquaintances no longer felt obliged to ostracise him. After all, Sir Matthew was still a powerful person, one who could wield influence and perform favours.

He smiled about him, yet still uneasy, conscious that he was a guest in his own house. It felt familiar yet strange to be here. He ached for times past when he belonged here, living in a loving and familiar environment with the children constant visitors. Maybe those good times would come again?

Henry, leaning heavily on a stick, stood talking to some friends. Georgina, followed by Rupert, struggled across the lawn carrying plates and glasses.

'Henry looks like a changed man,' Matt observed to his younger daughter. 'I hardly recognised him.'

Georgina, fiercely loyal to her mother, hadn't spoken to her father since his marriage, and seemed intent on ignoring him still.

'He's in constant pain,' Beth replied. 'He has the most terrible headaches, and brain damage has affected his locomotion. Georgina thinks they'll have to give up the farm.'

'But Michael . . . '

'He left. He and Henry kept on having rows. Henry has also been affected mentally, Dad. He has a very short temper.'

'That's awful.' Matt shook his head. 'And I didn't know, no one told me.' Suddenly he saw himself as others did: a selfish man, deeply engrossed in his own affairs, while things happened to his family that he knew nothing about.

They all knew his son was homosexual except him. No one told him; not even the wife he felt so close to. Had she really regarded him as a monster, too?

'I must go and have a word.' He looked anxiously at Beth. 'Will you come with me, darling?'

'Of course.' She linked her arm through his and together they walked down the steps, across the lawn to the table where the Timperley family were taking their seats.

Georgina finally met her father's eyes, briefly glanced at Henry, and then, going over to Matt, raised her mouth and kissed his cheek. 'Hello, Dad.'

'Darling, how *lovely* to see you.' Warm, emotional, Matt's lips brushed eagerly against Georgina's, his hands clasping her shoulders. 'And Henry – ' he stooped to shake his hand – 'how are you, old boy?'

'Much better, thanks, Matt.' Henry looked at him without smiling, something in his eyes deeper than pain; criticism, maybe. Contempt, perhaps.

'The going's been pretty heavy, Daddy,' Georgina said, moving away from Henry. 'But we try not to complain.'

'I hear Michael left?'

'Such a loss. We haven't really been able to replace him. He knew everything about the farm, had been with us for ages.' She leaned forward and said confidentially, out of earshot: 'Henry suffers from terrible swings of mood, and is very hard at times to put up with. I think, really, that's why Michael left.'

'The moods must affect you, too.'

'They do.'

'Oh, darling, and I didn't know.' Full of contrition, Matt put his arm round her waist. 'If only you could try and understand about me and Jenny and forgive me, we could all be such a loving family again. I miss it, I really do.'

'It was awful for us, Daddy, it came as a terrible shock; and then the attempt to get the house from poor Mummy added insult to injury.'

'But that's what strikes me as so illogical.' Matt angrily banged his fist into the palm of his outstretched hand. 'I can't understand why your mother – '

'Because she *loves* the house, Daddy,' Georgina said gently. 'It means a lot to her. It's her anchor.'

'I *understood* that she was quite happy to go and live with Maurice . . . '

'She would like to be with him, but here.' Georgina gestured about her.

'Well, anyway,' Matt said grumpily, 'he's now got another house as a wedding present, and a lovely place it is, with a beautiful two-bedroom cottage for your mother in the grounds.'

'Mummy's only in her mid-fifties, Daddy,' Georgina reminded him. 'She doesn't feel she wants to be treated as a case for the geriatric apartment just yet.'

217

'I didn't mean . . . '

'I know you meant well, but Henry and I thought it tactless. It reinforced the sense of isolation and inadequacy Mum had over your jettisoning her for a much younger woman, a ridiculously young woman.'

'Whom you've never met.'

'I played tennis with her,' Georgina said indignantly. 'I was here the day you first clapped eyes on her.'

'So you were . . . '

'Didn't you have any feelings of obligation – '

'Of course I had.' He interrupted Georgina before she could mention the word 'mother' again. 'But I couldn't spend the rest of my life living with one woman when I yearned for another. I tried but I couldn't.'

'You didn't try for very long . . . '

'Darling . . . Georgina.' He laid a hand on her arm, his expression pained. 'Must you? It's all over. It's done. I now want to mend fences, dam breaches. I want my family about me again. I want to live here with the woman I love, and have children. I'm a family man. I want you to make an effort to try and like Jenny, without in the least diminishing your mother. Believe me, I have missed my family and family life. I want to help you and Henry. How are things financially? Not a day has passed but I haven't thought about you and worried about you. Believe me, as well as loving Jenny, I have not forgotten all my duties and responsibilities.'

'Do you know, I think you mean it,' Georgina shook her head in bewilderment. 'I've heard of it happening before, and now it's happened to you.'

'Come and have your lunch,' Henry called, waving his stick at her, 'otherwise the flies will get it.'

Georgina glanced at Matt and then, followed by him, smilingly hurried over to the table.

'Darling, will you get Grandpa some lunch?' Georgina spoke to Rupert, who, nevertheless, went on eating his food. 'Rupert, did you hear me?' she said sharply.

'Yes, Mother. When I've finished.'

'Now, Rupert,' Georgina spoke with an edge to her voice, 'at once, please.'

'For God's sake let the boy finish his lunch,' Henry said irritably. 'We're not going to start running about at Matt's beck and call, are we . . . ?'

'Really, Henry!' Georgina looked outraged.

'It's quite all right, Rupert.' Matt assumed a casual air, a hand in his pocket. 'There are a few people I have to talk to; besides, I'm not really hungry . . . '

'Very *rude* to your grandfather,' Georgina, her face flushed, murmured *sotto voce*.

Matt lifted his hand in a casual wave. 'I'll see you later. Don't worry. I'm not hungry. Really.' He then wandered off while Georgina continued to chide her rebellious son, whose action was roundly and vociferously supported by his father.

Matt, aware of what was going on, felt rebuffed, angry, sad. Rupert had always been such a pal. But had he been fair to his grandson? Apart from sending money and a card at Christmas and for his birthday, he had made no real effort to bridge the barrier and see him. Yet he had adored him, and Alice.

What had happened to him, made him neglect them so while the focus of his whole life shifted to revolve round Jenny?

And now there was still Elspeth to face. He couldn't leave without seeing her, yet he felt that he desperately wanted to go. There was no place for him here; too many recriminations, refusals to abandon the past.

He made his way through the crowd, a crowd of strangers, really. People greeted him perfunctorily, some politely, some with embarrassment, one or two with warmth. Some he still did business with and stopped for a chat. One or two, mostly close friends of Elspeth, turned their backs on him.

'Have you seen your mother?' he asked Beth, who now

joined him in his slow progress across the lawn. 'I must have a word with her before I go.'

'Daddy, you've not eaten anything.'

'I'm not hungry.'

'Georgina beastly to you?' Beth eyed him sympathetically.

'No. It was Henry actually who wasn't very nice . . . and Rupert. I was *very* disappointed in him.'

'Well, Henry's not quite right in his mind,' Beth meaningfully tapped her head. 'And Rupert is at that awkward age.'

Matt shook his head. 'Georgina looks so sad, so much older . . . '

'Henry's a terrible burden. You don't know the half of it. Oh look, there's Mummy.' Beth pointed towards the terrace on to which Elspeth had emerged, shadowing her eyes and talking to friends. 'Shall I go and tell her . . . ?'

'Would you, darling?' Matt looked gratefully at her. 'She might take it better from you. Tell her to meet me in the old study. Try and get her to agree. Come with her . . . '

'I'll do my best.' Beth sped off and Matt watched while she spoke earnestly to her mother, whose eyes, still shaded, looked in his direction and then towards the house. She was either refusing or couldn't make up her mind.

Matt walked quickly back through the marquee and into the house via the hall. When he got to his old study it was empty. His hands were sticky, but not because of the heat. He got out his handkerchief, wiped his hands, and drew it across his brow. He reached for a copy of *Country Life* on one of the tables and began restlessly to leaf through it.

Time passed. Five minutes. Ten. She wouldn't come. He put down the magazine and was about to go when the door handle slowly turned and Elspeth stood on the threshold, very composed, gazing at him, hands folded.

'You wanted to see me, Matt.'

'Yes, I did.' He went eagerly towards the door and held it open for her. 'Please come in, Elspeth.'

'Thank you.' She entered the room with the air of someone who had come for an interview, and a very sticky interview at that. She looked as though she had taken a few moments to compose herself, maybe gone up to her bedroom and combed her hair, put on some lipstick.

'Do sit down,' Matt pointed politely to a chair. 'I see you've made some changes, Elspeth. Where's the desk?'

'Oh, everything is here, don't worry.' There was a note of irony in her voice. 'Nothing has gone to the saleroom.' She sat down, placing her hands in her lap as though greatly controlled, looked up at him. 'Matt, couldn't this have been done by lawyers?'

'Why go to the expense?' He sat down opposite her, hands on his knees. 'Goodness, Elspeth, we've been married over thirty years. Is there any reason to treat each other as strangers?'

'You treated *me* as a stranger, Matt. You were determined to get me out of Chudleigh. I was bitterly hurt. Up to then you'd been extremely civilised, said I could live here for life.'

'You could; but Elspeth,' he looked wildly around him, 'the place is huge. It was big enough for the whole family of six. However, maybe I lacked tact. I moved too fast. I didn't consult you. I want to say I'm sorry about the way I handled it. I want us to be friends, or at least be civilised to each other, and I want to see my children again.'

'Matt, they're all over twenty-one,' Elspeth said in her slow, precise voice. 'I've no control over them. They thought you behaved badly and, frankly, you did. Now you've bribed Maurice – '

'Bribed Maurice . . . ?'

'Yes,' her voice began to rise, 'bribed Maurice by giving him a more important job, and buying him a country house, at what expense I can't think.'

221

'It was a wedding present . . . '

'Maurice was happy to live here, Matt.'

'Yes, but – '

'You want to live here now with your dolly bird – '

'My *wife*!' Matt began to feel himself losing control of his temper.

'Why, Matt?' He thought tears glistened in her eyes or, if they didn't, they were not very far away.

'Because I love Chudleigh.'

'So do I.'

'But Elspeth, it has ten bedrooms, for God's sake. It is just not practical. Much too big for you.'

'But why do *you* want to live here? Why not buy a country house for you and . . . that woman somewhere else?'

There was silence.

'It's because *she* likes it, isn't it, Matt?'

Still no reply. Then:

'We both like it.'

'Yes, but *she* wants it. She is the one who wants to get me out.'

'That's not true. Look, Maurice said he wanted to divide the house. That I could not accept. It is a lovely mansion and it should not be divided into flats.'

'It could easily and skilfully be done so as to revert to its former use if necessary.'

'No,' Matt shook his head firmly, 'it could not. It would involve vast structural alterations that I was not prepared to accept.'

'So I'm to be tossed into a tiny cottage with two bedrooms?'

'Why do you need more?'

'Why do you need ten?'

'We're going to have a family.'

'I see,' she sneered, 'then the newspaper report *was* true. She is pregnant. Yet you told Maurice she wasn't.'

'She isn't.'

'Then why did the newspaper say she was?'

'They got the facts wrong.'

'Lying again, Matt?'

'I am not lying,' he said loudly, and felt the perspiration burst out on his brow. 'When did I lie to you?'

'All the time you were having an affair with . . . I can't bring myself to say her name. *You* know what I mean.'

'I did not lie.'

'Of course you lied! You were living a lie . . . all those excuses about where you were. Hong Kong. Henry lying seriously ill and you holed up with her in a Mayfair love-nest . . . '

'Don't be ridiculous.'

'Well, weren't you? You lied to me, to your children, to your employees and, doubtless, you had to lie to her. Apart from loving you as I did, Matt, I always respected you; but now I have no respect or love for you at all, only contempt. And furthermore, I shall not leave this house. It is the matrimonial home and to me it will remain that until I die . . . '

A terrible rage surged up inside Matt, one he knew he had to control or he would commit violence on her.

'You promised Maurice, Elspeth! You saw the house . . . you liked the cottage and, talking of lies and deceit . . . ' He paused, aware that he was hyperventilating, breathless with rage. 'For how long have you known that Philip was homosexual?'

Suddenly he felt her withdraw, eyes expressionless.

'I think I always knew,' she said at last. 'He always used to enjoy doing things with me. Remember? He was special, more so than Maurice.'

'Yet you never said a single word to me.'

'Philip never told me. I just knew in my heart.'

'It shows how much you trusted me.'

'Matt, would it have made you happier to know? I knew how you'd hate it. That's why I was glad he went to America, to spare you.'

'He's probably got AIDS.'

'Well, I hope you'd love and support him if he had.'

'Of course I love him because he's my son but nevertheless I find the whole thing repugnant.'

'And I find your attitude repugnant. What is it like to be a father in whom your son could never confide?'

'Nor could he confide in you, evidently.'

'If you like, we both failed him. Personally I find him a fine, charming young man, and if he chooses to live that life, let him. He can't do anything about it, you know. It's in the genes.'

'Rubbish.'

'It is. Medical research proves it.'

'You were always so over-protective. You spoilt Philip, made him a mummy's boy. I should have seen what would happen.'

'Matt, the scientists *know* it's genetic.'

'Then why is there suddenly such a lot of it? Because it's fashionable, that's why.'

'Because men who were that way now feel they can come out and talk about it. Formerly they were too frightened. Philip has talked to me a lot about it since he came back, because he had Russ there to help and support him. It's like a marriage, the sort of marriage you brutally and violently took away from me.'

And Matt knew then with certainty that Elspeth would never let him forget what he'd done.

He would never be free.

CHAPTER 12

Jenny threw the last piece of bread on the water, wishing she had more. They couldn't possibly still be hungry, but the greedy ducks and swans flocked to the side of the lake in Regent's Park, eager for more. The overweight pigeons strutted over from the shade to try and get their share, but the flocks of eager sparrows flitting down from the trees were too quick for them, and they stood around looking dejected. The swans that had reached dry land boldly stuck their necks out, their beaks pecking at her hands, but then someone else began throwing bread and the mad dash for food began all over again.

It was a lovely day, the sun sparkling on the water, which was full of rowing boats jockeying for position. In some was a solitary oarsman, seriously intent on making progress; in others amorous couples more interested in each other let the oars dangle in the water. Several contained families or groups, the boats weighed down on the lake, some almost too heavy to keep afloat. Passengers lay back, their hands skimming the surface, occasionally flicking another member of the crew, or causing irritation to a perspiring oarsman or woman. Much laughter echoed back to Jenny, making her look wistfully towards the cause.

Behind her, the small boating pool was full of over-excited toddlers and their parents and, further on, the swings and roundabouts in the playground were packed with revellers, the sound of excited, childish cries and screams piercing the air.

Throughout the park, people lay idly under the trees, some beginning a picnic as it was nearly lunchtime. More amorous couples energetically engaged in foreplay, imagining themselves hidden by tall grass or the leafy hanging branches of the trees.

Jenny put her paper bag in a bin and turned towards home, past the pool, the playground, across the bridge; past the kiosk where a queue had formed for snacks and ice-creams, and up the path along by the garden of the US ambassador's residence. She wore her trainers, jeans, a sloppy top with sleeves rolled back, her hair tied in a short ponytail. The park was full of people determined to enjoy a day's outing, happy people with lots of children, nationalities of every kind, who came from all parts of the Metropolis for a day in the sunshine. In the wide open spaces they could run about, play, entertain the children, listen to the band and, above all, enjoy the freedom of space, of air – perhaps not quite fresh, but fresher than in other, more built-up parts of London.

Jenny looked at her watch; it was shortly after midday. The wedding would be starting. She had never met Shirley or Philip, but Matt would be there in the front pew surrounded by his family. She could visualise him standing by Elspeth as Maurice waited for his bride. Then back to Chudleigh in a fleet of cars for the reception, a marquee on the lawn. Matt among family and friends, without her.

She had said she didn't want to go, but of course she did. She wanted to take her place by Matt's side, as was her right; but she knew she was excluded, perhaps for ever, by what she had done, what *he* had done, from that close family circle of which she would so like to have been a part. Yet he would always be part of it; she for ever excluded.

Maybe she hadn't quite realised what the effect on Matt's children would be of his desertion of their mother. Foolish perhaps, short-sighted, but she hadn't. If she had thought at all, in the excitement of the wedding, it was to suppose that, as they were grown up, they would be very adult and civilised about it, as her father and mother had been; Pehr welcoming Ingrid's son, and Angelo gracious towards Jenny.

But that was not the extended family in the English style, or rather as Matt knew it: cosy, intimate, exclusive.

How she'd longed to go with him that morning as she'd handed him his hat, removed imaginary specks of dust from the lapel of his immaculate, well-cut morning coat, and kissed him warmly on the mouth.

'Remember me,' were her last words, to which he had replied as he went through the door: 'Darling, how could I ever forget you?' and, turning, blew her a kiss.

But he would forget her for that day. Completely. Surrounded by all the family, his children, grandchildren, his son's bride and, above all, his first wife, he would have no time for thinking about the one he'd left behind.

Yes, she minded, very much. She could hardly admit it to herself. She envied the happy people crowding into the park on the summer's day and wished that, instead of trainers and jeans, hair screwed back from her head, she was wearing a couture dress, maybe a large picture hat, admiring and being admired, on her husband's arm for all the world to see. Instead she felt more of an affinity with the itinerant beggars who drifted by, clutching their worldly wealth in torn carrier bags or bundles tied up with string.

She came to the outer circle and waited for a break in the traffic to sprint across. Then over the grass along by the side of the canal towards the bridge, where she slowed to a walk again, looking up at the penthouse – its wide balconies towering over her – which was home.

Someone had said it was the most expensive apartment

in London when Matt had bought it just for her, and yet here she was feeling sorry for herself, envying the masses who were forced into the park because they had nothing else, not even gardens. Most of them lived in the high-rise flats which proliferated in that part of north London, or tiny cramped flats made from old Victorian houses with only back yards and scarcely a view of the sky.

Suddenly Jenny felt ashamed of herself for indulging in this rash of self-pity and, running across the road against the lights, dodging the traffic, she sprinted up the steps into the block, went up in the lift to the top, the penthouse, with its unrivalled view over London and the masses crowding into the park.

Selfish? Yes. Very. Selfish and spoilt. She was a woman who had everything she wanted, always had; yet there was that deep layer of dissatisfaction just under the surface, a sense of incompletion, of always wanting something else; being somewhere else; perhaps even being *someone* else.

She went into the kitchen, which had been left clean and sparkling by Maria, who had the day off. Putting ice into a glass, Jenny poured over it mineral water from a bottle, then took a long, satisfying drink. She wandered through the drawing room, on to the balcony again where, glass in hand, she leaned over, watching the crowds still streaming into the park.

Nearly one. The wedding would be over; photographs taken, cars massing outside the house, guests piling on to the lawn eating smoked salmon and drinking champagne . . .

Anyone would think she was deprived of this kind of life. She certainly wasn't. Only the night before there had been a dinner at one of the City livery companies, with superb food and wines, distinguished company; and they hadn't got to bed until one.

But for Matt to be alone without her, knowing she was not wanted, not even missed, made her feel lonely and deprived.

Selfish? Certainly.

The telephone rang and she went inside to answer it.

'Hello?'

'Hello, Jenny!'

'Eric!' she cried in delight. 'Where are you?'

'I'm at the airport.'

'Oh,' her voice fell, 'en route for somewhere?'

'En route for Newmarket.'

'Newmarket?'

'Newmarket, England. I'm seeing a bloodstock agent . . . Well, I have news for you, Jenny. I'm thinking of staying in England . . . '

'But that's *terrific*. You must tell me about it.'

'Maybe . . . '

'Come right over,' she said.

'You mean now?'

'I mean now, this moment. Matt is away for the day and I'm all alone feeling sorry for myself.'

'I sound like just the person you need.'

'You are.'

'I'll check in at the hotel and come straight over.'

'Where are you staying?'

'The Dorchester.'

'Have you cleared customs?'

'No, I'm at the carousel.'

'I'll expect you in an hour or so. Can't wait to see you, Eric.'

'Or I you, Jenny.'

She put down the phone, feeling suddenly alive again, exhilarated. Happy. An old friend of the family. Someone from home.

Eric arrived sooner than she'd expected. They embraced as he came through the door, hugging each other, the camaraderie of old familiars, childhood friends.

He looked wonderful. Blond, his face very youthful, taut, hardly any sign of beard, his eyes clear and blue like the sky, teeth very white. He wore green trousers, a light-weight jacket, green shirt, no tie. He smelt of some lovely herb-scented aftershave, his hands long, lean, with beautifully kept nails, squeezed both her arms. He stood back and looked at her.

'Jenny.'

'Eric, it *is* so good to see you.' She hugged him again, and then she stood back, gazing at him.

'And you, Jenny. You look wonderful.'

They spoke in Swedish, casually linking hands as they strode along the corridor to the drawing room. Of a size, tall; very alike. Could have been brother and sister.

'I say, this is spectacular.' Eric broke from her and went to the window. 'What a *wonderful* place. Where's Matt?'

He turned and looked curiously at her.

'At his son's wedding.' She grimaced and sank on to the sofa. 'I was feeling sorry for myself.'

'You weren't asked?' Eric frowned as she shook her head.

'Of course I'm being petty. I should try and understand.'

'Then I don't think Matt should have gone.'

'Oh, it wasn't that,' she held up a hand. 'He didn't want to go but I made him. Matt is very, very fond of his children, and they weren't too happy about our marriage. Needless to say.'

Eric helped himself to an apple from the bowl of fruit on the sideboard and polished it.

'You don't mind?' he asked, holding it up to examine it in the light.

'Of course I don't, really. Have you eaten?'

'I had a snack on the plane.' He shook his head. 'I'm not hungry.'

'You must stay for dinner. Matt won't be here until late. Oh Eric, it is *so* good to see you.'

He sat down beside her again and clasped her hand, his expression anxious.

'Jenny? *Are* you happy?'

230

'Well, today isn't a good day to ask, but – ' she nodded vigorously – 'yes, I'm happy. We have a fabulous life. This place . . . ' she gestured around and gave him a bright, an overbright, smile. 'What more could you ask? Now – ' she bent and touched his hand – 'what is this with horses?'

'Well, it's a new venture. Speculating.' Eric got up and began to pace the room, hands in his pockets. 'You know I was a ski-instructor during the winter? And then what to do next, I asked myself? One of the men who came for winter sports was a wealthy English racehorse owner. He may give me a job.'

'What as?'

'Maybe buying for him,' Eric shrugged. 'I hope that eventually that way I may get into eventing over here. You know, it's something I always wanted to do.'

'And you're good at, too. It's a wonderful idea. I didn't know you were that knowledgeable about horseflesh.' She looked at him doubtfully.

'Well, maybe not as much as he thinks,' Eric smiled. 'But anyway, it's a challenge, an adventure.'

'It's wonderful to see you again,' she said. 'I realise now that you're here how very much I've missed you.'

Matt put his key into the lock, eager to see Jenny, to relay to her the trials of the day; just, by her presence, to have the blues dispelled.

Jenny wasn't the sort of wife who warmed the slippers, not the sort to be found waiting by the hearth. But Jenny's cool, welcoming smile, her air of calm, of being in control, was as soothing and as important to him as any amount of cosseting from someone else.

He opened the door and heard voices. The dining room door was half open and the voices speaking in Swedish were quite loud. But the bantering tone, the familiarity, was not lost on him. He stiffened and stood there, feeling in his breast pocket for the small diary he kept as an

231

aide-mémoire and flicked hurriedly through the pages. No, the only engagement under the date was Maurice's wedding.

He walked along the carpeted hall and stood on the threshold of the dining room, feeling rather foolish in morning dress. Jenny looked up, surprise on her face.

'Matt!' she cried. 'You're earlier than I expected. Have you eaten?'

'I had enough to eat for a week, but . . . ' his eyes were on Eric sitting opposite his wife. Jenny languidly extended an arm in his direction.

'You remember Eric, don't you, Matt?'

'I do.' Matt went over to him and politely shook hands. 'How are you, Eric?'

'Fine, Matt. How are you?'

'Darling, sit down.' Jenny pointed to the chair between them. 'Sure you couldn't eat something?'

'I'm not really hungry.' Matt shook his head and went over to the sideboard, where from a collection of bottles and decanters he selected a fine old malt whisky which he poured into a tumbler. Behind him the two watched silently, the atmosphere suddenly became awkward as Matt's tension was perceived.

He felt movement, then the pressure of those long, thin hands on his arms.

'Bad day, darling?' Her cheek nuzzled against his. 'I should have realised.'

'Look,' Eric said getting to his feet, 'I'll go.'

'Don't be silly, Eric.' Jenny motioned him to sit down again. 'Matt would be very annoyed if you left. Wouldn't you, darling?'

'Very,' Matt muttered, and kissed her cheek. 'I had just forgotten he was coming.'

'No, I arrived unannounced,' Eric assured him. 'Or, rather, I phoned Jenny from the airport.'

'Are you staying?' Matt asked casually, taking his glass over to the table.

'At the Dorchester.'

232

'Excellent — ' Matt nodded his head — 'a good place.' He sat down, stretched his legs, felt himself begin to unwind, and gazed at Jenny. 'Sorry, darling, I'm a bit disorientated. The wedding was fine, superb, everything went off well. Shirley looked lovely, et cetera, et cetera . . . but I am glad to be back here, with you,' he leaned across and took her hand.

'I missed you,' she said. Matt looked pointedly at Eric. 'I had a long walk in the park thinking of you,' Jenny went on, 'wishing we were together. Eric rang from the airport at about one and I told him to come over.'

'Quite right.' Matt took a long drink. He felt a bit light-headed. 'You staying long, Eric?'

'Well, I'm not sure, Matt . . . '

'He's over here to see about work and, Matt . . . I have had *the* most wonderful idea.' Jenny leapt up excitedly and stood in front of him looking down. 'Please don't say "no". Listen to me first.'

'Go ahead.' Matt smiled and drank deeply from his glass.

'You know Eric is a superb horserider?'

'I think you told me. You're good, too.'

'Well, not like Eric. Darling, Eric wants to start buying horses for eventing — you know, the sort of thing Princess Anne does — and Matt, I thought of Chudleigh and what a marvellous place it would be. It has those old stables and lots and lots of room.'

'What are you trying to tell me, Jenny?'

'Matt, it's only an *idea*, but I thought — ' she turned to Eric for support — '*we* thought maybe we could buy horses and start a stable in the country.'

'Do you know what you're saying?' Matt began to burn with anger.

'Of course I know. Matt, it would give me a purpose, something to *do*. I hang around here all day waiting for you. It's not much of a life, darling. You've so much to do. I've so little. I was so busy before I married you . . . I thought you'd be *pleased*, Matt.' She flung herself down and, head propped on her hands, gazed at the table.

Eric, ill at ease, sat sideways, smoking, looking out of the window.

The anger in Matt's heart turned slowly to rage. He knew he must take care; not lose control. Eric was the last person he wanted to see, and this conversation the last one he wanted to have; one requiring decisions, new ideas which he didn't even want to consider. Absurd. He waited a moment or two, took a deep breath and said:

'I'm afraid Elspeth has changed her mind about Chudleigh.'

'Oh, no,' Jenny's head jerked up. 'I thought it was all settled.'

Matt shook his head slowly. 'I must confess, though, I thought so too.'

'But she can't possibly be allowed to change her mind.' Jenny's eyes were stormy.

'Well . . . '

'You must get the solicitors on to her immediately. It's too bad. You bought her a house . . . '

'Unfortunately there was no strictly legal agreement. Look, darling, can we talk about this some other time . . . ?'

'It will have to be soon. Eric is off to Newmarket about a job . . . '

'Then I think he'd better take it.' Matt rose to pour himself another drink, looked behind him as he stood at the sideboard. 'You can't suddenly *drop* these ideas on me, Jenny, not without thought. Anyway, for the moment Chudleigh's out of the question, so I suppose the whole idea has to be scrapped. In any case,' he turned with his whisky and came back to the table, 'I didn't know you were *that* interested in horses.'

'I am,' she said coldly. 'Very.'

'You have never once expressed to me any burning interest in horses.'

'Oh, she has always liked horses – ' Eric began.

Matt went on ignoring him. 'Never expressed a wish to go to the Derby or Ascot. Never studied form.' He was aware that his tone was increasingly verging on the sarcastic.

'Well, I do,' Jenny said quietly. 'Maybe it was because I knew you were not interested. You see, I'm not interested in opera, so I knew how awful it was to be forced to do something you didn't want to do.'

'I never forced you, Jenny!' Matt gazed stonily at her, whereupon Eric scraped back his chair and said, 'Actually, I *do* have to be going. It's getting late. I've had a long day.' He looked fixedly at his watch.

'Keep in touch, Eric,' Matt said pleasantly. He gave him a nod of dismissal. Jenny, looking very angry, rose and accompanied Eric to the front door, where they stood awkwardly, staring at each other.

'Sorry,' she said, 'he's in a hell of a mood.'

'Had a bad day,' Eric looked sympathetic. 'The wife is the problem, obviously. Anyway, thanks for the thought. It was exciting.' He leaned forward and briefly planted a kiss on her brow.

'I don't give up that easily.' She put a hand on his chest.

'I know.'

'And don't do *anything* yet. I'm serious about the idea. I like it.'

'Better go back and talk to Matt.' As she opened the door, Eric lifted his hand. 'And the best of luck.'

Jenny shut the door, then stood there for a moment before padding back along the corridor to the dining room, where Matt still sat at the table, chin slumped on his chest. He raised his head as she came in.

'I feel terribly tired.'

'You embarrassed Eric.' She sat down opposite him and stared at him hard.

'He embarrassed *me*. I didn't know he would be here. Jenny, hurling ideas at me about horses and eventing . . .

You can't expect me to take it in just like that. I'm not even sure I like that chap Eric.'

'Well, I do. I've known him since we were children . . . '

'Maybe you should have married him.'

'Don't be a fool.'

'He's young, he's handsome,' Matt waved his hand in the air. 'He rides beautifully . . . '

'I think you're drunk.'

'I'm not in the least drunk. Has he any money?' He paused and stared at her.

'He's not a gold-digger, if that's what you mean. I think he's what you call comfortably off but not rich.'

'He would, of course, pay his way in this horse business.'

'Yes, I suppose so.' She jerked up her chin. 'Anyway, it's not coming off is it? What's all this about Elspeth?'

'Well, it's as I told you.'

'I'm not standing for it, Matt.'

'Short of a legal battle, I don't know what I can do.'

'*I* don't mind going to see her.'

He sat back in his chair, folded his arms and looked at her. 'I believe you mean that.'

'I do. I shall say she has reneged on her word. You spent a fortune on a house for Maurice that would give her a home, too.'

'Well, that was the idea, but it was never actually spelled out.'

'How do you mean?'

'It was never stipulated that Elspeth must live there.'

'But I thought that was the whole point.'

'We thought she would want to.'

'You thought . . . ' Jenny rose to her feet and leaned threateningly over Matt. 'You're a renowned businessman, a captain of industry . . . '

'Business and personal life are very different.' Matt put a hand on his temple, which was throbbing. 'Please, Jenny, give me a break. I've had a horrible day. It was really awful.' He looked up. 'I say, can we go into the lounge and relax?'

236

'Of course.' Jenny abruptly left the table and preceded Matt to the drawing room. In the west, the sun was a golden ball, sinking below the treeline. Matt went and stood by the window, gazing at the view. Jenny sat down on the sofa and crossed her legs.

'My son's a pansy,' Matt said at last.

Jenny's control slipped and she looked shocked. 'Maurice?'

'Philip, you silly girl. The one you haven't met. He's over here from America with a boyfriend.'

'And you'd *no* idea?'

'None.'

'What a family.' Jenny gave a brief laugh and stretched her long legs along the couch. 'You don't seem able to communicate, do you? I mean, the thing about Elspeth and the house shows just how convoluted you all can be.'

'I suppose it does.'

'And not knowing your son was gay? I can't believe it. Are you sure?'

'Yes. Beth says so and Elspeth says so.'

'But it was never discussed? Never guessed?'

'They all thought I'd mind.'

'And do you?'

'Yes. Terribly.' He turned towards her, but her attitude on the couch was uninviting so, instead of sitting beside her, he sat opposite in one of the low Swedish armchairs.

'Well, you shouldn't.' Her tone was gentle. 'It's so common.'

'I still don't like it.'

'There's nothing much you can do about it, Matt, darling.'

'No.' He hung his head.

'But you *can* do something about Elspeth.'

'Well, I'll get the solicitors on to it if you really want me to. Try and get her to agree. I'd rather she went voluntarily than that she was pushed.'

'Naturally. Far better all round.'

He felt the atmosphere relax a little. 'It was really a ghastly, terrible day. Georgina looked awful. She's aged terribly and Henry is still not really well. It's mental as well as physical. You know he had this knock on the head; as well as headaches and a permanent limp, he now has wild changes of mood. Rupert, my beloved grandson, didn't address a single word to me, other than "hello" and "goodbye", and looked at me in a horrible, accusatory way. I felt like a pariah . . . and Elspeth hates me. Refusing to leave the house is all part of it.'

'Maybe neither of us thought this all through, Matt,' Jenny said gently after a while.

'Thought what through?'

'The consequences of what you did.'

'Of course we thought it through. We loved each other. At least I loved you . . . '

He looked at her but she didn't reply. Tired now and confused, still feeling lonely, unsure and a little afraid, her brief rocket of happiness shot down in flames, she didn't really know what to say.

'Maybe if we had a baby it would be all right,' Matt said later in the dark, whispering into her ear after they had made love. 'Babies do make families, you know. Just you and me alone . . . It's kind of incomplete.'

Long after Matt fell asleep, Jenny lay awake, pondering his words and the events of the day.

CHAPTER 13

Matt looked at the men assembled round the table, each one picked by him. A new team. A good team. The marketing director was doing his job, the financial controller was first class, the move to the new offices was proving successful and was thought to have improved business, orders were up even though there were signs of decline in the economy overall.

It was for this reason that Gerard Singer, also present, advised postponing the launch on the Stock Exchange. Matt agreed with him. He had never wanted to lose overall control of his company, and that was virtually what it would mean. But, personal preference apart, Gerard's arguments were cogent enough and his well heeled team accepted them.

'We don't want an issue that is going to be left with the underwriters,' Gerard concluded. 'It would have a devastating effect on the company, and if we are entering a recession, that's the last thing we want. Remember the collapse of the Stock Market in '87? It could happen again.'

Heads nodded gravely, in unison.

'Very well, gentlemen,' Matt said, after thanking Gerard for his lucid report, 'I think that concludes our business for today.' As they rose, he raised a finger in the direction of his son. 'Maurice, would you stay behind for a word?'

'Of course, Dad.' Maurice resumed his seat as the others slowly left the room amid a muted buzz of conversation.

'Well, I think that went very well.' Matt sat back in his chair, his expression one of satisfaction. 'Didn't you?'

'I still wish we'd gone to the Stock Market earlier.'

'Yes, I know you do, but I think you're wrong. Frankly I think we are in for a tough time economically, and it is best to rein in our horses. Now, to change the subject . . .' Matt drummed busily on the table with his fingers, ' . . . Settling in well?'

'I think so. There's a lot to do.'

'I think Shirley should give up her job.'

'Why?'

'Well, to help you. You can't be a busy ward sister and run a home effectively as well. Also, Maurice, I think you should consider a move to London, a flat in the Barbican just for the week. Weekends in the country.'

'I can't dictate to Shirley what she should do, Dad.'

'Naturally,' Matt nodded, and went on drumming, his expression thoughtful. 'No sign of a baby?'

'None planned, Dad.' Maurice smiled. 'Yet. We've only been married three months.'

'Quite.' Matt nodded again, and Maurice had the feeling that his father was stalling.

'Anything else on your mind, Dad?' He glanced at his watch. 'I want a word with Gerard before he leaves the building.'

'Well, think about what I've said and talk it over with Shirley. Oh, and your mother . . . '

'Ah!' At last his father was coming to the point. 'Well, you know that Mum doesn't want to go. I can't force her.'

'You have reneged on an agreement, Maurice,' his father said severely, changing from amiability to anger in seconds.

'I beg your pardon?' Indignantly.

'I offered to buy you a country home with cottage

attached as a wedding present. The cottage was meant for Elspeth.'

'But no one agreed to that. It was not a condition, just a suggestion.'

'I thought we had an unspoken agreement.'

'Not that I was aware of.'

'Well, either you're very naïve or very stupid, Maurice, and I don't think either is the case. But I would never have spent such a large amount of money on a house with a cottage if I'd thought your mother wasn't going to live there. It was *your* job to ensure she did.'

'Well, I didn't succeed, and nor did you. I think you brought it up at the wedding.'

'Jenny is getting agitated about it – understandably annoyed. She wants to start a stables.'

'A what?'

'Stables for horses. Breeding thoroughbreds. She's very keen on the idea. Chudleigh is ideal.'

Chudleigh was ideal because the previous owner had kept horses. It had a paddock and plenty of land, and the stables were in good order, used only for storage.

'So Jenny's not expecting?'

'Not yet,' Matt said briefly.

'It was a false alarm?'

'Yes.'

'Not a miscarriage, I hope, Dad?'

'She simply fainted and the papers made a meal of it. I told you that before.'

'But you did mention a family as the reason . . . '

'And I told you to get your mother out of that house,' Matt said, thumping the table. 'And pronto. I mean it, Maurice. I want her out. I hold you responsible, and if you can't manage to persuade your mother, I shall be rethinking my policy with regard to your future in this firm.'

Father and son glared at each other. Then Matt resumed his drumming.

'That sounds like blackmail to me, Dad,' Maurice said quietly.

'Call it what you like. But I think you blackmailed me over Stanfield Manor.'

'That is absolutely not true! You first saw the place; *you* liked it. We were almost pressed into having it. Mind you, I'm not saying we're not grateful. It's lovely.'

'Well, it sounds very ungrateful to me. I feel let down, betrayed. Jenny's very unhappy.'

'Maybe Jenny should have had Stanfield Manor?' Maurice's tone was ironic.

'Jenny doesn't want it. She wants Chudleigh, and so do I.' Matt stood up, a powerful figure towering over his son. 'Now, look here, Maurice. You get your mother out of Chudleigh and into that cottage. I don't care how you do it, but do it. Because if my marriage falls through because of it, you – ' he pointed a threatening finger at his son – 'are out of this firm. Do you understand?'

White-faced, tight-lipped, Maurice rose, gathered together the documents he had brought with him, and left the room without a word.

Shirley Ransom was the sort of nice, tolerant, sensible girl anyone would like having as a daughter-in-law. She was cool, not given to moods, yet affectionate, warm and responsive. She was liked by her staff and generally adored by her patients.

People thought she and Maurice were an ideal couple and, in many ways, they were. The only thing that irked Shirley, and always had, was the way Maurice seemed dominated by his awesome father. Maurice denied this, but Shirley wasn't convinced. It was Maurice's weakness; he was afraid of the old man.

Shirley had now been charged with the responsibility of trying to get her mother-in-law out of her home, and she resented it. It had sparked off the first row she and Maurice had had since that fairy-tale wedding in the grounds of this very house and, as she parked her Mini outside the imposing entrance, she visualised again that happy day and all it had meant to her.

Elspeth, expecting her for lunch on her day off, was waiting by the window, and as soon as she saw the car she waved and ran to the door, down the steps to greet her.

The women, who had always got on, embraced affectionately. Then, arm-in-arm, they walked into the house.

'Chilly today, isn't it?'

'Autumn is certainly upon us.'

'I've asked Ron to turn the central heating up.' Ron was the man who, together with his wife, looked after her and the house and lived in a flat in the attic.

Shirley shivered and rubbed her hands together.

'Sherry or coffee?' Elspeth said brightly as they reached the drawing room. 'I am so *happy* to see you, darling. You look well.'

'And I you.' Shirley felt rather guilty. She wasn't at all pleased to be here, annoyed at the task she had been charged with. She would rather have forgone her day off than be where she was right now. 'I think sherry,' she said looking surreptitiously at her watch. 'I haven't an awful lot of time and I had a coffee just before I left.'

'But you're staying to lunch?'

'Of course.'

'Good.' Elspeth, satisfied, went over to the drinks table and poured sherry into two large glasses.

'I feel I need a stiffener today,' she said, handing one to Shirley and raising the other in a toast.

'To you!'

'To you,' Shirley acknowledged the gesture, smiling. 'But why, is something wrong . . . ?'

'Oh, something is always wrong.' Elspeth sat opposite her daughter-in-law and drew the cardigan of her twin-set closely round her. 'I haven't got over Matt, you know,

243

what he did. Sometimes it bugs me more than others. Living alone, I brood on it.'

'Quite naturally,' Shirley said gently. 'But . . . '

'Yes?' Quickly.

'Well, it is time to try and rebuild your life, Elspeth. It's, what, over two years since Matt told you about Jenny . . . '

'Oh don't mention her name in this house, *please.*' Elspeth held out a hand as if warding off the sign of the Evil One.

'Elspeth,' Shirley said, firmly placing her sherry glass on the small table by her side, 'I am very serious about this.'

'About what?' Elspeth looked bewildered and, suddenly, rather frail.

'You starting a new life, getting Matt and . . . "her" out of your mind. And Maurice and I both think you should leave here.' She looked round the large drawing room. 'It *is* a huge place. It's expensive to run and economically wasteful. Now, in this little cottage – '

'I shan't hear of it. Did Matt send you?' Suspiciously.

'No,' Shirley chose her words carefully, 'not Matt . . . but Maurice *did* ask me to talk to you.'

'Oh, so it's a plot.'

'No, there is no plot. But Maurice has been threatened with the sack by Matt . . . '

'The *what*? I can't believe it.' Elspeth looked incredulously at the woman opposite her.

'Yes,' Shirley nodded to emphasise her words. 'He said that Maurice had reneged on a promise.'

'But surely Maurice never promised . . . '

'No, he didn't; but Matt said he bought the manor with the explicit idea you would move to the cottage.'

'Then he'd no right to.'

'Well, he blames it all on Maurice.'

'He's a monster,' Elspeth angrily shook her head. 'I simply can't believe it. I blame it all on that woman. She has made him very hard. The old Matt would never have behaved like this.'

'I tend to agree with you.' Shirley suddenly felt inadequate herself.

'Maurice is afraid of his father.'

'I think I agree with you there, too,' Shirley nodded.

'Always has been. That's why Philip went to America, maybe why Philip is . . . well, the way he is. Matt terrified them when they were small. The boys, that is. The girls he adored; even now, they are the ones who forgive him.'

'I think it's best to forgive.' Shirley's tone was decisive. 'No sense, Elspeth, in bearing grudges. What has happened has happened.'

'Is she expecting?' Elspeth asked suddenly.

'Not that I am aware of.'

'Matt said she wanted a family. Imagine him, nearly sixty, a father again. Personally I think it's obscene.'

'Try and put it all out of your mind, Elspeth. I'm sorry to sound harsh, but I think it's best for you. I really do. If you allow yourself to brood endlessly about what is now a *fait accompli*, you will become ill. You will do yourself no good at all.'

'I always thought you were my friend,' Elspeth said peevishly.

'I am. I really am, and I'm only doing this, and saying the things I'm saying, because I think it's in your own best interests.'

'And yours. Do you think Matt would really sack Maurice?'

'Yes I do, or move him, which he is always threatening to do. He once suggested *Belfast*.' Shirley shuddered. 'He is quite ruthless, business-wise, as you know, and yet I think he feels guilty about you. He is still certainly very fond of you. I don't think he'd do anything ruthless to you, but I think he would to Maurice. Look,' Shirley stood up and glanced at the clock on the wall, 'after lunch, why don't you drive back with me and have a look at the cottage again? I think it's lovely. I really do.'

*   *   *

245

In many ways it *was* a pretty little house, tucked out of sight of the manor, surrounded by trees. It had all been newly done up for its next occupant. Quite large, really, despite only having two bedrooms. Two was enough.

'The family can always come and stay with *us*,' Shirley said encouragingly, 'and then you won't have the bother. Guests can be an awful nuisance, you know.'

'I know,' Elspeth sniffed into her handkerchief, on the brink of tears, 'but somehow I feel I'm being put out to grass. Made redundant.'

'Not at all.' Shirley led the way downstairs again and into the pleasant living room which faced the lake. 'I think you will find life will *begin* again, Elspeth. Instead of brooding you'll have new interests.'

'Such as?' Elspeth sniffed again.

'Well, getting this place as you like it. Matt says you can have what furniture you like from Chudleigh . . . '

'Oh, how very *kind* of him . . . '

'Well, it's the least he can do.' Shirley, sensing victory, ignored the sarcasm. 'Then, once you're settled, you can take up some interests again . . . '

'Such as?'

'Well,' Shirley looked at her blankly, 'I know you're passionate about roses. What else are you interested in?'

'I *was* mainly interested in my family,' Elspeth said pointedly. 'They took up all my time, especially my husband. I shared his interests. We went up once, sometimes twice a week or more to London. We both loved opera – incidentally I hear *she* hates it. We attended a lot of dinners and functions. I had a very full life as Matt's wife and I enjoyed it. Suddenly that all went and I was left with nothing . . . ' and then she gave in to the tears that had never been very far away and wept.

Shirley let her have a good cry. There was nothing to sit on, so they sat on the floor, Elspeth cross-legged, handkerchief crushed in her hand, Shirley with an arm around her. It was cold and bleak. There was no sunshine outside, and

Shirley felt very sorry for her mother-in-law. She wondered if Elspeth did in fact move, whether she would indeed be doing the right thing?

Suddenly Shirley felt apprehensive, worried about the future, and slightly sorry that she hadn't let her husband do his own dirty work.

The gynaecologist was one of those smooth-faced, quietly spoken, very handsome men whom women patients invariably trusted, and some of them fell for.

It wasn't sexual love that one had for a gynaecologist – at least in most cases it wasn't. It was a sort of desperation, of trust, based on need. A woman needing the attention of such a doctor felt very fragile. He saw her at her most vulnerable, and was familiar with the most intimate part of her in the way that no other person, not even a lover or husband, was.

Jenny, however, despite Mr Vernon's charm and good looks, felt none of these things about him. Nor did she feel vulnerable. He had a job to do, and she had been told he was the best one to do it. The best person practising in the field of infertility.

And my goodness he knew all about her now, inside and out. The tests had been onerous, embarrassing, sometimes painful; but now, after weeks, including a few days in hospital and a general anaesthetic to 'have a really good look inside', as Mr Vernon explained, they were over and she awaited the verdict.

He didn't keep her waiting long in the discreetly opulent waiting room of his Welbeck Street consulting rooms, and she was shown into his presence by his nurse who withdrew, shutting the door gently after her. Mr Vernon sprang up, all smiles, and went round the desk to welcome his patient.

'Ah, good morning, Lady Ransom.'

'Good morning, Mr Vernon.'

He indicated a chair and she sat down, perfectly composed, handbag and gloves on her knee.

247

'And how are you, Lady Ransom?' Mr Vernon took his seat behind a large desk and drew some notes out of a folder.

'Fine.'

'Does the weather suit you?' He looked momentarily out at the icy street outside.

'It is much colder in Sweden.'

'Of course. Now Lady Ransom,' Mr Vernon huddled for a few moments over his notes and then looked up at her with a practised, professional smile. 'It is good news. I can find no reason why you and your husband cannot have children.'

'None at all?'

'None at all. Your uterus is fine, your ovaries and Fallopian tubes are fine; as you know, you menstruate regularly, so nothing wrong there. You release an egg which lodges in the right place at the right time . . . ' Mr Vernon hurriedly flicked through his notes, and Jenny thought it was as though he could actually visualise what he was describing – as indeed, after all this time, could she. The passage of the tiny egg, almost invisible to the naked eye, in its journey from the ovary, along the Fallopian tube to its home in the lining of the womb, from whence it was expelled, usually two weeks later, if fertilisation did not occur.

A mysterious and rather amazing process, really.

When he'd finished his account of what he had found in his tests, it appeared that he was right. She and Matt should by now be expecting a baby.

'The only thing I can think of,' Mr Vernon sat back and gazed thoughtfully at the ceiling, 'is that you and your husband may be incompatible,' and, seeing her look of concern, he hurried on. 'Oh, I don't mean emotionally. Not at all; I'm sure you're both very much in love. But it may be a matter of secretions; the mechanisms that lubricate the vagina may be too alkaline or not alkaline enough, and thus inimical to your husband's sperm.'

'Well, can't you do something about that?' Jenny found it hard to contain her dismay.

'Unfortunately I wish I could. I am, however, going to prescribe a vaginal douche, and would like you to use it every time you have intercourse – before, that is. It might neutralise the acid.' He looked at her gravely. 'On the other hand, it might not.'

'And that's all?'

'That's all.' He continued wading through masses of notes. 'As you know, his sperm count is fine . . . and . . . '

'What about implanting eggs, that sort of thing?'

'Not necessary, dear Lady Ransom. If you ovulate properly, and you do, there is no need for it. This is the sort of sensational stuff you read in the newspaper – pandering to people's ignorance. Now, let's see if the douche works. Let's give it a chance. The other thing,' he closed his file and looked thoughtfully at her, 'is psychological.'

'I beg your pardon?'

'Sometimes a woman doesn't *want* a baby.'

'Oh, how ridiculous.' Nervously Jenny laughed, crossed and then uncrossed her legs, fingers tightening over her handbag.

'No, I'm perfectly serious. Or, in her efforts to have one, she is too tense. I assure you I have known it happen. That's why some couples conceive after a number of years when they have almost given up hope. The woman thinks, "Oh well, I shan't have a baby, and I might as well adjust to that" . . . and hey presto, she conceives.'

'I don't think we can wait that long.' Jenny felt her caution begin to give way. 'My husband is nearly sixty.'

'I've known men become fathers at eighty . . . Mind you, I don't recommend it. Not that a man shouldn't be having sexual intercourse at that age, not at all; merely one has to think of the children.'

'Exactly.'

'On the other hand, you would be relatively young in twenty years' time, still able . . . '

Jenny opened her bag and grabbed a handkerchief, blew her nose hard to try and prevent the tears; but it was no use. Mr Vernon, all concerned at this display of emotion on the part of his very controlled and cooperative patient, got to his feet in concern.

'My dear Lady Ransom, I'm so sorry . . . '

'My husband so *wants* a baby,' Jenny sobbed. 'He's a family man. He already has a grown-up family, but family life means a lot to him. He would like us to have not just one child but two or three . . . '

'And you?' The doctor put his head on one side. 'Would you?'

'Well,' she dabbed at her eyes and then tucked the handkerchief back in her handbag, 'I'm a little afraid of babies, to be truthful; but I do want what he wants. I want to be positive about it, and I have decided to be.'

'Did you talk about it?' Mr Vernon perched on the side of his desk, gazing at her sympathetically.

'We didn't before we were married.' The handkerchief came out again. 'It was very silly, but I was young. I wanted to enjoy myself.'

'Quite natural.'

'I imagined that as he had a family he, well . . . ' She crumpled the handkerchief into a ball in her hand. 'We didn't discuss it and it was silly. But now there's a sort of tension in our love-making because Matt thinks it's for a reason. I find it hard to relax.'

'Ah-ah,' the gynaecologist looked triumphant and, bounding round his desk, scribbled something on a piece of paper. 'I'm going to recommend a very good physiotherapist who will give you exercises to relax you. That, and the douche, Lady Ransom . . . ' He held out a hand to help her to her feet. 'In no time at all you'll be giving me some very good news.'

*   *   *

When Jenny got home, to her surprise she found Matt already there sitting in front of the window, reading the *Evening Standard*, a glass of sherry by his side.

'Darling,' he said looking up, 'you're back already.'

'I didn't expect to see you,' she said, planting a brief, tender kiss on his forehead.

'Let me get you a sherry.' Matt got up with an expression of pleasant anticipation on his face. 'I've got great news.'

'Oh?' She sat down looking at him fondly, feeling strange because of the talk with Mr Vernon. Breaking down, not like her. Hoping Matt wouldn't notice she was still upset.

'Elspeth is leaving Chudleigh,' he announced as he put the glass of sherry into her hand.

'I don't believe it!' Her expression changed to one of amazement. 'Truly?'

'Honestly and truly. She has agreed.'

'Have you it in writing?'

'Yes.' He slapped his breast-pocket. 'There has been an exchange of correspondence between our solicitors and she will move out in a month's time.'

'Oh Matt, that's terrific.' She rose and, carefully putting down her glass, threw her arms round his neck. Then she stepped back and looked at him. 'Poor Elspeth . . . I mean, was there a lot of pressure?'

'Not at all. Shirley had a long talk with her. The house is *much* too big. Shirley then took her round the cottage and she decided after all that she liked it.'

'Oh, I'm so glad. I mean that it was voluntary.'

'Tell me, what did Vernon say?' His voice betrayed his nervousness, his eyes clouded with apprehension.

'Well, there's no reason why we can't have a baby, nothing wrong. He said it's simply a matter of time.'

'Oh darling . . . my cup is *very* full,' Matt said tenderly and, drawing her to him again, kissed her gently on the mouth.

251

CHAPTER 14

Jenny galloped towards the fence; her mare Clea hesitated just for a second, and then cleared it with ease and sped on towards the next.

Eric, his hands loosely on the reins of his own horse, Tomas, watched her with approval.

'Well done,' he called as she completed the course.

Her eyes sparkled and she patted Clea's flank. 'Good Clea – ' she bent to kiss the mare's glossy neck – 'a great girl.'

It was a fresh, sparkling morning, and the finishing touches had only been put to the four-railed fencing around the ring the previous day. The stables were complete and the first four horses already installed. Great care had been taken with the jumps, the angle, the height, the size.

Matt joked that she paid more attention to the stables and the jumps than to the house, but really very little needed doing that a professional decorator couldn't do. It had been redecorated, recarpeted, and many new pieces of furniture added. Elspeth's couple had gone to Maurice, and their flat had been decorated and prepared for a new couple not yet engaged.

There was something about indoor servants that Jenny didn't very much like. She felt they intruded on one's privacy. She was always aware of Maria shuffling about in the London apartment, listening, maybe, behind closed doors. Who could tell? However, until new premises were found for them – hopefully away from the house – any new couple engaged would have to have the flat now that the stables were in use. Just at the moment she was avoiding the evil day of appointing them.

Their move to Chudleigh had coincided with the beginning of spring. The lovely old house looked at its best, the white woodwork surrounding the windows, the pilasters of the porch gleaming with a fresh coat of white paint. The grounds were full of daffodils, the thick chestnut buds overhead unfurling on the giant trees that had been there for at least two centuries.

Jenny had had her sessions with the physiotherapist in Wimpole Street, meticulously applied the douche every time they made love, but still nothing worked, the periods regular as clockwork.

Mr Vernon thought that horses were a very good thing to take her mind off something that was threatening to become an obsession. He encouraged the idea of stables and eventing and pooh-poohed Matt's idea that somehow jumping would interfere with Jenny's insides, pointing out how many skilled horsewomen were also mothers.

The horses were thus seen as a kind of therapy, and Eric fitted into the scheme, entering with enthusiasm into the project, quite brilliant in some of his ideas and knowing where to get expert help.

They had Tomas, a stallion; Clea; Clea's daughter, Hibiscus; and April, a beautiful roan.

Seeing Jenny so happy made Matt happy, and he stopped worrying about the possible effect on her reproductive system. Vernon had told him in a private interview to stop agitating his wife about the baby. They all had a duty to relax.

Eric was happy too. He'd bought on Jenny's behalf all the horses, and had an eye on a couple more. He supervised the adaptation of the stables, the erection of the jumps, engaged the stable boy, Jim. He now sat watching Jenny, her head pressed close to Clea's neck, her hand stroking her flank. She looked magnificent on a horse, rode well and courageously, and was turning into a polished jumper, although her dressage needed a lot more practice.

'Now your turn,' Jenny called, but Eric shook his head.

'April isn't ready for jumping. I must give her time to settle down.'

'Right.' Jenny nodded her head in agreement, and cantered towards the stable. As Jim appeared to take the reins, she dismounted.

'Give her a good rub down,' Jenny instructed him, 'and then some nice oats.'

'Yes, Lady Ransom. When will the new horses be coming, my lady?'

'In a matter of weeks, maybe sooner.' She gazed up as Eric trotted into the yard.

'The new horses, Eric?'

'Can't say.' He shook his head as he dismounted and, taking a cloth from the stable door, began to rub Tomas down. 'Nothing we want to do in a hurry.'

'Of course.'

Jenny nodded, watching him. It was so good to be with Eric again. He loved the house, the countryside, the feeling of space. He finished rubbing down Tomas, threw the towel to Jim and, together, he and Jenny strode out of the yard towards the house.

Chudleigh Court had been built in the reign of George III, and was a very good example of the period of that long-lived monarch. A long, straight path led from the stables to the side of the house and, for a moment, Eric, a hand in the pocket of his jodhpurs, stopped and gazed at it.

Jenny stopped with him.

'It's a very beautiful place,' he said, looking down at her. 'I'm very lucky.'

'We're lucky to have you.' She linked an arm casually through his. 'It's just perfect you happened to come the time you did.'

As usual they spoke in Swedish.

'Jenny, the thing that bothers me – ' Eric freed his arm from hers and ran his hand through his thick blond hair – 'is the money.'

'Don't let it. We've got plenty.'

'But I do. I mean, I want to share in this as much as I can. So far you've paid for everything. It must have cost a fortune.'

'But we haven't paid you a salary.' She looked at him curiously. 'Is that what you're worried about?'

'The finances do worry me, I'll be honest.' He went on ruffling his hair. 'As you know, I'm not a rich man. I think I can manage on my allowance, but I can't make any contribution.'

'None is expected.' Her expression became serious. 'Don't let money come between us, Eric. It's not important.'

'It is if you don't have it.'

'Well, yes, perhaps . . . Would you like some sort of fee? Stipend, whatever they call it?'

'No, I don't want to be in your employ. It would alter the relationship between us. Besides, when I start winning competitions . . . '

'That will be different.' She linked her arm through his again. 'Then you'll be rich! Come on, cheer up. It's such a lovely day. A lovely place. I'm so glad . . . ' She paused, feeling awkward.

'But Elspeth is happy where she is, isn't she?' It was as though Eric could read her mind. He could. He understood her very well. There was such empathy between them, almost as though he was a bridge between her and Matt.

She looked gratefully at him. 'She's settled down very well. I just wish . . . the children were more natural with me. It would make Matt so happy. Me, too, of course.'

255

'Maybe now that you're here they'll come round. How anyone can resist you, I don't know.' Eric stooped suddenly and kissed her cheek, then put his arm around her waist.

She looked up at him, an expression of doubt on her face, almost as though she were afraid and, gently, she removed his arm.

It would never do to change the parameters.

The following day, Eric set off for Newmarket, and Jenny went off to London to fulfil a series of engagements with Matt. The company was going to the Stock Exchange after all, to raise more capital to offset the very high interest rates imposed by the government. There were a lot of important people to see, managers of pension funds who would be encouraged to buy shares in Ransom Engineering being prominent among them.

The beautiful Lady Ransom, on the arm of her husband or gracing the dinner table or the box at the opera, was seen as an asset. They were a glamorous, high-profile couple, and the next few weeks were exhausting but rewarding.

The Stock Exchange launch went well, considering the economic climate, although it was not oversubscribed and some shares remained with the underwriters. Not too many, however, and after the first few days of trading during which the price faltered and once fell below the issue price, the shares started to climb.

Half went to the public and institutions, and of the other half a quarter were offered to the staff. Matt had a quarter, Jenny a quarter, and the remainder was divided among the family. All of them became paper millionaires, and Matt added to his already considerable fortune.

But the greatest accolade of all came in June when he was made a life peer in the Queen's Birthday Honours, and took the title, Baron Ransom of Chudleigh in the County of Oxfordshire. A huge dinner was given in his honour in

London, graced by the prime minister, captains of industry, and other notables from business, the arts and entertainment.

In London they also celebrated their second wedding anniversary and Jenny's twenty-fifth birthday. She was beginning to feel old.

At the height of summer they returned to Chudleigh for a few weeks, inspected the two new horses Eric had bought, and threw a round of parties for people in the county. Of the family, only Maurice and Shirley came. Georgina had said she would come but didn't. Beth had joined a repertory company in the north of England and was trying to make up for lost time. She was getting on, too.

Jenny stood in the bathroom, the small pot containing amber liquid on the top of the table in front of her. She could have been a priestess officiating at the sacred mysteries. In a way she was. It was a solemn moment, fraught with consequences. Hand shaking slightly, she dipped the stick in the pot, left it for a few moments. She closed her eyes and wished. Six weeks since her last period. She was never late.

She opened her eyes and slowly removed the stick, examining it carefully in the light. Slightly pink – or was it? Her heartbeat quickened and she dipped the stick into the pot again and left it a good few minutes before withdrawing it, re-examining it, this time with the light on as an aid to the natural morning light. It was definitely pink. Well, pinkish.

She might, possibly, be pregnant.

She sat down on the stool and examined the stick again, turning it this way and that.

The instructions warned you of doubt in the early days.

She got up, threw the stick in the bin and her morning urine down the lavatory, flushed the bowl and went back to bed. Matt was lying on his side, fast asleep. She lay on her side, facing him, studying his relaxed features: he looked noble, handsome, maybe as a Roman emperor might have looked. She put her hand round his bare waist, and he stirred. As if aware of her gaze, his mouth puckered in a kiss, but his eyes didn't open.

'I love you,' he murmured.

'I love you.'

She left the hand on his waist, too excited to attempt to go back to sleep.

Later that day, she sat beside him in the back of the Jaguar, hands linked, as Peter drove them to the airport. It had been a busy morning getting ready. Dozens of things to do, faxes, telephone calls. All sorts of things. No time to tell Matt about the morning pregnancy test. Matt was off to Hong Kong for a week or ten days.

'Wish you were coming with me,' he said as the car devoured the miles on the M4, 'but you didn't want to.'

'I did,' she looked at him, 'but . . . '

'But what?'

'Well,' her hand tightened on his, 'I didn't want to tell you until you got back . . . but I think I might be pregnant.'

His eyes widened.

'Are you sure?'

'Not *sure*. I'm two weeks late with my period . . . I did the test this morning.'

'And?' She could see that, like her, he was trying to hold back his excitement.

'Well, the stick is supposed to go pink. You dip it in your pee. It went pink*ish* but not *quite* pink. Pink enough, I'd have thought.'

He bent towards her and kissed her cheek, gripping her hand hard. 'Wouldn't it be marvellous?'

'Marvellous,' she nodded, 'but I thought I'd just stay quiet here all the same.' She ran her hand through her hair. 'Besides, there is so much to do at Chudleigh still, Matt. Oh, and Matt, look, Eric isn't very comfortable at

258

the pub. I wondered if we could offer him the flat until we get someone?'

'What flat?'

'The flat upstairs that the couple had.'

'Well, I'll get a couple soon, especially if you're pregnant.' She could tell by his tone of voice he wasn't pleased.

'Yes, but until we do . . . '

'Do you think it's really a good thing,' he looked at her, 'to have him living in the house, especially at a time when I'm away?'

'Well, I don't see why not. If you mean what people might say – '

'Not just *that*.'

'You're still jealous of Eric, Matt, aren't you, and it's so absurd.'

'Well, wouldn't you be of a much younger man if you were me?'

'But I don't *want* a much younger man. I had lots of opportunities to have "much younger men", and I didn't. I wanted *you*.'

'Well,' he paused and looked uneasily out of the window, 'I don't really like it . . . '

'He hasn't much money. It's a way of helping. He won't take a salary or anything, and he has done an awful lot.'

'Yes, but he's benefited from it, Jenny, hasn't he? You haven't.'

'Oh, but I have. I love it. You remember what I said about achieving some independence? This helps me. It really does.'

'I'm not having you riding if you're pregnant.'

'I can still look after the horses. Darling, a purpose, a meaning to life besides everything else that I have: you, the house, perhaps a baby. It could be very full.'

'Well, if it makes you happy,' he said doubtfully. As they turned into the tunnel to Terminal Four, Matt leaned forward.

259

'Peter, you can just drop me off and take Lady Ransom straight home.'

'No,' she clasped his arm, 'I want to wave you off.'

'It's not necessary.'

'But I do.'

'OK. Peter, will you wait?'

'Of course, Lord Ransom. I'll pull over at the end of the terminal building, my lady.'

Matt always travelled light; a suitcase and a briefcase. A porter took his luggage and they followed him to the check-in. The airport was busy, frenetic, exciting, and Jenny half wished that, after all, she had decided to go with him.

They watched his baggage go, Matt checked his passport and tickets; then the call came for the plane for Hong Kong. They walked silently along the concourse and then stood by the barrier, looking at each other.

'I shall miss you,' he said, stooping to kiss her forehead.

'Me too.'

'Take care.'

'I will, and you.'

'Don't worry.'

'I won't worry.'

'The gynaecologist said not to worry.'

'I won't *worry*, I promise you.' She laughed and tapped the end of his nose with her finger.

'I wish I weren't going now.'

'I wish you weren't.'

They embraced briefly, and then he turned abruptly and went to the barrier, where he showed his passport and was immediately waved on by customs.

Long after he'd gone, Jenny still stood looking at the door through which he'd disappeared, and then turned slowly towards the exit.

Jenny sat at the window watching Eric put Clea through her paces. There was no doubt that Eric looked

260

tremendous on a horse; his fair hair flew over his head, his cheeks glowed with excitement. It was the same, she remembered, when he was skiing. He was a superb specimen of a man. It was no wonder, in a way, that poor Matt was jealous.

Jenny was tired, a little unhappy. Already she missed Matt, and she also had a sensation in her stomach, a bit like the forerunner of a period pain.

She'd been up early feeding and grooming the horses. She longed for a canter but didn't dare. Eric arrived soon after. They breakfasted together, looking at details of horse sales, the programme for the season. She didn't mention the possible pregnancy, and in the middle of breakfast Matt phoned. He'd just arrived in Hong Kong.

When Jenny got back to the breakfast room, Eric had gone and the cleaners were already busy with the day's chores.

Now it was mid-morning, and she was sitting by the window drinking coffee when, just behind Eric, she saw a tiny speck on the drive which, as it came nearer, turned out to be a red sports car with the top up. Eric took no notice of it, and the car continued its progress up the long drive until it arrived at the portico and stopped. She watched it with some interest, then the door opened and a very good-looking young man got out. He stood gazing round him and then, shading his eyes against the sun, watched Eric for some time before shutting the door and, glancing up at the house, running up the steps and pressing the doorbell. Jenny waited for one of the dailies to answer it, heard voices in the hall, and turned as the door of the drawing room opened.

'Mr Ransom, my lady,' Gladys said.

Mr Ransom?

'My goodness, you must be Philip.' She went towards the door, hand extended.

'Right first time.' His smile was charming. 'And you *must* be Jenny.'

'Yes, I'm Jenny.'

'You *are* indeed very beautiful.'

'Thank you.' A little taken aback by the candour, she gestured nervously to a chair. 'Would you like coffee?'

'I'd love it. Is Dad about?'

'He's in Hong Kong.'

'Oh, Hong Kong. For how long?'

'A week or so.'

'And you didn't go with him?'

'No I . . . ' she hesitated. 'There's so much to do here.'

'There's a lot to do.' Philip looked about him. 'It's funny to be in the old place again.'

'Do you miss it?'

'Not really.' He looked at her. 'You like living here?'

'I love it.' She paused. 'You are always *very* welcome to stay, as long as you like.'

'Thanks.' He stirred the coffee she'd given him. 'That would be nice. I say,' he jerked his head towards the window, 'who's that bloke riding the horse?'

'Eric Jorgensen, a very old friend of the family.'

'Of course, you're half-Swedish.'

'Yes.'

'Is he staying?'

'No. He's staying at The George in the village and looking for a house. We're in partnership. You know. Show jumping, eventing. Breeding thoroughbreds.'

'No. I didn't know.'

Philip seemed to find this information interesting, and continued to gaze out of the window. Then he got up and, cup in hand, wandered over to the window and continued to watch the rider.

'He's very good.'

'He is.' Jenny rose and stood beside him. 'He hopes to win some competitions.' She looked at him. 'Do you ride?'

'Oh yes. Love it.'

'Then you must come riding with us. Are you in England for long?'

'For keeps, I think.'

'Really?'

'My company have sent me here. I'm in computers, you know.'

'Yes, I know.'

'They're opening a branch in the City in an attempt to rival the Japanese.'

'That sounds most important.'

'It's interesting.'

'And you're staying . . . '

'With Mother in her little cottage.'

'Does she know you're here?'

'I said I was coming to see Father.'

'I thought she might know he was in Hong Kong.'

'I don't think the family talk to her too much about Father.' Philip turned slowly towards her. 'You can't blame her.'

'Of course not.'

She felt awkward and was glad of an interruption.

'More coffee, Lady Ransom?' Gladys put her head round the door.

'Is your friend coming in for coffee?' Philip asked.

'Call Mr Jorgensen, would you, Gladys?'

'Yes, Lady Ransom.'

'Why don't I go out and get him?' Philip moved towards the door. 'I'm sure this good lady has enough to do.'

Gladys nodded as if she agreed with him and, closely followed by Philip, left the room.

Jenny stood watching him as he sauntered along the drive, hands in his pockets – at ease; an English gentleman in an English country home. His home, really. Yet so far he seemed to like her, to accept her for what she was. Maybe if she acquitted herself well he would win over his brother and sisters. Philip could be a useful ally.

Seeing the visitor, Eric rode towards him. As he stopped his horse, Philip reached up and offered him his hand. Eric shook it and the two men immediately engaged in conversation for quite some time.

Almost, Jenny thought, until the coffee was cold.

CHAPTER 15

The Mapplington Horticultural Show had a reputation far beyond the original expectation of its founders. It had begun some time in the thirties, and attracted visitors not merely from the county but from all over England.

Held every July, its speciality was roses and, in the course of many years at Chudleigh seven miles away, Elspeth Ransom had become an expert on this beautiful, somehow typically English flower, and served on the committee of the show.

But for the last two years it had been an ordeal. Formerly it had been opened by Matt, and afterwards he, Elspeth, and other guests and notabilities would tour the exhibits. Elspeth was one of the rose judges; she also, as the wife of Matt, presented the prize to the winner of this section. Matt, as president of the show, presented the rest.

Like many other things they did together, this had fizzled out. After the divorce, Matt had resigned as president because he didn't want to embarrass Elspeth, to whom the show was so important. He had stepped down as well from numerous other local committees and societies, while Elspeth manfully struggled on, with a smile of forced cheerfulness, a typical display of that well-known English virtue – the stiff upper-lip.

Last year, the first since Matt's remarriage, she had wanted to stay in her shell, not to emerge and face the world, some of whom, rather than pointing the accusing finger at Matt, seemed to suggest that she was the one who, by some defect as a wife, had failed to hold her man.

For Elspeth the whole edifice of her life had crumbled. There was no firm religious faith to sustain her, although she dutifully attended church on the high feast days – Christmas, Easter and so on. She realised just how spiritually bankrupt she was, how slender her belief. But her comfort now was the family, especially Georgina, who nagged her mother into trying to make her life as normal as it had been before.

So, on with the annual Mapplington Show, where few guessed the extent of Elspeth's tormented mind. She looked well, she moved about serenely, always smiling, and when it came to judging the roses one was aware of her dedication, her knowledge, the expertise with which she examined every petal, inhaling the fragrance or sensing the lack of it in every bloom on show.

Finally she awarded the first prize to a new species grown by a local nurseryman, who came up to receive his rosette, face glowing with pleasure.

'Thank *you*, Lady Ransom.' He bowed as she pinned the rosette on his lapel and handed him a cup for the best rose of the show. They knew each other, and they had a brief chat about the technical qualities of rose-growing while the new chairman of the show, Colonel Hartley-Smythe, who had hastily been elected to succeed Matt, stood behind them looking important, a sheaf of papers in his hand.

Plump, grey hair topped with a straw hat, dressed in a silk floral-patterned summer dress and flat shoes, Elspeth looked the epitome of the typical English gentlewoman whose life was lived for good works and the well-being of her family. It seemed very wrong even to think of someone like that being let down, abandoned. But then, others suggested, you never knew what went on behind closed doors.

She shook hands with the nurseryman and turned to greet the chairman, who aligned himself next to her.

'Thank you very much, Lady Ransom.' He grasped the microphone and, unaccustomed to his role, spoke too loudly into it: 'And now I have a very special pleasure, one which it is an honour to perform.' He gazed at Elspeth above his half-moon spectacles. 'Lady Ransom, you have been on the committee of the Mapplington Horticultural Society for many years, and performed many remarkable services on its behalf. I don't think you have missed a show or a committee meeting in a dozen years and, as a judge of roses, you remain unsurpassed.'

Elspeth, blushing, was about to say something, but he held up his hand. 'It is therefore a particular pleasure to tell you that Jack Sprang has created a fragrant hybrid-tea which he has named in your honour. Jack, would you come forward?' The chairman beckoned to a local rose-grower who came slowly up to the platform, tenderly holding a shrub covered with a black plastic bag. He half stumbled on to the platform, was assisted up by Colonel Hartley-Smythe, who then helped him to remove the bag to reveal a beautiful deep yellow bloom which was just at its peak and which he now held out to Elspeth.

'I have named this rose Elspeth Ransom, in your honour, my lady.' He made a deep bow, began haltingly to say something, then lost his nerve and appealed to the colonel for help. Once again the colonel seized the microphone and spoke into it.

'Ladies and gentlemen, Lady Ransom, may *I* present the Elspeth Ransom, a rose specially developed in his nurseries by Jack Sprang, in honour of the chairman of the Rose Panel.'

A storm of applause broke out as Jack recovered his composure sufficiently to hand the bush to Elspeth who, equally confused, planted a clumsy kiss on his cheek. They both hastily set to examining the rose, discussing its finer points in great detail while the audience clapped, it seemed, for hours.

At the back of the hall, Henry and Georgina clapped as hard as anyone, and when Elspeth finally stumbled from the platform, they came up to her to offer their congratulations, Henry taking the rose from her while other people clustered round to shake her hand.

'What a lovely surprise . . . a great honour, my very own rose, like Elizabeth Taylor or Ena Harkness.' Elspeth, overcome with joy, seemed paradoxically also close to tears, and alternately sniffed the rose clasped in Henry's hand, or greeted some well-wisher waiting patiently in the queue.

'My very *own* rose,' she murmured again. 'What a *lovely* idea. I couldn't think of anything nicer.'

'You deserve it, Mother.' Georgina kissed her warmly on the cheek. 'Shall Henry put it in the car for you?'

'Isn't he coming back with us?'

'He's very tired, Mum.'

'I thought he was limping badly today.' Elspeth's expression of joy turned to one of concern.

'That's what I want to talk to you about,' Georgina lowered her voice, and Elspeth's happiness was once again clouded by apprehension. All too often this happened to her these days.

'Is he all right?'

'He just wants to get home. I'm sure you understand.'

'Of course.'

Georgina, who had been shopping in Oxford, had picked her mother up while Henry had made his own way in the Landrover. Henry was also an official of the horticultural show, chairman of the Young Farmers' branch, and an expert on judging cabbages and Brussels sprouts.

Tea was served in the marquee, which protected the participants from a sudden downpour. It had been a typically English midsummer day of sunshine and showers, but most of the events had managed to be held out of doors.

Finally, with Henry still hanging on to the slightly wilting rose, Elspeth and Georgina, their arms full of flowers, slowly made their way to the car, while well-wishers still pressed about Elspeth, showering her with their continued congratulations and good wishes.

Henry saw them to the car, carefully put 'Elspeth Ransom' in the boot along with the flowers and various items of produce they had bought from the stalls.

'Sure you'll be all right?' he asked.

'Sure *you'll* be all right, Henry dear?' His mother-in-law put her hand on his arm and looked up at him anxiously. 'Georgina says you've been in a lot of pain.'

'I'm OK,' he insisted, but his face was wan. 'I just thought I'd get home and put the leg up.'

'Albert doing the milking . . . ?'

'Well – ' he paused and looked at Georgina – 'we've sold the herd.'

'You've . . . ?'

'Last week.' Georgina nodded and looked agonisingly at Henry. 'It's what I wanted to talk to you about, Mother.'

'You and Georgina go and have a good natter.' Henry leaned forward and kissed her. 'She'll explain everything.'

He shut the door, stood back and waved, leaning heavily on his stick. Elspeth realised then how much Henry seemed to have aged. She'd been too wrapped up in her own woes to notice. Not only was he very thin, but his face had an unhealthy pallor not associated with the lifestyle of a farmer. Always thin on top, he was also getting increasingly bald.

'Henry looks *much* older,' Elspeth said as Georgina carefully reversed the car and then drove out of the field, waving to the man at the gate who had helped direct her. 'He really never got over that accident, did he? Are you sure they're doing all they can?'

'Well they say they are.' Looking thoughtful Georgina drove into the minor road which would take them past Chudleigh to Stanfield village. Elspeth settled back in the passenger seat.

'Well, what did you want to talk to me about?'

'I thought we'd wait until we got home.'

'That bad?'

'Well, not bad . . . At least, I don't think it's bad.'

She fell silent, observing from the corner of her eyes that Elspeth had her eyes turned to the right as their old home, standing well back from the road, became visible through the trees.

'I wanted to avoid this way,' Georgina murmured, 'but it's quicker.'

'Oh, I don't mind. I often drive past. One has to, or one would for ever be taking detours. I just never go in.'

'Do you ever want to?' Georgina looked in the mirror then glanced at her mother.

'No. Never. Fortunately all the roses were removed to my new garden. I still miss the house, though – or rather I miss the life we used to have.'

'It's inevitable, Mum.'

'Was it?' Georgina sensed her stiffen. 'What right did he have to do it? That's what I ask myself.'

Georgina didn't reply but kept her eyes on the road.

'Mum, one in three marriages, or something, ends in divorce. It's a huge statistic, and it often happens to middle-aged couples. I sometimes think the education system should be changed to prepare people for the fact that their parents might not always stay together; that women and men, but especially women, might eventually find themselves on their own.'

'But if people were prepared for it, we'd always be on our guard.'

'Well, maybe we should be. Then the shock wouldn't be so bad.'

'You can't spend your life "on guard",' Elspeth retorted indignantly. 'Your father and I were married in the old days when vows were exchanged in church and meant something.'

'But that's just it, Mum, they didn't. By the "old days", you're talking about the fifties. They were not the "old days", they are post-war, modern. What happened to Dad has happened to a lot of men . . . '

'I hope that's not what you're going to tell me about you and Henry,' Elspeth retorted, almost discouraging a confidence.

'Well, here we are, anyway.' Heart sinking, Georgina drove up the drive of Stanfield Manor, past the house and on to the cottage which was about two hundred yards away, finally coming to a halt outside the pretty front door surrounded by climbing roses and clematis.

'It *is* a lovely place,' Georgina exclaimed, sitting back. 'You must be very happy here, Mum.' She gestured towards the big house. 'So nice to have Maurice and Shirley next door.'

'I hardly ever see Maurice,' Elspeth said plaintively. 'Now he's talking about a flat in London. Of course, Matt should have left him in charge at Oxford. The journey every day to the City and back tires him. I think it was a way of Matt bribing Maurice, tying him to his apron strings. He has done all he can to alienate my children from me.' Elspeth's voice broke into a sob. '*That's* what I can't forgive.'

'Oh Mum, that is not true . . . '

'When he first married that woman you all said you'd never go near them. Now you're a regular visitor.'

'Not quite – ' Georgina began defensively, but her mother interrupted her.

'Philip and your father *never* got on, but now Philip stays with them in London *and* at Chudleigh, when I'm only a few miles away.'

'I think Dad wants to make amends.'

'Amends for what?'

'Well, for what happened with Philip, for breaking up the family which he knows he has. He does feel guilty. He does feel responsible.'

'Good. That doesn't help me though, does it?'

'No, because you will never agree to meet Jenny.'

'And she would never want to meet me! Imagine the two of us on either side of Matt. Beauty and the beast . . . ' Elspeth flung back her head and her body shook with artificial laughter which turned suddenly and predictably into tears.

'Oh, Mum, please . . . ' Georgina put her arm round her and bent over.

'I'm sorry,' Elspeth hastily wiped her eyes. 'I didn't *mean* that to happen. I didn't *plan* it. I'm all over the place you see, at sixes and sevens. One day I'm OK. The next day I feel awful. I never know what to expect. Up one minute, down the next.'

'Have you seen the doctor?'

'He says there's nothing clinically wrong. I know that. He's given me a mild tranquilliser, sleeping pills, but you know how scared doctors now are of prescribing these things. Besides, *I* don't want to get addicted either.' Elspeth sniffed, seemed to feel better, produced a handkerchief and gave her nose a good blow. 'No, I accept that it is a difficult time and one which I must make every effort to get over by myself. And I shall. Now, darling . . . ' She wiped her eyes, blew her nose robustly again, and turned to Georgina. 'Let's have another cup of tea, or maybe it's time for a sherry?'

'Time for a sherry, I think.' Georgina gave her a broad smile and opened the door.

It took a few minutes to unload all the stuff they had in the boot. Shirley appeared by the side of the car and offered to help.

'Had a good day?' she asked, kissing her mother-in-law.

'Lovely. They named a *rose* after me!' Elspeth looked out from the boot of the car and proudly held it up. 'Look: "Elspeth Ransom".'

'Oh, but it's beautiful.' Shirley leaned forward to inhale its fragrance.

'Such an honour,' Elspeth said, pleased, her tears forgotten. 'Are you going to come in for a drink, Shirley?'

271

'No, thanks,' Shirley shook her head. 'I've just put the dinner on. Maurice will be late again, and then he's off first thing in the morning to Edinburgh.'

'Oh, that's too bad!' Elspeth closed the boot with a bang that seemed to imply overwhelming disapproval. 'He's overworked.'

'Oh, he seems all right. I think he's a workaholic, like his father.'

'Matt always knew how to enjoy himself as well,' Elspeth began, and then, as if aware of the *double entendre*, stopped herself.

'Give him our love,' Georgina called from the doorstep, arms laden, 'we don't see enough of him or you. Try and come over.'

'I will.' Shirley stood back as Elspeth joined Georgina, and together they went into the pretty sitting room with its chintz-covered sofa and armchairs and dumped their things. 'Elspeth Ransom' was carefully stood on a table. The evening sun was just disappearing over the trees, and it was a very peaceful, tranquil scene, the air pungent with the scent of flowers coming in through the open window from the garden.

'Oh, that's nice.' Elspeth sank on to the sofa, removed her hat and kicked off her shoes. 'I don't think I sat down all afternoon. You know, I wish Shirley would give up work.'

'Why?' Georgina was pouring two large sherries from a decanter on the sideboard.

'So that she can be a good wife to Maurice.'

'But I think she *is* a good wife to Maurice.'

'Oh, I suppose I'm old-fashioned.'

'A bit, Mum.' Georgina gave her mother her glass and sat down next to her. 'I've always been a working wife – '

'That's different being a farmer's wife.' Elspeth gazed sideways at her. 'Now, what's this about selling the herd? Has it got anything to do with what you want to tell me?'

'A lot.' Georgina also kicked off her shoes and curled her

feet under her on the sofa. 'You know Henry hasn't been at all well. He never recovered properly from the accident. We've seen doctors, we've seen specialists, and they think he's about as well as he ever will be. He may even deteriorate if he gets arthritis in the leg, and his memory isn't good.'

'Oh dear!' Elspeth, crestfallen, ran a hand over her face. 'That *is* depressing news.'

'Well, we have to be practical. We have to face up to it, the situation as it is. We got quite a nice sum from the insurance, and we have decided . . . to start a new life.'

'A what?' Elspeth looked at her uncomprehendingly. 'What do you mean "a new life"?'

'A new life – you know. Go somewhere different, maybe abroad.'

'Abroad?' Elspeth looked aghast.

'Spain or France. We fancy Spain for the climate and it's cheaper.'

'Spain!' Elspeth echoed in the same strangulated tone.

'Well, Mum, it's not the other side of the world.'

'I can't believe this. And no word to me . . . '

'Well, we didn't want to say anything until we were sure. Last week we sold the herd . . . '

'Does your father know?'

'Er, yes,' Georgina ventured cautiously.

'Oh, of course he would. You *would* tell him first.'

'I didn't tell him, Mum, Maurice told him.'

'Oh, Maurice knows too. I see. The whole family knows, I expect.'

'Mum . . . we knew you would be very upset.'

'Yes, I am upset. Upset to be the last to know.'

'That's not the point, Mum.'

'Well, what is the point?'

'We know you've had a rough time. This might seem like the last straw.'

Elspeth was silent for a moment, finishing her sherry. Then she rose and poured herself another before turning to face her daughter.

'Yes, it does. It *is* the final straw. Do you think I'll see you often if you live in Spain? No, I shan't. I shan't see my grandchildren grow up . . . '

'Oh yes you will. They're remaining here at boarding school, and you can come over to see us often. We thought Alicante or even the Balearics – you know, Majorca. It's not decided, Mum. It's not settled. Only, as Henry feels he no longer has the energy or even the will to farm, he might as well give up.'

'And what will he do?'

'Well,' Georgina shrugged, 'nothing.'

'You mean retire? He's only thirty-five.'

'Thirty-six,' Georgina corrected her.

'Thirty-six is still very young for retirement.'

'Oh, he'll potter. We got a good sum from the insurance; we hope to get a lot for the farm. We both have a bit of money put by, and Dad says he'll help anyway with the school fees. They're taken care of.'

'Oh, I bet Dad will help,' Elspeth said with a snort. 'Anything to get in your good books. No doubt he and "that woman" will be frequent visitors to Spain, too.'

'Oh Mummy, please try not to be bitter.' Georgina leaned over and kissed her. '*That's* why I didn't want to tell you. I knew it would be an ordeal.'

'I just feel all the family are ganging up against me, isolating me.'

'That's not true. It's not a *bit* true.'

'That's what it feels like to me. I'm an appendage, an outcast. I don't belong any more.'

'Mummy, we all love you, we want you, we need you. But we also have to lead our own lives.'

'Of course you do. I'm not saying you don't.'

'Why don't you come and live in Spain too?' Georgina said suddenly.

'Are you mad?' Elspeth looked at her.

'It's an idea; not with us, but near us. Why don't you come over and have a look while we look for property?

then you wouldn't be very far away. Not with us but near us. Just as we are now. You could start a new life, Mummy, like us.'

'Not with us but near us.'

The phrase haunted Elspeth through the evening after she had waved Georgina off. Even going back into the house after her departure made it seem desperately empty. She had another sherry, her third, made it quite large, then after a couple of sips she topped up the glass. She wasn't a drinker, but today she felt like drinking. She'd been holding back, holding herself in for so long. Being noble about Matt, magnanimous about the house, brave about Philip preferring the glamour of St John's Wood and Chudleigh to staying with her. She had always been smiling, cheerful, composed, someone who could cope.

Did people know that, inside, her heart bled continuously? Still?

People admired her, she was sure; but she didn't want that sort of admiration. She hadn't had it before. She wasn't admired for being Matt's wife; but she was for being his 'ex'. It was the sort of admiration in which pity was the main component. In all the time she had been the jolly, cheerful, outgoing chairman of the Rose Panel of the Horticultural Society, they had never thought to name a rose after her. They never would have, but for the fact that she'd been abandoned. 'Elspeth Ransom'. It was a pretty name for a lovely flower, now standing, a little the worse for wear, on the kitchen table, its noble head drooping a little, like hers. She went over to the tap, drew water into a jug and watered it carefully. She needed a drink and poor 'Elspeth Ransom', her namesake, needed one too.

She took her drink back into the sitting room, realising she was feeling a little bit drunk, light-headed, but not happy. Definitely not happy.

Drink made you maudlin, everyone knew that. She slumped into a chair and gazed about her: empty. The room was empty, her life was empty. At one time she never had a free moment; now she had too many.

And the thought that Georgina, her bulwark, her rock, would even contemplate uprooting herself and her family and leaving her mother: it was like an act of treachery, making her more alone, more isolated than even before.

Georgina and Henry abroad, Maurice caught up in his business, his wife, and soon, perhaps, the first baby. Beth doing rep in Nottingham, Philip starting an exciting new life in London. Matt about to be a father for the fifth time. That woman . . . well it didn't do even to think of her.

Elspeth went into the kitchen and carefully put away all the things they had bought: the pots of home-made marmalade, honey and strawberry jam, the cake which she would give to Shirley tomorrow, the home-grown peas, cabbages, marrows and cauliflower; the pots of herbs – she had plenty already – and, finally, she looked at the rose 'Elspeth Ransom' and burst into tears.

Poor Elspeth. Tomorrow she would find a home for it, a place of honour in the rose garden. Eventually she dried her tears and sat at the kitchen table looking morosely at the rose.

She glanced at the kitchen clock and was surprised to see it was nearly nine. She hadn't eaten, but she wasn't hungry. She did, though, feel she needed another drink, and refilled her glass to the brim with sherry. Was this her fourth or fifth? She stared at the glass, feeling decidedly muddle-headed. Well, who cared? She tossed half of it back. She went, a little unsteadily, into the sitting room, turned on the TV and realised she had missed the news headlines. Well, she didn't want to see it anyway; all the gloomy news about the economy and refugees in Somalia no one could do anything about, certainly not her.

She turned it off and sat, glass in hand, staring at the blank screen.

What would she *do* without Georgina? They saw each other almost daily. She was fond of Shirley, but Shirley still worked at the hospital and was out all day, or most days. How could Georgina contemplate doing such a thing when she knew how much it would hurt her?

Why, Georgina didn't care. None of them really cared. She had no place, no function any more.

No one would care if she died.

She went upstairs and drew back the covers of her bed. Sat there for a long time, staring at the floor. She realised she was losing control and must pull herself together. She had been depressed before in the past three years, but had felt nothing quite as bad as this. It was the sheer emptiness of her life that appalled her.

She opened the bedside drawer and took out her bottle of tranquillisers. It had one of those difficult caps and she nearly couldn't unscrew it, feeling so awkward, all fingers and thumbs. Finally she did, and in the act the bottle overturned and some of them fell on to the floor. She sat staring at them and realised she was rather drunk. Very drunk, perhaps. Four or five, maybe six, large sherries and nothing to eat. She shut one eye and studied the label on the bottle. NOT TO BE TAKEN WITH ALCOHOL. Well, she would just take one or two. It would steady her, although probably tomorrow she would have a frightful hangover.

She undressed unsteadily, frequently pausing to sit on the bed and stare. Then she went into the bathroom, combed her hair, cleansed her face and brushed her teeth. She sat on the end of the bath for a while, looking at the tub.

She felt very strange, like someone in a trance, but actually better. It was quite pleasant. She went back into the bedroom, took off her gown and got into bed.

But Georgina going away. It was too awful. How could she contemplate it? It was an act of treachery; terribly, terribly cruel. She thought she was sobering up and decided to take a sleeping pill. Maybe another tranquilliser as well, and perhaps a couple of sleeping pills — two or three. One could so easily lose count.

She tipped the bottle and shoved a handful into her mouth.

It was still dark. Not quite five. The alarm had gone off at four. Maurice hadn't wanted her to get up but she had insisted. Besides, as a nurse, Shirley was used to what were called 'unsociable hours'.

He wouldn't have breakfast. That he would have on the plane, but first there was the drive to the airport, so he agreed to have a cup of tea.

She saw him to the door and, before opening it, he kissed her. She was still rubbing the sleep out of her eyes. Maurice ran down the steps with his briefcase in one hand, suitcase in the other.

'I should have gone to see Mother last night,' he called from the bottom step. 'Tell her I got in late, will you?'

'Don't worry.' She waved and blew another kiss, then she looked over towards the cottage, half obscured by the trees, and saw that a light was on in Elspeth's bedroom. Maybe she'd gone to spend a penny.

Maurice started the car, his arm fluttered from the window. She waited there until he drove out of the gates and then she looked across at the cottage again.

Silly to be alarmist. But Elspeth's moods recently had worried her. She seemed to be trying just that bit too hard to behave as though nothing had happened; frequently Shirley had seen the mask slip, and knew that she was still suffering. Always bright, always cheerful, never complaining. It was unnatural. Sometimes you wished the woman would just sit down and have a good weep, howl maybe. Well, perhaps she did. Perhaps she was doing that now.

Shirley went back to the bedroom and, undecided, sat on the side of the bed. Her hand went towards the telephone. But if Elspeth was asleep, if she'd fallen asleep

278

with the light on, the phone at five in the morning would scare her to death. What else could it be besides bad news?

She looked out of the window. The light was still on. Dawn was just breaking in the eastern sky, and it was going to be another lovely day.

Shirley hurried across the room, along the corridor, back down the stairs and into the kitchen where, in a cupboard, they kept a spare key to the cottage. Then she went out of the kitchen, across the yard to the back of the cottage.

She let herself in by the back door and listened.

All was still: Elspeth must have fallen asleep over a book. Yet she didn't remember seeing the light on when they went to bed, quite late because Maurice was late back. The last thing they always did when they drew their own curtains was to look over the lawn to Elspeth's house. Maybe last night, because they were so late and had to be up early, they'd forgotten.

Shirley went through the kitchen, along the corridor and stood at the bottom of the stairs. She could see the beam of light from Elspeth's room illuminating the landing.

Despite her training as a nurse, her alleged nerves of steel, she felt apprehensive and quickly mounted the stairs. When she got to the top she could see straight into Elspeth's room. Elspeth was lying in bed, looking as though she was fast asleep, as she was, but on her lap was a bottle of pills, some of the contents of which had spilt on to her bed and on to the floor.

'EX WIFE OF PEER IN APPARENT SUICIDE ATTEMPT'

The fifty-seven-year-old ex-wife of Lord Ransom of Chudleigh, the wealthy industrialist, was rushed to hospital in the early hours of yesterday morning after being found in a coma by her daughter-in-law Mrs Shirley Ransom.

Mrs Ransom had been worried that her mother-in-law's bedroom light was on at five in the morning when she saw her husband,

Maurice, the Ransoms' elder son, off to the airport. On investigation she discovered Lady Ransom and called an ambulance. Mrs Ransom is a
nursing sister, and it is probably due to her prompt
action in resuscitation that Lady Ransom's life
was saved, though she remains in a critical condition.

Police who are investigating the incident gave
no indication that a note had been found. Lady
Ransom's children and her ex-husband went immediately to the Radcliffe Hospital where Lady
Ransom remains in intensive care.

Lady Ransom divorced Lord Ransom two years
ago, whereupon he immediately married a beautiful half-Swedish woman, Jenny Holstrom,
daughter of a wealthy shipowner who is thirty-
four years his junior.

The whole family is said to be very upset by the
incident, which was totally unexpected.

Lady Ransom was seen in apparently good
spirits earlier in the day at a horticultural show
where she was presented with a rose named after
her.

Jenny put down the paper and sat for a long time staring in
front of her. How Matt would hate this. How she hated it.
He had been called by Shirley from the hospital and had
immediately gone to Oxford. For a time Elspeth was not
expected to live, but began to revive after her stomach was
pumped out, which was found to contain a near-lethal
mixture of drink, tranquillisers and sleeping pills. Maurice
received the news on the plane to Edinburgh, and turned
round as soon as he arrived. Beth had been summoned
from Nottingham, and Philip had gone with his father.
They had both been staying in the London apartment.
Georgina went to the hospital after being called by Shirley.

The only one not wanted in this drama was her, the
guilty, second wife, the seductress. Somehow, she realised

now, in the back of her mind, she'd always been frightened something like this would happen: that in a trice, in a moment, her happiness would be destroyed.

Matt had sounded so strained relaying the news on the phone, almost as though he'd been accusing her.

And how did she feel now that she knew for certain the effect the break-up had had on Elspeth? Had guessed at, certainly, but now knew for sure.

Had she tried to blind herself? What did other people do? How could you cushion grief?

Do unto others as you would have them do unto you.

Jenny put the paper down and crossed the room. She leaned out of the window. Eric, who had now moved into the house, was practising his jumps and when he saw her he waved. Listlessly she waved back. He completed the round, then left the ring and came cantering over to her.

'Any more news?' he shouted.

'Come in and have some coffee?'

'Well,' Eric hesitated, then nodded. 'OK, I'll just take her back to the stables. I'll be over in ten minutes.'

'Fine. I'll put the percolator on.'

Jenny felt restless, unhappy. She went into the kitchen, which was immaculate as always. From upstairs she could hear the sound of hoovering.

She filled the percolator and plugged it in, then stood for a while watching while the water began to bubble vigorously.

She fetched two cups and saucers, put them on a tray, got some biscuits out of a tin.

After a few minutes the back door opened and Eric came in, wiping his boots on the coconut mat.

'I don't think they're too dirty.'

'It doesn't matter,' she shrugged and unplugged the percolator.

'Here, let me,' Eric said going over to the tray.

'You take the percolator, I'll bring the tray,' he said to her.

Jenny led the way, kicking the kitchen door open to let Eric precede her along the unlit hall to the drawing room.

'It's a beautiful day,' Eric said cheerfully, putting the tray down on a table.

'Huh! You can say that again.' Jenny closed the door behind them and put the percolator carefully on the tray.

Silently she poured the coffee, handed Eric a cup and the plate of biscuits. He took the cup but shook his head to the biscuits. 'I really am terribly sorry, Jenny. I mean, for you. It's an awful situation.'

'Did you see this?' Jenny held out the paper and Eric took it and started to read.

'And that's only one paper,' Jenny said. 'God knows what's in the others. You know what the tabloids are. I think Elspeth's crazy. You must be crazy to do something like that.'

'You're sure it was a suicide attempt?' Eric looked up from the paper as Jenny shook her head.

'They don't know. She's still unconscious but coming round. But there was no note.'

'So I see. Oh well . . . ' He put down the paper, went over to her and took her arm. 'It's not your fault, Jenny.'

'It's just so bloody awful,' she said, sinking on to the sofa. 'Matt feels terrible. The family dislike me enough already.'

'I thought they were beginning to like you. Besides, it's hardly your fault. You and Matt have been married two years.'

'Exactly. It's more the fault of Georgina, who apparently told her mother the day she . . . did this that she and her husband were emigrating to Spain.'

'To Spain?'

'Well, you know the husband hasn't been well. He was injured on the farm. The farm's too much for him. Georgina said her mother was very upset, and she noticed she was drinking, which she doesn't usually do. Georgina left around six, so they can only surmise that Elspeth spent the evening brooding. Maurice was supposed to go and see her and didn't. He was flying to Scotland the next day, said he'd say goodbye but he got home late; too late, he thought, to disturb her. It does *look* like attempted suicide, I'm afraid. What the effect on Matt will be I can't think. You know – ' she gazed reflectively at Eric – 'it's sort of like a time-bomb that's been ticking away. In a way I'm relieved that at last it's exploded.'

'You mean you expected something like this to happen?'

'No, because I never really knew Elspeth, but I suppose I always felt guilty, wondering how she felt. You must have a terrific degree of selfishness, you know, to take away another woman's husband.'

She finished drinking and suddenly put her head in her hands. Eric swallowed his coffee, replaced his cup, and then came and sat next to her.

'If he was out of love with Elspeth . . . '

'He did chase me. He pursued me. I was weak.'

'You were very young.'

'Then I desperately wanted this house.' She screwed back her hair with both her hands so that her knuckles showed white. 'Maybe that's what triggered it all off. Oh, if only we could undo the past . . . '

'Well, we can't.' Eric put a hand on her shoulder. 'Not every abandoned wife tries to kill herself; most adjust to it. Jenny, it's a part of everyday life . . . '

'Ask yourself how you'd like it,' Jenny murmured, as if she wasn't listening to him. 'I never did that.'

'Would it have been any different if you had?'

'I don't know. I guess if I thought at all I felt the guilt lay with Matt. But, truthfully, I didn't think.' She paused and then she said, 'I think, I hope, I'm pregnant. If I am, if it's confirmed, it will help Matt get through this.'

'That's terrific news.'

'But maybe if I am pregnant it will only make things worse for Elspeth.

'Whatever happens, our lives can never be the same again.'

CHAPTER 16

Matt opened his eyes wide, jerked awake by he didn't know quite what: a noise, a dream? He lay blinking in the dark, then put out his hand to feel the space next to him: empty. He could hear vague noises from the bathroom.

It was unusual for Jenny to get up in the middle of the night, though not for him. He usually felt the call of nature in the small hours of the morning, but it never seemed to disturb Jenny, who was a sound sleeper.

He lay for a few moments, listening to the sounds coming from the bathroom, aware of that sense of depression that had afflicted him on first waking ever since Elspeth's foolish act. It had turned his family upside down, and Jenny not least of all. The excessive concentration of the family on Elspeth had made Jenny feel isolated, neglected. Matt felt too that their relationship had changed, even though he tried so hard to reassure her that he loved her as much as ever.

Did he? He scratched his head in the dark. Yes, of course he did. No agonising on behalf of Elspeth could diminish that. Agonising, but also rage, anger. By overdosing, whether deliberately or not, she had turned the tables on them all; made herself, inevitably, the pivot, the centre of attention.

But it had also made him aware of divided loyalties. The children blamed him, and society blamed him, thanks to the tabloids, which were having a field day.

Jenny was a long time in the bathroom. He put on the bedside light and looked at the clock. Ten to three. A terrible time. The worst time of night.

'You all right?' he called.

No reply.

He swung his legs out of bed, sat on the side for a moment rubbing his eyes, and went over to the bathroom.

'Are you all right, darling?' he called, knocking at the door. At the same time he turned the knob and pushed the door gently open.

'Oh my God!'

Jenny was sitting on the floor, her head propped against the side of the lavatory, blood streaming from between her legs.

'Jenny!' Aghast Matt went into the room, crossed the floor and knelt beside her. 'Darling . . . '

'It's OK,' she said weakly. 'I'm OK.'

Matt's head sank on to his chest. 'I'll get a doctor . . . '

'No need,' she pointed to the lavatory pan.

'You saw . . . ?'

'Nothing to see. Just like a heavy period. Could you pass me the towel, Matt, please?' She pointed to the towel rail and Matt clambered to his feet and passed her a thick bath towel which she put between her legs.

'I'm so terribly sorry, Matt . . . '

'Not *your* fault, Jenny. Not your fault.' He knelt beside her again and began gently to stroke her brow. 'Are you in pain?'

'Just a few cramps. I felt this pain in bed and rushed to the bathroom.' She began apathetically to rub herself with the towel. 'I'll be OK, Matt, but please leave me. I want to get tidied up. All this bloody mess . . . '

'Darling, don't worry about that. It's you. I'll go and ring Dr Hardy.'

'There's no need to fuss. There's nothing he can do. Maybe a cup of tea?'

'I'll go and make one straight away, darling. Sure you don't want me to call . . . ?'

'I don't want you to call *anybody*.' There was a note of irritation in her voice.

Matt went down the stairs to the kitchen, switching on the lights as he went. He filled the kettle, and plugged it in. He heard a sound behind him and turned to find Eric knotting the cord of his dressing gown.

'Is anything wrong, Matt? I was reading and thought I heard a noise.'

'Jenny's had a miscarriage.'

'Oh my God! Is she OK?'

'She says she is.' The kettle boiled and Matt stood there helplessly, not knowing what to do, where to find things. The geography of the kitchen was, to him, like a strange land.

'Tea bags?' Eric said helpfully, opening a cupboard. 'Would you like me to do it for you while you go back to Jenny?'

'No thanks,' Matt said coolly, watching him drop two bags into a pot he had produced from a shelf. 'You do know your way around, don't you?'

'Jenny's very good. The kitchen in the flat is very basic. I like to cook.'

'I see.' Matt watched him produce milk, sugar. Obviously a man completely at home in his surroundings.

He leaned against a bench watching Eric as, finally, he put a cosy on the pot.

'I want to call the doctor, but she says she's OK. She says,' he swallowed, 'it was like a normal period.'

'Of course.' Eric looked vaguely embarrassed, discussing these womanly things with someone he scarcely knew. 'Is there anything else I can do?'

'Nothing.' Matt prepared to take the tray. 'But thanks for asking.'

'You're quite sure?'

'Quite sure.' Matt felt a bit irritated. 'Oh, you could switch off the lights after me as you go upstairs.'

286

'Of course. And my best to Jenny, Matt.'

'Thanks.'

Matt made his way up to the bedroom, again feeling vaguely annoyed about the intrusion of the unwelcome guest.

When he got to the bedroom, Jenny was lying between the sheets looking pale but composed. She had put on a clean nightie and looked gratefully at Matt as he carefully put the tray by the side of the bed.

'Thank you, darling.' But seeing his frown as he put the tray down she went on: 'Did you find everything OK?'

'Eric came down,' he said. '*He* knew where everything was all right.'

'Oh, he does. He's very domesticated.'

Matt poured the tea and handed her a cup. Then he sat heavily down on the bed beside her, and gazed anxiously at her.

'I'm so sorry, darling.'

'*I'm* sorry.'

Jenny gratefully finished drinking her tea, handed the cup back to him, and lay back with her head resting on the pillow.

Matt returned the cup to the tray and took her hand.

'It wasn't your fault . . . '

'I'm sorry that . . . ' Tears began to run down her cheeks. Almost angrily she brushed them aside. 'Sorry that, well, you wanted it so badly.'

'It isn't the end of the world.' Yet he sounded defeated, unconvincing, his voice curiously lacking conviction. He did, in fact feel extremely disheartened, let down, as if in some way Jenny had failed him. His hand tightened over hers. 'Never mind. The main thing is that you get well. It isn't as if children are the be all and end all of life. We all know that.' Grimly he removed his gown, switched off the main lights in the room, and climbed into bed beside her. He lay there for some time staring at the ceiling, hands laced across his stomach. 'What a bloody *awful* time we're having just now. Elspeth scarcely out of the wood and now you.' He turned his head and studied her pale face. 'You're sure you *were* pregnant?'

'Not *completely* sure.'

'You never saw the doctor?'

'I made an appointment for next week. Now it won't be necessary.'

She felt tears, just below the surface, well up inside her again, but tried to keep them at bay. She wanted Matt to take her in his arms and comfort her. But maybe he didn't know how. She was a good-time girl, a trophy wife, and they were not expected to experience failure, pain or disappointment.

Abruptly he put out the light and lay as he had been on his back, sighing deeply.'

'You OK, Jen?'

'Yes.'

''Night.'

''Night, Matt. I'm terribly sorry.'

There was no reply, and after a few minutes she could hear the deep, regular breathing that always signalled sleep.

Suddenly she was aware that a gulf had opened between herself and her husband. She felt isolated, alone . . . and a little afraid.

Dr Hardy entered the drawing room, put his case on the floor and took the chair indicated by Matt.

'Drink, Doctor?'

'No, thanks.' The doctor held up his hand. 'Not while on my rounds.'

'How is my wife?' Matt didn't think this stricture applied to him, helped himself to a whisky, and went and took a chair opposite the doctor.

'As far as I can tell, she's fine. One can't examine too thoroughly in this condition, but I ran the rule over her and she seems perfectly all right. Of course, a woman the age of your wife would miscarry quite naturally, just as if it were a normal period; that is if it *were* a miscarriage, and not just a heavy period.'

'How do you mean "if it were a miscarriage"?'

'Well, did she really know she was pregnant?'

'Well, she said she was.' Matt's tone was irritable. 'She tested herself. Look, I know nothing about these things.' His irritation seemed to grow.

'A pregnancy kit. Yes she told me.' The doctor nodded thoughtfully.

'We didn't have that kind of thing when my older children were conceived.' Matt sounded peevish.

'No, it was a long time ago, Lord Ransom. A very different age. Usually these kits are quite reliable. I understand anyway, she was coming next week to see me.'

'She could have been mistaken?' Matt looked at him suspiciously.

'Well, she could have been. She told me she wasn't sure. It could be she was just at the beginning of a pregnancy and the fertilised egg, lodged in the lining of the womb, didn't take.'

'My first wife had absolutely no trouble in conceiving. Just the opposite, in fact. Look, Doctor, will Jenny ever be able to carry a baby full term?' Matt stretched his legs before him and studied the doctor as though he were interviewing him for an executive position in his company.

'I don't see why not.'

'We have been married for over two years, and trying for eighteen months.'

'Sometimes it does take that long, or longer.' Dr Hardy appeared slightly nervous. 'Why don't I arrange another appointment with Mr Vernon? You are very keen to have a baby, aren't you, Lord Ransom?'

'Yes, I am. I'm used to families.' Matt swept out an arm. 'I want to fill this house with children as it used to be. I have not had an easy time, you know, Dr Hardy, and this business with my ex-wife is . . . ghastly.' He shook his head.

'An accidental overdose, I understand?'

'So she says,' Matt nodded. Hardy was a new man to the area, and not Elspeth's doctor. 'You see, you don't know the truth about anything, do you?'

'How do you mean?' Dr Hardy was by now thoroughly confused.

'I don't know if Elspeth meant to kill herself, and I now don't know if Jenny meant to deceive me into thinking she was pregnant because she knew I wanted her to be.'

'Well,' Dr Hardy's head started to buzz, 'I can't help you, I'm afraid, especially about the first Lady Ransom. As for your present wife . . . I imagine she wouldn't *want* to deceive you. The whole thing seems perfectly straight-forward to me. Many women, of all ages, miscarry in the early months of pregnancy.'

'Jenny might have pretended, to please me.'

Dr Hardy scratched his head. 'I'm sure she wouldn't. She told me she wanted a baby very much. I don't see why she should attempt to deceive you, or raise your hopes for no reason.'

'I suppose you're right.' Matt shrugged, got to his feet and the doctor did too. 'It's one of those things. Well, thank you, Doctor. I'm sorry you've been troubled.'

'No trouble at all.' The doctor picked up his bag. 'I just hope you're not too disappointed, Lord Ransom, and if Lady Ransom wants a proper examination, I suggest she sees her London gynaecologist as soon as possible, and seeks his advice.'

Matt ushered the doctor to the front door, saw him drive off, and thoughtfully shut the front door. He then made his way upstairs to the bedroom, where he found Jenny propped up against her pillows, leafing through a magazine. She looked up from the pages, and tried a brave smile.

'He's a nice man.'

'He wasn't sure you were pregnant.' Matt's tone was plaintive.

'I wasn't sure. I didn't deny it.'

'I wish you had been before you said anything to me.'

'And I wish *you'd* try and be a bit more understanding about me.'

'In what sense?' Matt didn't sit on the bed but on a chair a few feet away from the bed, as though he wished to put distance between himself and his wife.

'You seem to think I'd planned all this deliberately.'

'I don't think that at all.'

'Still I feel the suspicion is there. The onus of blame seems to be on me.'

Matt ran his hand across his forehead before looking up.

'I'm sorry, Jenny; maybe if I was a younger man I'd understand about these things more. Maybe that's when age tells. I was excited, you'd built up my hopes. I thought about it all the time when I was away . . . '

'Do you think *I* didn't?' Jenny's voice was strained. 'I wanted one, too, to please you as well as myself. It has become a challenge for me. How do you think I feel when, every month, my period comes on again? I feel a failure, inadequate, not like Elspeth, who was *so* fertile. I've had exhaustive gynaecological tests. I've done all I'm supposed to do. I've even prayed. How do you think *I* felt when I missed my period? I was very excited, ecstatic. I didn't tell you at once but waited until I'd tested the urine. It looked encouraging. I was bursting with pleasure, with hope and, as you were going away, I wanted to share this with you. Yet now you make me feel guilty.'

'There's no need for that,' Matt mumbled, as if her words had chastened him. 'We go on trying.'

'I'll get so screwed up, Matt. I can feel the tension even now.'

Matt stood up and went over to the window, where to his relief he saw that the ring was empty. At least one irritation was removed. He didn't have to watch Eric cavorting about on a horse, flaunting his youth. He turned round and looked at the person lying in bed, no longer

291

a remote, desirable, beautiful young creature, but a suffering, vulnerable human being. All too human.

Something in Jenny seemed to have changed. She had come down to earth, fallen off her pedestal. Sad, but true.

'Look,' he said, flicking his head towards the window. 'Just how long is that fellow going to stay here?'

As she frowned, he said brusquely: 'Don't pretend you don't know who I mean. Eric.'

'Matt, he's not doing anyone any harm.'

'We're going to need that flat soon. We're going to have to get a couple in.'

'Why? We've got two dailies and a full-time gardener and groom.'

'Well, for this sort of thing. If anything goes wrong in the night.'

'Matt, "this sort of thing" isn't going to happen often . . .'

'And if next time it was OK . . . And we have a baby . . . '

'Well, we'll wait for that to happen. Then we'll decide.' Looking dejected, Jenny put her magazine to one side as if she'd lost interest in what she'd been reading.

'Frankly, I don't like Eric in the house.' Matt walked across to the window again. 'I don't like him here alone with you.' He put up a hand. 'And don't tell me he's just an old family friend.'

'He is.'

'Well, I don't like it, and people will talk.'

'Have people talked?' She looked accusingly at him. 'Your family, for instance? Is that what you're trying to say?'

'I don't know if people have talked or not. They wouldn't talk to me, you can be sure of that, but what with everything that's happened recently, Elspeth, and now this . . . Well, I'd rather that fellow had a place of his own, and that's the truth.'

'Matt, how *can* you be so jealous of someone else when you're the one I love. You're the one I need?'

'I'm not *jealous* of him. I just object to him knowing where everything is in *my* kitchen. I don't like it.'

'You're being petty and unreasonable.'

'Well, so be it.' Matt raised his chin stubbornly in the air, an attitude he adopted when he intended to take a stance.

Jenny pulled the sheet up to her chin and closed her eyes. 'I really am very tired, Matt,' she could anticipate the argument growing, becoming more heated. 'Besides, I find this conversation too upsetting. Please leave me alone now.'

Matt looked as though he was about to reply, lowered his chin while glowering at her, and then, making no attempt to go near her again, went out of the room and down the stairs to the drawing room. There, although it was not yet noon, he emptied the best part of a quarter of a bottle of whisky into his glass and put it to his lips, longing for oblivion.

Matt Ransom was no sportsman, but he had belonged to The Sportsman's Club – tucked away at the end of a cul-de-sac off Curzon Street – ever since he'd been introduced to it by his father, who was. Not only had Edmund Ransom been a patron of the turf, a good amateur cricketer, but he had also been quite a boxer in his youth and, as a result, had sported a broken nose.

Matt very rarely went to The Sportsman's. It had a slightly raffish air, not the sort of place one really liked to be seen in, but he hardly ever did see anyone there who he knew or who knew him. It was a place where you could have a meal, a few drinks in anonymity, which was not the case at the gentlemen's clubs to which he belonged in St James's, where you knew almost everybody and everybody knew you.

There was also a gambling room; sometimes he had a few pounds on roulette or chemmy. You could also pick up a woman there, as it was patronised by both sexes and, although some of them were the perfectly respectable wives or girlfriends of members, he always had the suspicion that possibly one or two might be on the game. It had occurred to him that the club might even have maintained informal links with a Mayfair brothel or call-girl agency, although, as he never felt the need of the services, he never asked.

Nor did he feel the need of the services tonight as his taxi stopped outside the club and he got out and paid the driver. He just felt miserable; lonely, yet with a need to be alone and not be subject to the stares of members of his St James's clubs, curious ever since Elspeth's overdose had been loudly trumpeted in the tabloids.

There was no doorman at the club. He rang the bell and, after speaking into an intercom, was admitted by a pretty girl with a cheery smile: just what he needed.

'Good evening, Lord Ransom,' she said brightly.

'Good evening, Bridget. How are you?'

'Very well, thank you, Lord Ransom. How nice to see you again. Will you be dining?'

'Yes, and a little gambling I think. Are there any players for chemmy?'

'Not quite yet, Lord Ransom,' Bridget consulted a dainty gold watch on her wrist. 'Maybe you'd like to have a drink first?'

And with the practised smile of the professional hostess, she led the way into the bar and pointed to an alcove in the corner.

'What would you like, Lord Ransom?'

'A double Glenlivet, and spare the water.'

'Of course, Lord Ransom.'

She gave a gentle, melodious laugh, and conveyed the message to the barman. While she was waiting for him to complete it, Matt eyed her morosely. Bridget served as the hat-check girl, receptionist, hostess. The manager was a man who was seldom seen; Bridget represented the front of house and did it really well. She couldn't have been more than about twenty, and was very pretty with her

294

brown-eyed, dark-haired Irish good looks, and a very faint lilt, a suspicion of the brogue.

She was a very calming, tranquil sort of person, moved gracefully and always dressed tastefully and well and, as she brought his drink over to him on a tray, Matt patted the place by his side.

'Come and sit with me, Bridget. I could do with the company.'

'Oh, Sir Matthew, why is that?' she said, momentarily forgetting he had been ennobled. 'You always seem to me to be so content.'

'Not at the moment, my dear, not at the moment. Are you drinking, Bridget?' he asked as she sat down next to him, seeming intent on giving him her complete attention. She was the sort of woman, one imagined, who lived just to make men happy.

'No thank you, Sir Matthew, I mean Lord Ransom.' She put a long, well manicured hand to her mouth. 'I keep on forgetting. I never drink on duty.'

'And what do you do when you're off duty, Bridget?' he enquired, smiling at her.

'Well, there's *very* little time for that, Lord Ransom.' She tactfully inspected her dainty wristwatch. 'Especially at the moment as we're short staffed and rather busy. Now, why is it you're out of sorts? It's not like you.' Her dark Irish eyes melted with sympathy.

'You must have read in the papers about my former wife, Elspeth?'

Bridget nodded. 'I was *so* sorry about that.'

'It was an accident.'

'So the papers said,' she murmured.

'But a lot of them don't believe it. You can tell. It's because she seemed to swallow such a lot, had to have her stomach pumped. Difficult to believe it was done accident-ally. As if that's not all, with the consequent opprobrium and innuendoes cast on *me*, my present wife loses the baby we were expecting.'

'Oh, I'm *so* sorry about that, Lord Ransom.' Instinctively Bridget put a comforting hand on his arm. 'Maybe it was the shock?'

'Well, she was only *just* pregnant . . . if pregnant at all,' Matt said pensively, looking into space.

'*Plenty* of time to try again.' Her hand on his arm tightened, and then she hastily removed it.

Matt held out his glass. 'Get me another of those, will you, please, Bridget?'

'Certainly, Sir Matthew.' She got up and took the glass from him.

'And don't spare the Glenlivet,' he jokingly called after her, already beginning to feel a little drunk.

Three hours later, Matt was very drunk. He continued to drink before dinner, with his dinner and afterwards, when he lost quite a lot of money as a result in the gaming room.

At about midnight he called for yet another whisky and, though the place was not full, one or two of the members murmured, and the barman ignored his order.

'I said – ' Matt began belligerently, but at that moment Bridget glided into view and, taking him gently by the arm, led him once more to the alcove in the corner where the evening had begun.

'I really think you've had enough, Lord Ransom,' she murmured very softly, discreetly, so that no one could hear. 'Let me call you a taxi, or is Peter outside?'

'I want another bloody drink,' Matt demanded. 'My wife was telling *lies* about that baby, Bridget.' He looked at her in that comical, lopsided way that inebriated people do when they are losing control of their features.

'I'll call you a taxi,' Bridget said in response. 'Now will you be all right?'

'My wife is a bloody liar,' Matt banged the table again. 'She was not pregnant. Now why should she say she was?'

'I've no idea, Lord Ransom.' Bridget signalled to the manager who had mysteriously appeared and now stood in the doorway looking at her.

'His lordship would like a taxi,' she called over to the manager, whereupon Matt began to slide sideways along the bench, saved just in time by the manager who rushed over and, catching his arm, pulled him upright.

Matt sat there feeling very groggy, while Bridget and the manager, Justin O'Leary, who was a compatriot, engaged in whispered conversation with each other. Finally the manager came back and firmly took hold of Matt's arm.

'Your apartment is on Bridget's way home, Lord Ransom. She lives in Kentish Town, so she can easily drop you off.'

'Thas *very kind* of Bridget,' Matt said, wondering why he was unable to find his feet, 'very, very, *very* kind.'

'No trouble at all, Lord Ransom,' O'Leary said diplomatically and, gesturing to the barman, got him to take Matt's other arm so that they half dragged, half carried him to the door, where Bridget stood waiting in her coat, a taxi ticking away by the pavement outside.

Matt put his hand tentatively on the place next to him in the bed. It was empty. He opened his eyes and shut them again very quickly. He had a terrible, throbbing headache. He lay there for a few seconds, wondering where he was and what time it was.

He opened one eye, then another, and gently raised his head.

He was in the St John's Wood apartment, but he had no recollection as to how he'd got there, or of going to bed the night before. The sunshine outside was bright, too bright, so it must be mid-morning. He looked at the clock on the bedside table and gulped.

Eleven thirty! He had never slept until eleven thirty, and he had a vague feeling that he had a meeting planned for the day, something important in the City.

He closed his eyes again, only aware of how wretched, how awful he felt. The room seemed to swing gently around him. The door slowly opened and he waited until whoever it was was standing beside him. Then he opened his eyes.

The girl from the club was looking down at him. For a moment he couldn't remember her name, and dragged the rusty, dusty confines of his memory to find one.

'Er . . . ' he began.

The girl bent solicitously towards him.

'How do you feel, Lord Ransom?'

'What happened? Er . . . ' he still couldn't remember her name.

'Bridget, my lord, Bridget from the club . . . '

'Ah, the club,' he clutched his head and screwed up his eyes. 'What happened, Bridget?'

'You had *rather* a lot to drink, Lord Ransom. Justin O'Leary, the manager, was worried about you and, as I live quite near you, he asked me to drop you off in a taxi.'

'And did you?'

Bridget, who looked just as fresh and well groomed as she did at the club, smiled.

'I felt I couldn't leave you, sir. You couldn't stand up properly and the night porter helped me up here with you.'

'God! How awful. Does Maria know, the housekeeper?'

'She was in bed asleep, Lord Ransom. The night porter . . . and I put you to bed. I didn't want to leave you in case you became ill in the night. You hear so many dreadful things . . . '

'*Very* good of you, Bridget. Most considerate.' Matthew ran his tongue over his cracked lips. 'Be an angel, would you, and pass me a glass of water?'

Bridget obediently poured out a glass from the bottle of mineral water on the table. It was then that Matthew noticed an empty bucket by the side of his bed.

'Was I sick?' he asked a little fearfully.

'Dreadfully *ill*, Lord Ransom.'

'You're very good to me, Bridget.' He reached out for her hand. 'I just don't know how this happened to me. Maybe it was something I ate?' He looked at her hopefully.

'I'm afraid, sir,' Bridget replied as tactfully as she could, 'that you came to the club in a very unhappy mood.'

'Oh yes, I remember.' Matt sank back on the pillow. 'Elspeth . . . Jenny.'

'Your wife had a miscarriage.'

'Yes, I remember.' He closed his eyes again. 'And Elspeth, an overdose. My life is in an awful mess, Bridget. I am a very unhappy man.'

'I'm terribly, terribly sorry, Lord Ransom.' She sat by the side of the bed, her hand still clasped in his.

'Of course Maria knows everything?'

'I said you were taken ill and that I was asked to bring you home. I don't think she was very concerned about it, sir. She didn't seem to understand very much.'

'Her English is poor,' Matthew acknowledged. 'However, I must be sure this doesn't get back to my wife.'

'She didn't seem to *me* to be the kind of person who would tell tales, Lord Ransom. Also, when she came in to the sitting room this morning I was asleep on the sofa.' Matt, studying her, felt drawn by her womanliness, her sympathy and, not least, her looks.

'I'm enormously grateful to you, Bridget. Do you think you could get some Paracetamol out of the bathroom and then, maybe, I could have a cup of tea? Oh, and could you pass me the small diary you will find on the inside pocket of the jacket I wore last night? I think I had a meeting today.'

Bridget nodded.

'You had, sir. Your son rang – '

'Oh my God, did you speak to him?'

Bridget shook her head. 'Your housekeeper did, sir. She told him you were ill. He said he was sorry and he would ring again.'

'Thank heaven for that.' Matt lay still while she went to the bathroom, where he could hear her rummaging round. How calmly and sensibly she did everything. No histrionics, no reproaches, just calm acceptance. Jenny wouldn't have taken his behaviour as lightly as this, and Elspeth would have fussed about with an air of silent disapproval.

Only he never remembered, with either woman, being as out of control as he obviously had been the night before.

'I don't know what I would have done without you, Bridget,' he said, shaking the pills from the bottle she handed to him and drowning them with great gulps of water. 'It would have been an absolute disgrace if I'd been found drunk and incapable in Mayfair. I owe you, and Justin, a great debt . . . '

'Especially, Lord Ransom – ' Bridget paused and then handed him a newspaper she seemed to have been con-cealing behind her back – 'Since I'm afraid your name is in the papers again today.'

Matthew, reeling with shock, read the banner headline.
'WHAT MAKES A MAN GO FOR A BIMBO?' There was a large picture of him and Jenny at some social occasion over a smaller one of him and Elspeth, looking her age, at their thirtieth wedding anniversary bash. Underneath there were smaller pictures of a number of elderly men in the company of much younger women.

'Oh my God!' Matt said, covering his eyes. 'What did I ever do to deserve this?' Then after a moment he opened them. 'Would you pass me my reading spectacles, dear? I think you'll find them in the pocket of the same jacket.' He held out his hand as she groped in his pocket and handed them to him.

'You are a dear, Bridget. Thank you.'

'Here. Let me help.' She propped up the pillows behind him and, as he lay back on them, she said, 'Should I get you a nice hot cup of tea now?'

'Would you do that?' He smiled gratefully at her. 'I hope I'm not keeping you from your work?'

'Oh no, Lord Ransom,' she smiled reassuringly back, 'I don't start until six this evening. But I should go home and change at some stage.'

'You're a wonder,' he put on his reading glasses. 'You look marvellous. Never think you'd spent an uncomfortable night on the sofa.'

The picture of him and Jenny was in colour. She did look marvellous, far better than the wives or girlfriends of the other men, contemporaries of his, featured in the article. He adjusted his glasses and started to read the column, written by a woman known for her acerbic tongue.

> Although the recent overdose taken by the first wife of tycoon Lord Ransom of Chudleigh was attributed to an accident, it does emphasise the plight of women discarded by their husbands of many years for a younger woman.
>
> Lady Elspeth Ransom was married to the then Mr Ransom over thirty years ago. She supported him through his career but, alas, she is only the latest in a long line which includes . . . ' [and then the names of several well known men were mentioned.]
>
> What *is* it that attracts a man, mature in years, a highly respected citizen, ennobled, as so many of them are, to a . . . bimbo?
>
> The present Lady Jenny Ransom is a stunning strawberry blonde of twenty-five. She was only twenty-one when the then Sir Matthew first set eyes on her, and twenty-three when he married her. Jenny Ransom is seen on the arm of her husband at all the most sociable functions in London. She is a skilled horsewoman and is establishing a stable at the family home in Oxfordshire, out of which the first Lady Ransom was ejected, allegedly much against her will, a year ago . . .

'Oh I can't take any more of this.' Matt threw the paper to the floor, removing his spectacles, as Bridget came into the room carrying a tray.

'Now then,' she said gently, putting it by the side of the bed. 'A nice hot, *strong* cup of tea. Maria wants to know if you would like any lunch?'

'Heaven forbid!' Matt shuddered. 'I really overdid it last night, didn't I?'

'Maybe understandably in the circumstances,' Bridget replied tactfully.

'I feel my wife doesn't understand me, Bridget.' He leaned forward and took the cup from her hand. 'Maybe she never really loved me . . . '

'Oh, Lord Ransom, I'm *sure* she loves you.' Bridget replaced the cup on the tray. 'She is *so* beautiful.' She gazed at the picture in the paper lying on the floor.

'She *is* beautiful,' he agreed 'but we have so little in common. She doesn't even like opera. I can't stand horses. She was quite determined that my ex-wife should leave the family home, which I'm sure caused her to overdose – '

'Then it *wasn't* an accident, Lord Ransom?' Bridget looked interested at this piece of news.

'Well, Elspeth *says* it was; but she took a heck of a lot of pills. Whatever the reason, she was very unhappy. No one disputes that and, you see, it makes me feel so responsible. If she'd died I would never have forgiven myself. My children would have blamed me for the rest of my life. And Jenny was no help, no comfort. I almost think she had this so-called miscarriage to refocus attention on herself . . . '

'Here, Lord Ransom,' Bridget decided she should put a stop to this prattle, 'have another sip of tea and then try and have a good sleep.'

Matt looked up at her gratefully, sipped his tea and then, as she removed the cup and replaced it on the table, made a grab for her free hand.

'Bridget,' he said in a wheedling tone, 'why don't you take some of your clothes off and get into bed with me? Just for cuddling, you know, nothing more.'

302

PART IV

The Wise Father

It is a wise father that knows his own child.

Shakespeare, *The Merchant of Venice*
Act II, scene 2

CHAPTER 17

Georgina Timperley stood at the window of her bedroom watching Henry cross the yard. Haltingly now, with a stick, he had the gait of an elderly gentleman. Yet he was not yet forty, a man in his prime to whom fate had dealt a cruel blow.

A farm without animals was like an empty shell. Even the cats and dogs seemed out of place. The barns, especially the one where the accident had happened, were locked and out of use. All the farm machinery had now been sold, together with the livestock.

They were able to make ends meet but only just. They had intended to sell the house and buy a place somewhere cheap like Spain. Then Elspeth had taken an overdose.

Whether deliberately or accidentally would never be known; she probably didn't know herself. But, as sure as anything, it had changed their lives just as much as the divorce had. Nothing could ever be the same again after that, and now a question mark hung over Spain.

She could see the emptiness, the despair, on Henry's face as he looked around the yard and turned towards the house. Then, raising his head, he saw her. His expression immediately brightened and he raised his stick.

Time for coffee.

Time, time, time. There was a lot of it – too much of it – hanging on their hands.

She finished tidying the bedroom. When she got downstairs Henry was in the kitchen waiting for the kettle to boil. Their mugs, with coffee in, stood on the table. Henry was useful in the house. He liked to be kept busy. He had taken up carpentry and had set about restoring some of their antiques, possibly with a view to selling them.

The accident had left him not only lame, but with a very short span of concentration. He found it difficult to keep his mind on anything for too long, so woodwork and household tasks suited him admirably. So, paradoxically, would life on a farm, but the responsibility had been too onerous, and all the paperwork caused by European Community regulations much too much, even with Georgina's help. Anyway, he had developed an aversion to cattle which, in the circumstances, was not surprising.

'Coffee up,' he said, turning with a smile as Georgina came in, her arms full of dirty washing. She went into the utilities room off the kitchen and filled the washing machine, set the programme and closed the door. Henry was pouring water into their cups. She took hers, and with a heavy heart sat facing him on the opposite side of the table. What she had to say would not be easy.

'Darling,' she began. 'Henry . . . '

'Yes?' He looked expectantly up at her.

She took a long, steadying drink.

'I think we should reconsider Spain.'

'We should what?' He appeared not to understand what she meant.

'You know, rethink the wisdom of going there.'

'But Georgina, we have to. We can't afford to keep this place. We have no option but to sell . . . '

'Well, I thought we could . . . You see, Henry, I don't really want to leave Mummy. She's awfully vulnerable just now. I'm terribly worried about her.'

'But your mother has Maurice and Shirley practically next door, and now Beth has forsaken her acting career to

306

stay with her for as long as she likes. What else could your mother possibly want?'

Georgina fiddled with a kitchen knife on the table. 'But it's detrimental to Beth's career. She can't live with Mummy for ever, and she has already turned down a TV job to be with her. I don't want her to turn into the spinster daughter spending the rest of her life at home.'

'But she won't do that. Beth's very resourceful.'

'I feel she might.' Georgina wriggled uncomfortably. 'She was very, very worried and upset about Mummy.'

'We all were.'

'Who, incidentally, is not all that resourceful, as events have shown.'

'I still don't think, Georgina,' Henry said with the slightly halting voice he had developed since the accident, 'that that is enough to ruin *our* lives as well.'

'But we won't ruin our lives, Henry! How can you say that?'

'Your mother living with us — I suppose that's what you're suggesting — would ruin our lives. I like her; always have, but I don't want to live with her. You are bound to give her more attention than me, and I feel I have first claim on that, as well as your love.'

'But Henry, you do and will have them.' Georgina rose and, walking round to him, leaned over him. 'You *do* have them, always will,' she repeated.

'You can't put us both first, and I know what it will be. Always watching Elspeth to see she isn't knocking back the sherry. Making sure the pill bottle isn't going down too fast, quietly opening her door if she sleeps late to make sure she's all right . . .'

'Oh, it won't be like that . . .'

'But it will. I see it, if you don't . . . or won't. We don't know for sure whether or not your mother intended to take her life. None of us does. Do we?'

'No.' Georgina went back to her chair and sat there, head bowed. 'I don't think she does either.'

'Momentary despair. She could do it again. Well, she has Maurice and Shirley, a trained nurse; I believe she now keeps the pill bottles.'

'Yes, she does. Gives Mum what medication she needs.'

'Well, there you are.' Henry made a gesture of impatience with his hand. 'Now, let's get out that estate agent's brochure and have another look. I quite liked that place in Alicante . . . '

'Henry,' Georgina anxiously kneaded her hands in her lap, out of sight under the table, 'I *can't* leave Mummy. I just can't. Not now, not so soon after. Besides, Daddy has said he'd help us.'

'Oh, has he? You've discussed this with him then?'

'Of course,' Georgina looked surprised. 'He's as worried about Mummy as we all are.'

'And yet he drove her to it.'

'He did *not* drive her to it.' Georgina gazed indignantly at her husband.

'Of course he did. He left her. Married a much, much younger woman, just to rub salt in the wound. Then he kicked her out of her house. You think it didn't fester? You think that wasn't why she did it? I'm quite sure it was. Quite, quite sure, and that it was deliberate. I think you all know that and won't admit it. It was a cry for help, a cry to have you all running round her, and that's just what is happening now. That stupid newspaper article painting your father as a randy old goat didn't help much either.'

'That was horrible and unfair,' Georgina nervously bit her lip.

'Anyway,' Henry gazed abruptly at her, 'I thought you were right off your father. Suddenly you've changed your mind, you're defending him.'

'I was not "right off" him,' Georgina replied defensively. 'And, of course I thought, and still do, that he treated Mother badly.' Georgina paused, her expression one of anguish. 'But blood is thicker than water. He's my father, and the whole thing has got thoroughly out of hand now that the papers have got onto it.'

'Once they start they'll go on, you know.' Henry seemed to enjoy pressing the point. 'They'll watch your family like a hawk. One false move and the hounds of Fleet Street will start baying again.

'But papers are, I agree, largely irrelevant to what is happening *here*. Beth has a fragile career threatened, Shirley and Maurice's marriage is in jeopardy, and now you want to put *ours* in jeopardy too.'

The more quickly he spoke, the more he stumbled; by the time he had finished, Georgina felt Henry was close to collapse.

'Henry!' she cried. 'Our marriage is *not* in jeopardy.'

'Well it will be if you go ahead with your plan. If you have *your* mother here, I'm off to Spain alone. Make no mistake about it.'

'But you can't.'

'Oh yes I can.' Henry got awkwardly to his feet and, grasping his stick, shook it at her. 'And I will. What do you think staying in this house does to *me*, Georgina? I hate it, you know. I hate the bloody place, here where I lived the best years of my life and had them cut short. Did you ever think of *that*? *Did* you?'

By now he was shaking so much that Georgina got up and went over to try and calm him, taking him by the arm and forcing him to sit down again. She began to stroke his head, like a cat or a dog.

'Yes, I did. Of course I did. I saw you this morning walking round the yard: I know you hate it.' She straightened up. 'Very well then, Henry. We'll sell up and get somewhere else, but somewhere local and somewhere where we can have Mummy. I'm sorry, Henry, I'm quite adamant about that.'

'Then I'm quite adamant about going to live abroad – ' Henry thumped his stick several times on the floor – 'and that is a decision, my darling wife, that you and only you can make.'

Georgina felt her pulse racing at speed, too fast. She'd have to slow down. Didn't want another accident, another tragedy in the family.

Henry had stormed out of the kitchen and then she heard him thumping about upstairs, as if deliberately making as much noise as he could. Much as she loved him, Henry could be trying, always had been, and more especially so since the accident. She knew that part of the damage done to the brain made him revert at times to childish behaviour that was quite untypical of the Henry of old. The old Henry could be difficult but not childish. The new one threw tantrums and did his best to get her attention, just like the children, so that instead of having two about the house in the holidays when they were home from school, she felt she had three.

Shortly afterwards Georgina left the house without telling Henry where she was going. She drove the seven miles to Stanfield, turned into the drive of the manor and saw that the garage doors were open and there was no sign of either Shirley's car or of Maurice's.

As she stopped in front of the door, it opened and Beth emerged and ran to greet her, flinging her arms round her neck.

'George, *darling*. How lovely to see you.' She kissed her sister enthusiastically, and then stepped back to look at her. 'Everything OK?'

'Everything's fine.' Georgina turned to shut the door. 'How's Mum?'

'Mum's all right.'

'Sure?' Georgina turned and anxiously studied her sister's face.

'Sure. Sure . . . '

'But darling,' she linked arms with Beth as they walked up to the house, 'you can't stay here all the time looking after Mum. You've your career to consider.'

'I know, but Mum needs help . . . '

'Shirley and Maurice – '

'Not the same. Shirley's marvellous, but she's awfully busy.'

'But your career – '

'Can take second place. Anyway, Dad's here.'

'Dad's *here*!' Georgina looked surprised. 'How long has he been here?'

'About an hour. He's going to stay for lunch. Isn't that nice? We can all have lunch together, like old times.'

'Well, I don't know.' Georgina's expression turned to amazement. 'Dad would never have done that a year ago.'

Just then Matt, looking relaxed in flannels and a jersey, appeared at the door and held out his arms in greeting.

'George!'

'Dad!' They embraced. 'What a nice surprise. Are you at Chudleigh?'

'For a few days.'

'Taking some holiday?'

'Not really. I have some work to do, a report to write, and it's quiet. Jenny's very busy practising her jumping. Out practically all day.'

Matt's voice was non-committal, but Georgina thought she detected a note of disapproval.

'It must do her good. All the fresh air.'

'I suppose,' Matt nodded. 'And how do you find your mother, George?'

'I think she's fine.'

'Do you really?' He looked earnestly at her. 'I feel so responsible, so guilty.'

'We all do. Why, I was *there* on the day. How do you think *I* feel?'

'Did she seem depressed, more than usual?'

'Well . . . ' Georgina paused doubtfully. 'She *was* delighted about the rose being named after her, but she was upset about us leaving and then, of course we did have a few sherries. They might have made her maudlin.'

'We can't leave her, you know now, darling.'

'I know, Daddy.' Georgina resisted pointing out that he was responsible, adding 'That's why I'm here.'

'Oh?'

'We'll talk about it over lunch. I'm so *glad* you're staying.' She put her arms around him again and hugged him, echoing her sister. 'It will be just like old times.'

Upstairs Elspeth could hear the sounds of Georgina's arrival, the noisy welcome and then the suddenly lowered voices murmuring away in the hall.

About her.

Well, it was time someone thought about her, as she had spent most of her life thinking about them. She stooped to examine herself in the mirror and tucked a stray piece of her snow-white hair into place. Then she stood up, pulled her dress well down over her tummy, and looked at herself full length, pleased with what she saw. She'd lost several pounds in weight.

Today she had dressed carefully, applied make-up carefully, done her hair with special care using the heated rollers. She thought she looked good, still too plump, and it was too late to change the colour of her hair. She was certainly no Jenny. But then she had never pretended to be, didn't want to be, never had been.

It was lovely to feel surrounded by family again; surrounded, wanted and protected. Everyone was at her beck and call, and it made her know they cared. For so long it had seemed that no one cared at all, and maybe when she'd reached for those pills, it had just been to let them all know . . .

She squirted some perfume on the top of her dress, glanced at herself again, got a handkerchief from her drawer, scented that and then, with a last look at herself in the mirror, walked across the room and out of the door on to the small landing from where she could see them in a huddle.

'Hello there!' she cried gaily, waving from the top of

the stairs, gratified to see the way they instantly sprang apart.

'Hi there, Mummy!' Georgina waved and took a couple of steps to greet her. 'How are you?'

'Fine,' Elspeth called preparing to come down. 'And you, darling?'

'Fine.'

'You look well.' In fact, she thought Georgina was beginning more and more to resemble her, putting on a bit of weight.

Mother and daughter greeted each other affectionately at the foot of the steps, and then they walked into the sitting room where Matt had preceded them and had the sherry decanter in his hand. This he held up in the direction of the two women. Georgina shook her head.

'Elspeth?'

Elspeth was about to say 'yes', then decided at the last moment to refuse. Didn't want them to think she was *drinking*. Beth popped her head round to say lunch would be ready in five minutes.

'Need any help?' Georgina called, but Beth shook her head.

'It's just soup and cold cuts.'

'Lovely.'

'Cheers.' Matt held up his well-filled glass. 'Good health, Elspeth.'

'Thank you, Matt.'

'George, how's Henry?' Matt replaced the decanter on the table.

'Well . . . ' Georgina paused, 'that's why I'm here really.'

'Something wrong with Henry?' Elspeth looked concerned.

'Mum,' Georgina sat next to her mother and pressed her hand, 'I'm not at all *happy* about us going to Spain.'

'Oh, good,' Elspeth clasped her hands together.

'You don't like the idea, Elspeth?' Matt asked.

313

'No, I don't. I like my family about me: who doesn't? But I don't want to be selfish, and if it is in their best interests that they go, then go they must.'

'But what made you change your mind?' Matt sat opposite his eldest daughter and studied her. Together, side by side, he too suddenly saw how like Elspeth she was getting.

Georgina clasped her mother's hand again. 'I don't like leaving you, Mum.'

'Is that all?' her mother stared at her. 'Because of me?'

'Mainly, yes.'

'But darling, I've got Beth and – '

'Beth has her career.'

'Maurice, Shirley . . . '

'They're terribly busy.'

'Philip is always popping over . . . '

'He's got a job in London, and is looking for a place of his own in the country, isn't he, Dad?'

Matt nodded. 'I think it's a waste of money, but that's his affair. He seems to have plenty of the stuff, so he can do what he likes with it.'

'He wants independence, Daddy, you can understand that. Personally I don't think Mum should be left all alone . . . '

'Darling, I'm not a *baby*, nor an *invalid* . . . '

'No, Mum, but you did worry us. Made us see things we didn't see before. How vulnerable you were, how lonely.'

'And what does Henry say to all this?' her father asked, his eyes on his glass.

'He doesn't like it.'

'I can see why.'

'But I think Mum has to come first.'

'Not before *Henry*, darling.'

'Not before, but as well as. That's my point. I also think we're better off in England, where the medical facilities are good, better than Spain.'

314

'No doubt about that,' Matt nodded agreement.

'But,' Georgina went on, 'Henry doesn't like the farm. I mean the house. He wants out. It has unhappy memories for him. I think we could get another house here in the locality, and maybe a cottage like this so that we can keep an eye on Mum.'

'Well, it's very kind, very thoughtful.' Elspeth looked doubtfully at Matt. 'What do *you* think, dear?'

'I can't really see the point.' Matt got up and re-filled his glass. 'Elspeth is very happy here. She's well looked after; Shirley and Maurice are within call. Shirley is a trained nurse. I don't see why Georgina, much as we'd love to keep her in this country, should feel responsible for her mother rather than her brain-damaged husband.'

'I do feel responsible for Henry, Daddy, and *please* don't refer to him as "brain-damaged". It sounds horrible.'

'Also not true,' Elspeth added.

'Well it's partly true,' Georgina corrected her. 'His brain function is impaired; but he's all there mentally, and almost all there physically.'

'Let Henry have a good few years in the sun,' Matt said. 'He deserves it. You know you can come over here as often as you like, always plenty of places to stay.'

'It's not the same, Daddy . . . '

At that moment Beth reappeared to say lunch was on the table, and they all rose and went into the dining room.

It was all so lovely, Elspeth thought, looking round. Flowers on the table, the family silver, wine in a decanter, cut-glass wine glasses even for a light luncheon. Just like old times. Oh that those times had never ended. She looked affectionately across at Matt, who glanced up and smiled at her.

'A penny for them, Elspeth?'

'I was thinking how nice it was, dear, for the family to be together.' She realised that she hadn't referred to him as 'dear' for many years. But he had been so sweet, so

315

attentive since the accident. It was very easy to forgive someone one still loved, as she did Matt.

'Yes, it is,' he agreed.

'We must — ' she paused, not wishing to be considered pushy — 'try and do this sort of thing more often.'

'Well . . . we'll see.'

'Would Jenny mind?' Anxiously.

'Jenny wouldn't be consulted. After all, she doesn't consult *me* about everything.'

Tactful pause.

'She has gone crazy over this horse business, which excludes me. Riding, riding, all day long. When did she consult me about that?'

'I'd supposed she would.' Elspeth studied the pattern on her plate.

'Well, she didn't. She's spending her money and, as we said about Phil, she's entitled to do what she likes with it. But horses, horses, horses . . . All I hear.'

'With that attractive Swede,' Beth said meaningfully.

'Don't be bitchy, darling.' Georgina gave a conspiratorial smile.

'Well,' Matt paused, 'he's an old friend. I must say I'm not keen on him. It doesn't make things any easier.'

'*Bitterly* disappointing about losing the baby . . . ' Elspeth began.

'Oh, Elspeth, don't be so *nice*!' Matt said his voice rising. 'You're not disappointed. None of you is. It's just all been damned difficult. Now I've got myself in the public eye. My board don't like it. I hate it . . . '

'I bet Jenny wasn't too pleased either,' Beth glanced slyly at her sister.

'Poor Jenny was deeply, deeply hurt. Calling her a bimbo! She is a very intelligent woman.'

'It was scarcely flattering about *me*.' Elspeth shuddered inwardly at the memory of first reading the article. The sense of humiliation she'd felt, but also a secret joy at the unflattering reference to Jenny.

'If only one could sue, but it makes everything worse. One day the press in this country *has* to be controlled. Well, anyway, it upset us all deeply, and it *was* unfair. Still, the damage is done. I wish – ' Matt paused and joined his hands together on the table – 'sometimes I wish . . . ' He paused again awkwardly, looking round at the three pairs of eyes all fixed on him: his dear, familiar family; wife – well, ex-wife now – and two daughters.

He sighed. 'Well, I wish . . . '

But he didn't say it.

Couldn't say that he sometimes wished he hadn't met Jenny.

The three women stood on the steps of the cottage waving as, later in the afternoon, Matt drove himself off. Peter had taken Maurice to Heathrow to meet an important client whom Matt would see the following day.

He waved out of the window, disappearing with a toot round the bend in the drive.

Georgina linked her arm through her mother's and, with Beth following in the rear, they walked back into the sitting room, where Elspeth flopped on to the sofa with a sigh. Beth sat next to her, while Georgina strolled over to the window and stood looking into the garden.

'It *was* nice to be together,' Elspeth gave a deep, deep sigh. 'Just like a family. Just like old times.'

How many times had she said that? Georgina slowly turned and sat opposite her mother and sister, face thoughtful, hands linked in front of her.

'That's what worries me.'

'What worries you, darling?'

'Your expectations. Dad's solicitousness. I don't want you to think he's changed.'

Elspeth gave her daughter a knowing look and wagged a finger at her.

'Don't forget I lived with your father for over thirty years. You don't live with a person that long without

317

knowing them very well. Instead of marrying Jenny he should have had an affair with her. Got it out of his system.' She held up a hand as Beth started to protest. 'No, let me finish. I could see that Jenny wasn't Matt's sort at all. He was obsessed by her, carried away. He thought she was a goddess, not flesh and blood like poor old me. Do you think he's happy with her? No. Of course he's not. She's human after all; loses babies. Why should he want a baby but to recreate his family? Us. Now I think he misses us and wants to put back the clock.'

'I never heard him talk so disparagingly about Jenny,' Georgina mused. 'Never heard a word of criticism before.'

'I said it would last two years. I was right. I can see the signs of Matt's restlessness. I know him. I know my man. And do you know what I think?' Elspeth paused and gave a conspiratorial smile. 'You know what I *really* think?' As the others shook their heads and pretended they didn't know she went on, 'I think that eventually Jenny and Daddy will get divorced and that Daddy will come back to me. You see, one day we'll be together.'

'And you'd *have* him back?' Beth gasped.

'Yes,' Elspeth said with the same secretive little smile. 'Of course I would. You'll see, one day we'll all be united as a family at Chudleigh again, and that will solve all our problems, won't it?'

Paul Vernon finished making his notes and looked across his leather-topped desk at the woman who, fully clothed now, emerged from his examination room and sat opposite him, perfectly composed. She wore a fine, houndstooth woollen suit, in a sort of greeny brown, over a yellow polo-necked jersey. Brown boots, brown gloves and handbag completed the outfit, her blonde hair, casually tossed back to one side, curled very slightly under her ears. He glanced at his notes again to check the date he'd last seen her and realised, with a most unprofessional pang, how much she'd changed. She was pale, thinner, and there

318

were dark rings under her eyes; even her lovely hair had lost some of its lustre.

'Lady Ransom,' he said earnestly, leaning forward, 'you must take more care of yourself.'

She smiled very slightly.

'How do you mean?'

'I think you've lost half a stone at least since I last saw you. You look as though you don't sleep. You are far too pale. How long since you had a holiday?'

'We were due to have a holiday in the summer, but what with Matt's first wife's overdose and my supposed pregnancy, somehow we never got round to it. I do a lot of riding . . . '

'That's not the same as a complete change of scene. It might also help you with your current problem.' He referred to his notes again. 'Lady Ransom, I can still find no reason why you can't bear a child. Nothing has changed . . . '

'Then do you or don't you think I was pregnant?'

'I think possibly you were, as your periods are so regular. Unfortunately it was an early miscarriage. What I am saying, what I can't emphasise enough, is that if you relax more, don't think that every time you have intercourse you might become pregnant, it might happen. I would advise a long restful holiday in the sun, maybe, or in your home in Sweden . . . Although I find you in perfect condition physically, I am less happy about your mental and emotional state. Are there any – ' he paused – 'difficulties in the marriage?'

'I wouldn't say "difficulties" exactly,' Jenny said after a while. 'I don't think things are *quite* what they were before . . . Well, both events coincided – the overdose and the miscarriage, or whatever it was. They made a big strain on Matt . . . '

'And you too, I imagine.'

'Yes. I didn't feel as guilty as Matt did about his former wife, but I was very upset. I was more upset that I didn't

319

give him the child he wants. Perhaps that's very selfish of me, I don't know. You see Elspeth, the first wife, was very fertile. She had no difficulty in producing children. Why can't I?'

'You who would appear to have everything,' the gynaecologist murmured. 'Beauty, youth, why can't *you* conceive? Well, I'm sure you can and will. You must give it time.'

'You see,' Jenny suddenly found herself wanting to confide in this sympathetic professional, 'when you marry an older man whom you admire, you realise you're lost in a time warp. You have to give up your life for him, however young in heart he is — and Matt is very young in heart, very energetic. But there is a whole generation between you, different points of view.'

'Does he compare you unfavourably to his former wife?'

'Oh no, except, as I say, in her ability to conceive; but since her overdose he sees her when he didn't before. He telephones her quite often. I have the feeling they have become close again and, inevitably, I am excluded from this . . . I do feel a little jealous. Unworthy, isn't it?'

'Not at all. It seems quite natural to me. This woman felt abandoned and made a cry for help which was answered.'

'Not only by her former husband but her four children *and* their spouses. She is now very, very well looked after.' There was a trace of bitterness in Jenny's voice.

'And you feel neglected?' Then, seeing her expression change, Vernon said hastily: 'I'm not a psychologist, Lady Ransom, please understand that. It is simply a situation I can visualise, and one which isn't too uncommon. We are very sorry for the first Lady Ransom. Lord Ransom undoubtedly does feel some guilt which may rub off on you. But you both made the decision to marry, and I think your life should be lived in the present, not the past. Now, enough of this talk. I am going to change your douche and suggest that Lord Ransom comes and has a talk with me . . . '

320

'Oh, but I should hate you to say . . . ' she began, but stopped as he held up a hand.

'As I said, I am *not* a psychiatrist. I shall just be discussing the physical aspects of intercourse, the benefits of relaxation, because I am quite, quite sure this is a mental problem, Lady Ransom, and not a medical one at all. By all means come together, if you wish, but if I see him by myself I can talk to him man to man. I know this may sound chauvinistic and old-fashioned, but, sometimes, it helps with a man of his age.'

Matt, arms folded, stood brooding by the window in the drawing room. A few hundred yards away the horsemen jumped the fences, the woman practised the slow, meticulous, incredibly intricate steps of the dressage to the far side of the ring.

It was a scene of youth, of skill, and one in which he felt he had no part. Excluded. Jenny, Eric and Philip had been at it since breakfast, and it was now nearly lunchtime. They never seemed to tire.

It was true he had work to do, papers in his study that needed examination and careful thought. But he was restless, irritable, out of sorts, his mind not on his work or his home, but on that dark-eyed beauty who had so unexpectedly stolen Jenny's place in his heart.

Matt turned impatiently from the window and went over to the telephone, lifted the handset and punched in some numbers. At the other end he heard the ringing sound and, for a moment, he thought there would be no reply. Then she answered in that quiet, soft voice that was so restful, so infinitely alluring.

'Bridget, is that you?'

'Matt!' Even his name spoken by her sounded different.

'How are you, darling?'

'I'm very well. Matt, where are you?'

'In the country.'

'Oh!' Disappointment. 'I thought you were going to say we could see each other today.'

321

'I'm afraid not, darling. My son is staying here and I have a lot of work to do. But Monday . . . Monday afternoon?'

The afternoon was the time they met and made love, almost the only time they could get, because Bridget's flatmate had a day-time job, and the St John's Wood apartment was far from secure.

'That will be lovely, Matt,' she said softly. 'Are you all right?'

'So-so. Wish I was with you . . . '

He heard the sound of voices in the hall and whispered urgently into the phone. 'Must go. Love you. Goodbye.'

And before she had time to answer, he replaced the phone in its bracket. When the door opened, he was standing by the fire, idly flicking over the pages of the *Stock Exchange Gazette*.

'Matt, there you are.' Jenny, face flushed, ran over to the fire and warmed her hands. 'Golly, it's cold. The trouble with dressage is that it's so slow.'

He looked up as Philip and Eric came into the room laughing, as if sharing some private joke.

'You OK, Matt?' she asked, her tone changing as she looked up at him.

'Fine,' he smiled at her. 'Hungry.'

'I'll go and see if lunch – ' She straightened up.

'Ready in ten minutes. I just asked. Well,' he threw the journal down on the sofa, 'how was the morning?'

'Excellent.' Looking highly pleased with himself, Philip rubbed his hands together.

'I think he'll make a jumper,' Eric said.

'He's excellent,' Jenny agreed. 'And yet you never kept horses, Matt?'

'No one was interested in them in my family. I think Philip had riding lessons, maybe Georgina, too. I can't remember.'

'I really took it up in the States.' Philip walked over to the drinks table. 'Vodka, sherry, anyone?'

'I'll have a sherry,' Matt said, 'that'd be nice.'

'Jenny?' Jenny shook her head.

'Sherry for me too, please.' Eric sat down on the sofa and took up Matt's magazine.

'Interest you, Eric?' Matt asked, an edge to his voice.

'No. Not a bit.' Eric closed the magazine and put it down again. 'I'm afraid I'm hopeless at figures, Matt.'

'So it seems.' Matt accepted a glass from Philip with a cursory smile. 'Thanks, Philip.'

'Oh?' The smile left Eric's face. 'What does that mean, exactly?'

'Well, you said you weren't any good at figures, and I said, "so it seems". Nothing wrong with that, is there?'

'It's a strange remark to make, Dad.' Philip sat down next to Eric, a drink in his hand. 'It sounds vaguely un-pleasant.'

Jenny too was looking at him, a booted foot on the fender, one hand on the mantelpiece.

'I'm sorry if I said the wrong thing. Forget it.' Matt raised his glass. 'Cheers!'

'I'd appreciate it if you could elucidate what you said, Matt,' Eric persisted, and Matt sighed loudly.

'I just *wondered* how long you were going to stay on in this house, accepting our hospitality, that's all. It may be a petty thing, but it's beginning to irritate me. You seem to make no real progress with your horse jumping. Where are all these competitions you were going in for? Forgive me if I've got it wrong, Eric, but I assumed you were eventually going to pay your way and find somewhere of your own to live after a decent interval. Well, I think that a decent interval has elapsed, and I think it's time you thought of shifting yourself. Besides,' he looked at Jenny, 'we'll be needing the flat for a couple.'

'Why, is Jenny expecting again?' Philip looked surprised.

'No, but that's not the point. This is our house and we want it to ourselves; except for you, Philip, of course, and such of our family who want to come here. They are always *very* welcome.'

With an exclamation, Philip rose and, placing his empty glass on the table, turned to his father, face white with fury.

'Dad, that is one of the rudest speeches I think I've ever heard.'

'Not very nice, Matt.' Jenny anxiously looked at Eric.

'Well, if that's the case . . . ' Eric made to get up.

'Don't be silly. Stay where you are.' Philip pushed him back with his hand. 'I guess you've got something to say, Dad?'

'What do you mean?'

'That you're sorry?'

'I'm not. This has been festering in my mind for some time.'

'So it seems . . . '

'There *is* such a thing as taking advantage . . . '

'Matt, I do wish – ' Jenny began, but the door opened and Gladys announced that lunch was on the table.

'Thank you, Gladys. We'll come in a few moments,' Jenny said hastily.

'I think we'll go out to the pub, if you don't mind, Jenny.' Philip pointedly ignored his father. 'I think after this outburst of Dad's – '

'It was *not* an outburst, it was a statement of fact,' Matt protested. 'However, maybe I could have done it more tactfully.'

'You can say that again.'

'Then I'm sorry for that.'

'*I* really am sorry. I apparently outstayed my welcome.' Eric, very pale, looked shaken.

'You didn't outstay your welcome, Eric,' Jenny cried. 'This is my house too and you're very welcome. Welcome to stay as long as you like. Now let's all forget about this and go into lunch . . . '

'I really couldn't,' Eric began.

'Please.' She took his arm and gave him an encouraging smile. Then, with her other hand, she beckoned to Philip and led them towards the door.

324

'Oh, very well.' Philip looked angrily at his father who, as if slightly bemused by the fuss he'd caused, brought up the rear.

It was not a happy meal. During the course of it there was little conversation. Eric hardly spoke at all, except to ask for condiments or the butter. Philip glowered at his father and, as soon as the meal was over, he asked to see him alone.

Jenny watched them from one end of the table, chin in hand, and, when the door had closed, turned to Eric, saying in Swedish:

'*I* really *am* terribly sorry. I had no idea that Matt felt so strongly.'

'I think he's jealous of me, you know.' Eric gave her a sly smile.

'Jealous?'

'Didn't you ever think he was jealous? I did, the way he looked at me. I knew he never liked me, but I thought there were other reasons.'

'What reasons?'

'Never mind. I should have gone a lot sooner. Being here alone with you I suppose looked odd to a lot of people.'

'But people don't think like that any more.'

'Yes, they do. Matt's generation does.' Eric got up and, coming round the table to her, bent down and tenderly placed a hand on her head. 'You are a very sweet person, Jenny.'

'That's rubbish.' She reached out and caught his hand.

'And I love you for it,' Eric murmured, bending down. His lips brushed her cheek.

'I think I'll go back to the jump, behave as normal,' he said, straightening up. 'As far as one can. We don't want to turn it into a feud.'

Jenny, chin still in her hand, watched him go.

Yet it would be very difficult now to carry on as normal, to pretend that nothing had happened.

*   *   *

Philip and Matt eyed each other warily like gladiators in a ring. Matt stood in front of the fire and lit a small cigar.

'Well, I'm sorry,' he said, forestalling his son. 'I apologise. I really do.'

'You should have said *that* to Eric.'

'I'm not sorry about what I said to him. It needed saying. I'm sorry to you, *and* Jenny. I embarrassed you both. I let my feelings get the better of me, but I do want the fellow out.'

'But why? There's masses of room.'

'Because I do. Even the family talk about him.'

'You mean about him and Jenny?'

'Yes. It makes *me* look a fool, a cuckold!'

An expression of enlightenment spread across Philip's face. 'Is *that* why we had this outburst?'

'Partly.'

'Couldn't you have been politer, more discreet?'

'Perhaps, but the fellow annoys me. I never did like him very much. Jenny has spent a fortune on those stables and the horses. I believe he's hardly contributed a penny.'

'I believe he's not very well off.'

'Then he should have chosen something less expensive to do.'

'He was about to go and work for a bloodstock agent when Jenny made her offer.'

'I never knew that.'

'Well, it's true. He's a very old friend of the family.'

'And her lover?' Matt looked belligerently at him.

'Surely you don't believe that, Dad?'

'Why shouldn't he be?'

'You're jealous, then?'

'I'm not "jealous". I just don't want him buzzing around my young wife.'

'But he isn't. I can assure you of that.'

'How do you know?'

'Because I do.'

Matt stared at Philip and Philip returned the stare. And then, at last, Matt knew too.

'We never did talk about this, Dad.' Philip's tone was more gentle as he interrupted the silence that had fallen between them. Matt sank on to the sofa as one carrying a great weight. 'About me being gay.'

'I'd rather not.'

'It's something you just don't want to face up to, isn't it?' Philip put several logs on the fire and poked the embers into life.

'It causes me such pain,' Matt said at last in a broken voice.

'But Dad – '

'I don't care what you say, or how you try and explain it; it does cause me pain. It hurts. I can't understand it, you see.'

'I exiled myself so that I could spare you, Dad.'

'I know. I know.' Matt nodded several times, his eyes fixed on the flames now licking round the logs. 'I still don't understand it. I *can't* understand it. That my son . . . '

Matt suddenly put his head in his hands and, to Philip's extreme consternation, began to weep. 'I'm so unhappy,' he moaned, 'so unhappy.'

'Oh Dad, come on.' Philip bent over his father and put his arms round him. 'I'm still your son. I love you.'

'And I love you, Philip, but I *don't* understand.'

Philip had never seen his father cry. Hadn't imagined he could; that such a robust, controlled, forceful man could have a weakness. It disturbed him a lot.

'Maybe I should go back to the States, Dad . . . '

'No,' Matt flapped a hand in front of him, 'I don't mean *that*. It's just that my life at the moment is so *miserable*, so full of guilt . . . Your mother . . . Jenny . . . What I don't understand is why, at my time of life, should all this be happening to me?'

Jenny lay quietly by Matt's side, knowing that he wasn't asleep. Philip and Eric had, after all, abandoned jumping and driven off at about three, and had not returned. Jenny spent what was left of the short winter's day messing about with the horses; grooming them, feeding them, fussing over them as if they were her children – which perhaps, in a sense, they were. She knew Matt was in his study pretending to work. She too was surprised to see traces of tears, and suddenly felt angry with Philip, with Eric, the whole bloody world.

She and Matt had an evening meal alone together where the conversation was again desultory, stilted, the air vibrant with tension.

Jenny wondered just how long it could possibly last.

'Matt? Are you awake?'

'Yes.'

'I thought you were.'

'I am. What a terrible day . . . '

'Matt, Paul Vernon would quite like you to go and see him.'

'Vernon? Vernon?' Matt said in the dark.

'The gynaecologist.'

'Oh, yes. You saw him again?'

'I saw him last week.'

'You're not . . . ' Matt reached over and put on the light, looked at her.

'No, no, I'm not; but he still says there is no physical reason. Thinks it's psychological. He says he'd like to talk to you, man to man. Thinks maybe we should have a holiday together . . .'

No response.

'Well, it would be nice,' Jenny said after a while, a little nonplussed at his apparent lack of interest. 'We haven't really been alone for any length of time since our honeymoon. Perhaps it would . . . help, Matt. Matt, are you listening?'

'I'm listening,' Matt said and, stretching over, put out the light. 'But my mind can't focus, Jenny. I'm too overwrought. Too exhausted. Let's talk about it tomorrow.'

Jenny lay there almost until dawn, wide awake, full of pain, full of hurt, wondering when, if ever, this unhappy time would end.

CHAPTER 18

'Good evening, Lord Ransom.'

'Good evening, Bridget.' Matt winked as she came forward to greet him. This formal welcome when he arrived at the club always amused him, vaguely titillated him. 'And how are *you* today, my dear?' He looked round and then furtively kissed her lips, tightly clutching her hand.

'I'm fine thanks, Lord Ransom,' she replied with the usual quick, nervous smile in case they were observed. 'Are you going to dine?'

'I wondered if you could dine with me?' he whispered.

'It's against the rules, I'm afraid,' she said loudly. 'A drink but not dinner.'

'Let's have a drink, then?' He looked at his watch, then once more, *sotto voce*, 'Maybe we could eat when you've finished?'

'After midnight?' She pretended to be surprised.

'Why not? I can wait.'

'Well . . . ' She lowered her head and gave that shy, sexy smile he so loved. 'If you're *sure*, that would be very nice.'

'We'll have a drink. I'll have a sandwich to keep me going and then a couple of hours at the tables. I'll wait for you round the corner in the car.' Then he slipped his arm through hers and they walked slowly towards the bar, heads together, deeply engaged in conversation like two old friends, people who had known each other a long time.

Bridget only drank low-alcoholic wine while on duty. Justin O'Leary didn't really approve of it, but Matt was an important customer, and there were others like him, people of power, money and influence whom the club liked to keep happy. Besides, Lord Ransom had only recently started to visit them regularly, and he thought he knew why. Bridget had that effect on a lot of men, which was why she was such a valuable asset. He walked over to where they sat in the corner, heads close together, and bowed:

''Evening, Lord Ransom.'

'Good evening, Justin,' Matt said jovially. 'Will you have a drink?'

'Never have a drink on duty, Lord Ransom.'

'Then have a glass of low alcohol wine or orange juice, like Bridget.'

'Well, maybe a low calorie lager then, Lord Ransom. Thank you very much.' He went over and gave the order to the barman, then he joined his valuable customer and the member of staff.

'We are seeing quite a lot of you, Lord Ransom. Have you moved permanently to London?'

'Oh, no. But I spend several days a week here.'

'Lady Ransom well?'

'Very well, thank you.'

'She prefers the country, I expect?'

'Yes, as a matter of fact, she does. Tell me, Justin, are you a family man?'

'Alas no, Lord Ransom.' Justin took a sip of his lager and shook his head sadly. 'I am wedded to my work. But maybe one day . . . ' He smiled and glanced at his watch. 'Bridget, I think, if you don't mind . . . if you can spare her, Lord Ransom.'

'Of course,' Matt said amiably. 'I know she has a job to do. And I'll have a sandwich and another whisky and a couple of games of chemmy.' He looked up as she rose and winked. 'See you later, my dear.'

'Not eating with us tonight, Lord Ransom?'

'Not tonight,' Matt said and, as the manager turned his head, he winked again at Bridget and patted her gently on the behind.

Later, as he sat at the back of the car waiting for her, he realised that she fascinated him in the way Jenny had. Only she was more willing and malleable than Jenny had been. With Jenny sex was an orgasmic upheaval, but with a nineteen-year-old night-club hostess it was a jolly rollicking affair, exciting and inventive, and a lot coarser than it had been with Jenny. It had begun just like this with Jenny: fascination leading to obsession. Jenny, all fire once she got going, had been like an iceberg at the start, hard to crack.

And now here was Bridget, peering through the window, looking as fresh and delightful as if she had not been working hard all night trying to please men in noisy, smoke-filled gaming rooms and a crowded bar; taking coats, carrying drinks, filling in for the barman, the croupier and, sometimes, the waiters if necessary. All things to all men. Not much of a life.

He opened the door with a wide smile of greeting, and then she was in his arms, a passionate kiss in the back seat while Peter started the engine and the car purred north-wards towards St John's Wood.

Peter put them off outside the block, then said goodnight. The night porter let them in and they went up in the lift, pressed close together, tactile.

The flat was in darkness except for two low lights in the drawing room, a shaft of light from the half-open dining room door.

Matt helped Bridget off with her coat, kissed her shoulder, and then they went into the kitchen, opening the door of the fridge to see what Maria had prepared for them. Salmon roulade and cold beef. A bottle of Sancerre. Perfect.

'You take the starter, darling, and I'll bring up the rest,'

Matt said, fetching the chilled wine from the fridge and extracting the cork. 'I'm terribly hungry, aren't you?'

'Starving.' Bridget excitedly put the plates on a tray and led the way into the dining room.

She thought it such a lovely, luxurious room, with the contemporary furniture, all that polished teak and steel, the dazzling lights of London twinkling away beyond the park. It was a far cry from a bed-sit in Kentish Town, inducing in her a feeling of luxury and opulence she had coveted all her life; coveted but never expected to find outside a cinema or the intimacy of the TV screen.

She put the plates on the places laid for them by a discreet woman who, even if she cared, would never ask questions, certainly never tittle-tattle to Lady R. – the roulade in front of them, the beef to one side, the bowls of salad centre table, the vinaigrette, the rolls and butter. Then she looked up with grateful, sparkling eyes as Matt began to pour the crisp, amber liquid into the tall Swedish glasses.

'To you, my darling,' he said, raising his glass.

'To you, Matt.' She raised hers and looked into his eyes. Linking arms, they kissed, then drank from the other's glass.

Such happiness. How long could it last? They ate in silence for a few moments, both clearly hungry, then Bridget broke the silence.

'Aren't you worried your wife might find us here?'

'I'm sure she'd let me know if she were coming to London.'

'Does she ever come?'

'Not as much as she did. She would never just turn up, here I mean. Don't worry about a thing.'

Bridget, puzzled, laid down her knife and fork and looked at him. 'But you're not *estranged* in any way, are you, Matt? Not out of love?'

Matt joined his hands together, elbows on the table, and looked across at her.

'Jenny and I do not exactly see eye to eye. It's been like this for some time. It's nobody's fault. We're different people. She likes horses. I don't. I adore opera, she doesn't . . . '

'If I were married,' Bridget said guilefully, 'I should make it my business to do what my husband liked.'

'Exactly. My first wife liked what I liked; she went out of her way to fit in with me. And I with her. I was not, never have been, an unreasonable man.'

'Then why did you fall out of love with *her*?'

'My dear, after thirty years – ' he waved a hand vaguely in the air – 'you can't remain "in love". No one can. I loved her and I still do. I was desolate when she took the overdose. It made me feel very guilty, as if I hadn't explained to her just how I felt. Frankly I was obsessed by Jenny. I should have had an affair with her, but she wouldn't have it. She forced me into marriage and now,' he looked at her, 'I'm in love with someone else. A woman, I suspect, with a little more wisdom than my dearest Jenny, whom of course I still love. You see – ' Matt reached over and helped himself to more slices of good red beef – 'in the Orient men *understand* all about this. They take another woman while still loving the first, and then another while continuing to love the first *and* the second. It's all a question of sex drive, which in a man is very strong. After many years I have come to the conclusion that monogamy is unnatural. On the other hand, there *may* come a time when someone like me, at my age, finally meets a woman who suits him in every way, and then he has no need to look further.'

Matt looked over to her, his expression soft, sentimental. 'You know the song: "when he thinks he's past love, it is then he meets his last love and – "' Matt, slightly inebriated, started to sing, conducting himself with his hand as he swayed back and forth – '"he loves her as he *never* loved before."'

'Oh Matt, that is *very* sweet,' Bridget cooed appreciatively when he'd finished, and then he put his hand on her knee, took a large gulp of wine and, leaning over, filled her mouth with it.

Later Bridget sat on the bed and began to undress. Matt disappeared into his dressing room, from which he shortly emerged in a towelling robe. She was quite nude now, vulnerable, sitting gazing at him. He knelt on the floor, parted her legs while she lay back on the bed and gave herself up to the extremes of pleasure.

Finally Matt rested his head on her lap. 'Bridget, I am *so* happy with you. If only you knew how much. You have given me new life.'

He then took off his robe and climbed into bed while she lay alongside him, her expression thoughtful, apprehensive rather than amorous.

'Bridget?' He gazed at her. 'Worried about something?'

'Matt, there is something I must tell you. I've been trying to tell you all evening, for days really, but the words can't come.'

'What is it?' he cried in alarm, sitting up. 'Don't tell me you're leaving London?'

'No, *no*,' she said reassuringly, pushing his head back on the pillow. 'But it *is* serious, and I think you should know, though it's going to be perfectly all right.'

'You're ill?'

'Not at all. I think it was the first night . . . rather, the morning after. You remember I brought you home, you were so drunk? Well, of course I wasn't expecting it . . . '

'Don't tell me you're pregnant?' His face reflected a myriad of emotions. 'And it is *mine*?'

'It's definitely yours, Matt. I had no other boyfriend. I wasn't on the pill, you see, and didn't like to refuse you. Of course I went to the doctor and put myself on the pill after, but . . . well, the doctor says it is *quite* definite and it is about twelve weeks . . . '

'Pregnant. My God!' Matt covered his face with his hands.

'Of course I've arranged to have a termination. It *is* a little late, but I only knew for sure last week.'

'Termination!' Matt again managed to struggle to a sitting position. 'Are you mad? Don't you know my wife and I have been trying to have a baby almost since we were married?'

'But Matt . . . I couldn't possibly *have* it.'

'Why couldn't you?'

'What could I do? Where could I go? It wouldn't be fair, Matt.'

'There's no *question* about what you must do or where you must go.' Matt began frenziedly to rub his hair with excitement. 'I still have a flat in Mayfair where you can live until we find something better. Of course, at the moment marriage is out of the question. You must realise that.'

'Of course, Matt,' Bridget said humbly.

'It would cause a stink, not only in my family, but it would not be good for me in the world of business.'

'I *do* understand . . . '

'The press have their piggish little eyes on me. There's already been an unsavoury article about me marrying a "bimbo". You can guess what they'd say . . . ' He didn't finish, perhaps realising just in time that his words might cause offence. 'I would, of course, support you and the child. I am a very wealthy man and there is no problem about money at all . . . '

'I never did it deliberately, Matt.'

'I believe you and I understand. But I'm glad it happened. Believe me, I'm delighted. I love children and they love me. You would never want for anything. Nor the child. I think I can make you very happy, Bridget.'

He looked at her, his expression a curious cross between that of a lover and an excited schoolboy.

'You already have, Matt,' Bridget said, nestling back, putting her head on the pillow beside him.

'Well, gentlemen, I think that concludes the business for today. Sorry that Lord Ransom couldn't be with us. I don't quite know . . . ' Andrew Rose looked interrogatively at his

335

secretary who, head bent, was scribbling the minutes. She shook her head without looking up.

'Maybe he mistook the day.' Fred Archer, a large, red-faced construction engineer, looked annoyed. 'I came all the way from Tyneside for this meeting.'

'I know, Mr Archer.' Andrew got up and went over to him, as the others, who had been gathered round the table, also rose. 'Believe me, I'm terribly sorry.'

'Can't you take any decisions without him?'

'Not really; but I hope we'll get back to you with an answer without another meeting being necessary. If not, Lord Ransom will come up himself to see you.'

'Maybe he thinks he's too bloody important,' Archer muttered, addressing the underling he had brought with him.

'I assure you he does not, Mr Archer.'

Maurice, who hitherto had been silent, interrupted him. 'Something very urgent must have come up. I'm sure Father will telephone and apologise. I know he's very keen on this deal . . . '

Maurice trailed off as an obviously angry-looking Andrew Rose took Mr Archer by the elbow and steered him out of the room. He was followed by Gerard Singer and all the other executives who had attended the meeting, with the exception of Mark Strong, the finance director, who stayed behind, obviously something on his mind. The last to leave shut the door, whereupon Mark turned to Maurice, his face grave.

'I know, I know,' Maurice held up a hand as Mark was about to speak. 'It's very *naughty* of Dad.'

'It's more than "naughtiness", Maurice.' Mark sat on the side of the table, swinging his legs. 'Does your father really have the interests of this company in mind, or doesn't he?'

'Of course he does,' Maurice said indignantly.

'Then what's happening to him? His behaviour is getting increasingly erratic. He misses meetings without any explanation. He takes unilateral decisions, sometimes with disastrous consequences.'

'Like?' Maurice said aggressively.

'The purchase of Arbuthnot Clifford . . . a second-rate machine-tool firm.'

'Dad didn't think they were second-rate.'

'He didn't do his homework. When we looked into their financial situation, it was ten times worse than we imagined. Another lightning decision of your father's, taken without sufficient consultation. You remember what happened to Ferranti? The same thing will happen to us. We are now a public company and will have to be doubly responsible to our shareholders, as well as to our employees.'

'Well, you'd better talk to Dad about it, not me.' Maurice looked up as Andrew Rose came back into the room, the same expression of hostility on his face.

'I see Mark has been talking to you.' Andrew Rose stuck his hands in his pockets.

'Yes. I'm not trying to defend Father – '

'But you are.' Mark pressed the point home. 'We're talking to *you*, Maurice, in the hope that with your influence over your father you will be able to knock some sense into him. Otherwise . . . '

'Otherwise?' Maurice looked from one grave face to the other.

'We might take steps to remove your father from the chairmanship, even from the board of directors.'

'But you can't do that.'

'We can,' Rose said sweetly. 'We can call an extraordinary general meeting of shareholders and you will find that we have a clear majority – or will have as soon as we explain the situation and the possible disastrous losses as a result of acquiring Arbuthnot Clifford. We haven't even begun to realise what a pig in a poke we've purchased and, frankly, your father is directly responsible. Did it with no consultation at all. He seems to think the function of the board is merely to rubber-stamp everything he does.'

Maurice turned his back on the two men and went to stand by the window. He gazed out at the traffic rushing along London Wall. In front of him was the old City, behind him the new, ugly Barbican complex. He thought, sometimes, that his father represented the old paternalistic working ways, and these thrusting, ambitious men in front of him the new. He, as the grandson of the founder, a Ransom through and through, was somewhere in between.

'I'll have a word with Father . . . '

'"A word" isn't good enough,' Mark said firmly.

'Then what do you want me to do?' Maurice spun round.

'A serious talk, followed by a formal meeting with the board.'

'What, to eject him?'

'To censure him. To warn him what will happen. We want a lot more communication and consultation, or we want the resignation of your father who, it seems to me since he acquired that glossy new wife, has lost interest in the business.'

'That is not true.'

'Then see to it, Maurice,' Andrew wagged a finger at him and, after nodding to Mark to follow him, left the room.

'Sorry . . . ' Mark began looking chastened by Andrew's vehemence. 'I wouldn't have put it so strongly myself . . . '

'Don't worry, I'll talk to Dad.' Maurice remained tight-lipped. 'I'll put it to him, as you've put it to me.'

Maurice felt very isolated and alone as the men left and shut the door. The boardroom seemed a large, deserted place. He felt that if he was to keep his own position in the company, he had better play his cards carefully. These new-style executives were completely lacking in sentiment in a tough, competitive world struggling with recession.

Perhaps they were right.

338

He looked at his watch, gazed on to the road again and then hurriedly left the room.

He popped his head into his secretary's office, told her he was going out for lunch, and then got the lift to the ground floor, ran down the steps on to London Wall, and hailed a taxi.

Cutting through Clerkenwell, Holborn and Camden Town, it took about twenty minutes to get to the apartment block in St John's Wood, where he paid off the taxi and, for a few minutes, stood looking up at the top floor.

The first thing he saw as he lowered his eyes was the green Jag with Peter sitting in the driving seat reading a paper.

'Morning, Peter.' Maurice popped his head in.

'Oh, good morning, sir.' Peter looked up, startled.

'Is my father there?'

'Er,' Peter seemed momentarily confused, 'I think so . . .'

'Well, you'd hardly be waiting for him here if he wasn't, would you?' Maurice said brusquely, and ran up the steps and pushed through the front door before the porter had time to open it for him.

Upstairs, Maria opened the door. When she saw Maurice she too looked startled.

'Is my father here, Maria . . . '

'I,' Maria looked behind her and, gently, Maurice pushed past her and went swiftly along the corridor to the dining room, from which he had heard voices that now stopped. He looked in and saw his father casually dressed in shirt and flannels, sharing the table with a woman he had never seen before. They appeared to be enjoying a leisurely lunch, or maybe it was a late breakfast, as the smell of bacon and eggs lingered.

Matt looked as though he had just removed his hand from the hand of the woman — or girl, rather. Despite her apparent sophistication, she looked no older than eighteen or nineteen, a fresh-faced, dark-haired beauty with huge brown eyes, now opened wide, and sensuous lips.

Maurice stood at the door, looking at his father, who gazed at him before half rising and pointing to the woman beside him.

'Maurice,' he said, and then stopped as if he wasn't sure how to proceed. 'May I introduce Bridget Murphy? Bridget, my dear, this is my son, Maurice.'

'How do you do, Miss Murphy,' Maurice said politely, but did not attempt to shake hands with the woman, who looked rather shell-shocked. 'Dad, could I have a word with you?'

'Certainly,' Matt said immediately, and looked down at Bridget. 'Shan't be a moment, my dear.' He then went towards the door and through into the corridor, as Maurice, without another glance at the girl, stood aside to let him pass, shutting the door after them.

Matt preceded him into the drawing room, still clutching his table napkin, for once looking ill at ease.

'Maurice . . . ' he began, as Maurice followed him into the room.

'Dad, what *is* going on? Who *is* that woman?'

'She's a friend.' Matt threw down his napkin and stuck his hands in his pockets.

'*Friend*!' Maurice was almost beside himself with indignation. 'Do you realise you missed a very important meeting this morning with Archer Construction? They were on the verge of concluding a very good deal with us, and now they may be changing their minds.'

'Heavens, I completely forgot.' Matt clapped a hand to his mouth. 'I thought my diary was clear.'

'Dad, *Peter* is downstairs waiting for you. Surely Peter knew you had a meeting?'

'Well, yes . . . '

'Peter came, and I suppose you told him to go away.'

'Maria told him to wait,' Matt mumbled. 'Said I wasn't feeling well.'

'No phones answered,' Maurice stabbed a finger at him. 'Dad, you knew *quite* well about the meeting. I guess you

340

were holed up with that woman . . . Dad, I really can't believe this of you. What *is* going on?'

Matt collapsed in a chair and ran a hand over his face. 'I'm very unhappy, Maurice. I'm fifty-nine and I've made a mess of my life.'

'You certainly have, recently anyway. But it won't help if you go round screwing other women. This one looks even younger than Jenny was when you met her.'

'She is; but she's awfully sweet . . . '

'Well, Dad, you must get rid of her at once, or you'll have a first-class scandal on your hands. And, what is more, Rose and Strong are out for your blood. They want you out of the chair unless you pull yourself together.'

'What a bloody nerve.' Matt, recovering himself rapidly, looked indignant. 'What colossal cheek.'

'They have discovered that Arbuthnot Clifford's accounts were all wrong. They are ten times more in debt than the accounts showed. Rose thinks a Ferranti-type scandal might ensue.'

'What rubbish! Neither we nor Arbuthnot are anything *like* the size of Ferranti. That was fraud on a massive scale.'

'We're a public company and growing. Frankly I don't think they consider you're fit to be in charge.'

'I see.' Matt fell silent for a moment. Then: 'And what do *you* think, Maurice?'

Maurice, sensing a thaw, if not capitulation, sat opposite his father and leaned forward, a hand on one knee. 'I think you're a first-class businessman and industrialist, one of the best in the country. But I think something has happened to you, throwing you off course, and I think it's since you met Jenny.'

'Did they say that?'

'They called her your "glossy wife", no doubt referring to the number of times you appear in the papers, as well as her youth.'

'Bloody cheek!'

341

'I don't think anyone would say anything, Dad, if you didn't neglect the business – or rather I should say, didn't try to run it single-handed.'

'It always worked in the past. You know I hate all these meetings, committees; such a waste of time.'

'Yes, but we're now a public company, responsible to shareholders, and we've got some very tough men on our management team. Rose is one of the best and, believe me, if he says he will vote you off the board, he will.' Maurice stood up. 'Now get rid of that . . . that girl, and we'll go to the office and tackle Rose.'

'If you think I'm apologising to him I'm not. It's my company. My father founded it and I built it up. If necessary I will buy it back . . . '

'Then you will be in trouble.' Maurice gave a brief laugh. 'Look, Dad, what you do with your own life is, I suppose in the last resort, your affair. But having completely messed up one good marriage with an apparently unsuitable woman, as you don't seem to be faithful to her, please don't tell me that you're stricken all over again. What *has* got into you, Dad?'

'I suppose I didn't sow my wild oats in the past.' Matt's usually strong voice had turned into an uncharacteristic whine. 'I was always a good and loyal husband. And please don't call Jenny unsuitable. She is a very beautiful woman but she isn't easy. Jenny's got a very wilful, independent streak and, frankly, at my age, I want a more compliant wife. Jenny and I have grown apart. I'm not one of these modern men like you, you know. I believe in a man's place and a woman's place.'

'Then you should have found out more about her before you ruined your marriage to a woman who *was* compliant and did please you. Mum lived for you.'

'She did,' Matt sighed loudly. 'She was a wonderful mother, *is* a wonderful mother. But I can't explain to you what happened to me. I shan't try. I was obsessed by Jenny . . . wanted her at all costs. But I want an easy life too. This desperate business to have a baby . . . You can't think what we've been through. It's not what I want at my time in life. Now this dear little thing, Bridget, she adores me. Worships the ground I walk on. She makes me feel important, on top. I've no real time for all this equality . . . '

'Don't tell me you want to marry *her*.'

'I don't yet know *what* I'm going to do, to be honest.' Matt worriedly scratched his head. 'But I tell you one thing,' he gazed earnestly up at his son, his expression at once bewildered and pathetic, 'I'm beginning to think I'm in love with her. Just in the way I first loved Jenny.'

Maurice had always been the solid, sensible one of the family, the calm, practical, good-natured elder son, responsible and mature from an early age. But he knew he had been dominated by his father. In a way he wanted to be *like* him, and it was a shock to him to find that this revered parent, whom he had always wished to emulate, had feet of clay.

A lot of Maurice's safe world fell apart when his father deserted his mother. Maybe that accelerated his own decision to marry, to put in new roots to replace those which had been dug up.

Shirley – solid, sensible, practical like him – was an ideal helpmeet, and the young Ransoms, although they were unaware of it, to some extent mirrored their elders as they'd been thirty years before. Maurice had a strong sense of country, family, loyalty. He was conservative in every sense. Voted for the party in power, believed in old-fashioned values.

He wanted to continue Ransom Engineering as his grandfather and father had done, and he now began to fear he might be driven out of the company, along with his father, if common sense did not prevail. He knew he was only tolerated as the son of the chairman, perhaps resented, and Ransom's would not be the first company to find itself taken over by people without the ideals of the founder.

Maurice pondered the situation in the course of the hour's drive from London to his home, eager to seek the advice of beloved, sensible Shirley. In all this turmoil, he realised how much he now valued his secure home, loving wife, the near presence of his mother, his sisters, and now even Philip, who, although they didn't see him so much, hovered comfortingly in the background. Like his siblings, Maurice would have liked nothing better than to see his parents united again. Now that hope had been dashed completely. He realised that Matt seemed intent on going down the slippery slope of many men when they sensed old age approaching.

'Dad is completely going off his rocker,' Maurice observed to Shirley when, after a stiff whisky, he told her about his day, the missed meeting, the comments of the management team and, finally, the encounter with the latest love in his father's life.

'And you say she's only nineteen.' Shirley's face bore the same astonished expression it had as the story had unrolled.

'Well, not much more.'

'A *night*-club hostess,' Shirley went on. 'I can't believe it. Is he going to *divorce* Jenny and marry her?'

'Of course he's not. The whole thing's absurd. If he does he will have to resign from the chairmanship of the company, whether he wants to or not. We can't support that sort of scandal.'

'Jenny, of course, knows nothing?'

'As far as one knows, absolutely nothing. She wouldn't stay on with Dad a moment if she did.'

'I don't know how he gets the opportunity. They have such a packed social life.'

'Less now than before. Jenny has taken to country life and they turn down a lot of invitations. Dad spends most of the week in London, Jenny in the country.'

'And your father's financial position? Is that safe?'

'Oh, very safe. Chudleigh belongs solely to Dad, and his private fortune is absolutely secure and independent of the company. But, I mean, it's just not *good* enough, is it? To have your father playing an old goat at his age.'

'Your mother was talking about his sixtieth birthday.' Shirley refilled her glass and Maurice's, handed his to him.

'Yes, that's coming up. I'd forgotten about that. She really has started to forgive him, hasn't she? She realises the fascination with Jenny is on the wane, but she doesn't know that he has someone else.'

'People do remarry, of course. Poor Elspeth. It will be a double shock to her.'

'I'm going to try and talk some sense into Dad before that happens,' Maurice said grimly. 'Try and make him behave like a man of his years, and not a silly old fool people will begin to feel sorry for.'

The bell rang. Shirley looked at the clock on the wall of the kitchen where they'd been talking while she prepared dinner. A person who left nothing to chance, the planned meal for that night was well advanced. Stuff had been prepared days beforehand, and taken out that morning or the night before from the deep freezer.

'That will be your mother and Philip,' she said. 'Let them in, dear, would you?'

'My goodness, I haven't washed or changed.' Crestfallen, Maurice looked down at his crumpled suit.

She gave him an appraising glance. 'You look fine. Give them a drink and then change into something more comfortable.'

'Not a word to Mother about all this,' Maurice warned her.

'Of course not,' she vehemently shook her head. 'The very idea.'

Maurice went to the door and opened it. His mother and brother, arms linked, stood smiling on the threshold.

345

'Here we are,' Elspeth said brightly. 'Not too early, I hope, dear?'

'Oh no, Mum,' Maurice stood back to admit them. 'I haven't been in long, but I'll get you a drink before I go and change.'

'What a lovely day it's been,' Elspeth said. 'Warm for the time of year. Was it in town?'

'I hardly noticed.' The weather that day had been the least of Maurice's preoccupations.

'Sherry for you, Mum? Philip?'

'G and t would be nice.' Philip, casually dressed in jeans and a thick sweater, threw himself into a chair.

'Where's Shirley?' Elspeth hovered at Maurice's elbow. 'Shall I go and see if she needs any help?'

'She doesn't.' Maurice passed her her drink. 'Look, you and Philip have your drink, and we'll be with you in a jiffy.'

'Did you see your father in town today?' Elspeth asked.

'Er, yes,' Maurice hesitated by the door.

'And how is he?'

'He seemed well.' Maurice gave a little wave and, feeling fraught, ran upstairs to change. After the sort of day he'd had, he felt he could have done without the family.

He too got into jeans and sweater. When he got downstairs he found Philip on his own.

'Mum couldn't resist helping, I suppose.' Maurice got a drink and perched on a chair near his brother.

'Naturally not.' He smiled lazily at Maurice. 'You look tense.'

'It's been that sort of a day. This commuting between Oxford and London gets on my nerves. It's too much.'

'You should stay at the flat. Dad loves company.'

'Oh, does he?' Maurice looked at his brother, wondering what he would say if he knew. Or perhaps he knew already. Philip was a dark horse, always had been; difficult to fathom. A younger brother who, in many ways, seemed older. 'I'd never see Shirley.'

346

'Quite!' Philip put his glass to his lips. 'Mother's much better,' he said as he lowered his glass.

'Much better.'

'She's started to enjoy life again.'

'We must be sure she doesn't get depressed. She doesn't really want to live alone, you know. She doesn't like it.'

'Has George really given up the idea of going to live abroad?'

'I think so. They've also convinced Henry he shouldn't be domiciled abroad for the sake of his health, and I agree. He's not going to get better but worse. I think they may try and buy an apartment somewhere and go for long periods, maybe taking Mum, but they're not going to live abroad permanently.'

'That sounds like a good idea.' Philip took another sip of his drink.

'They'll sell the farm, get somewhere larger round here and Mum will move in. That will free Beth to pursue her career and Shirley and I will have less to worry about.'

'Worry? Who's talking about worry?' Shirley breezed into the room, wiping her hands on a cloth. 'Everything is ready if you'd like to go in, gentlemen.'

'Shirley, you didn't have another drink?'

'Your mum and I had one in the kitchen. She's in sparkling form. I haven't seen her so well since – well, you know – since the divorce.'

Elspeth's good form seemed set to continue throughout the evening. The dinner proved, after Maurice's misgivings, to be a jolly affair. Shirley, in addition to her other accomplishments, was a splendid cook, and Maurice always kept a good cellar.

Beth had gone up to London for an audition, and the prospects seemed promising, so she occupied their attention for a while.

'I feel I mustn't stand in the way of her career,' Elspeth looked a little nervously around the company. 'Beth isn't getting any younger, and they do say after the age of thirty . . .'

347

'Oh, Mother, there are some splendid older actresses,' Philip protested. 'But I do know what you mean . . . '

'She gave up the rep for me. She's so loyal. She's never once agreed to meet that woman . . . ' A shade darkened Elspeth's face for the first time that evening.

'Mum, if you're having a dig at us,' Philip calmly poured cream over his home-made chocolate mousse, 'I personally feel no guilt. Dad and I have been estranged enough in the past without making it into a family feud . . . '

'But I didn't mean – '

'I can't ostracise Jenny. I think she's rather a nice person . . . '

'Philip, do be careful,' Maurice muttered.

'No, Maurice, I have to say it. I do. We can't just not talk about Jenny, pretend she doesn't exist because of Mum.'

'It won't last, anyway,' Elspeth recovered her composure. 'I can read the signs. I may once have felt bitter about her but no more. Everyone talks about her and that man anyway.'

'What man?' Philip looked up sharply.

'The Swede,' Maurice said briefly. 'Eric.'

'There's nothing between Eric and Jenny, Mum.' Philip pushed back his chair and started to laugh. 'I'm sorry to disappoint you, but there isn't.'

'And how do you know? She has bought him horses, and paid for an elaborate ring with jumps and fences, entirely out of her own pocket.'

'That was for her sake as well. Eric is a *very* old friend of the family. Jenny was keen to have her own interests apart from being Dad's wife, which is where you went wrong, Mum. And, anyway, I happen to know that Eric has another romantic interest in his life, someone else.'

'Oh?' Shirley looked across at him enquiringly, put down her spoon. 'Who?'

'Me. As a matter of fact we're looking for a place in the country, Gloucestershire maybe, with enough room for horses and a ring so that he can continue his training career.' Unperturbed, Philip looked round the astonished faces of his family. 'I've already got my eyes on a property, so it could happen quite soon.'

CHAPTER 19

Bridget lay in bed drinking her morning tea, eyes on the TV at the foot of the bed. One thing about a small, cramped room was that you could see the TV everywhere. When she was at home she watched it a lot, because there was not much else to do.

She had not slept well, but still she was awake early; she had cramps in her stomach which alarmed her a little. She got up and made tea, felt better, returned to bed and put on breakfast television as the bright, chatty presenter was introducing some gossipy item of news.

'And Her Royal Highness attended . . . ' Bridget sat up and took notice. Matt had been going to the royal première of a film the previous evening, in the company of royalty. He was chairman of the charity in whose aid the film was being premièred, one of the many good causes with which Matt was associated. The car drove up to the front of the cinema, the crowd surged forward, and the princess alighted and gave her customary practised smile. The camera followed her inside and there, resplendent in full evening dress, waiting to greet her, was Matt, who stepped forward, bowed and shook hands. Then he turned to a very beautiful, elegant woman just behind him. 'Lady Ransom being presented to the princess . . . ' intoned the commentator.

Lady Ransom smiled, curtsied. She looked ravishing. She

wore a royal blue evening dress split up one side, with a décolleté neckline and a wide sash to accentuate her slim waist. Her beautiful hair, almost pure gold in colour, was swept up and secured by a tiara of small pearls and diamonds. She carried between her hands a bouquet similar to the one which Matt had presented to the princess.

'*Beautiful* Lady Ransom,' the presenter clucked, adding, with a cheeky little smack of the lips. 'Isn't her husband a lucky man?'

One of the stars of the film was in the studio, and she turned then to interview him. The glamorous royal party faded into the background, and Bridget's eyes lingered on her rival. It was the first time she had seen her in the flesh, as it were, and she wished in many ways she had not.

How could Matt possibly prefer *her*, Bridget Murphy, entirely unknown, to the goddess she had seen on the screen, who easily, in Bridget's opinion, rivalled the overrated beauty of the princess?

Of course, she'd seen photos of Jenny; not many, just one or two in the St John's Wood apartment; one of her and Matt on their wedding day, another when she was a bit younger.

She was very Scandinavian looking, vibrant, alive, exciting . . . Yet, of course, she had one drawback: she didn't understand her husband. How many times had Bridget heard that worn, tired old phrase before? How many men of about Matt's age had she comforted and cosseted since she'd come to London at the age of sixteen, already with hints of the mature woman she was later to become.

Bridget's brown eyes and dark good looks had led her straight to a model agency, which had taken her on to its books. But the relentless trudge of photographers, magazines, dress designers and assorted neurotic ad-people had not only yielded little work, but took its toll of her physically. Never strong, she became seriously ill with pleurisy and decided to give it up.

Through her Irish connections, she knew someone who knew someone who gave her the telephone number of Justin O'Leary. At the time he happened to be looking for a hat-check girl: Bridget admirably filled the bill. She was appealing and good to look at, and also she was naturally subservient to men. She definitely regarded them as superior beings sent by the Almighty to rule the universe. None of men's little foibles annoyed her. She was at home in their midst, comforting them, administering to them and, occasionally, sharing their beds.

Bridget was not poor, but she was parsimonious. She was a saver, putting money away against that rainy day which many young women brought up in near poverty in the suburbs of Dublin were taught to expect. She could maybe have had a bigger room, a flat of her own, but, apart from the money that went on clothes, which she regarded as an investment, she put it all away after sending a little home to the long-suffering mother who had taught her five daughters that men ruled the roost.

What made Matt any different from the rest? Well, nothing, really. He was not young, but he was attractive, he was important, he was a lord. One or two lords, not many, patronised The Sportsman's. She had had absolutely no expectations of Matt, and didn't even know why she'd told him she was pregnant. Maybe she had a hunch that her luck was about to change.

And change it did. But was this for the better? Gnawing her nails as she looked at the TV screen, she wasn't sure. He was a very busy man, had a very beautiful wife. He had so far failed to install her in this much-talked-about Mayfair flat he'd promised her, saying that it still had a tenant in.

True or false? She didn't know. All she knew for sure was that she was getting bigger, thicker, every day. It was now far too late to have an abortion – her Catholic conscience wouldn't let her at this advanced stage – and she would shortly have to give in her notice before she was booted out of the club.

The breakfast television programme finished. The news, another glimpse of the princess at the gala evening the night before, but not of Matt. She flicked off the TV and lay down in bed, feeling rather sorry for herself, insecure, alone in a big world and still not quite twenty.

Marie, her flatmate, had gone to work. She had nothing to do now until evening. She felt a curious apathy descend on her, and she was about to snuggle down and try to sleep again when the doorbell rang.

Nine fifteen. The post? There usually wasn't any. She knelt on the bed and looked out of the window, which was next to it. Across the road stood a dark green Jaguar with the engine still running.

Bridget flung open the window, leaned over the sill and waved. 'Hi!' she called.

'Hi!' Matt, who had been gazing anxiously at the door, stepped back and looked up at her. 'Hi!'

He hadn't been inside the Half Moon Street flat for nearly a year. It looked very much the same as it had when he last saw it, only more impersonal, as places which have been let out for rent often do.

Somehow looking round made Matt uncomfortable, reminding him of his excitement the first time he'd seen it; he'd shown it to Jenny. Now the furniture — new then — was a little worn, the carpet stained. One of the beds had a loud, irritating squeak it hadn't had before. Bridget excitedly threw herself down on all of them. She ran through the flat like a small girl, flinging open doors, exclaiming, admiring. Bridget was so uncritical, easy to please.

He watched her with amused tolerance, thinking just how unlike cool, rather spoilt and critical Jenny she was.

'Well,' he smiled down at her when her inspection was complete, 'will it do?'

'Oh Matt, I can't *believe* it. That it's *mine*!'

'Whenever you like.' Matt tossed the key down on a table. 'It will all have to be cleaned and redecorated.' He looked critically down at his feet. 'I think we can do with a new carpet, but for the time being . . . '

'"Time being", Matt?' Bridget suddenly felt insecure again, nervous.

'Well, my dear, you can't live here all your life, not with a baby, a young child. This is purely temporary. We shall have to see about getting you a nice little house, some-where in the suburbs or, maybe Hampstead or Chiswick. Chiswick is better for me, of course. What do you say, dear?'

'I say,' she went up to him and, stretching, for he was so much taller than she, put her arms around his neck, 'I say you are a very, very kind person.'

'And you're a dear, sweet girl,' he said impulsively, stooping to peck her nose. 'Now I really have to get to my office soon; as there's nothing here, we've just time for a quick coffee round the corner.'

Round the corner was Shepherd's Market, bustling with activity at eleven thirty in the morning. It was sunny, cold, and people hurried past the window of the café where Matt and Bridget sat sipping coffee.

'The only thing wrong is that it's so terribly near the club,' Bridget said after a while.

'What's wrong with that? You'll have left soon, anyway.'

'Well, I just wouldn't want to . . . bump into Justin, people like that.'

'Well, my dear, you can start looking for a house as soon as you like. I'm so terribly busy I'll have to leave it entirely to you. All well at the clinic?'

'Oh yes,' she smiled at him gratefully. There would be no NHS baby for Lord Ransom. She was seeing a Harley Street gynaecologist and was booked into a private clinic near-by. 'You're just so good to me, Matt. Incidentally – ' she stirred her frothy cappuccino – 'I saw you on the TV this morning.'

'Really?' He looked surprised.

'At the gala last night.'

'Oh, was that on the TV?'

'On breakfast TV. They were interviewing one of the stars, I forget his name. Not someone I know terribly well. I suppose you met them all?'

'Yes, we did.'

'Did you enjoy the film?'

'What I saw of it.' He smiled and put his hand over hers. 'I'm afraid I slept through most of it. It had been a long day.'

'Your wife – ' Bridget paused – 'Jenny, is very beautiful, Matt.'

'Oh, you saw her, too?'

'When you presented her to the princess.' Bridget sighed. 'She's lovely.'

'Yes, she's a good-looking girl.' Matt sounded prosaic, matter-of-fact. 'But you're lovely, too.'

'Not like her.'

'No, different.'

'I could never . . . *be* like that, Matt: elegant, graceful.'

'Nonsense, didn't you tell me you were once a model?'

Matt began to feel uncomfortable. What was she getting at? Hadn't he made it perfectly *plain*? Was all *any* woman wanted still marriage? He'd thought modern attitudes had changed all that.

'Oh, don't look so worried,' she said quickly, with that almost uncanny way she had of seeming to read his thoughts, interpret his every wish. 'I know you'd never marry me, Matt, never leave Jenny for me. I wouldn't expect it.'

'It would cause such a scandal,' he said, sighing with relief.

'But I understand, Matt . . . really I do.'

'Bless you, Bridget,' he said, thankful he could relax, unwind in the presence of this wise, understanding, yet not terribly well educated young woman who satisfied a part of him that Jenny would simply never understand.

*   *   *

355

As well as the fact that Justin O'Leary and Bridget Murphy shared a nationality, they had much else in common. They were both good at their work, in a sense dedicated professionals; they were both careful with money and also meticulous and secretive. No one knew where Justin lived or anything about him, whether he was married or single, straight or gay. He was usually the first at the club and the last to leave.

He was the sort of man married to his work. Even his age was indeterminate. He could have been anything from twenty-eight to forty.

Although younger, Bridget was the female counterpart of Justin, working almost as long a day as he did. She too had seemed wedded to her work, until the last few months when, to everyone who knew her, she seemed pre-occupied; her attention to customers slightly half-hearted, her enthusiasm for her duties a little lukewarm.

It was therefore not a great surprise to Justin when, one day early in December, she appeared in his office and put before him an envelope with his name written on it in Bridget's neat hand.

He took it, studied it, and then, without opening it, looked at her.

'Is this your notice, Bridget?'

'It is, Justin. One month, as stated in my contract.'

Justin gazed at her for a few seconds more and then, taking up a paper-knife, slit the envelope, looking at her once more before perusing the contents.

He then glanced at the calendar and, drawing his diary towards him, opened it and scrawled a few words on one of the pages.

'Well,' he said at last, 'we shall be sorry to lose you. Are you taking up other employment, Bridget?' He gestured towards a chair in his small office at the top of the house, whereupon she sat down and folded her hands in her lap.

'I'm going to have a baby, Justin.'

'Ah, as I thought.' Justin bent his head and considered his desk top for a few moments. 'It has not escaped my notice, Bridget, that you have changed your shape.'

'I'm five months pregnant.'

'In that case you have concealed it well.' He looked up at her with a reassuring smile. 'No need to ask who the father is, is there, Bridget?'

'Oh, you guessed that, too?'

'Well . . . do you have any plans, or is His Lordship looking after you?'

'I think he will take care of me, Justin. He is a very good man.'

'In that case, I hope you won't be severing ties with the club, Bridget. After all, it is where you met.'

'I'm sure we won't, Justin.' She stood up and pulled her dress well down over her stomach. There was no doubt she was putting on weight fast now. Justin stood up too.

'Look, Bridget,' he said after a moment's thought, 'I'll have a word with the owners, but I don't think there's any need for you to work out your notice, unless you want to. I dare say you'd like that, wouldn't you?'

Bridget seemed surprised. 'I would but – '

'I'll get a temporary replacement.' He loftily waved a hand in the air. 'You go off and take good care of yourself, and mind you come and see us now with the baby after it's born.'

Just like Bridget, Justin O'Leary had ambitions to rise beyond his calling as the manager of a Mayfair club where, all things being equal, he might well spend the rest of his life. Like Bridget's, his parents too were of humble stock. He too was not well educated, and had started his career as a waiter – first in Dublin, then later Birmingham and finally London.

He was not poor, but he was not rich, and the temptation to acquire a sizeable sum of money for very little work proved in the end irresistible.

One day, not long after Bridget's departure, he picked up the telephone and asked for the news desk of a well-known daily tabloid, whose speciality was sniffing out the foibles, indiscretions and peccadilloes of the famous and publicising them for all it was worth.

Jenny sat at her desk shifting apathetically through the post. Matt's pile there, her much smaller pile here, joint invitations in the middle. 'The presence is requested of Lord and Lady Ransom at a banquet to be held . . . ' Reject, accept, discuss. These, too, went into different piles. There were an awful lot of them. No wonder she felt tired.

And for what, she wondered? What did one really achieve by attending all these pointless functions, except to see and be seen; she wasn't much interested in either, especially as the company was mostly around Matt's age, titled people like themselves.

She felt sometimes that she could see the years stretch endlessly before her, doing the same kind of thing, leading the same kind of life.

The telephone rang and she rose to answer it, looking out of the window to see if there was any sign of Eric. The field was empty. Eric was packing up preparatory to his departure in a few days' time.

'Hello?'

'Oh! Is Lord Ransom there?'

'Who's speaking please?' Pleasantly.

'Well it's his daughter, Beth.'

'Oh . . . ' Awkward pause. 'Beth. This is Jenny.'

'Yes. Is my father there, er, Jenny?'

'No.' Puzzled. 'Have you tried his office?'

'He isn't there either. No one seems to know where he is.'

'Oh dear, he does seem to be disappearing a lot these days. I tell you what, we have a function in town tonight. If you don't get him . . . Is it urgent?'

'No. Not really. It's just that I've been offered a part . . . '

'Oh, he *will* be delighted. Congratulations. May I ask what in?'

'I'd rather tell him myself, if you don't mind.'

'Of course.' Jenny felt chastened, but also a little indignant at the pointed snub. 'Oh, and Beth . . . '

'Yes?'

'We really *would* love to see you here or in London one day. Is there any chance you could come and stay, or come for dinner? You'd always be very welcome, and it would give your father such pleasure. Me, too, of course.'

'Thank you. I'll think about it. Goodbye.'

'Goodbye, Beth.' But Matt's daughter had already replaced the receiver at her end.

Jenny walked disconsolately back to her desk, looked out of the window on the grey December day. Well, one cheerful spot on the horizon was that they had planned a Christmas break in the sunshine. A friend of Matt's kept a yacht in Grand Bahama, and they were off to Freeport for Christmas. The Wilsons were even older than Matt. Henry Wilson, a retired High Court judge, had been a boyhood friend of Matt's, and his wife, Edith, a lifelong pal of Elspeth's. This was not a holiday to which Jenny was especially looking forward. But give her sea, and plenty of sun . . .

There was a tap at the door and she called, 'Come in.'

'Hi!' Eric put his head round the door.

'Hi!' Jenny spun round in her chair. 'How're things going?'

'Fine.'

'Did you want coffee?'

'I'd love a cup.'

'Tell Gladys . . . '

'Gladys saw me come along. She'll be bringing it for both of us in a minute.'

Eric sauntered into the room. He wore jeans and a T-shirt and appeared unshaven.

'Nearly all done,' he said, slumping into a chair. 'All packed up.'

'I'll miss you.'

'And I'll miss you, but we won't be far away and it's excellent that we can carry on here.'

They had come to an arrangement that, for the time being, the horses would stay where they were.

'Excellent for me, too. I also like the fact that Philip will see his father more regularly. Matt so loves his family, and it's so difficult to persuade them to come here.'

'Still?'

'Still. I just had Beth on the phone. She was looking for Matt, but I said we'd love to see her here. Do you know I haven't seen her since we were married? Of course she gave me a colossal snub.'

'Ridiculous. You'd think they would behave in a more grown-up way.'

'They still deeply resent me. Maurice is reasonably civil, and I like Shirley. We've had them both here . . . but Beth,' she shook her head sadly, 'I really think she hates me. Georgina, of course, is very much her mother's girl, so – ' Jenny gave him a bright, but rather artificial smile – 'I'm glad about Philip.'

'Oh, Philip's all there.' Eric stretched out on the sofa. 'He knows that not only will he get affection from the old man, but also money. He'll need a lot of cash to do up the farmhouse, even with me doing all the work. A lot needs doing to it structurally.'

'I'd love to see it.'

'You must come over. Let me get one or two of the rooms habitable . . . '

The door opened and Gladys came in, carrying a tray on which there were two cups of coffee.

'Will you be having lunch, Eric?' Jenny asked, putting his cup in front of him.

'Well, if it's not inconvenient?'

'Lunch for two then, Gladys. Thanks.' Jenny smiled at her and waited until she'd closed the door.

'Don't you think you should have the rooms habitable before you move out?'

'I want to get out of here, Jenny. Matt was *so* unpleasant . . . '

'Yes, but that's when he thought you were after me. Oddly, he seems more reconciled to the fact that the object of your affection all the time was his son.'

'That's not exactly true.' Eric stirred his coffee and then lit a cigarette. 'Philip made a play for *me*. We felt we had to be very cautious about the whole thing. Didn't know how the old man would react.'

In fact Matt's mildness had rather surprised Jenny when he learned that Philip and Eric were to share a large, decrepit farmhouse just over the Gloucestershire border, which Philip had got at a knock-down price because of the collapse of the housing market.

Maybe it was because, of all his children, he seemed to respect Philip the most. Philip argued with him, stood up to him, would not let himself be bullied by him. Matt had even lent him the money to buy the property to save him getting a mortgage. Matt obviously wanted Philip's love very much indeed.

'What are you going to do, Jenny?' Eric asked suddenly, looking across at her.

'Do?' Jenny, aroused from her reverie, looked up at him.

'This isn't the life for you, you know. Idle – '

'It's hardly idle.'

'I don't call going to all these social functions exactly making a contribution to life, do you?'

'Well, they help, they're all worthy causes . . . '

'Which would get along perfectly well without you.'

'I suppose so.' Jenny fell silent for a moment. 'I think I'm beginning to accept that I'll never have a child, at least with Matt. The specialist says there's no reason why I can't conceive and, as we know, Matt has already had four children . . . '

'Oh, but people do after years, don't they?'

'I know there's a possibility, and of course we don't give up. But something's gone out of our relationship recently.

361

Since the summer it seems as though Matt doesn't really care all that much. We never discuss it.'

'Perhaps he's accepted it too.'

'Perhaps he has, but you're right. There *is* a lack of point in my life. I seem superfluous to needs and, sometimes, I don't really know what to do about it.'

Eric rose and, walking across the room, stopped in front of Jenny and put his hand on her head, gazing at her fondly.

'I do love you, you know. You are a very special person for me. I love you, and I always will, and if ever you need me I'll always be there.'

Jenny grasped his hand and squeezed it. All at once her eyes filled with tears, and it took some time for Eric to comfort her or understand the cause of her grief.

Jenny was jolted wide awake and lay there, heart pounding, not knowing what had so rudely shattered her sleep. Then she heard it again: the strident sound of the doorbell. She put on the bedside light, looked at the clock, saw that it was four a.m. The doorbell at *four a.m.*

Her first reaction was one of horror, of fear: something had happened to Matt, to one of his family, to her father . . . She jumped out of bed, seized her dressing gown, and went to the door of her room as the bell rang again, someone keeping their finger on it for a long time.

She opened the door, but before she had time to switch on the hall light saw the light come on over the stairs leading to the top floor, and heard the sounds of feet hurrying down. Thank heaven Eric was still here.

Eric, his hair tousled, was also tying the cord of his dressing gown, and reached her just as she put on the light.

'Who on earth *is* that?' he asked.

'I haven't any idea. I can only think it's something awful . . . '

'Is Matt here?'

'No. He stayed in town.'

362

'I'll go down, you stay here.' Eric brushed past her and ran down the stairs.

'Take care,' she called out after him. 'Don't let anyone in, until – '

'Don't worry. I'll find out who it is.'

Jenny was now convinced that something really dreadful had happened, and sat at the top of the stairs to try and calm herself. Eric put on lights throughout the house as he hurried across the hall to the front door.

'Who is it?' Jenny heard him call, and she strained forward to try and catch the reply.

'Is that Lord Ransom?' came a voice from the other side of the door.

'Who wants him? Do you know what time of night it is?'

'Would you open the door, Lord Ransom? It's the *Daily Reporter.*'

'What do you want?' Eric asked angrily.

'We want you to comment on an item in the paper, Lord Ransom. Please open the door.'

'An item? What about?'

'You won't know until you open the door.'

'How do I know you are who you say you are?'

'Telephone the newsdesk,' the voice replied, and gave him a number.

Jenny stood up and took a few tentative steps down. She saw Eric undo the bolt, unlock the heavy door, and peer round it. Something was thrust in his face, and he stepped back, a newspaper in his hand. He was followed by a pleasant-looking man in a tweed suit.

'You're not Lord Ransom,' the reporter said accusingly, looking at Eric in surprise.

Eric, scanning the front page of the paper, shook his head in agreement. 'I'm a house guest.'

'Is Lord Ransom here?' In the nick of time, Jenny scurried back up the stairs in her bare feet as the man looked around.

'He's away,' Eric shook his head. 'Where do you get this garbage?'

The man didn't reply to his question. 'Is Lady Ransom here?'

'No, she's away too.' Eric again shook his head.

'Are they together?'

'I've no idea. I suppose so.'

'Do you know whether she had any knowledge of this affair . . . '

'I'm sure she didn't, but it's none of my business. Even if true.'

'Oh, it's true.' The man looked disappointed. 'You're sure he's not here? It will save a lot of trouble . . . '

'I tell you, neither Lord *nor* Lady Ransom is here, and if you don't remove yourself I'll phone the police. You have no right in the grounds anyway. This is a private house . . . ' And he opened the door wide, stuck his hand on the newshound's chest, and pushed him outside. As soon as he put the bolt back into place, Jenny ran down to join him.

'What *is* it, Eric? What on earth is it?' She stretched out her hand for the paper but he held back.

'It's just garbage, Jenny. I don't want you to see it.'

'But I *must* see it.' Her hand remained outstretched. 'What on earth is it to make them come to the house in the middle of the night?'

'Come and sit down.' Eric handed her the paper. 'This is the sort of thing you better take with a drink.' And he led her into the drawing room, switching on the lights while Jenny came slowly after him, reading the paper.

Eric went at once to the drinks table and poured something into a glass, but she slumped in a chair, still reading, and waved him away.

'I don't need anything. Thanks.' She looked up and gave a weak smile. 'This is *incredible*, isn't it? I suppose it's true.'

Headed, 'THE CASE OF THE PEER AND THE NIGHT CLUB HOSTESS', it detailed an alleged affair between 'Lord Ransom, the well-known industrialist' and one Bridget

Murphy, aged nineteen, daughter of an unemployed labourer in Dublin, who was supposedly expecting Matt's child.

It went on to explain how fifty-nine-year-old Lord Ransom already had a young wife he had only married two-and-a-half years before, having jettisoned the first: 'grey-haired, plump, in her fifties.'

Bridget had worked as a night-club hostess at a discreet club in Mayfair, where she met the peer earlier in the year, just after his present wife was believed to have had a miscarriage. The paper surmised that 'the second marriage then came under threat'.

There was a large colour picture of Matt and Jenny on their wedding day. Underneath was a fuzzy black-and-white picture of Bridget with the legend: 'Night-club hostess expects peer's baby'.

The story continued on a centre spread, where there were pictures of the club in Chesterfield Street, the outside of the Ransoms' London flat, 'the most expensive penthouse in London', and a picture of Chudleigh taken from the road, probably the day before.

It went into some detail about the Ransom family history which, up to now, had been impressive but relatively scandal-free. The article kept on referring to them as 'the new rich' and called Beth 'an up-and-coming actress' who had recently been cast in a new series for the TV. Little was known of Jenny except that she was a 'prominent society beauty', though they were on the track of it and had already despatched reporters to Sweden. They knew anyway that her father was 'enormously rich'.

Apparently a lot of unnamed people had believed there were 'storm clouds' hanging over the second marriage, as 'Lady Jenny Ransom' was a 'beautiful, feisty young woman who liked her independence'.

'My God how do they *know* all this?' Jenny said at last, letting the paper fall to the floor. Then she looked up at Eric, who had stood by the mantelpiece while she

365

read, gazing at her. 'Perhaps I *will* have a brandy now, Eric.'

'Is it true?' he asked.

'How do I know?'

The phone rang and they looked at each other.

'It might be Matt,' she said.

'I'll get it.'

Eric went over to the phone and picked it up. 'Hello?'

A voice spoke rapidly at the other end.

'No, I am not, and I don't know where he is, and Lady Ransom is *not* here either.'

He banged down the phone, let it rest for a moment, and then lifted the handset and switched it to 'off'.

'We don't want any more of *those*.'

'Who was it?'

'ITV News. They've read it in the *Reporter* . . . '

'What if Matt tries to ring?' Jenny looked anxiously at the handset.

'Where is he? Do you know?'

'I *assumed* he was at the flat.' She gave a twisted smile. 'But it appears there's a lot I don't know. It's true Matt *has* been very elusive recently. Perhaps this is why.'

'Maybe you should ring Maurice?'

Jenny shook her head and sipped the brandy Eric had given her. 'I don't feel like talking about this to anybody except Matt right now.'

'I can understand.' He came over to her and took her hand. 'I'm terribly sorry, Jenny. Life has *not* been kind to you recently.'

'Life has not been kind,' she echoed.

'Maybe you should fly back to Sweden at once? If I can get you out of the house and on to a plane . . . '

'And run away?' She shook her head. 'If I scuttle home I'll look ridiculous. On the other hand I am not going to be one of those wives who "stands by her husband" when he makes a fool of her . . . though he has made more of a fool of *himself*, if it's true. *Nineteen*!' She gave an incredulous laugh. 'It makes me feel very old indeed.' She pressed his hand. 'Thank God you were here, Eric. I don't know what I'd have done without you.'

'Now, why don't you go up to bed?' Eric pulled her gently to her feet and then, as they looked at each other, he put his arm round her. 'You know I love you, Jenny, and will do everything I can to protect you.'

'The whole thing is absolutely *unbelievable*,' Elspeth said, turning back to the front page of the newspaper, staring at it again. 'Poor Jenny.'

Georgina looked at Beth, who pulled a face. It was the first time either of them had heard their stepmother being referred to as anything other than 'that woman'.

'Poor Jenny!' Maurice exclaimed in a tone of outrage. 'What about the rest of us? You know what the press are when they get on to a story like this. They won't leave Dad, or us, alone.'

'But is it *true*?' Elspeth, still unable to believe the evidence, looked from one to the other. 'Did *you* have any idea, Maurice?'

'No. No,' Maurice lied, sticking his hands in his pockets and looking thoughtfully up at the ceiling. 'But Dad has been behaving oddly. I mean, rather in the way that he behaved,' he glanced apologetically at his mother, 'when he was having an affair with Jenny without your knowledge.'

'Oh you knew about that?'

'I knew there was someone. There was a flat in Mayfair.'

'How sordid, Elspeth said, shaking her head wearily, 'The *depths* to which a man will sink! I've decided that I never really knew your father. He must be ill.'

The full story was only in the *Reporter* which seemed to have an exclusive, but there had been a brief item on the ITV news and it featured on the front pages of the papers held up for inspection on BBC 1.

As yet the rest of the family had remained unmolested,

though Maurice supposed, as it was only nine in the morning, it would not be long before they were after his mother, his sisters and him.

'What the effect of this will be on the share price, I *daren't* say,' he said despairingly.

'But why should it affect *that*?'

'Because the markets are so fragile. You remember what happened to . . . ' He named a well-known businessman whose company went into a decline after news of an illicit romance surfaced. 'It's awful. It's *deeply* irresponsible of Dad,' Maurice went on, 'and, if true, and if it does damage the business, the board will demand his resignation. As it is,' he looked at his watch and shrugged, 'I suppose I'll have to face the music alone.' He went over to kiss Shirley. 'Look after yourself, and Mum. I'll be in touch.'

'What do we do if the *press* turns up?' Shirley, having, unusually, lost her composure, clutched at his sleeve.

'Don't let them in. Come to think of it, I'll call the police and tell them to keep an eye on the gate.'

Eric had made a call shortly after seven to alert them to what had happened, to confirm that Matt was not at Chudleigh. The police had stationed a car and two men by the gate to keep away a small crowd of reporters and a newsreel cameraman which had already formed. Jenny was keeping out of sight. Yes, deeply upset, but coping.

'Take care.' Shirley saw Maurice to his car parked in the drive. 'Isn't it a perfectly *dreadful* thing to happen, especially when your mother was so much on the mend?'

'Dreadful to happen, but especially dreadful to let himself get found out,' Maurice said testily, switching on the ignition. '*That's* the worst part.'

When Maurice drove up to the factory there were already police on the gate.

'You'd think my father was an international figure,' he said, showing his security pass as he leaned out of the car window.

'It's something like that, sir,' the policeman touched his cap. 'I'm afraid the papers love a scandal.' He stuck his head confidentially through the window of the car. 'You don't happen to know where your father is, do you, sir? Is he inside the building?'

'Not that I know of, although he's due. No, we don't really know where he is. Maybe he had a whiff of what was to happen and went to ground. He has to surface sooner or later.'

'I'll keep an eye out for him, sir.' The policeman touched his cap again and stepped back, waving Maurice through and shutting the gate firmly after him.

Half the board was already gathered in the boardroom when Maurice entered, all with the offending newspaper laid out before them. They all looked up as Maurice came in, and Andrew Rose stood up and went towards him.

'Maurice, had you any idea . . . ?'

'Of course I hadn't. And nor, I should imagine, had he.'

'You mean he mightn't *know* the girl is pregnant?'

'What I mean is, he didn't know it would be in the papers. Nor do I know where he is. He's gone to ground.'

'And your stepmother?'

'It was a complete shock to her. She has no idea where he is either.'

'Then it *is* true?' Andrew slumped into a chair and put his head in his hands, his eyes once more going over the story in the paper.

'We're not *sure* that it's true until we talk to Dad.' Maurice sat down next to him, deeply resentful of the way he had, in a sense, become his father's accomplice in a gigantic falsehood.

'Do you know the girl?'

'Never met her.'

'Or where she lives?'

'I know absolutely nothing about her. I've never been night-clubbing with my father. I didn't actually know *he* did either. He kept it to himself.' Maurice gazed at the

369

gloomy faces around him. 'I think I should go up to London and, if you give it your approval, Andrew, see not only if I can find my father – I have one or two ideas where he might be – but settle the London office.'

'It's under siege,' William Lumsden shrugged his shoulders. 'Once in I've told the staff not to go out. The commissionaire is keeping the press out.'

'I'm afraid you'll have to flush out your father *and* get him to make a statement. For God's sake consult a solicitor first.' Andrew Rose had difficulty concealing his annoyance. 'This is terribly bad for business, especially as the half-yearly figures are soon to be announced . . . '

'And they are none too good,' Mark Strong concluded. 'Sales right down.' He jerked his thumb towards the floor.

'Oh *hell*!' Maurice looked from one to the other.

'I think I should make a statement too . . . or you, Andrew.' He looked at the managing director.

'What sort of statement?'

'About the business.'

'I don't want to make a statement. The less said the better.'

'OK. As you like.' Maurice again glanced at his watch. 'I'll leave by the back gate. Andrew, may I borrow your car?'

'Why?' Andrew looked puzzled.

'So that no one will recognise it as mine.'

'Oh, I see. Very well. I'm not at *all* pleased about this, you know, Maurice.'

'Do you think *anyone* is happy?' Maurice replied coldly as he left the room. 'And, incidentally, I'm not my father's keeper.'

As he ran up the steps of London Wall to the office, Maurice saw the small crowd gathered round the entrance and paused abruptly. He began to go back down the stairs in order to find another entrance, then changed his mind and ran up to the top again, where he was spotted by the reporters, who crowded round him.

370

'Have you any idea where Lord Ransom is, Mr Ransom? Can you give us your comments about recent events? Did you know anything about it? Do you know the woman concerned? Have you ever met her?'

Maurice paused, smiled, and spoke clearly into the microphone nearest to him.

'I have only a short statement to make, ladies and gentlemen, and that is that my father's personal life is his own affair. I am a married man and what my father does is of no direct concern to me. I should also like to say that nothing in his private life has, nor, I imagine, ever would, detract from his skill as an entrepreneur and businessman. As such he has the complete confidence of the board of Ransom Engineering.

'That is all I have to say, except that my family and I would be *immensely* grateful if you could now leave us all alone. The publicity this business has engendered is deeply unsettling and distressing for us, and is also quite uncalled for. Thank you. Good afternoon.'

Then, with a smile, he disappeared inside the building, from which the press had been barred by the commissionaire, and rang the bell for the lift. He had done his best, but he knew, in his heart of hearts, that if he thought he had heard the last of this, he would be wrong.

It was not an enjoyable afternoon at the office. The staff were nervous, morose, resentful. Telephones never stopped ringing, and little work was done. He made several telephone calls but could not establish the whereabouts of his father. According to Maria, he had had a midnight caller, presumably from the press, and left shortly after by the service exit.

Justin O'Leary was not available at the club. The staff there hadn't seen him all day. The telephone at the Mayfair flat, which Maurice knew had no tenant, rang continuously but remained unanswered. Maurice felt very annoyed, very unhappy, very frustrated.

Just after five he left the office and went down in the lift to the basement, where he found his way out on to the street via the boiler room. Picking his way carefully, he made for his car, looking cautiously around, but observing no followers.

He drove out into the traffic heading for the West End. Unfortunately it was close to rush hour. He reflected bitterly that it was a terrible reflection on society that one had to behave like a fugitive in one's own country when one had actually done nothing wrong. He also thought, in passing, how much life had changed since his father had abandoned the stability and happiness of a long marriage for the life of a philanderer. He had always before admired his father, been in awe of him, modelled himself on him, but now he felt nothing but exasperation and a kind of contempt.

He got to Mayfair, and found without difficulty a meter in Curzon Street, as it was the hour when people were heading for home. He put a full complement of coins in the meter, then walked briskly up Curzon Street, along Half Moon Street and, pausing outside the house that had been converted into luxury flats, looked upwards. There was a light in the window. His instinct had been right. He rang the bell, waited a long time, but there was no answer. He thought there might not be. He rang the bell of the flat below, and when a voice answered he muttered, 'Paper, could you let me in?' He was hoping for someone rather indifferent to security, and to his relief the entry buzzer sounded. Once inside, Maurice summoned the lift which took him up to the third floor.

Maurice rang the bell of the flat owned by his father. As he feared, there was no reply. This time he left his finger on the buzzer, and was finally rewarded when a woman's voice said timidly, 'Who is it?'

'It's Maurice Ransom. Is my father there?'

There was no reply. He knocked softly and said in a low voice, 'Please let me in. I urgently want to contact my father.'

There was a brief silence and then finally he heard the chain being unfastened, the lock turned, and there, in shirt sleeves and the trousers of his business suit, looking a little crumpled, stood Matt. He had not shaved and looked as though he hadn't slept either.

'May I come in, Dad?' Maurice said, looking at him.

Silently Matt stood to one side. Maurice entered and stood looking nervously about him in the hall.

'How did you know I'd be here?'

'It was obvious wasn't it?'

'It's a terrible business.'

'You can't hide for ever, Dad,' Maurice said angrily. '*And* you've led me a terrible dance . . . '

'I simply didn't know what to do.' Matt, looking suddenly relieved to see him, took his elbow and steered him towards the drawing room.

'Come and say "hello" to Bridget. She's distraught by the whole thing. She only moved in here a week ago. Hardly a thing's been done to the place.' It was true it looked rather sordid, with all the signs of a hasty occupation.

Although the effects of prolonged weeping were evident on her face, Maurice could see that Bridget was coping. She really did look very big, and he felt rather shocked to realise she was carrying his father's child.

'Hello, Bridget,' he said politely, holding out a hand.

'Nice to see you again,' she replied morosely, her handshake very limp. He thought she was frightened, but excited at the same time.

'Did anyone follow you?' Matt looked towards the window.

'No, I don't think so, though there was a crowd at the office. I made a statement saying that what you did was your own affair.'

'We heard a report about it on the four o'clock news.' Matt heavily sank on to a chair. 'God, you'd think I'd *murdered* somebody. Something has to be done about controlling the press in this country. What it's doing to Bridget is terrible.'

Bridget collapsed on to a chair next to Matt and started weeping again. Matt reached for her hand and squeezed it.

'Is there any way you can get us out of here, Maurice?'

'But where to?'

'Somewhere abroad – anywhere.'

'Dad, you just can't run away. You've got to face it.'

'But what can I do? What can I say?'

Maurice sat down and unbuttoned his jacket, feeling suddenly important, like the one in charge, the one in control, a position formerly occupied by his father. 'You'll have to make a statement.'

'About what?'

'About the situation. I mean, it is true, obviously, isn't it?' He looked pointedly at Bridget. 'But how did they *know*? I'm assuming it wasn't Bridget or she wouldn't be looking so terrible.'

'She thinks it was the manager at the club. Justin O'Leary.'

'I tried to ring the club to see if they knew where Bridget was. *He* hadn't been seen all day.'

'There you are. A sign of guilt.'

'He was the only one who knew,' Bridget said tremulously. 'He *guessed* it was Matt.'

'Didn't your parents know?'

Bridget reddened. 'My sister lives in London. She knew and she told my mother and father. But no one knew who the father was. Not even my sister.'

Maurice found it hard to believe that she wouldn't tell her sister something like that, but he didn't say anything.

'Have you been in touch with Jenny?' Maurice looked solemnly at his father.

'I tried but she doesn't answer the phone. Have *you* been in touch with her?'

'Eric rang us. They had the reporters at the house at four this morning. Like you, I imagine – ' he looked at the socket in the wall – 'she has the phone unplugged so as not to be pestered by incoming calls.'

'I feel absolutely terrible about poor Jenny. To hear like this . . . '

'To hear any way couldn't have been pleasant, Dad.'

'It was never my intention to tell her, not yet. Bridget was very understanding about the whole thing.'

'I rather think Jenny may *not* be quite so understanding.' Maurice looked severely at his recalcitrant parent, who hung his head like a schoolboy caught in a misdemeanour.

'What *shall* I do, Maurice?' He gazed forlornly at his son, in a way Maurice had never seen before, as if he looked up to *him*, rather than the other way round.

'We must control the situation,' Maurice said authoritatively. 'You'll have to make a statement to steady the share price. Tomorrow they're expecting a large fall on the market.'

'But that is absurd.'

'It may be, but it is a fact. Look what happened with Maxwell, Nadir . . . Once there's a scandal, any scandal, the market loses confidence in the shares.'

'But there have been no financial irregularities. It's quite preposterous.'

'I agree it's preposterous, and it's unfair; but it is a fact. I'll call a press conference for some time tomorrow but . . . you must talk to Jenny. I mean, what are you going to do?'

'I don't know. I never thought about it.'

'You never *thought* about it?' Maurice looked incredulous.

'What can I say?'

'Tell her the whole story.'

'She'll be most dreadfully upset. The baby . . . Bridget's baby was quite unplanned, but Jenny wanted a baby, too, you see. Life really is *most* unfair, isn't it, Maurice? That something that can be so easy for one is so hard for another. It became quite an obsession with Jenny, and me, too, of course. It was something we both desperately wanted, and our failure did nothing to improve our marriage.

'But, of course, if you can arrange for me to see Jenny in private, I'll explain everything to her, and try and get her to understand.'

CHAPTER 20

The item came just at the end of the news, heralded by a smirk on the face of the announcer:

'And finally, in an extraordinary development today, in an effort to halt the slide in the price of the shares of his company, Lord Ransom the industrialist, made a short statement to the press at his London office about his affair with a night-club hostess who is expecting his child.'

The picture then went from the studio to the boardroom at London Wall, where Matt, flanked by Maurice, Andrew Rose, and the company's solicitor, and looking extremely uncomfortable, started to read from a prepared statement.

'I would just like to say how much I deprecate this intrusion into my private life, and the effect it has had on the price of the shares of Ransom Engineering. I intend to continue as chairman of the company, and an active member of the board. The person or persons who betrayed a confidence made by Miss Murphy has or have a lot to answer for. I am prepared to stand by her and support her child, but I love my wife and am sorry for the distress I have caused her and my family.'

He then stopped, folded the crumpled piece of paper, and a barrage of questions began.

'Have you been in touch with Lady Ransom, Lord Ransom?'

'What does your first wife say?'

'What do your children think?'

'Do you expect this to continue to affect the share price of Ransom Engineering?'

The lawyer got up and held out both hands in an attempt to stem the tide.

'Thank you, ladies and gentlemen. Lord Ransom declines to answer questions. We ask you to respect the privacy of him and his family . . . '

The picture then faded and Jenny, slumped in a chair, zapped it off, wishing that she'd never put it on in the first place.

'Sorry' for the distress he'd caused her. That was rich. He had not only caused her 'distress'; he'd condemned her to a life as a prisoner locked up in the fortress which Chudleigh had become, unable to go out or show her face. She hadn't been outside the gates since the story broke. One of the photographers had fallen out of a tree beyond the grounds and broken his leg while trying to photograph her riding, and since then she hadn't even exercised the horses.

Eric came and went and, of course, it would have been possible in theory to lie on the floor of his car and be spirited away like that. But where would she go? Just where *did* one find refuge, peace, in a situation like this?

Rage, anger, despair; all these emotions came and went with terrifying rapidity, but nothing was enough. There was no escape, no way out of an appalling feeling of claustrophobia.

She crossed the floor of the TV room and went out into the hall. The house was in total silence. Gladys had gone, Eric was at the farmhouse he and Philip were doing up, and night had settled in.

She ran up the stairs and into her bedroom, *their* bedroom. Suddenly the rage which came and went seized hold of her again and, going into the bathroom, she took the bottle of douche from the bathroom cupboard and emptied the contents down the basin. Then she got hold of the elaborate equipment and stuffed it into the waste bin.

This act of destruction gave her a lot of satisfaction and, yet again, with it went the thought of the humiliation she had endured on Matt's behalf, the endless examinations, the protracted conversations, the bitter disappointment when each month produced a period, the endless contortions one got up to in the act of sex to try and produce a baby.

All futile. Not much happiness there, and yet this woman, this night-club hostess of nineteen, had managed to achieve with apparent ease what Jenny, in two years, had not.

Jenny flung herself across the bed and took up the letter from the table by its side.

Dearest Jenny,

It may be very hard for you to believe, but I am suffering as much as you are. I wish I could be with you and try and explain, but I'm a virtual prisoner, as I know you are.

This incident will have shocked you enormously, and I can find no way to excuse myself. My affair with Bridget was an absurd folly, the act of a tired and rather desperate man. It started in the summer after Elspeth's overdose and your miscarriage.

I never meant it to be like this, and hope that, in time, you will find it in your heart to forgive and welcome me again.

Your very loving husband,
Matt.

Come to think of it, it was the first letter she had ever had from him. The curious courtship was all verbal.

That morning she'd wept and, in the course of the day prowling restlessly about, she had read it a dozen times more, as if in its rather stilted words she would be able to find a solution to the mystery. Why? But there was no clue. She knew the letter by heart, and now she hauled herself up on the bed and tore it into tiny fragments. Then she went again into the bathroom and stuffed it into the wastebin after the remains of the douche bottle and rubber apparatus.

Suddenly she stood up, alert, because she thought she'd heard the doorbell. She looked at her watch and saw it was just before seven. She was in the house by herself but there were still police at the gates, back and front. She was not exactly afraid, but she was still apprehensive. She listened and the bell rang again. She went swiftly through the bedroom, along the corridor and down the stairs. Crossing the hall, she stood for several seconds by the door.

'Yes?' she said after a while.

'It's the duty officer at the gate, Lady Ransom, P. C. Burns.'

'Yes, Constable Burns?'

'I have a gentleman with me, madam, who says he is your father . . . '

'My father . . . ?'

'Darling,' Pehr's welcome voice said in Swedish, 'I have come to see you.'

'Oh, *Father*!' she cried, also in Swedish, and flinging open the door fell into his arms. For several seconds father and daughter stood there, hugging each other. The policeman, who took his duties very seriously, was gratified. Those wily reporters could disguise themselves as anything, even Lady Ransom's father; but the sound of the Swedish tongue reassured him, even if he didn't know exactly what was going on.

'Thank you very much, Constable Burns,' Jenny said, still with her arm round her father.

'I've got a case in the car, Jenny.' Pehr kept his arm round her.

'I'll get it for you, sir.' Constable Burns saluted smartly and, running down the steps, produced the case from the boot of the car and hurried up with it into the house. But already Lady Ransom and her father had disappeared into the drawing room and, with a furtive look around, the policeman put the case down and quietly closed the front door behind him, conscious of a job well done.

Jenny and Pehr again clasped each other, gazing into each other's eyes in relief and excitement.

'However did you manage it?'

'Easily,' he shrugged, released himself and lit a cigarette. 'Got a plane, hired a car, and here I am.'

'No press, no nothing?' She continued to look astonished.

'They didn't know who I was; but darling – ' he took her arms again, his cigarette still burning between his fingers – 'I am most terribly sorry about this, this . . . disaster. Have you seen Matt?'

Jenny shook her head. 'We're prisoners. All the family are staying where they are, except Maurice who travels around, as he has to, pursued by a cohort of hacks.'

'I was terribly worried . . . you must be so unhappy. Is Eric here?'

'Eric comes and goes. He has relative freedom. He usually is here at night because I don't terribly like being alone, even with the police at the gate. There are police with dogs patrolling the grounds, but the reporters seem prepared to go to any lengths to get near me. Eric is not here tonight. His flat is almost empty.'

'Only the English would let a trivial matter like this dominate the news. They are obsessed with sex.'

'Yes, but it's such a nice fat, juicy scandal: a night-club hostess and a peer, plus a baby. What more could you want?'

'Darling, Jenny – ' he reached for her again – 'what are you going to do?'

'I haven't decided. It's all happened so quickly.'

'You have to speak to Matt, Jenny.'

'I don't terribly want to speak to Matt. What can we say?'

'There has to be an explanation.'

'He wrote to me.' Jenny stepped away from him and ran her hand through her hair. Pehr thought she looked extremely pale and unwell. That man, Matt Ransom, had robbed his precious daughter of her youth. She looked nearer forty than twenty-five.

'Come sit with me,' he said, and beckoned her to the sofa where he enclosed her hand in his.

'He said he was very sorry, and so on and so forth. Wished we could meet. Could explain – '

'May I see the letter?'

Momentarily her face lit up with a wry smile. 'As a matter of fact I destroyed it just before you came. I shoved it in the wastebin in the bathroom, together with all the rubbish I've been using to try and give Matt the baby he wants so badly, despite the fact he already has four grown-up children. I've come to the conclusion that man is a child at heart.'

'Perhaps all men are,' Pehr said quietly.

'You're not,' her hand tightened in his. 'You're a rock.'

'Darling, I think you should come back home, at least until this blows over.'

'How can it "blow over"? With a child involved it will run and run. You remember what happened to the Tory MP, Parkinson? There will be no end to it.'

'Then come home for good.'

'I don't understand you.'

'Look, later I'll explain. Now, if you can give me a chance to have a little wash, change my clothes, and maybe pour me a whisky, I'll be more human. I feel I have been travelling for days.'

Pehr had been up early and, regardless of climbers in trees, he had gone to the stables to inspect the horses. There Jenny joined him, and they had enjoyed a quiet hour together with the groom, feeding the horses, seeing to their comfort and well-being, but not riding them.

Gladys had arrived, escorted as usual by the duty police-man. She half enjoyed the notoriety, half resented it. For once in her life she was famous, but it was not the sort of fame she would have wished for, given a choice. She knew the papers were after her, and offering money, but she was too afraid of the consequences if she accepted. Besides, her husband was against it, and he more or less dictated her life. The shame, the notoriety of telling all would outweigh the possible gain of a few thousand pounds.

It had been one thing to work for Lord and Lady Ransom when they were respectable, admired, even envied mem-bers of the community. But now, well . . . Gladys filled the percolator and began to make the coffee and toast which was all Lady Ransom ever had for breakfast.

Jenny and Pehr had meanwhile returned from the stables and were strolling around the house. Upstairs, from the windows of the flat, which was almost bare, Pehr looked across at the panoramic scene of the beautiful Oxfordshire countryside, which now included a slightly diminished horde of photographers at the gate.

'They get fewer every day,' Jenny said, following his gaze. 'When they're all gone I'll go out.'

'And where will you go then, darling?'

Pehr, hands in pockets, turned to her. She'd obviously enjoyed a better night's sleep, maybe comforted by his presence, and looked more rested, less fraught, though still too pale and much, much too thin.

'Well, have my hair done for a start,' she said, tossing it about her head.

'Jenny, for weeks, months, you will be recognised. You won't have any peace at all.'

'You think so?'

'I know so. You said so yourself last night. Your face is well known. Everywhere you go you'll be recognised.'

'I'll think about it,' she said, smiling suddenly at him. 'Let's go and have some breakfast. I'll introduce you to Gladys.'

Just being with Pehr was relaxing, wandering about, showing him the treasures of Chudleigh, which he had never seen, listening to his admiration – he loved antiques. Her only regret was that it couldn't be a normal visit. If Pehr had come the previous year as he'd intended, how different things would have been. But Ingrid had been ill, and there had been some problems with the business.

In the afternoon they rode, avoiding the jumps but choosing the fields behind the house, which were still surrounded by the high, red-brick wall. With her father here, Jenny didn't care anyway whether she was photographed or not. She felt protected once again; protected and loved as she had been all her life, up until now.

'It's such a feeling of rejection,' she told him over tea, which was always served by Gladys just before darkness came and she left. Gladys felt happier about leaving for the day now that Jenny's father was here. The drawing room curtains were drawn and a fire roared up the chimney. Pehr and Jenny, still in jodhpurs, sat side by side, nibbling the newly baked scones, one of Gladys's specialities.

'You mustn't feel rejected,' Pehr shook his head.

'What else can I feel?'

'Betrayed maybe,' he suggested. 'Deceived. But I'm sure Matt didn't want to reject you. He just wanted you as well as . . . this other woman.'

'A night-club hostess of nineteen! Not very complimentary.'

'It hurts your pride. It's natural.' Pehr finished his scone and wiped his lips on a napkin. Then he drained the tea in his cup and, sitting back, put his hand once again on Jenny's.

'Darling, it is early days, and you won't come to any sudden decision. But I have been thinking about this ever since the news broke and I must tell you I'm not surprised.'

'Not *surprised*?'

'Matt obviously hankers for adventure, for younger fertile women. I tried to warn you about this, but you ignored me. Heaven knows what goes on in the mind of someone who starts behaving like he has. Maybe it is a change in biochemistry, something in the brain because, apart from anything else, he must know he is not only hurting a number of people he really loves, but he's making a fool of himself and damaging his business, maybe irreparably.

'What exactly *does* Matt get out of all this? Nothing, if you ask me. I am prepared to accept that this affair was something he didn't think would be very serious but, like a number of people before him and, doubtless, lots after, he's been caught out. As he is a public figure and the British love a scandal, especially nowadays, he has got far, far more than he bargained for, and frankly, in my opinion, more than he deserved. I don't know why these days a woman has to get pregnant unless she wants to, but obviously this girl did. It may have been to trap Matt. I wouldn't know. The thing is, Jenny, you want to think not of him but of you. Do you want Matt back?' He waited but, as she didn't reply, he went on, 'You probably haven't thought about it. Naturally your instinct is to reject him, but you might change your mind several times.'

'I don't think I'd change my mind,' Jenny said, slowly shaking her head back and forth several times. 'I'm not Elspeth. I'm not a devil for punishment.'

'Then it's final? The break *is* final?'

'Final,' she said firmly, but almost in a whisper, as if she wasn't quite sure, still bemused by the whole situation.

Pehr appeared to take a deep breath. 'I do hope so, my darling. I do *hope* that you mean it and will stick to it because it is my opinion that you can never again be happy with Matt. You will never trust him. He says he is going to support this woman and her child. What sort of life would it be for you, especially since you have found yourself unable so far to get pregnant?

384

'Also, Jenny, in my opinion you have never done yourself justice. You are not only a beautiful woman, but a clever one. Your grades at school were always excellent. I wanted you to go to university yet you wouldn't. What I want to suggest is why don't you consider now a couple of years of study?'

'Study?' Jenny gasped as if she didn't quite understand.

'Why not?' Pehr shrugged. 'At home in Sweden. You would get straight into university with the grades you got, and you are still only twenty-five. Jenny, life is in front of you, not behind. And I think what you want to ask yourself is this: do you want to go on being Lady Ransom with this large, very beautiful house but a husband you can't trust, and yet who is so much older than you? Everywhere you go, all the occasions, opera and so on, people will look at you. You will never feel the same. You will never be allowed to forget.

'Jenny, as is too often the fate of beautiful women, you have always been a man's woman. You like older men, too. George was older than you were; Matt a lot older. Why is it that you need all the time the protection of older men? Is it because of me?' He pointed a finger at his chest. 'Did *I* not set you free? Well, I am advising you, Jenny, to try and achieve that freedom. Come home, not to Stockholm, but maybe to Uppsala, one of the greatest and oldest universities. Get a flat there, register for a degree. You will meet people who are not only interesting, but more your own age . . . '

'But Father, I'd be so much older . . . ' However, a glimmer of interest had replaced the defeat, the dejection so clearly reflected on her face.

'No, you won't. There are graduate students as well as undergraduates. Meet people of your own age, with your ideas . . . Then, after two years or so . . . there is no need to make up your mind immediately. Just try and create a little space for yourself, Jenny . . . time to think again, and take stock of your life.'

*   *   *

The large, indignant-looking Irish family sat clustered round a thin, weasly man, with the pink nose and bloodhound eyes of one over-fond of the drink.

The shot moved to the TV reporter, microphone in hand, whose own expression tried hard to emulate the indignation of the family. She thrust the mike towards the weasly man, whose hand shook slightly as he put his glass to his lips, lowered it and wiped the froth off his mouth.

'So what do you think of the situation in which your daughter has got herself, Mr Murphy?'

'I think it's terrible,' Bridget's father said in a whining tone. 'Lord Ransom promised to marry my daughter. If you ask me he was a vile seducer who deserves to be hanged.'

'Isn't that a little extreme, Mr Murphy?' the reporter asked with a wink to the cameras.

'No, it is not.' The large woman next to Mr Murphy stuffed her handkerchief into her eyes. Obviously this was Mrs Murphy, her wedding ring buried deep in her fat finger. She pulled her cardigan protectively round a large, bra-less bosom. Together they looked like Jack Spratt and his wife, and the family gathered round resembled them in various degrees.

Watching the scene, Matt shut his eyes, only too thankful that Bridget didn't look like her mother . . . yet.

'Turn it off,' Bridget said, her eyes streaming with tears, just as her mother's had been.

'I just want to see it all.' Matt held on to her hand. 'We've got to know what they say.'

Mrs Murphy finished wiping her eyes, and said in a tremulous, scarcely audible voice, that Bridget had always been a good girl who went regularly to Mass, but God-alone-knew what had happened to her after she left the safety of Dublin for the sinful streets of London. The reporter asked when they had last seen their daughter; they didn't seem to know.

'Then how do you know that Lord Ransom promised to marry her?'

386

Mrs Murphy stuck a podgy finger into the side of the pretty girl next to her, clearly one of Bridget's sisters. 'Well, didn't you, Maire?'

'I thought, Ma. But I wasn't sure . . .'

'And now I return you to the studio,' the reporter said quickly, rather as a QC, thinking he or she is losing their case, might decide to call the next witness.

'Huh!' Matt zapped off the machine.

'I don't know how she *could*,' Bridget blubbered through tears. 'That is our Maire.'

'They only do it for money.' Matt put a comforting arm round her. 'People will do *anything* for money.'

They'd stayed holed up in the Half Moon Street flat because it was the only place the reporters hadn't seemed able to find. Matt's statement had done nothing to stop the fall in the price of Ransom shares, though it levelled off after day three and the story stopped making the front pages, to be succeeded by another sensation, this time of a political nature.

After that dreadful performance from Bridget's family, though, Matt was sure the whole affair would be revived and the share price would begin to slide again.

He suddenly began to wish that a girl called Bridget Murphy had never come into his life, and reflected on the good old days with Jenny, and the even better ones with Elspeth, when he had gone from work to home and back again with a welcome monotony, and the news had been something that happened to other people.

Maurice stood looking round at his family, like one presiding at a wake. And indeed their attitudes, the way they sat, stood, or waited listlessly for him to speak, were those of dejection, even bereavement.

Maurice had a copy of the latest tabloid article in his hands, which christened Matt 'Randy Ransom', went into intimate details about his two spouses and, after the revelations of Bridget's family, discussed the prospect of a third. There was a particularly unflattering portrait of Elspeth which they had tried to keep from her, unsuccessfully.

387

'I know I'm no beauty, but . . .' followed, not unnaturally, by tears. Everyone was so pent up, so volatile, that normal life was impossible.

Elspeth's tears had dried, but the family remained deeply worried about her. Beth had been recalled from the cast of the TV series, and there was now another question-mark about her future. She sat with Elspeth, holding her hand. On the other side of Elspeth was a worn-looking Georgina. Henry, who proclaimed himself fed up with the whole thing and glad his name was not Ransom, had refused to attend.

Philip stood leaning against the mantelpiece, feigning nonchalance. But in reality he was very concerned, because his name *was* Ransom, and here he was trying to start up a new software company in the City.

Ransom was not the kind of name easily forgotten. It was particularly unfortunate that it alliterated so well with 'Randy'. 'Randy' Brown wouldn't have sounded half so exotic. But 'Randy' Ransom had caught the fancy of the gutter press, and they made use of the new nickname freely.

For Shirley it had been a time of great anxiety, trying to keep the disparate family strands cohesive and together. There was anxiety about the effects of this crisis on Elspeth's fragile nervous system, and talk of Shirley giving up her job at the hospital.

Shirley had finished handing coffee round to everyone, and now she squatted on the floor in front of the sofa on which the three other women were sitting. All eyes were on Maurice.

'What I have to say isn't at all pleasant,' he began, 'and it gives me no pleasure to say it. Of course it's about Father,' he waved the scandal sheet in front of him. 'I don't think coverage of his misdeed is going to end until a new scandal crops up to take their wretched minds off it. It did seem to have abated, but the revelations of the wretched girl's family have had a disastrous effect on the price of our shares. We have finally had to ask for a suspension in dealings on the Stock Exchange.'

'What does that mean?' Beth, pinched and unhappy, looked at him.

'Well, in order to prevent the price falling even lower, and making us vulnerable to a takeover bid which we don't want, we have asked the Stock Exchange to suspend dealings. That means that no one can buy or sell until trading resumes. The price stays at 352p per share, which is over 100p lower than they were when the news broke. We can't go on sustaining a loss like this. The board, therefore, at an emergency meeting yesterday, decided to ask for Dad's resignation.'

There was a swift collective intake of breath, and Elspeth began gently to weep again.

'There, *there*, Mother.' Maurice bent down to pat her shoulder.

'And what did your father say?' Elspeth asked in a tremulous voice.

'Well, he flatly refused, and left the meeting in high dudgeon. We continued, however, and agreed that if he continues to refuse we shall call an extraordinary general meeting of shareholders and try and get them to vote Father off.'

'I think that's terribly unfair and humiliating to Dad,' Philip said. 'Just because of a little scandal – '

'Phil, it is not a "little" scandal, as you call it,' Maurice said heatedly, 'it is momentous. We are all losing a great deal of money, and if we did fall prey to a takeover, we should lose a great deal more.'

'I thought you made money when you sold?'

'Only when the price is high and it comes as a surprise, not when the price has been deflated by gossip and innuendo.'

'I see . . . I'm still against it. It's disloyal to Father.'

'It is possible you are influenced by the fact that Dad has recently helped you financially.'

'Don't be despicable – ' Philip began.

'Boys, please don't fall out.' Georgina, as the eldest

sibling, felt herself in a position, not for the first time, to call her brothers to order.

Maurice, however, only hesitated long enough to allow her to have her say.

'Whatever Philip says, I'm hoping to take the rest of the family along with me. Shirley and I have talked about it and we agree that, hard as it is, we shall have to let the vote go against Dad. I'm hoping that when he realises how strongly people feel about this, he will resign. Then, with a new chairman and chief executive, we can get started again and put the past behind us. Dad . . . Well, frankly I feel Dad can do as he likes. As a family we have pretty much had it up to the neck in terms of what we can take from him . . .'

'He changed *completely*,' Elspeth murmured.

'Right, Mother. He is *not* the father we knew, loved and respected . . .'

'I love him, but I don't think I respect him.' Beth's expression was more than usually tormented. So much of her young life in the past few years had been thoroughly disturbed by her father's behaviour. As the youngest she was also the most fragile. 'However, I don't think I could let my shares be used against him.'

'My dear, you've practically had to give up your acting career because of him,' Maurice protested. 'Didn't you say they were all ragging you at being the daughter of "Randy Ransom"?'

'Well,' Beth looked defensive, 'they were small-minded. People like that don't really matter. I came here to be with Mum and make sure she was all right.' Next to her, Elspeth gratefully squeezed her hand.

'I think I have an idea,' Georgina spoke up again. 'We should agree to give our votes by proxy to Maurice, to let him do as he thinks fit . . .'

'Well, that's very generous.' Maurice looked at her gratefully. 'That's a splendid idea.'

'I, for one, completely trust Maurice,' Georgina went on, 'and I know that what he does is for our good. He has had a hell of a time. He has had to keep the ball rolling, defend Father as well as cope with all of us.'

'He's taken a lot of flack,' Philip agreed, 'but I want to do with my shares as *I* think fit.'

'Right, that's your privilege.'

'I trust Maurice, too,' Elspeth said in the same low, broken voice. 'I shall give him my proxy and then I shan't think I have been personally involved in Matt's downfall. Despite his atrocious behaviour I know how much the company means to him.'

'Mother, it's *not* a downfall.'

'Your father is being squeezed out of his own business . . .'

'I shall be there.'

'You mean you might head it?' The expression on Beth's face brightened.

'Eventually. At the moment Andrew Rose will probably succeed Dad, but it will be a step up for me. Not – ' he added hastily – 'that I shouldn't have preferred it another way; but my concern is Ransoms and that there should be a Ransom there eventually to lead it.'

Beth felt a sudden flood of relief. 'I think George's idea is excellent. Then none of us can say that we pushed Daddy over the edge. I go along with that.'

'I'll still hang on to my shares,' Philip said. 'Father has been generous to me, and I do reserve the right to do as I like when the time comes.'

'And what of Jenny in all this?' Shirley wondered.

Maurice looked at his watch. 'I'm going to see Jenny tomorrow or the next day. I haven't any doubt at all that she'll go along with us; if so, her large shareholding will certainly be sufficient to sink Father.' He paused and examined every face. 'It is a *very* painful day for all of us, our loyalty has been stretched to the limit, but let's face it, Dad has ruined our lives. None of us is the same as we were four years ago.

'I wonder whether we can ever forgive him?'

391

CHAPTER 21

There was a tap on the door. Jenny didn't reply and, after a while, it opened quietly. She raised her head from the pillow and watched as Gladys crossed the floor, a tray in her hand.

'Shall I put it here, Lady Ransom?' she asked, standing by the side of the bed, the tray poised over the bedside table.

Jenny shook her head. 'Put it where you like, Gladys. I'm not hungry.'

Gladys pushed the things on the table to one side and gently slid the tray on to it. Then she straightened up and looked at the woman lying in the bed.

'You *must* eat, Lady Ransom. Starving yourself won't help anybody.'

Jenny shook her head. 'Not starving myself. Just not hungry. Thanks, Gladys.'

Gladys hesitated, but finally left the room.

Jenny looked at the clock. Ten a.m. After watching some TV in her room she'd put the light out at about eight; but her night had been full of nightmares, abrupt wakenings, palpitations.

Pehr had gone and she missed him dreadfully. He was such a rock, yet she knew that to have gone with him was not the answer; only the postponement of an answer. In the course of her life Jenny had seldom been thwarted, wronged, neglected, ignored. If anything it was the opposite: she had been a privileged person, the centre of attention, one around whom things revolved. She had known she was beautiful. Even when she was very small she had been conscious of people whispering about her. Many actually told her to her face. 'Oh, isn't she pretty!' 'What a lovely little girl!' As if a small person was incapable of understanding such things, or being spoiled by them.

The only really bad thing that had happened in her young life had been the divorce of her parents, though even that had been effected in such a way as to make her feel she was the one who mattered, the one they were most concerned about. They even continued to keep on good terms specially for her.

But if the divorce taught her anything, it was that women were less trustworthy than men, fathers stronger than mothers. She cleaved to her father, she cleaved to Matt. They were secure.

If she looked into herself now she could see what sort of person she had become: rather superficial, really; selfish; liking power and admiring it.

She propped herself up on an elbow and looked at the tray by the side of the bed. Rather tasty-looking toast, a pot of marmalade, teapot, teacup, milk, hot water.

She poured herself a cup of tea and took a piece of toast, popped it into her mouth without marmalade, swallowed it. It felt good.

She sat upright, shook her head, brushed her hair away from her face and finished the tea, ate three pieces of toast.

Then she got out of bed and drew the curtains. It was an iffy kind of day, sunshine but plenty of clouds massing in the east. Maybe later it would rain.

A movement across the park caught her eye, and she saw Eric emerge from the stables on Clea. Eric was busy working on the farmhouse, but he spent plenty of time with her, supporting her, talking to her.

As she watched he circled the ring and then prepared to make the first jump. He cleared it easily; then the next, then the next.

Thoughtfully she recrossed the room and, sitting on the side of the bed, poured another cup of tea and finished the toast, now cold, but good. She imagined it was how people starved for several days must feel; they'd eat anything.

She had never known starvation, want, grief, until now. She had been spurned, rejected and deceived, pushed off her pedestal by a man she thought had worshipped her. Some people might have thought she deserved it, though she had never as far as she knew had enemies, unless the Ransom family could be classed as such – maybe the small consolation they had from the present situation was what it had done to her: she had been well and truly put in her place.

She went into the bathroom, ran the bath, and indulged in a good, long soak, bubbles coming up to her chin. She was out and towelling herself when a shadow fell across the doorway and Gladys called out:

'Someone to see you, Lady Ransom.'

'Well, if it's the press . . .'

'It's Mr Ransom, Mr Maurice. He's in the drawing room, Lady Ransom.'

Jenny held the towel up to her face. 'What did you tell him?'

'I told him you were in your room, my lady.'

'Well, tell him I'll be down in ten minutes.'

'Yes, Lady Ransom.'

'Oh, and I had the breakfast.'

'So I saw.' Gladys sounded gratified. 'No use taking it out on yourself, you know.'

Ten minutes later, wearing trousers and a silk shirt, Jenny walked into the drawing room and held out a hand.

'Hello, Maurice. Nice to see you.'

394

'Hello, Jenny.' Maurice shook her hand. He thought she looked very cool and composed. 'I hope I didn't disturb you?'

'No, just having a lie in.'

'I expect you needed it,' he looked at her sympathetically. 'It's been very, very trying for us all.'

'It has.' Jenny sat opposite him and joined her hands. 'Gladys will bring us coffee in a minute. How are you, Maurice, and the family?'

'Well, bearing up as far as we can. It's all, of course, so terribly unexpected . . . like a bereavement. Sometimes in a way I wish it had been . . .'

'How do you mean?' She tipped her head on one side.

'Well, of course we would have been sad to lose Father, but we wouldn't have been in this mess. We could have kept our dignity. Have you seen Dad yet?'

'No, not yet.' She ran her hand through her hair. 'Frankly, I don't want to. I don't know what to say to him, or what he could say to me. Sometimes silence is best. My father has been here for a few days, made some useful suggestions which I'm pondering. The future . . .' She held out her hands. 'I don't really know. I don't think I'm the sort of woman to "stand by my man" when he makes asses of us all . . .

'Now, Maurice, is there any particular reason for this visit, or is it just a courtesy call?'

'Well . . . yes, there is a reason. I mean, I wanted to see how you were, but there is another reason.' Maurice took a newspaper from his briefcase which he held out to Jenny. 'I don't know if you saw this?'

She appeared to freeze, but did not take it from him.

'I have not been seeing the papers.'

'Well, I think you should see this.'

'I'd really rather not. I imagine it's nothing nice.'

'Very well,' Maurice kept it in his hand. 'My board, the board of Ransom Engineering, is taking the whole thing very seriously. The newspapers are not going to leave Father alone, and the publicity is having a disastrous effect on the price of our shares. There is also wind of an unfavourable financial report which will be published in a few days. Very bad timing, but our half-yearly figures are not good. We attribute a lot of it to the economic downturn. Many companies are experiencing the same kind of thing. We have had to ask for dealings in our shares to be suspended on the Stock Exchange.'

'Maybe I'd better see it.' Jenny held out her hand for the newspaper, which Maurice passed to her.

'It means we think Dad will have to go.'

'RANDY RANSOM TO WED TROPHY WIFE NO. TWO?' screamed the banner. Then:

'LOOK! They get younger.

'The first Lady Ransom: well past her prime.'

There was an unflattering picture of Elspeth judging at a local flower show in a homely blouse, cardigan and skirt, low-heeled shoes.

'The second: past her sell-by date too – ' Here there was one of the many attractive pictures of Jenny taken in the past year – 'and she's *only* twenty-five.'

'The third Lady Ransom?' There was a picture of Bridget, possibly provided by her family that made her look about fifteen. 'A new Irish beauty: now that *is* the ticket! Only nineteen *and* pregnant . . .'

'I can't read any more of this.' Jenny handed the paper back to him. 'Has he definitely said he's going to marry her?'

'Her father gave an interview on the TV. Said he had. Matt denies it.'

'Well it *is* a terrible mess, no doubt about it.' Jenny, feeling less brave now, smiled wanly. 'But I can't see why it should ruin your father's career. Can you?'

'That's magnanimous of you, Jenny; but the fact is that we do think Dad should go. If he won't resign voluntarily, we propose to call an extraordinary general meeting of shareholders and vote him off the board.'

'Then why are you telling me this?' Jenny got up and poured the coffee which Gladys had brought in.

'Because I want your support.'

'*My* support?' Jenny turned to look at him.

'Well, you have a lot of shares. We want to muster as many as we can against Father.'

'I see.' Jenny passed him his cup, her expression inscrutable. Then she sat down and faced him, stirring her coffee. 'You know, Maurice, I have spent a lot of time in the past few days thinking about this débâcle . . .'

'I'm sure you have.'

'With my father and without him. It was a sort of self-examination. Something I don't think I've ever done before.'

'How do you mean?'

'I saw myself as a cosseted, spoilt person, someone brought up to think mainly of herself. Maybe I should have thought more about your family when I allowed Matt to court me, more about Elspeth. Whether we consciously thought about her or not, she made us feel guilty, and this came to a head with her overdose.

'I've been punished now; so has Matt. I can't understand his irresponsibility, but I am unable to hate him. I also would never dream of using shares given to me as a gift *by* him *against* him.'

She finished her coffee and got up. 'I'm sorry, Maurice. Matt hurt me badly, but I would never try and unseat him from the head of the company to which he has given his life and which now, perhaps, is the only comfort he has.'

Andrew Rose took the chair and the members of the board fell silent as he began to speak.

'Gentlemen, we are here to perform rather an unpleasant task, which is to ask for the resignation of our chairman and chief executive, Lord Ransom. As you know, he refuses to resign, and has asked that we summon a meeting of shareholders. Our company is in a parlous state, and we need to take drastic action if we are to stay in business. Now by article 17 (a) of our constitution . . .' He continued in this vein for about ten minutes, outlining all the possible options the board had but, in the end, he had only one conclusion:

'I feel we have no option but to summon a meeting of shareholders, recommend them to vote against him.'

He sat back. The other members of the board murmured among one another. Finally Maurice spoke:

'I must tell you, Mr Acting Chairman, that my family and I have considered the matter carefully and, although we as individuals believe it would be in the best interests of Lord Ransom were he to go, I don't think we'll carry the shareholders.'

There was a burst of chatter among the members of the board, and Maurice waited for it to subside. 'If I may finish speaking . . . My father and the present Lady Ransom control over half of the family shares. Even if we all vote against him – and it is possible my brother will also refuse . . .'

'You don't mean Lady Ransom will support her husband?' Andrew asked incredulously.

'Yes, I do. I've seen her. She will not vote against him. With the possibility of Philip also opting out, I don't think you'd carry the vote and, in that case, we'd all have to resign.'

'Well, I don't know.' Rose hit the table with his hand and looked angrily around. 'Has anyone any ideas?'

'I have.' Gerard Singer spoke out. 'It did occur to me that Lady Ransom, indeed the whole family, might support Matt, in which case we would have stalemate. I agree with Maurice that Matt has a fine standing in the business community, and by the time the EGM is called this – ' he tapped the paper on the table in front of him – 'which we deeply deplore, might have been forgotten. A nine-day wonder. The public has a short memory and the fact that Lady Ransom supports him will undoubtedly be in his favour.

'My proposal is, therefore, a very simple one. Matt is waiting outside for our decision. We should ask him to come in and attempt a compromise.'

'And what is that?' Rose asked.

'That he should resign as chairman and chief executive in favour of yourself, and become president of the company. There is good precedent for this, and it is a way of saving face. He retains his seat on the board, and if Maurice would consent to becoming deputy managing director, he would continue the family presence in the company founded by his grandfather, which we are all anxious to see. It would reassure the public, shareholders and, not least, the financial press. We could all begin to breathe again.'

Eric stopped the car outside Terminal One and turned to look at Jenny in the seat beside him. Just a few yards in front of them was a familiar green Jaguar, a man hunched at the wheel reading the paper. It brought back memories to Jenny of those early days of courtship and, with them, a lump in her throat.

'Thanks for everything,' she said to Eric, leaning over to hug him.

'Shall I come with you?'

'No. I'd rather you didn't. Look after the horses.' She put a hand on his arm and tried to smile.

'I will.'

Eric got out of the car and beckoned to a porter. There was, in fact, very little luggage, maybe denoting a woman who was undecided about her future.

They kissed again briefly, and then he got back in the car and sat watching her as she entered the terminal building. Sadly, because he felt it was the end of a chapter, he switched on the engine, put the car into gear and drove past the Jaguar, aware that Peter didn't even look up.

Jenny followed the porter to the SAS check-in and, as few passengers seemed to be catching her flight, or maybe she was early, she was soon through.

She felt very vulnerable, very alone, as she made her way along the concourse to the VIP lounge, where she knew Matt must be already.

But more than ever, as she stopped outside the door, she remembered the day Matt had come unexpectedly to see her off just before Christmas all those years ago. That was before they were courting, before they were lovers. How highly charged and full of sexual tension the encounter then had been.

She wished she hadn't come; wished she'd arranged to meet him somewhere else. Perhaps Matt had chosen this place deliberately.

She pushed open the door of the lounge. Matt saw her immediately and came towards her. It was a cold January day and had been snowing. He wore a heavy overcoat. She thought he had lost weight, and remembered very vividly the day she'd first met him.

'Jenny!' he cried, putting both arms round her.

'Hi!'

She gazed up at him and thought what a long time it was since she had seen him. Six weeks? Something like that.

'What will you drink?'

She looked apathetically at the bar.

'A glass of champagne?' he suggested. 'Just like old times?'

'Why not?' She flung back her head, managing a smile, and his gaze lingered on her as though he, too, was remembering that day.

She went over to a table and sat down and, very soon, Matt joined her with two flutes. 'Cheers!' he said.

'Cheers!' She raised her glass and sipped the liquid. It tasted bitter.

'I'm very glad you agreed to see me, Jenny,' he said, sitting down next to her, unbuttoning his coat. 'I wanted to thank you for what you did. It was very generous.'

'It was in everyone's interests not to let the share price fall to the bottom,' she said, with what she hoped he'd notice was a trace of irony.

'Still, you've been very, very good . . . Jenny . . .'

'Yes, Matt?'

'I hope this isn't the end, just a holiday. I love you, you know.'

'Oh do you indeed?' she said sarcastically. In reality she felt like hitting out, at least verbally, but as she'd held herself in control for so long now, it would be a pity to spoil it.

'I do love you, and I think you love me or you couldn't have behaved so well.'

If only he knew. She swallowed.

'What about Bridget, Matt?'

'Well,' he gazed at his well-kept nails. 'Bridget is no problem. She is a sweet girl and I never promised her marriage, whatever her dreadful family said. I never did and she knows it. I swear to you.'

'Matt,' she stamped her foot impatiently, 'you're lying to me again, aren't you?'

'No, I am not.' His expression was wounded.

'Yes, you are. You lied to me about Elspeth – '

'I did not.'

'You said your marriage was over before you met me.'

'In a sense it was.'

'Sense! Elspeth loved you and continued to love you. She tried to kill herself . . .'

'That was – '

'Matt, we *know* she tried to kill herself. Well, you've tried to deceive us and yourself about *that*, as well as about everything else. It's time to face up to the truth, Matt. Now it's Bridget. You have to support her, and the baby . . .'

'It's a wretched situation.' Matt abandoned the argument and shook his head. 'Happily people forget in time. There's the house, Jenny, Chudleigh, you love it. There are the horses, me . . . we all need you.'

The call came for the flight to Stockholm. Jenny felt relief surge through her.

'There's my flight.'

Matt finished his champagne, but Jenny left hers almost untouched. They both stood up.

'Why don't you stay here, Matt, and have another drink?'

'But I want to see you off.'

'I'd rather you didn't. Please.' It reminded her too much of the time before.

'But Jenny, you will write, telephone. You will keep in touch . . .'

'I can't miss my flight,' she said, rather breathlessly.

And with a wave she left.

401

AFTERWORD

The ancient city of Uppsala was only an hour from Stockholm by train. It was one of the oldest cities in the country, with the largest cathedral in Scandinavia, the Domkyrkan, which contained the relics of Sweden's patron saint, St Eric.

The university was founded in the sixteenth century, and among its famous alumni were the botanist Linnaeus and Anders Celsius, inventor of the temperature scale.

Though parts of the university buildings dotted around the town were of almost equal antiquity, the current building, mainly used for lectures and seminars, only went back to the nineteenth century, though its imitation Renaissance architecture blended in well with the rest of the old town.

The student in the middle row of the lecture theatre was a serious-looking woman, maybe not quite as young as the rest, but with a beauty which she seemed intent on disguising. Pad on her knee, pencil in her hand, she occasionally made notes, peering purposefully through a pair of horn-rimmed spectacles.

She wore jeans, a T-shirt, just like the others. Beside her was an equally serious-looking man, also in jeans and a T-shirt, also with horn-rimmed glasses, though he wore his all the time, whereas she slid hers down from her brow to make notes. He made fewer notes because he had spent

402

years studying, knew the subject well, whereas Jenny was only in her second year. Sig, however, liked to go with her to classes and seminars when he could.

She liked his company, but she was not in love with him. She thought it would probably be years before she could love again, and by that time she would have a degree in philosophy and psychology and, maybe, a career. She was proving an enthusiastic and adept student, thus fulfilling her father's prophesy, justifying his faith in her.

She had a small flat in an old building not far from the botanical gardens which had been laid out by Linnaeus in the eighteenth century across the river on Linnégatan. She lived there by herself, though occasionally Sig stayed, and fellow students were always coming to call.

There were parties, there were dinners, lots of beer and coffee drunk, plenty of talk into the small hours. There was time for reading, time for walking by the beautiful River Fyrisån which flowed through the town, time for learning to cook, an art which hitherto escaped her. Most of all there was time to make up for experiences lost when, as a younger woman, she had always been in the company, not of her peers, but of older men and, inevitably, their friends. With hindsight she was able to see just what an appendage she had actually been, almost like an object to be praised, flattered, admired, looked up to but, above all, used; not a human being.

Still, often in life it is not too late to make up for the mistakes of the past.

Every now and then she went back to Stockholm for a weekend, but home was in Uppsala. It was no longer with her father, no longer Chudleigh Court, or the duplex in St John's Wood. She was no longer Lady Ransom but Jenny Holstrom, second-year student in the Department of Philosophy.

Everything about her now was far removed from the days when, as Lady Ransom, she appeared at all the fashionable openings, all the first nights, and whose picture was continually in the paper.

No one from that time would recognise her now, and for this she was glad.

It was a summer afternoon, hot in the theatre. Some students drowsed, but she remained alert, awake, interested. Sometimes she exchanged glances with Sig who was a psychology graduate and lectured part-time in the university. He was as unlike George or Matt as it was possible to be.

The lecturer looked at his watch and began his concluding remarks. One or two sleepy students jerked awake. Jenny looked round and momentarily closed her eyes, feeling so happy, so at home among this large, friendly but mainly anonymous crowd, where nobody knew about her past or, possibly, cared.

The variegated blues and lilacs of the massed banks of delphiniums, the pinks, yellows and whites of the lupins, the brilliant red and orange of the poppies brought a splash of bright colour to the south east corner of the garden which had been sadly neglected in recent years.

Now everything was changed, and from her return the previous winter Elspeth had worked tirelessly, with the help of two additional gardeners, to repair the damage that had been done to the gardens of her beloved Chudleigh during its years of neglect.

The weeding, the hoeing, the mulching in spring, the sowing of seeds and planting of fresh young shoots of perennials and annuals, had taken most of the spare time she had in settling in.

She stretched, adjusted her sun hat and, with a contented smile, looked towards the terrace where Matt and the two girls sat chatting over the evening aperitif. It had been a day of bright sunshine, and she strolled along the path by the herbaceous border, pausing to snip off a dead head here and there, stooping to remove a clutch of obtrusive and unwelcome greenfly between her thumb and forefinger, and then paused by the beloved rose garden.

404

Many of the hybrid teas and floribundas dotted among the tall standards were in full bloom, most of them in bud. There was not a trace of black spot or mildew to be seen she noted, stooping keenly to inspect them. And there in the middle was a circle of the pride of them all: Elspeth Ransom, finally come into its own. Like her, it had come home.

As she approached the steps of the terrace, Georgina looked up, put down her drink and rose to greet her.

'Mummy, we wondered where you were. I'll get some fresh ice.' She paused to look into the empty bucket. Elspeth put a restraining hand on her arm and then removed her hat, placing it on a bench before sitting down next to Matt.

'Don't bother, darling. I am happy with sherry and I don't need ice.'

'I'll get it,' Beth said jumping up and running into the house. Sherry. It was only recently that Elspeth had started drinking it again because there was no fear now, no need to worry that she would ever again be tempted to drink too much, to surrender to that awful despair that had led . . . well, it *had* been deliberate hadn't it? In her heart of hearts she knew it had, and so did everyone else.

'Just a small sherry,' she said as if aware that the memory still lingered, would never really fade and, as if in compensation, she smiled brilliantly at Matt.

'Had a good game of golf, Matt?'

'Excellent,' he replied.

'And I expect they were all glad to see you again.'

'Everyone very civil,' he murmured as if reluctant to pursue the subject.

There were, alas, so many things now they would prefer not to remember, so many skeletons locked in the family cupboard.

Beth reappeared from the french doors, a glass of sherry on a small silver tray. Elspeth took it and smiled up at her.

'Thank you, darling. Any news from the TV people?'

Beth shook her head. Yet another disappointed dream. It was such a difficult field to break into. One small part was followed by months of periods of 'resting'. Frequently in the past year she had gone down to Monte Carlo where Matt now lived, having bought a large apartment with a spectacular view of the bay. It was two years since Jenny . . . well since it all happened; two and a half, as they were now half way through the year.

So many things had happened, so many changes. It had seemed at one time that disasters would never stop. Not long after the news broke about Matt and Bridget, Georgina had returned home one day to find a note from Henry in which he informed her that he had gone off with the physiotherapist who had been treating his leg, and they now had a home in Spain.

Georgina, ever the conventional stereotype of the re-sourceful Englishwoman with the stiff upper lip, had promptly put the house on the market, whereupon Matt told them of his decision to go and live abroad, and offered Elspeth Chudleigh as her home. And if Georgina would like to move in with her . . .

It all worked out perfectly, and from then things did seem to improve. By the following year they were back in Chudleigh. Maurice and Shirley now had a son. Georgina's divorce had just come through, and Matt was on one of his regular visits to the family.

Somehow in many ways it was perfect.

Surreptitiously, Elspeth touched the wooden arm of her chair. She sipped her sherry slowly, aware of a feeling of great, all pervasive, calm and contentment. She wanted to reach out for Matt's hand, but knew it wouldn't be in order, not yet. Maybe not ever. There was no point in *hurrying* anything. Officially, though divorce proceedings had started, he was still married to Jenny. Suddenly Elspeth sighed deeply, and Matt turned to her with a smile.

'A penny for them, Elspeth?'

'Just happy' she said impulsively. 'Happy to be back here, happy that things have improved and happy . . . ' and finally, at last, she did reach out her hand, 'to see you.'

He took her hand and lightly clasped it. His touch was fraternal rather than passionate, that of a comforting presence, an old, valued friend. Maybe it would always remain like that and, maybe, it would be better if it did.

But Matt was far away, his eyes on the tennis court now overgrown with weeds because no one seemed to play there any more. In his mind's eye he could see *so* vividly that day – how many years ago now – six, eight? – when he had watched the beautiful girl throw the ball in the air, lean forward to serve . . .

It was as though between then and now a lifetime had elapsed, not just a few years. The world had turned upside down. In many ways he now felt he had been slightly deranged. The only memories that survived of that time were the occasional niggling jolts when some reference to the abandoned Bridget and her baby Sarah appeared in the columns of a tabloid paper. A baby he had never seen, did not want to see, and never would see. She and her mother were well looked after, lived in some style in a house near Berkhamsted. Poor little Sarah, who could not be blamed for her birth, reminded him too vividly of that dreadful period of his life and he could never bring himself to see the child who had unwittingly been the cause of so much misery. Occasionally the press enjoyed resurrecting the memory, rubbing salt in the wound.

Matt's grasp of Elspeth's hand slackened, and she withdrew hers altogether. The shadows lengthened on the lawn. The hoot of Maurice's car was heard in the drive and, with one accord, the three women rose to greet him and Shirley, who were coming to dinner. But for a moment, Matt remained where he was, sitting in his chair leaning slightly forward, his eyes on the neglected, overgrown court.

She raised her arm and threw the ball high in the air. Her fair hair, held in place by a white band, gleamed in the sun and he caught a glimpse of her hairless armpit, aware of the slight curve of her breasts, the sight of her thigh as she jumped high in the air from the baseline as her racquet thudded down on the ball.

It was wonderful to be once again in the bosom of the family, to be surrounded by those he loved and who, indeed, had shown that they still loved him.

However, reluctantly, almost sadly, Matt Ransom abandoned his vision of the past on hearing his name called, and slowly heaved himself out of his chair.

Then and now; but he knew that, although he might not see her again, he would never forget her, never really say goodbye in his heart to that girl.